# Chosen

## of the

# Elements

Soel

# Chosen

*of the*

# Elements

A Novel by

*Soel*

*Chosen of the Elements*
By Soel
Cover Design by Laurelei Black

ISBN-13: 978-1-956765-16-8 (paperback)
ISBN-13: 978-1-956765-17-5 (digital book)

Copyright 2023

Asteria Books, a division of Asteria Projects

# The Land of Paelencien

Paelencien is a world of seemingly little magic. In actuality, it is a world full of magic. The lands and inhabitants of the world are in a delicate balance with the magic and nature. The inhabitants unknowingly owe their lives to the balance.

The world is full of unpredictable and powerful storm patterns. Rain falls often and the wind storms are concussive. In some areas of the world, there are element specific terrains that are beyond dangerous: one where it quakes and spikes, one that is cold, frozen, and blinding, another that is a field and ever-storming sky that crackles with continuous lightning bolts and electricity, another that rains down flaming balls to the ground while fire shoots out from the ground, another that has water so turbulent that no ships may go near it or be doomed to have a deep and permanent grave, and yet another that has nothing but amazing and deadly wind storms on a constant basis. There is a field of death where as you walk on the land, it sucks the life force from your body, and conversely a land of eternal life. Other places with unique oddities also exist throughout the lands.

Paelencien has creatures made of magic and creatures of nature. Most people just see the creatures of nature. The most notorious of the creatures are goblins. The 3-foot tall, grey-skinned creatures covered in warts have a slight intelligence, enough to brandish human-made weapons. Because of the sharp claws on their tiny hands, they don't need weapons. However goblins want to be better than their animalistic instinct and use the weapons of humans. They are populous in the tree-covered hills around Ishta, burrowing under the ground in little caves. Goblins reproduce quickly, faster than humans, but since they are only slightly intelligent, they loose a lot of their numbers to regular hunts by the humans. The hunts keep the population under some control, though the hunts are still dangerous. They began many years ago after the goblin population grew too large and devastated the region containing Ishta and several other cities in the middle of the continent, Wildia. The region never recovered fully and has gained a reputation that drives most people away. Nothing dares to eat the goblins. They aren't poisonous; they just taste bad. They are carnivorous, vicious creatures that go after anything living as food. If encountered in numbers, they are very dangerous. Goblins are just one of many dangerous creatures of the land.

The humans of the world have several kingdoms and are the most populous. As a lingering remnant of the old world and what humans used to be, occasionally a human child will be born with dark-sight or other unusual features. Sometimes both can occur, but that is even more rare. The dark-sight allows the human to see in the dark, and the other unusual abilities are usually heightened senses or altered features. No one remembers about the old world humans, as it has been too long ago. Humans used to be friends with the elves, but not in this age. A catastrophe happened that severed the link and altered the humans of old from the humans today. The elves that once had many forested lands, now only have one large forest. They are very protective of their forest and tolerate no incursions from anyone.

Before humans came to be in Paelencien, powerful beings lived in and controlled the lands. Not much is known about them. They are only mentioned in legends and far-fetched tales. There are a few in the world who know more about them than they are willing to tell. When the lands changed, humans came, the old beings "died", and new gods were formed and worshipped. One of the most prominent gods is the god of secrets. In a land that holds so many secrets, it makes the god of secrets one of the most powerful and most worshipped. Evidence of the old world and the beings that "died" has been mostly erased over time.

Paelencien is under the control of numerous deities of varying power. There are often schemes and battles between them, and it tends to spill onto the humans. The deities are also eternal, so for all their rivalry and fighting between one another, they cannot destroy each other. Only one deity is able to wield the power of giving life to someone dead whose soul has left the human body to The Beyond. This power belongs to only one for a good reason. And as such, it has kept a balance between the gods and the world of Paelencien. The Beyond is the place all soul energy collects into once the body expired. Once there, it is only a matter of time before the soul is unreturnable. The Beyond holds the soul energy for only so long, then the deity who the soul belongs to can claim it for their own. Once the soul is claimed by the owning deity, it cannot be returned to the body and they use it however they see fit.

There is a dark presence in Paelencien, who has been here for a very long time. Some human kingdoms fight the Dark Lord's forces avidly. They seek to rid the land of his darkness. He is the most feared being in the land. Most who enter his lands never return, and it is speculated that they become undead. Most assume he is not human, for no human can be that cruel. No one knows what he is or where he came from, but he was there as long as the humans of this age could remember. His cruelty is well known, so most stay far away from his territories.

The plants are vibrant with green life, and in Paelencien, plants grow unbelievably tall and large. One could get lost in the grass fields alone. There is little issue with food in most areas of the world, since the crops and plants are very abundant and healthy. Many plants even have magical properties, but you have to be careful when trying to harvest, eat, or use such plants. They grow so well because of the magic and the suns and moons.

Paelencien has 3 moons and 3 corresponding suns per moon. Isis is a purple colored moon that corresponds to the vibrant light violet sun. Isis and the purple sun are the most common bodies in the sky. The other named moon, Cassius, is blue with a hint of green. The corresponding sun to Cassius is rarely seen. Its green tint is faint and can hardly be seen unless someone knows how to look for it. Once about every ten years a light pink moon and a peach sun can be seen, but they don't last long. Those celestial bodies have a mystery about them that no one has been able to uncover. The sky is a different color depending on which suns and moons are prominent.

Paelencien is an old, beautiful world, but treacherous, deadly, and unpredictable. It is a land of deep mystery and many secrets. From the deities who control it, the chaotic and powerful weather, and the humans and creatures both magical and not, the world is never lacking for intrigue and excitement. Some take the excitement and intrigue by the hand willingly. Others are simply more secure in staying put.

# FIRE, ICE, and EARTH

# Chapter 1: The Birth

The skies of Paelencien darkened and rain poured down while small white flowers sprang instantly from the ground as each raindrop hit the earth. The villagers of Ishta watched in awe from their windows at the darkness that seemed to threaten them, but also at the white flowers springing to life, which gave them comfort. An ominous aura and comfort pervaded the air like a think cloud of static. This was surely a sign from the Gods. Judith Merril had just given birth to her newborn son and daughter. They were twins, though they did not visibly seem so. Marcus Merril was outside the room awaiting the news. The midwife came out to tell Marcus the wonderful news of the births and he sighed with relief. He had been concerned about the birth since Judith had been having complications and unusual pains with her pregnancy. She was exhausted from the ordeal and needed to rest. Marcus went to his wife's side and gently kissed her on the forehead.

"Goodnight my love. Rest well, for you have been through more than I can even well imagine," he whispered to her as she drifted off to sleep. He was anxious since he still hadn't had a chance to see his newborns. The midwives removed them from the room without showing them to their father. He would just have to wait till the next morning, as hard as it would be to wait.

Morning broke rather dark and dreary. Still it rained. In fact, it was supposed to rain all week, according to some. Since it was only the beginning of the week, it would be dreary for a while. Though the joy of her new children filled Judith's heart, she could not be completely happy. She still hurt so much and there was some odd force that seemed to keep her from being truly happy. Marcus felt the same way but he did not want to burden the woman he loved so much with his own concerns. She had been through enough the night prior. He could not bear to hear her screams of pain during delivery. It was over now and their children were healthy and fine. They were given two lovely children that they longed to have. Marcus and Judith wanted something that would be truly theirs, to love and cherish.

As the anxious Marcus waited to see the children for the first time, he could hear a woman scream from children's room. One of the midwives ran out of the room and straight to another. Others ran to the scene to see what had happened. Marcus had run to the scene to make sure the children were alright. Marcus was almost frantic with worry. This was the last thing Marcus wanted to hear happening. "Are my children alright? What is going on?!"

A midwife responded to his concerns by checking in on the children. "They seem to be perfectly fine, sir, now if you'll excuse me...I must find out what has happened here myself." She took off towards the screaming.

Marcus understood and said "by all means". The sooner they found out, the sooner he would as well. He was comforted and pleased to know the children were safe, though he was still anxious to see them. The screaming woman, now somewhat calmed, came out and sobbed and mumbled something unintelligible. The others tried to calm her further but to no avail. The distraught midwife shrugged off attempts at comfort and fled the home quickly.

The one who checked on the children returned to the parents. "She just had some personal problems. She'll be fine with some rest. I will bring the children out to you right away."

Marcus gave a sigh of relief and was anxious for her to return with his babes. She and a helper went to the children's room and gathered them gently. Ellis Canri, they decided for the boy, was born first and had dark hair and dark brown eyes. They were so dark that they could be mistaken for black if not given a closer look. Ellis was presented to him first. Marcus was so elated to see his new son. Ellis seemed to be a happy child though the father could not help but feel that there was something strange about his son. Ellis exuded an uneasy feeling to those near him. He seemed to be a happy baby though. When Ellis stared at his father he seemed to stare into the mind. The nurses interrupted the silence and held forth his daughter Angeline, who was the happiest child he had ever seen. Her presence was soothing and quite cheerful. Angeline Jeann was born second. She was a darling child with bright red hair and blue eyes. Her eyes were the color of a bright blue summer sky, which was not a common color for the people of her village, though the red hair was only slightly uncommon. While holding her he felt as if everything would be alright. He felt warm and alive with her in his arms. Angeline kept reaching up to him with her small hands and tiny delicate fingers and smiled at him so much that he couldn't help but smile and laugh lightly.

"Let's go meet mom, shall we?" He said soothingly and he held her close to him. The nurses followed Marcus into the room with Ellis in hand. Judith seemed to be deep in thought. She stared out the window seemingly endlessly, almost as if she were somewhere else entirely. Marcus called to his wife and she slowly looked over at the three walking into the room. Marcus presented Angeline to his wife. Judith smiled as she stared at her and held her in her arms. She held her for what felt like an eternity, filled with joy and love. Angeline had her mother thoroughly enthralled.

"She really is an angel isn't she?" Judith couldn't stop smiling at her.

Marcus lifted the shining girl from her mother reluctantly as the nurse then brought Ellis over and offered for her to hold him. Judith seemed reluctant to hold him but did anyway. She just looked at him and shivers ran through her entire body while he was in her arms. Then her face turned blank as if she were in thought again when suddenly she burst into tears. The nurse took Ellis from her and Marcus tried to calm her but all she could say between her sobs was that she wanted to be left alone. The nurses took the children back to their room and Marcus continued to try to calm his upset wife. After they were alone he asked her what was wrong. She didn't answer for a few minutes and then finally spoke.

"Do you love our children? Do you think they are just perfect?" she said sobbing.

"I do love them. You know I do."

"Don't you notice something wrong with Ellis? I know he looks normal but he doesn't feel normal. A mother should love her children but I can't stomach to hold him or be near him at all. He's creepy. Something is wrong with him. He's ....off. He seems to be the exact opposite of his sister. I love holding her but I can't be near him. There's something else too." She paused. "Never mind, you wouldn't believe me if I told you. I need some rest right now." She started to stare out the window again.

Marcus tried to comfort his wife and try to ease her fears, but he could not deny her observations. "I do notice something odd about our son. He is a little creepy but we can't push him away for that. We should embrace him and love him. What kind of child do you think he'll turn out to be if we shut him out of our lives based on that petty of a reason? He is ours... our baby. Could you live with knowing that we turned our son into an uncaring, unloving person who could potentially grow up to hurt people because his mother didn't love him or want him? Could you really live with that?"

Trying to respond calmly, but not really succeeding, "I just can't do it. There's something about him that frightens me. I want to give him to someone else. I couldn't live with myself for making him into that so I shouldn't be the one to raise him. Maybe someone else in the village will care for him better than I will."

"Then I will." Speaking with a firm resolve, "We aren't throwing him away. We can't do that to him. I will raise him and will keep him from bothering you. I can't give our child away no matter how creepy he seems to be."

"Fine then. You deal with him because I can't." Her firm tone had anger in it. Perhaps it was anger at her husband for not supporting her huge decision she felt was best for everyone. She turned from him and asked to be left alone when he didn't immediately leave.

He was concerned for his wife, but what more could he say to her? He didn't understand. She clearly made up her mind and now they would just have to cope with the issue at hand. Those two precious children needed their parents. And clearly he needed to be the one to take charge of seeing them grow up knowing love and support.

# Chapter 2: Ishta

Most small towns are notorious for residents snooping in an outsider's business. Ishta was no exception. Not all travelers liked Ishta, so those few who came often stayed on the outskirts. The town was surrounded by a dense forest with only a few fields open for farming. Travelers opted to deal with potential goblins rather than entering town. The presence of the goblins helped the Temple of Arah though, by helping to shield their secrets.

A small temple to Arah, a lesser goddess of secrets, was built in Ishta before any of the current residents could remember. Arah was under Thornakai, the greater god of secrets. There were a number of lesser gods beneath him who corresponded to different regions. Arah's charge was the region Ishta was settled in. Her temples were grey and nondescript to keep inquisitive minds away. Becoming a priest or priestess of Arah was very difficult. She had to choose you, which usually happened during dreams. The process of the Arahian dreams were enlightening and excruciating. Human minds were barely equipped to handle them. Most people did not know about Arah's followers, nor did they want to have anything to do with them because they appeared as poor needy folk with the ability to heal. This was another way they detracted attention from inquiring minds. The only time people would want to enter the temple was to have severe wounds healed, which the nurses could not mend.  The newcomers that knew of her felt uneasiness at the thought that their own secrets, what few they could keep in such a small town, would be revealed.  Others just felt generally uneasy, not knowing why.

Ishta had only a few buildings and ten houses.  Merk, an older gentleman, owned the general store.  He knew most of the gossip in town.  He was a secret keeper in his own rite, but not clergy of Arah.  He was also the most knowledgeable about the outsiders that arrived since his shop was the first, and often only, place they stopped.

Jake was the main bartender and innkeeper at the local inn and tavern, called Ishta's Finest.  He could contend with Merk in the learning and keeping of secrets if not for the fact that many people did not want to stay the evening in town.  Those brave enough to stay liked Jake.  He was a great listener and always was able to give good advice when needed.  The villagers greatly respected him.  Judith worked for him during the night shift, but most of the people who stayed up in the evening would never mention her.  They would often leave early before the locals awoke.

Keeping Ishta small was good but it did limit exposure of many aspects in the children's lives.  There was a school and it had to be responsible for all knowledge.  On occasion, outsiders needed to repay a resident of Ishta, which usually consisted of teaching a new subject at the school.  Defense was also taught considering the size of the town and in case the town was besieged by goblins.

There was a lawkeeper in town that kept the peace and made sure everyone remained orderly with one another.  He was a capable warrior who could defend the town when needed.  His largest task was keeping the children from town safe since they had tendencies to want to explore the Outside.   There were several children who were unable to be saved over the years.  One group of children did slip past him into the woods and were set upon by goblins.  They survived, mostly due to the teachings of Kaahn, a traveling martial arts master who decided to stay in town. The loss of children was something that never left the minds of the townsfolk.  In a town so small, the loss of any child was devastating, but children have ways of getting around their confines.

Most of the houses were small farmhouses since the town had to often survive on their own without the supplies from other cities and the surrounding forest didn't allow for large fields.  Most traders didn't stop and trade.  Some protections were set along the perimeter of the town to ensure the goblins did not steal any of the precious food or other wares.  It did a good job at keeping the goblins out, but not effective at keeping all the children in.  Outsiders also were outside the protections because they chose to be.

The adults did the best they could.  Sometimes situations were just out of their control.  Losses were had and felt deeply by the community.  It was a close-knit community, but they held more secrets than most could realize.  The presence of Ellis and Angeline greatly impacted the dynamic when they joined the community.

Judith and Marcus were from Ishta.  They were both born there.  They were sweethearts their whole life.  The bond between them was unshakable, until the birth of their twins.  That night, many things changed.  Much changed that people didn't even realize.  The polarity of the town was forever altered with the birth of Angeline and Ellis.  It would take time for the residents to fully realize the impact.  It was like a secret about to burst.  By the time further events would unfold and all was said and done, all Paelencien would know of Ishta.  The inevitable destruction of what should have been an eternal bond was just the beginning.  The twins would shake the core of their world.

## Chapter 3:  Growing Up

Weeks went by and the twins began their life.  Marcus took care of the children while Judith worked.  Judith worked quite a lot, actually.  She kept herself busy so she would have an excuse not to come home and spend much time with her son.  She wished she could spend more time with their daughter, but if she treated one a certain way, she'd have to treat the other the same.  She decided that working as much as possible and letting her husband take care of the children was the solution.  It made her quite sad that she felt the need to be like that with her own children.  After all they were her children but she didn't have the strength to deal with them.  Giving birth to them was only the beginning of her loss of strength.  She was haunted by nightmares every night since the birth.  They needed the extra money anyway since Marcus was staying home to care for the children.  He used to be the sole provider.  Marcus was doing great with them, but so long as he cared for the children, Judith couldn't be there.  She still felt strongly her son needed to be removed from the family and into a better home and family.

The villagers acted strangely when they were around Judith after the birth. She paid them no mind. They also reacted oddly when the children passed by. Glances were varied in emotion depending on which twin was seen first. Angeline brought at least some measure of happiness while Ellis brought on revulsion. With the two together it seemed to be resentment. The children hadn't yet figured out their presence was resented. Marcus had a measure of respect from the community, but whether they spoke to him depended on the child with him at the time of the meeting.

During those few weeks, Marcus noticed odd things happening. He was having nightmares about his wife dying and the children becoming ill. The nightmares of his wife were the most frequent. They troubled him, but then he would wake up and check on Angeline first thing. It was his daily routine. She always took his fears away and gave him nice afternoon dreams of the entire family being together having fun. It was the only time he and his wife were together since the births. Angeline usually slept quietly through the night and never cried. She would always smile, which always brought smiles to others. Ellis on the other hand was always up all night and slept most of the day. He cried frequently but would stop once Marcus came in to check on him. Ellis seemed to want Marcus around all of the time, but he couldn't be. Marcus wouldn't have been able to handle it.

Marcus also noticed strange things going on around the house. The candles used to brighten up the house were always melted half way then frozen. Little scorch marks would appear but be cold to the touch and frosted over. He would wake up with sores and scars in the mornings, but by the evening after his naps he would examine them and they were gone. It appeared as if they were never there. This cycle went on for years and the strange occurrences still happened. As the children grew older, the problems became bigger. The scorch marks were larger and the candles would be completely melted and both were colder to the touch as well. It was something that no one could explain. He'd have people reluctantly come to look at it but they could find no reasonable answer for why these oddities happened. People tended to exit very quickly after these inspections. The phenomenon was too weird for them in addition to being in the same house with the twins. The house had a mixed aura after the children arrived.

Also as the children grew, they fought more often. Ellis always picked on his sister but he was never able to do much damage, try as he may. It frustrated him to no end that nothing he did to his sister worked. She was always the same happy child as she had been since they were born. Ellis was always unhappy even though he seemed to get more attention from daddy. He didn't want part of his father's attention, he wanted all of it. He just couldn't stand that his sister got such positive attention from everyone and they would usually shy away from him. The only person who spent time with him was Marcus. Ellis wanted to hurt his sister by taking daddy's attention away from her. He wanted her to feel the pain of rejection that he did. I want to hurt her period, he thought. He tried but the wounds he inflicted on her always healed before they could start. He hated her for her pureness and her happiness because he could never feel that way. He felt he would forever feel unloved and unwanted by the world. He hated how people stopped and stared at him as if he were a freak, but they looked at his sister and compared her to an angel. It didn't help that they named her after one!

Marcus began to see how much Ellis disliked his sister and tried to discuss it with him. That was another aspect about the children. They learned to walk and speak at an astonishing rate. They weren't being tutored much either. It was as if it just came to them naturally. Marcus tried to talk to Ellis about why he picked on his sister so much. Ellis would just reply that all he wanted was dad to be around forever. Ellis would often ask why people avoided him like they did. All Marcus could say was that they were just odd and not to worry about them. Of course that never satisfied the boy's desire for an answer. That was not a real answer!

Angeline became interested in art. She loved to paint. Painting brought her a sereneness she could not fully describe. She would paint scenes of people and wondrous things. All of her paintings brought happiness to all who would look upon them. She painted scenes of places she had never been, but were real places, and just as wondrous to behold. She would close her eyes and paint and not look until they were finished. It was as if she was actually viewing those places and scenes. But some of her paintings were strange to the viewers, as if they depicted future events. People would see what she painted and ask how she knew about it. When asked she would respond, "I paint from my dreams". They just dismissed it as pure luck mostly, but she could really see the future at times. She never bragged about what she saw, nor did she brag about her artwork. She was quiet and polite. She often just concentrated on her artwork.

As she became older, she would tend to the wounds of others and heal people with a touch. She didn't know why or how she could heal, it just happened when she touched the wounds. She didn't remember that she'd do it as a baby to counter her brother. She knew she and her brother were unlike everyone else they knew. She was grateful for her abilities because she could counter her brother when he lashed out, and he did that often. She still never bragged about her natural abilities and the people just thought their conditions healed naturally.

Ellis became fond of making weapons such as knives and daggers. He made other things that looked more like torture devices, but he kept those to himself. As he got older, he helped out in the local weapon shop. He did various things for the owner and was often praised for his craftsmanship even at a young age. People were still a little scared of him, but they eventually dismissed it as them being silly, thinking that they had nothing to be afraid of. He would also gather poisons from the local plant and animal life and make potions in secret to use on the weapons he made.

The time came when Marcus thought the twins were of school age and should go to school. They would learn valuable skills and knowledge. The parents and the children's readiness determined school age. It was usually around 5 years old. Marcus withheld the children from school for a while and taught them at home. The townsfolk were the main reason. He did not want his children ridiculed by all the others. He knew how cruel children could get at times. He wanted to protect his angel and was scared how Ellis might have responded to other kids' cruelty.

Of the few non-residential buildings, the school was the largest. It was well kept, but not fancy. It had what it needed to fulfill its function. School was devoted to teaching the local children about history, arts, construction, religions, and defense. Each general class had specializations. It offered a few classes that were only for specially selected kids, and those classes were very secret. Merk and Jake had attended the secret classes as children, and not even their parents knew. They were the last children to be in it by the time Angeline and Ellis were brought to school at the age of 7. In the general courses, children had their choice of what they wanted to learn, though all children had to learn how to read and write. There was a part of the building used as a training hall where children could learn to defend themselves with various weapons of their choice.

Angeline thought school was great. She loved learning about history and art. She liked to learn as many different languages as she could. She preferred not to participate in the weapons training and defense classes, but did eventually agree to unarmed combat classes when her father said she had to take at least one defense class. She also learned about which herbs and plants could cure ailments and which were edible or poisonous.

Although no one else knew what Ellis was up to, she did. She could hear his thoughts as clear as if he were only inches away and speaking to her aloud. She knew that he hated her for the attention she received and that he wanted to make her life miserable. Luckily she could hear his thoughts so she could counter whatever damage he planned on doing to their home or others before it was too late. She always stuck close to him to watch and protect him, but not close enough to be considered hanging out with him. Even though her brother hated her, she didn't hate him. She loved him because he was her brother. He was the only sibling she had and she felt a bond with him, even if he didn't. It was okay with her if he didn't like her, because she still loved him unconditionally. He certainly did keep her on her toes with his actions in school, town, and at home.

He hated how she was always near him. He hated how she always followed him around and smiled at him if he glanced over at her. He often wondered why does she always have to smile and be wretchedly nice to me all the time? Isn't it obvious to her that I hate her?! She should know this instinctively. Can't she tell? She must be doing this to torture me. She's being spiteful, that's it, spiteful! Can't she tell I want her dead?! Ellis tried to make that as obvious as he could. She frustrated him with her incessant compassion! I will wipe that smile off her face someday and then I will be the one smiling! If only he had her foresight to know the things he would actually end up doing for her.

Ellis continued his training on plants and poisonous things in school. He also spent most of his time focusing how to better wield his daggers and swords. He improved his weapon-making skills and made weapons with spikes and points so the weapons would inflict more damage and pain upon people. He received pleasure out of seeing people in pain. He particularly loved to make people dream about their worst fears and watch them suffer day by day. After all, why shouldn't they suffer for shunning him and making his own heart hurt? They should be in as much, if not more, pain than he had to endure. In fact, they should be in more pain for making him suffer. He made his father suffer for several years because Marcus could not devote all attention to him. Instead, Marcus paid attention to that sister of his that everyone loved so much, at least in his mind. Ellis' memories of those events began to change over time. Even his mother was not spared pain. It served her right to suffer from a vision he put in her head after she pushed him away before she even got to know him. Judith was to be eternally tormented by what she saw, though it would never really be enough to satisfy Ellis's cruel intentions. At least she suffers from many causes now, so she will always suffer as she deserves to.

One day after school, when the children were 14 years old, there was a local boy, a bully, who picked a fight with Ellis because he thought Ellis looked at him the wrong way. Ellis and that boy had never gotten along and quarreled on and off. The boy decided to pick a time and place to fight, and after school they went there. Ellis did not brandish any weapons and the boy had a dagger. The bully was very adept at weapons. He was one of the best in his class. He lunged at Ellis and Ellis simply dodged by moving aside with ease.

"You will never leave this alley alive, freak!" the boy threatened.

Ellis just coolly said, "If till death is the way you want it, then so be it." He simply stood in place and grinned as he made cuts and wounds appear all over the boys body as if a master at blade-use was right next to the bully, slicing him to bits. Ellis was several feet away from the boy.

Blood stained the boy's white shirt and black pants. He doubled over in pain and was quite confused as to what just happen to him.

"Have you had enough yet you crying coward? You talk a lot, but that's all you are. Talk, talk, talk..." said Ellis in a cool and calm, but seething tone with underlying pleasure at his torture mixed in. Ellis wanted to hurt him more. He was simply toying with him that time. The next action Ellis took would be the clincher. The boy could stay there and bleed to death or Ellis would finish the job cleanly and quickly, though still quite painfully. Ellis would have preferred to watch him suffer, but would've been glad to finish it his own way without his annoying sister around to ice him down.

The bully changed his tone and begged for mercy. He pleaded with Ellis to go get a priest or nurse, but his plea was not very intelligible.

"Too late...you brought this on yourself remember, till death...those were the agreed upon terms of leaving the alley," he reminded the boy. "And far be it from me to alter those terms. Your death can be quick or slow, your choice." His eyes narrowed with a bloodlust longing to be released into fruition.

The boy cried and pleaded with him to get help again. Ellis didn't want to listen to whining so he made the boy combust into flames in a mere second. Moments later there was nothing left of the bully but ash that blended with the dirt and got carried away by the wind. Pleased with the events, he went about the daily routine he had for years and had a special smile on his face for the rest of the day.

While Ellis was with the boy, Angeline could hear and even see everything that happened clearly in her head. She began to weep in the middle of her class and all eyes stared in disbelief because they had never seen her cry before. The teacher approached her to inquire what was wrong but she did not speak. She felt the need to protect her brother from the harm that would befall him should she speak of the horrible murder. She couldn't even say anything about the boy because she didn't want to have to answer questions about what happened. Her silence, which spoke volumes, was best.

That boy in particular had picked on her constantly and made her feel like a freak though she never showed him her feelings. She just smiled and shrugged at him. It was his own fault for picking the fight with Ellis, even though he didn't realize the odds he faced. It was also her fault for not being with her brother to stop him. Had she done so, the boy would be alive and well. Instead, no one would ever find him. They would just assume he ran away and probably fell prey to goblin attack. Perhaps it was best to spare the suffering of thinking he had died. Thinking the child merely missing would at least give them hope. Hope was better than hopeless sorrow.

She went straight home to her room, and did not come out for the rest of the evening. One of her teachers went to the house to tell Marcus that she saw Angeline crying that day. She encouraged him to find out what was wrong since Angeline wouldn't say during class. Marcus was concerned by this news and tried to find out what she cried about, but Angeline just said she didn't want to talk about it. The response gave Marcus even more cause for concern, but he did not push further. It was very odd behavior for her. She never held back from him, but he could tell she was holding something back now. He was sure something was drastically wrong, but if she was unwilling to share, he could not and would not force it out of her. Maybe she will tell me in time, Marcus thought.

Ellis came back home later with not only a smile, but also an added curious look on his face.

"Why is she crying? " Ellis asked his father.

"No one knows, she won't tell me or anyone else for that matter," he said with a concerned look on his face. It was the first time Marcus had seen Ellis smile so much. "It has been a very odd day today," and Marcus said nothing more about it. He didn't want to see the smile fade from his son, but the fact that Ellis was smiling meant something was wrong.

Ellis went up to his goody-goody sister's room and knocked. There was no answer from the other side. He opened the door and found her in a meditative state that they both used when they needed time to themselves.

"What's wrong with you today?" He got no response other than her opening her eyes to look at him. "You're awfully quiet today." He still got no response from her but while he stared into her eyes he found his answer. I have done this to her. She knows about the incident today. I finally made her cry! What a smile he had on his face then. It lasted the evening and all the next day. One thing puzzled him though, why, if she knew, did she not tell anyone? Surely that wouldn't be great torture for her to turn me in. He could not figure it out, but he still received great pleasure out of knowing he'd made her cry for once.

She, knowing Ellis thought he made her cry, had still won that round. It wasn't her brother that made her cry. She cried at the loss of the boy's life. His spark went out in a blaze and was silenced in just a mere moment. No matter how mean he was, he didn't deserve that. It wasn't his time yet to go the Beyond. Even though the boy picked on me, he did not deserve his death. At least he didn't suffer as long as Ellis would have preferred, she thought. Oddly enough, she was glad for her brother. For once in his life he was smiling, even if it was at hers and the dead boy's expense.

# Chapter 4: Missing

The next few days after the incident with the bully went by as usual in the Merril household. Things seemed to return to the way they were with the twins normally. Ellis kept trying to make his sister cry again. He gloated about his achievements. He was trying to make her feel lesser again. Angeline just took it in silence and smiled at him.

One evening, years later when the twins were 16, Judith didn't return home from work and Marcus began to worry about her. She never stayed out all night. She came home for a few hours of sleep, and then left before anyone woke up.

Angeline could feel her father's tension and fear. "What's wrong, daddy?" Her voice was calm as she tried to sooth his worries even though she still had concern in her voice.

"Your mother did not come home last night, but I don't think we need to worry quite yet. I am concerned for her. This is highly unlike her." Concern was clearly taking over his emotions.

"Try and get some rest," Angeline told her father soothingly as she lightly petted him, "she should be home soon enough."

"You're right," he agreed. He went upstairs to bed. Even though he lay in bed, he could not sleep. Eventually his eyes just became so heavy that he had no choice.

That morning Angeline left the house early to try to find her mother. She soon discovered mentally that her brother awoke a little earlier than he usually did and noticed she was no longer there. He wondered where she went and thought at least I can have one morning to myself without her following me around. When she didn't return in about an hour, Ellis began to wonder and decided to follow her for once. However, he did not know her location. She wasn't hard to find usually, so he figured he'd find her in no time.

Marcus slept in and upon waking realized how long he'd slept. He looked around for his wife in case she came home while he slept. There was no sign of her. Marcus immediately rushed out of the house to the lawkeeper's building to report his wife missing.

Angeline decided to check the general store to see if Judith had been there, and when she might have left.

Merk, the storeowner, said he hadn't seen her since she left the previous day. "She was supposed to be into work yesterday morning, but alas she never showed."

"Mom never came home last night, which is unlike her, and father is really worried about where she might be." The concern in her voice was clear.

Merk shared her pain. He'd never heard Angeline sound concerned before. He wanted to help however he could, and ease her worries. "I'll let Marcus know if she makes an appearance. I will also send some people to look for her. Do not worry, dear, we will find her. I think there are people still searching for Lew. He's been missing for too long."

That news made her happier knowing others would also be looking for her mother. Angeline then went to Ishta's Finest to see if her mom was still there. Judith worked the inn and tavern late at night for those travelers who arrived after midnight. Angeline went into the inn and tavern and noticed only a few people there, but none of them her mother. There was a female singing light songs for the morning. She was in the corner of the bar on the stage. Sometimes the elven songstress, Lira, performed her entrancing songs there. The bar was usually packed when she came into town.

Angeline asked Jake if her mother had left the inn and tavern last night.

"Nope Angel, she never came to work last night, at least she wasn't there when I showed up in the morning and I rarely see her when she just gets in. No one had tended the chores that needed to be completed, which means she never arrived. I'm sorry to say it, but if she continues this way, then I'll have to ..."

"She never came home either." She knew what he was about to say and things were bad enough.

Jake looked concerned.

"Have you seen anyone or anything unusual in town this morning?"

"Sorry sweetheart, I don't have the manpower to document everyone who comes in here and when. It could've been that some people came in last night without me knowing. Normally your mom would take care of writing down who comes in during the night."

Angeline decided it would be best if she looked in the rooms upstairs and Jake gave the go ahead for the search.

Ellis decided to check the school and found his sister wasn't there. He overheard some say they saw her go to the general store. He followed the lead to the store and before he was able to enter, a few locals left in a hurry. His curiosity was definitely piqued now. He went inside to find Merk cleaning the store up a bit. Merk saw Ellis, and before Ellis could speak, Merk said "there's no sign of her yet, but I'll let Marcus know whenever I found out about her whereabouts."

Ellis was confused and didn't know what to say for a moment. "What are you talking about?"

Merk looked surprised and informed Ellis about Judith being missing, and that he was sorry for the pain Ellis might have been going through. Ellis looked surprised momentarily, but then went expressionless.

So that's where Angeline is, Ellis thought. She's looking for mom. I'm intrigued as to where she ran off to as well. I hope something happened to her. She deserves it. Maybe she ran off with a "customer"... "Do you happen to know where my sister ran off to?"

Merk said he didn't know. Ellis then thought about it for a moment and deduced that she must have gone to their mom's other place of work. Ellis knew what his mom did at that inn and tavern, but he knew his father didn't. His father would be heartbroken if he found out his wife spent her nights keeping the travelers company in their rooms. He then smiled at the thought of the look on his father's face at the first discovery of the news. I should save that bit of information for a later time. I should save it for a time when it will hurt the most.

Ellis went over to Ishta's Finest and heard the songstress's voice and knew who it was. He had her in bed once when he was 15 years old, though no one ever knew about it. He always hated her singing, but her other noises weren't so bad. At least when they were together, he had her occupied doing other things.

He walked into the building and saw Angeline heading up the stairs with a number of keys in her hands. She stopped on the stairs and turned to look back at him and turned to continue on her way up. He was surprised she looked at him, but then again, she did that a lot. She seemed to know exactly what he was up to and thwarted his plans. That was another thing he hated about her. She could predict his actions when he couldn't do the same in return. Ellis decided to follow his sister to see what was going on...out of curiosity.

Angeline went to the first door and knocked on it. There was no answer and as she was about to open the door, her brother came up behind her. She just looked at him and smiled, then proceeded into the room. The first room had not been touched all night. The bed was still made and it was quite clean. There were no clothes or anything else in the closet. There was nothing on or under the bed, and the dresser was empty. Ellis took this chance to talk to his sister.

"So, what are you snooping around for? It's not like you to go snooping." Ellis was grinning as he spoke to her.

"I'm looking for anything to clue us in as to where our mother is. Not like you care about her anyway. Why don't you just go do whatever it is you do in the morning?" She was short with him because she didn't need him making it more difficult for her.

"No way! You always follow me around and now I'm going to give you a taste of your own medicine. You're right though. I don't like her. She was never there for us." Even though you didn't need her attention, I did and she refused to give me any. I could really care less if Judith were found dead.

Angeline just glared at him and said in a firm tone "If you insist on following me, do not get in my way. And by the way, I know you could care less if she is found dead, but you don't need to say it."

Ellis just looked at her and grinned. They proceeded to the next room being satisfied that the first room held nothing of importance.

Room 2 was quiet upon approaching the door. Angeline knocked and after a few moments, they could hear some movement from the other side of the door. A brown-haired, scruffy middle-aged man answered the door in his underwear.

Angeline filled with embarrassment and turned her head while she spoke. "Excuse me sir, would you mind terribly if we searched your room for a brief moment? We know someone who thinks they left something precious in one of these rooms and we are here to search for it."

And for the first time she was really caught off guard by the guy's reaction towards her. He seemed to like her brother more than her and was reluctant to let her in.

"It will not take long," Ellis chimed in and they were allowed in. They searched the room and found nothing of importance. The only things in there were a few undesirable "toys" for the man to use with his women. Ellis ended up having to search for clues by himself because the guy was too creepy for Angeline, and not because of his reaction to Ellis, but because he just had a weird vibe. She ended up waiting for Ellis outside of the room while the man kept staring at her with a strange look on his face. The stranger was examining her in several ways. Ellis noticed the look and decided to prolong his search in the room just to watch his sister squirm.

He eventually exited and said, "I didn't find anything fitting the description of the item being searched for. Thank you, stranger, for letting me search, "and for making my sister so damned uncomfortable! That was worth every moment!

They continued onto the next room. The guy slammed the door shut as they moved onto the next room.

"You know he wanted to use some of those implements on you," he laughed as he taunted his sister. "You might actually learn something by going in there!"

Angeline was not amused by her brother's insinuations, but she was glad he was able to search. "I need not have learned any lesson from him aside from what kind of people to stay away from! I think he liked you more. Perhaps he would have preferred you in there more than I. I get the feeling he would have enjoyed your…company." She smirked at her return taunting because both of them were thinking it, Ellis was just not as amused by the thought as his sister seemed to be.

As they approached the door to the third room they could hear two people, a man and a woman, doing something in the room. Angeline really didn't want to knock on the door but did anyway for the sake of her mother. The noises stopped and they could hear someone putting on clothing. A moment or two passed and a woman answered the door. She had sheets wrapped around her body and asked them what they wanted. Angeline gave the same story to her as she did the guy in room two. The lady let her in after motioning something to the other person in the room. Ellis had been hoping that it would be their mother that answered the door just to see his sister squirm. He was disappointed when a different woman answered the door. They searched that room and found nothing relating to their mother once again. They thanked the woman for letting them look and apologized for disturbing them. The two seemed to be slightly put off by the event, but not angry about it.

Moving onto room four they found it was empty as the first. There were only two more rooms left to search and upon going to those rooms they found that the fifth room was unoccupied as well. Room six had some dirty towels and dirty sheets but no one occupied the room. The twins figured whoever had the room had left early in the morning. They found a bloodstain on the sheets but the placement of those spots spoke volumes, which made them certain their mother had not been there.

Angeline was about to give up when she and her brother noticed something small and shiny on the floor of the hallway, in the corner crevice. Upon searching the area, they found a small earring that Angeline recognized as their mothers. It was near room five. In fact, upon closer inspection, they noticed it was considerably cleaner than the other unoccupied rooms. That one had been cleaned especially well, as if to hide or cover up something that happened in the room. Angeline ran down the hall and down the stairs. She told Jake that she found signs of her mother being up there, but she wasn't there in person. She asked Jake not to let anyone into room five until the lawkeeper instructed to do so. She then ran out of the inn and tavern and over to the lawhouse. She hardly knocked on the door before she rushed into the room to speak with the lawkeeper. The lawkeeper and Marcus were talking before her entrance, but they stopped abruptly to look at Angeline.

"I found something at the inn and tavern. I found mom's earring just outside of room five. Ellis and I both noticed that the room had been cleaned exceptionally well. I think you need to search the room for more clues as to where Mom is." Angeline was nearly out of breath at that point.

Marcus moved toward his daughter and held her. "I will search the room Sweetheart, with anyone else the Lawkeeper wants to send with me."

The lawkeeper agreed with Marcus' decision and walked into an adjacent room momentarily. He returned with a blond-haired boy that was his apprentice. The young adolescent seemed eager to investigate.

"Angel, go home and don't worry about a thing," Marcus instructed. "We'll take care of it." He kissed his little girl on the top of her head and held her a moment longer.

It was comforting, but she could not just simply go home. She nodded in agreement, but in her mind was not in agreement. She planned on searching for more clues elsewhere.

Ellis looked around the area a little more but found nothing. He decided to follow his sister and soon found her exiting the building with Marcus and the apprentice. He saw Angeline exiting in a different way than Marcus. Marcus approached his son. "Ellis, would you keep an eye out on your sister? I need you to ensure her safety."

Ellis agreed with a clever smile that was really a hidden smirk. Ellis followed after Angeline as Marcus and the apprentice went on their way to the inn.

Marcus and the apprentice searched the room five as well as the others but could only uncover what the twins had already discovered. The worried husband was very disheartened and decided to go home to ponder other places she might have gone. When he arrived home and looked for Angeline, he realized quickly she wasn't there. At least her brother is with her.

The lawkeeper called for a few of his men to gather at the lawhouse, and a few of his apprentices arrived eagerly. "I need you to go and look for Judith. She's gone missing. She was supposed to return home, but never did. Some of you will need to search Outside. And be careful! I need you to split up to cover more ground." The men searched the village that evening and then Outside the following morning to find her.

Meanwhile, Angeline wasn't going to waste time in finding their mother. She planned on leaving that day and to camp along the way. Ellis watched as she packed her things and he followed her to the general store. She noticed her brother was there and said nothing to him. She knew he was only going along to pester her, but it didn't bother her as much as the situation with their mother. She purchased some supplies and food to sustain her along the way. She didn't have much coin, but it was enough. The nearest town was a few days away by walking. Ellis bought some provisions as well for his use on the trip. Why is she not saying anything to me about following her around? He wanted it to bother her, though it didn't seem to.

While at home looking for his daughter, Marcus noticed something small and white. Angeline left her father a note, but Ellis tore it up and threw it out before he left the house. Luckily Angeline expected her problematic brother to pull something like that and made another, which Marcus found on his bed.

"Father,

I'm fine but I'm concerned for mother and am going to look for her myself. I'm pretty sure Ellis will be traveling with me at least for a little while. Don't worry about me, please, because I'll be fine. I love you and we'll bring mom home to you soon. Your loving daughter,

Angeline"

Marcus was still concerned for her, but as long as Ellis went with her it made him feel slightly better. He hoped that she was right and that they would return soon. He was now all alone, left with nothing but wonder and concern for all those he loved dearly. He decided to get some rest and the next morning he went to inform the lawkeeper that the children also decided to expand their search for Judith. The lawkeeper was very concerned for them, since they were only children of sixteen years, but there wasn't much he could do about it. Plus, the town would rest easier without Ellis there; though the folk would likely miss Angeline's smiling face. He quietly wished them a safe and quick return.

# Chapter 5:  The Journey Begins

Angeline took her first footsteps out of town. She had never been away from home before. All she knew about The Outside was that there was another town a few days walk away. At least it would be an adventure. She liked to experience new things every now and then.

Ellis traveled behind her, but not closely. He kept a comfortable distance from her. He was going to really enjoy watching how his annoying sister would react and respond to certain situations. He was gleeful from the thought of her falling to pieces in her first fight. He knew there were goblins around somewhere. If she ran into trouble, he questioned to himself, would I help her? He really wasn't sure. I'll just have to see how I feel when the time comes that she needs my help, which is inevitable. She's always had daddy looking after her. Well, you're not in daddy's world anymore. He grinned.

She simply kept on going and tried her best to ignore her brother. She was taking in the newness of the world, absorbing its vastness and beauty. Every sound was exciting. Every step was like it was her first, and it would lead her to a new place, perhaps even a better one. The sky was the color of her eyes, ever such a light blue with hints of purple. The sun, though she had seen it before, seemed a new and awesomely vibrant light violet. As she took more and more steps away from the place she knew as home, she knew that she was doing the right thing.

She only looked back once and whispered, "I will return, Daddy." There was a deep sincerity in her voice as her thoughts turned to what it might be like upon her return, with her mother at her side and a more appreciative brother at her other side. She smiled, and then turned her attentions to the present and future.

Angeline traveled on throughout the afternoon on a mostly untrodden path through forest. Since few travelers came to her town, the forest was pretty well intact. Even though her neighbors used wood as building material, the trees grew very quickly. She decided to stop to eat a little something, and besides, her feet hurt. She wasn't use to so much walking around and especially with a pack of things on her back. She decided that she definitely needed to rest for a moment. Ellis soon caught up to her.

"Wow, not twenty feet away from town and you have to stop already?!" he poked… "And you think you'll make it where? You can't handle this. Admit it and turn around now…don't worry, I'll look for mom." He was hiding a grin, but barely. He was jesting, but trying to sound sincere. Angeline knew better.

She disregarded his comment and took a few more minutes to rest before she got back on her feet. "Why do you get such joy out of pestering me, brother? I don't treat you that way."

Ellis just smiled and shrugged. *You bother me in other ways, with your kindness, with your spoiling of my fun, oh yes. You bother me more than anyone else on this land could ever manage, even if it is just for the simple fact that I cannot remove you from my life. I am stuck with your incessant …everything!* His face smiled, but inside he wanted to scream the more he thought about her and her annoying traits. He wanted to squish something. He then tried to think happy thoughts, such as Lew, the boy he killed. Angeline was disturbed by this, but remained silent.

They walked silently down the rough dirt and only lightly trodden weed path that the locals called a road. It could hardly be called that, but it was. They heard the sounds of the forest creatures, like songbirds and insects, and little else. They walked on further and when night started to fall, Angeline took out her bedroll and her pillow and set them up just off the path. Off the "path" meant sunken into the tall grass and weeds. She didn't dare go further into the woods for they were very dark and she didn't know what lurked in them. She felt safer by the road and oddly she felt safer with Ellis there to protect her. I know he thinks he would not protect me given the choice, but he wouldn't be here if he didn't care. She knew he'd never admit to it of course, but she knew he cared about her on some level. Really, she figured that she was all he had, since he hated that their mom and dad liked her better than him. She thought about that as she dozed off. Ellis just took out his own sleeping items and proceeded to go to sleep as well, though he'd keep his ears perked for anything strange in the night.

Sometime in the night, Ellis awoke to the sounds of odd jittering coming from all around their camp. He wasn't sure if he should wake his sister up or not. Ah, let her sleep, she'll just be in my way. He sat up and glanced around. Little glowing eyes were seen around the perimeter of the camp and he prepared to have some fun while she slept. He didn't even need weapons, though they were also fun. The creatures began to converge on the camp and the jittering became louder. He wondered how many of them were out there. Who cares, the more the merrier and there's no time to count them, unless I count the heads rolling. He focused on some of them that he could vaguely see outlines of. Flames shot out of the center of the unknown creatures, bursting the little bodies and lighting up the camp. There were jittering screams and the sound of many little feet running away. Some were infuriated even more and tried to move in to attack him. Before they could get to him though, or become visible, they went up into flames as well.

Angeline was now startled awake and wondering what was happening. All she could see was flames bursting all over in front of her. She was lucky that none hit her, but they came close. The foliage from the woods was somewhat on fire. When the fury of flame died down she could see burnt pieces of things that she couldn't identify. She used her ice to cool things down so the forest wouldn't catch fire completely and burn down from the attack.

She turned to Ellis, "What happened?"

"Just go back to sleepy-land; it is all over with now. You need not worry your annoying little head with it."

She couldn't help but worry or at least wonder what those things were, but Ellis seemed to have taken care of whatever came in the night. She slowly went back to sleep and awoke a few hours later. She ate some more rations, as did Ellis when they awoke. Ellis was oddly quiet in the morning except to suggest they should get underway. She just nodded and thought, it would be wise not to pry about what happened last night. For now I will leave it alone.

# Chapter 6:  New Friends

When they set out in the morning, the skies were slightly cloudy.  The wind was slightly chilled in the morning.  It soon warmed up to a temperature that was almost too hot for both of them.  Somehow they managed to endure the heat. They said nothing to each other all day, but nothing needed to be said.  They were accustomed to not speaking to each other.  Neither of them minded it at all.  In fact, if either of them did say anything, the other would just tend to ignore them anyway.  That was just how they were and it worked for them.  Angeline didn't want to provoke bad behavior from Ellis showing off, and Ellis didn't want Angeline thinking he liked her.

They stopped for a brief lunch and continued on their way.  Angeline's feet hurt but she didn't want to complain because she didn't really enjoy Ellis when he became irritated.  He would get irritated if she complained about anything, so she just decided to keep her mouth shut and deal with it.  The newness of the adventure was still there, but she wanted to rest her feet.  Afternoon turned to nighttime before they realized it. So much time had passed.  It felt like a lifetime.  They could eventually see the next town up ahead.  Angeline couldn't wait to get there and take a bath and sleep in an actual bed.  Ellis was just looking forward to having some time away from her for the night.

They reached the town of Raist in short order, and went straight for the inn and tavern whose location was pretty obvious.  They were both tired and cranky and needed time to themselves.  When they reached the inn and tavern, the lights were out except for a candle in the window.  The dark streets were empty.  The twins made their way over to the inn and Angeline began to knock on the closed door. Ellis just pushed it open in front of her.  As they entered, a little bell rang lightly.  An old man came out of the back and seemed surprised to see visitors, but he was happy to rent them some rooms.  Angeline pondered asking about her mother, but she really just wanted some sleep so she figured she'd ask in the morning.  Ellis didn't even think about their mother and went straight upstairs.

Angeline looked at the innkeeper and politely asked, "by the way, would it also be possible for a bath to be drawn for me? But only if it won't be too inconvenient to ask."

"Yes, young lady, it is not a problem.  Let me call for my niece, Jenny, and have her prepare it for you right away."  The innkeeper was more than happy to please his customers.

Jenny was sleepy-eyed, but did as she was told. Jenny seemed to be about the twins' age. As she prepared the bath, and Angeline watched, Jenny turned her attentions to Angeline. "Just wanted to say welcome to The Twilight Inn and Tavern. If you need anything at all don't hesitate to ask." Her voice was sweet, but shy. Angeline suspected that she hadn't been working for her uncle long.

After Jenny left, Angeline disrobed and put aside her traveling clothes. The room was cool, but she quickly warmed back up once she began to put her first leg into the tub, which was set into the floor of the bathroom. Angeline enjoyed her bath which was the perfect temperature and extremely relaxing. It was definitely helping her aching feet as well. She lingered in the bathtub soaking in perfection, reflecting on the day's events and all the new sights and sounds. She was happy with her first adventure out of Ishta, but she was exhausted, more than she thought she would be. Her soaking time came to an end when the water cooled down too much, and she prepared herself for bed. It was her chance to rest her feet before resuming the search for her mother.

Ellis went to his room, took off his boots, sat on the bed, and leaned back. He was tired, though he'd never admit it. He reflected upon his first day away from Ishta as well. He thought about the new sights and sounds, the feel of the tall grasses upon his hands as they walked. The feel of the ground was still moist beneath his boots, but firm enough not to sink. He thought about being hidden away and free for once. He was free without constraints, and the possibility of his future freedom was a shining light. The only thing standing in his way of true freedom was his sister, but if he wanted to, he was free to choose to whether to leave her and abandon her to her foolish quest. He thought about the slaughter by firestorm of the invading unknown creatures and drifted into sleep happily. Angeline didn't need to wonder what all happened the night before, as she got the jist of anything she might have missed. Both of the siblings got their well-needed rest and were up bright and early in the morning.

Angeline awoke cheery and ready for the new day. She felt renewed again and ready to resume the search. She headed down the stairs to the bartender to ask about her mother when she realized a different person was tending the counter. The new guy was in his twenties with long brown hair and deep brown eyes. He had a few scars that were very telling of adventuring at some point in his young life.

"Good morning Miss, I am Marku. Is there some assistance I can give you?" He gave her a slight bow.

She smiled at his courteous nature. "I am here because my mother has gone missing and I was wondering if you or anyone here has seen her." She described her mother as best she could.

He didn't seem to recognize the description of her but said, "I don't always see who comes in as I am not the only one working here. Would you care for something to drink sweetheart?" He thought she was beautiful. He hadn't ever seen anyone like her before. Though she was in a better mood, concern for her mother still showed on her face. It is a shame for such a beautiful creature to have to go through this, Marku thought.

"Just some water please."

He poured some into a glass with ice for her. Items were generally frozen by the nirka flower. Nirka flowers grew in the coldest of climates and maintained the coldness for the extent of their life cycle. It wasn't a rare thing to see them in use, but they were costly for those wanting to purchase harvested nirka flowers. Some travelers made their money by hunting these white flowers with a glittery blue sheen. While alive, the flowers glowed brightly. You could tell how old the plant was by its glow.

She took her drink and walked over to a table to wait for her brother to wake up. As she looked around she saw that the tavern and the town were bustling with people in the streets and others coming out of their rooms. A few people were already starting to drink, but not too many.

Ellis entered the inn through the front door of the inn and tavern, which surprised Angeline since she was expecting him to be sleeping. His mind was silent that morning so she had no idea he was already awake.

His expression was blank. "We should look around town for the things we might need."

"Marku said he hadn't seen our mother, but that's not to say she can't be around town."

She was ready to start her search and Ellis was ready to see what had been missing from their small town. I really want no part in this hunt for that whore, and she certainly cannot be considered my mother, though everyone seems to think so. Why is my brat of a sibling so insistent upon this goal? It is meaningless, but then again she always concerns herself with meaningless tasks like "helping people". I don't see why that matters since it is merely a waste of time. I'd rather help myself and he often did so. Angeline sometimes had a difficult time trying to understand why he was so unwilling to help people. As long as he was with her though, she could deal with his attitude.

Looking around at Raist with fresh new eyes and sunlight, the town of Raist was larger than Ishta. Raist was mostly composed of wooden buildings that needed some repair. There were a few stone buildings, but not many. At night, Raist was dead, but sunlight seemed to breathe new life on it.

Angeline decided to go to the local church to Aria, the goddess of love, to look for clues as to where her mother might have gone. The church was the only building in town that was colorful and kept up. The walls were made from red, pink, and white rocks. It was not a typical place Judith might go, but Angeline had to check. As she approached the door to knock, it was opened by a blond woman in a red and pink dress. The priestess invited her to enter. "What can I do for you today ma'am?" Her voice was sweet and soft. It had a calming effect on Angeline.

"My mother went missing and I wondered if you or anyone you know has seen her." Angeline described her mother again, as she thought she would have to do over and over again. A thought that threatened to darken her mood, but the priestess's aura was calming.

She expected the priestess to say "no", even though she hoped for the best. Angeline's surprise came when the priestess informed her that she did indeed see a woman matching that description with a group of gentlemen a while ago.

"The men were hardly gentlemen actually, but it wasn't really my affair to interrupt. The woman did not seem to be harmed at all, but she seemed tired or out of sorts. I reported the incident to Priestess Sana and she said she would look into it. In fact, Sana went after them to investigate and still hasn't returned." The blond priestess looked concerned. "Could you, in your search for your mother, look for Sana also? She has red hair and green eyes and wore a pink and white dress. Sana also had a necklace with a ruby pendant in the shape of a 's'."

"I will look for her along my way as I search for Mom."

"Thank you my dear, any help is appreciated."

"Which direction did they head off in?"

"East."

Angeline took her leave and quickly went east through town. She finally had a lead and some hope.

When she arrived on the east side of town, she noticed it was much worse off from her entry point in Raist. This side had trash and filth all around on the street and there were numerous filthy, scruffy-looking men causing a commotion down a side alley. She passed the alley quick enough and was thankful for it. She kept her cool and continued walking. Eventually she arrived at a rowdy inn and tavern, but didn't really want to go in. She had to enter if she wanted to know more about where her mom was.

Angeline entered the Naughty Man's Inn and Tavern and observed quite a few people in there. There were all kinds: gamblers, swindlers, and scoundrels. She knew she had to get through this to know more, but she dreaded staying there even a few moments. She decided to try to alter people's moods in her favor. It was something she discovered she could do when she was growing up, but like the ice, never really knew where it came from.    The effect would make them slightly more pleasant to be around. She concentrated for a few moments on the thoughts of a less rowdy bunch of people as she stared at them, and it was done. She noticed the difference right away. A group of guys playing cards started playing fairly instead of their normal method of cheating. They were not the only table like that to be affected. A few groups of people playing different games started playing fairly. Confusion and shock set in for the gamblers when they oddly admitted that they had been cheating. The people they confessed that little tidbit to took it in and thanked them for being so honest. She found it humorous, but knew she had to get out of there as soon as she could.

She approached the bartender/innkeeper and asked "have you seen a group of men carrying off a woman..." and she described her mother. She was quick and to the point so she could make a quick exit before the effect wore off. She had never tried it on so many people and was unsure of its duration.

He thought about it for a moment. "Lady, men carry women off all the time in this neighborhood, especially here, but from your description... yeah it does sound familiar. They checked out a few days ago and went east, but they're quite the...colorful group of personalities, even compared to the low lives around here. If you're concerned for her, you'd better get to her soon. There's no telling what they'll do to her, let alone what they've done to her already! They even tried to hustle me but failed." He smiled at Angeline. "Would you like something to drink with me later, beautiful? Oh and I'll have to ask you to pay me for that information. I don't snitch people out for free. I only told you this ahead of time because you look like an honest person, unlike my usual clientele."

She had to think about it, but figured that it would probably be a good thing since she could get more information from him. She paid him some coin and accepted his invitation for a drink on the condition that it was on a better side of town. "Why don't we meet at the Twilight Inn and Tavern?"

He happily agreed. "I'll see you there in 5 hours...roughly."

"Great, I look forward to it." She was looking for more information to help her and didn't want to be rude to him by denying his request.

While Ellis watched his sister go off on her pointless search, he was going to look around the town a bit. He went around to the shops to peruse what they had to offer. He was surprised at the vast selection of items because there were so many more things to get in Raist compared to the little town of Ishta. It never had the things he needed or wanted to own. As he was shopping, a cloaked and hooded man approached him from out of nowhere and put a piece of paper in his hand. As Ellis read the note his face lit up. He followed the directions on the note, which led to an alley where a large burly guy was just standing and leaning on the wall.

As Ellis approached, the guy looked him over and asked him "what's the greatest thing in the world?" His voice was deep and almost intimidating. Anyone else would have run in fear.

Ellis replied "a woman with her mouth sewn shut" and grinned as he said it. The burly guy looked at him and laughed.

"Go on in." He stepped away from the wall and a door opened before Ellis.

"Love the answer by the way. I must meet the person who came up with that!" It just tickled Ellis. It was the funniest thing he'd heard in a while.

The doorman smirked and said, "and I never get tired of hearing the answer."

I know just who it fits too, if only I could do it!

As a curious Ellis entered, he found that he had to descend a number of stairs to finally arrive in front of an iron bound wooden door. There was no handle on the door so he decided to knock. The door opened quickly and he found himself in a room with a number of vendors sitting on the floor with various wares spread about pieces of cloth. There were a few people there who were making some purchases. As he looked around he saw the cloaked and hooded man coming toward him at a casual pace.

"Hello, I'm glad to see you made it. I was hoping you'd arrive," the man told him. "So what's your name?"

"Ellis. And yours?"

"Jacar." Jacar's voice was almost like a sinister whisper.

"Nice to meet you. I love the password by the way. It's true. So why did you pick me to hand the note to? I could've been anyone and you could have been in trouble since this place is obviously secret." Ellis was curious about this place and this new person. His interest was piqued.

"I just sensed something about you and knew that you would enjoy what we have to sell. You seemed quite interested in some of the common items up above. But the rarer relative items would really interest you I figured."

"Yes, but everything looks ordinary here too, aside from you trying to keep this place secret."

"Everything may look ordinary here but it isn't." Jacar picked up a cane and pulled a sword out of it. He picked up a leather strip and showed Ellis that it could hold daggers and knives discretely. That item could be concealed easily as well. He showed Ellis some boot knives and buckle knives and other things that interested Ellis tremendously. These were hidden weapons and the means to hide other normal weapons. "We even carry such things to ensure the deaths of your enemies in quick succession should you need such a thing for a very sturdy living foe. It does not effect the undead however, and we are far from priests here." The last part received many laughs from around the room.

"I think I like this place already." Ellis was very pleased with it. This place will be of great use to me, even though I don't technically need weapons. Jacar could be a great contact.

Jacar was thinking the same about Ellis. "Please, come into my office, there will be plenty of time for shopping later." Ellis agreed with a nod and Jacar lead Ellis up a few stairwells and through a few doors and hallways. They finally came to a door plainer than the others. It almost made it look like a broom closet. Jacar tapped on the door a few times in certain places and the door opened. The tap spots seemed almost random, but he figured that was intentional. Jacar invited him in his office and they talked.

"I heard about your encounter with the goblins that tried to attack you and your female companion in the forest. They exploded into flames...," he seemed to be fishing for an explanation. "You?"

Ellis had no reservations or fears of others knowing what he could do. He actually preferred it because then they stayed out of his way unless they had a death wish. "It is something I have been able to do since I was born, and most of the times I tried when I was young, it failed," though Ellis didn't say why. "I enjoy it tremendously when it works." Ellis grinned a wicked grin at the thought of pleasant memories.

"So where is your female companion?"

"Don't know and could care less. In a ditch I hope." His answer was blank and cold.

Jacar looked surprised about that, but said nothing more about it. "Well then, perhaps some shopping to brighten the mood, perhaps some potentially illegal and deadly supplies?" Jacar, after a moment of silence in thought said, "You know, the streets aren't safe for a woman such as your companion to be wandering around alone. Women have been turning up missing lately. Whether you care about her or not, you had better find her before she disappears as well. Just a suggestion, take it or leave it."

Ellis just shrugged and said, "I'm really not concerned about her in the streets. Perhaps she'll get attacked, but until I'm damn well ready to leave, she's on her own." Ellis walked out of the office and turned for a moment to say again, "it was a pleasure making your acquaintance," then turned around and shopped.

Jacar was surprised at Ellis' response regarding his female companion and figured he should go find her if Ellis wouldn't. Jacar's girlfriend disappeared and he just couldn't understand why Ellis wouldn't go after his traveling companion. He left the area a different way than Ellis entered and found one of his co-workers. Jacar asked them if they had seen the "Fire Starter's" girlfriend around.

"I saw her walking east, but I wasn't able to follow," said the lackey informant. "I got distracted by normal business. Was I supposed to follow her?" The question was an excuse, but Jacar agreed that he never gave him those instructions.

"I just wanted to know so I could tell if she was safe, or if she needs assistance."

Jacar headed east quickly, looking around him as he went, and watching carefully for any sign of her. He saw a group of scruffy guys in an alley and made his way over to see what was happening. He found that one of the bums in the neighborhood had been murdered and the guys were just trying to see if he had anything good to steal. Jacar passed them up and headed east again, since the bum was not his issue to deal with. Jacar's presence was invisible most of the time. He preferred it that way unless he meant to be visible and known. It was actually fairly common in Raist for muggings and occasional murders to occur. It was far from safe, but some parts of town were better than others. He finally arrived at the Naughty Man's Inn and Tavern. He knew this bar was notorious for people disappearing so he decided to check it out. As he walked in to scope the room, he found Angeline and the bartender smiling and talking. He knew the bartender there because they used to be co-workers. At least she is safe for the moment, he thought.

She began to walk away from the bartender and turned back around for a moment. She looked rather embarrassed. "I'm sorry", she blushed, "I never asked your name."

The bartender smiled at her as she blushed, "the name's Laic, sweetheart." She was cute when she blushed.

She smiled back, still blushing. "See you in a few hours." Then she walked out the door. As she headed back to the other inn and tavern, Jacar followed her. She kept feeling like she was being followed, but she didn't stop to find out if her feelings were true. She hurried back to the Twilight and stopped to eat lunch upon her return. The food wasn't great, but it was edible. The mystery stew she was given needed more spice to enhance the dull and lackluster flavor.

Jacar followed her to the Twilight and then turned back thinking she was safe. He wanted to speak with Laic. He waited for Laic to get off work and caught Laic in a nearby alley.

"Hello Laic." His voice came from behind the surprised bartender. "I want to know about the girl."

As Jacar asked him about her, Laic realized he never got her name either. He didn't worry about it though since he would be seeing her soon. "Jacar, you spying on me now?"

"Only when I have to, and no this isn't about you. It is about her." His matter of fact tone wasn't surprising to Laic.

"Got nothin' to say yet, forgot to even ask her name. Go ransack a wizard's home or something. You're cramping my style." Laic dismissed his presence to go on his date with Angeline. He wondered what her story was.

Jacar decided to follow him and listen in on their conversation.

The two headed for the Twilight, but they stayed separated. Jacar remained in the shadows and trailed Laic. When Laic arrived, he didn't see his exotic-looking date anywhere. He had never seen a woman like her before: the long and slightly curled strawberry red hair, opaque sky blue eyes like a frosted over sky with a bit of light purple, 5'5", slender but built legs, nice hips, and healthy sized breasts. Laic definitely wanted to get to know her. He began to wonder if she had stood him up when he couldn't find her. After he realized that the possibility of her standing him up was the least likely, the thought occurred to him that maybe she was kidnapped like the other girls. He went to the innkeeper and asked him where she was. Laic had to describe her because of course he didn't get her name, which on many levels seemed suspicious. Still, the innkeeper obviously knew who he was talking about.

"She left shortly before you arrived," was the only information he was given.

Laic decided that he should look for her and just as he was about to go through the door, Angeline and Laic ran straight into one another. She nearly fell, but he caught her just in time. He noticed her face was turning a bright shade of red while he unknowingly and unintentionally held her close to him for a few minutes, still in the doorway. As soon as he realized what he was doing, he released her.

"You okay sweetheart?" He still felt a bit thrown by the situation. Being so close to her was sending odd signals to his body that almost paralyzed him. He wasn't sure how to react, but he wanted to be a gentleman, at least for now.

She was still blushing and yet confirmed her safety. She had never been so close to someone like that before. It was odd for her too. She didn't know how she was supposed to react. She was paralyzed and speechless for a minute. After composing herself, she went to sit down at one of the tables as he followed her.

Laic was a gentleman only a few inches taller than her, medium brown hair, brown eyes. He was simply dressed, in browns of various shades. He wasn't a large burly man, nor was he tiny. He was slender, but decently built from what she could tell. He wasn't extremely handsome either, but he wasn't ugly by any means. He was very much average looking in several ways. He seemed to be just a little older than her, but she didn't ask. Still there was something about him that caught her attention. She liked the way he spoke to her, the way he treated her. It was something new.

They began to drink and talk.

"So you got my name, but somehow I managed to miss yours. Such things are not common occurrences for me. I apologize." I got lost in your eyes.

In a happy tone, "oh that's okay, I understand. I nearly forgot to ask you as well. My name is Angeline." She smiled and blushed as they spoke. Laic seemed like a nice guy. She asked a lot about her mother and the guys who she was seen with.

Laic told her "they've been coming in a lot with different girls each time. I've had my suspicions about them, but you must understand those people on that side of town always do that. Most men who frequent that bar have a different woman with them every night. That bar is certainly no place for you to be. It's bad enough for whores, let alone beautiful women who aren't. It is a dangerous time to travel right now with a lot of women disappearing off the streets like they never existed here."

She seemed surprised by the description of the place he worked at. She seemed disturbed about it, but said, "I knew a few were missing but not as many as you make it sound. And how do you know I'm not a ..."

"Sweetheart, I've seen enough whores to know you do not behave like one. You could never be one. For one thing...they don't blush like you do when a man looks at you. And believe me when I say there's a shortage of women like you, especially here in Raist. It is a sad fact."

She blushed even more. Once she composed herself a bit, "so why do you work there if it's so terrible?" She was trying to change the subject.

"It's a job," he said plainly. "Plus it's good to keep an eye on what's going on. Are you traveling alone? If you are, then I must insist I keep you company. I don't want to see you get hurt or snatched. I just met you, and I am looking forward to getting to know you. Plus I hate working at that inn and tavern anyway."

She smiled. "Your offer is sweet and I thank you for it sincerely, but I travel with my brother and I honestly do not know how he will react to you. He's um...difficult at times where strangers are concerned. He tends not to play well with others."

Jacar was surprised to hear that they were siblings, but was relieved. Jacar was in the corner under the cover of shadows, listening to every word. He was only relieved for a moment though since that meant her brother didn't give a damn about what happened to her. This then led to thoughts of how much danger Angeline was truly in.

Laic seemed noticeably disappointed. "I'm at least glad that someone is with you in these dangerous times."

Angeline felt guilty about making him feel bad. She thought he seemed nice, but she really didn't know how her brother would react.

"So where are you headed off to next?" He paused.

"East of course, since they seem to have taken my mother that way. I must find her, Laic."

Jacar instantly thought of an idea about how she could be escorted by Laic. He smoothly exited the shadows so it looked like he just walked in, and approached Laic.

"There you are. I have a job for you if you aren't too busy." Jacar glanced over at Angeline. "I need a few...supplies from Rokk. I need you to get them as soon as you can. Someone will be waiting for you to pick it up." He then turned to Angeline. "Excuse me, my lady, I did not mean to interrupt your conversation."

Laic gave Jacar an odd look, but knew what he was trying to do, and agreed to the task. Jacar exited just as quickly as he entered, though he still listened in on the conversation from nearby. Laic looked to Angeline, "seems we're headed in the same direction. What do you say? Will you have me with you or will I need to travel alone? It would be a shame to have to travel alone, and to think about the beautiful woman I could've been traveling with."

Angeline really didn't want him to travel by himself if he was going the same way, so she agreed. Ellis will just have to deal with it. She never asked Ellis to come along anyway.

Laic was happy that she said yes. "Angeline, you should stay in your room this evening. I am concerned for your safety in these rough times. I will be by tomorrow morning to travel with you. Goodnight my lady, till tomorrow." He smiled at her and gave her a wink and a slight bow. He wanted to do more, something more, but thought better of it.

"Alright, goodnight to you as well then."

With a bow, he took his leave. Laic hurried home to prepare for his trip. Once he was home, he discovered Jacar was also there. "Follow me for long?"

Jacar laughed lightly. "Just all the way from the inn. You're too easy to follow."

"Really? Well I wasn't making myself hidden so there isn't much to that. So what brings you in to grace my house with your presence uninvited?"

"I gave you the excuse to go because her brother has no concern for her safety. He simply could care less what happens to her. She needs more than Ellis for a traveling companion, especially in these times."

Laic began to wonder just what kind of brother Angeline had, and why he was even traveling with her. Laic looked forward to finding out all that information the following day. He got all of his gear and provisions for travel together and had a nice meal at home since it was doubtful he'd have another one anytime soon. Laic lived alone after his last girlfriend left him. His family didn't live too far away though. After she left him, he kept the house, and opted not to move back in with his parents. Laic went to sleep and awoke bright and early. He looked forward to the new day.

Ellis continued shopping, went out drinking, and even had a few girls for company that evening. He never once checked to see if his sister was alright. He convinced himself he didn't care and didn't think about her at all after his talk with Jacar. He just had his fun and woke up early. He didn't look forward to moving on with his sister, but he was still determined to make her miserable, so he would endure her annoying sweetness. He was curious what she found out, but not because he cared at all. Not about what happened to their mother, no..."her" mother. He just wanted to know what she found out. He wasn't going to help her with anymore information gathering on this trip. That was a burden she would have to shoulder. He just wanted to see the world and enjoy life outside of that nowhere town they grew up in. When he was finished getting ready for the trip in the morning, he went downstairs and ate a morning meal.

Angeline went to her room after the meeting with Laic and sat on the bed in thought. She wondered if their mother was alright. She hoped so, but she feared the worst, not only for their mother, but also for the other missing women. She didn't know what she would find, but she had a feeling it was very bad. She also caught her brother's thoughts that night and she eventually tuned them out because she did not want to know how he felt and what he thought while he was enjoying the company of strange women. Nor did she enjoy his thoughts lately on the topic of their mother. She knew that she would be doing this alone, but she also didn't see why he just had to come along to be a pain in her side. He could have just parted ways, but he didn't because he wanted to see her suffer. In her mind, that type of behavior was not normal. She went to sleep after tuning him out of her head and woke up bright and early only to be pounded with his thoughts of making her suffer. She was accustomed to getting that first thing in the morning, but she was not in the mood that particular morning for his attitude. She went downstairs to eat her breakfast and wait for Laic.

## Chapter 7: The Darkness Begins

Angeline was the first to arrive downstairs for breakfast, where she awaited Laic's arrival. She was quiet as her brother came down and made some random smart ass comment. Ellis also decided to sit down right next to her. He was quite cheerful and quite annoying that morning. He tried to goad her into saying something, but she wouldn't give him the satisfaction. She could tell it was making him irritated because he was trying so hard. Laic walked in the door and saw the twins sitting next to each other. This was the first time he had seen her brother and could tell by the look on her face that she was really annoyed. Laic decided to break up the discomfort by sitting on the other side of her and saying "good morning". He then turned to Ellis who looked very surprised and irritated himself.

"Who the hell do you think you are approaching my sister that way?!"

Laic just smiled and said, "oh so sorry, and a good morning to you as well. I met your sister yesterday, as she had to travel alone through the city. Someone had to watch out for this beautiful woman's safety with all the disappearances of late. Times are dangerous...sorry what was your name? Mine's Laic."

Ellis was deathly silent and giving Laic the evil eye. He knew that was a jab at his "brotherly" skills.

"I didn't see you at all yesterday. I would have thought you would join your lovely sister for dinner while in a strange city. You know, she could've easily been abducted were it not for my company. Maybe it is not my place, but it would seem as if you have little care for her where safety is concerned. Would you have known what happened, if she was abducted, upon your return? Not likely." Laic was politely not backing away from this.

Angeline just sat there smirking on the inside, but tried to keep a straight face on the outside. She could hear all the words that were going through her brother's mind and they were quite humorous, though dark. She knew she would have to calm her brother down or things were going to get ugly quickly. Ellis was thinking of all kinds of things to say to this jerk who all of the sudden seemed to be imposing himself and complaining about Ellis' ability to be a brother. He was starting to think about setting him on fire and watching him scream and burn to the ground when he felt his sister's cool touch on his shoulder that distracted him from his thoughts.

Angeline smiled at the two of them and said, "if we plan on traveling together, the two of you will have to learn to get along." She turned to her brother. "Laic is right Ellis, you weren't anywhere around to even try to look after my safety, but I'm sure you were doing your own research to find mom. For that reason only, I will excuse your lack of duty. You have cared for my well-being, but were not always able to be around. And to me, that's fine. I don't always want you around and I know on that we both agree."

"I meant no offense, sir. Sorry if you took it as such. I was just... surprised no one was looking out for her."

Ellis was still pissed and glaring at Laic. "You will not be accompanying us and that is my final say." He even slammed his hand down on the table of added emphasis.

Angeline really wasn't in the mood to put up with her brother that morning so she excused herself from Laic's company momentarily and pulled her brother aside and away from Laic before he could hurt him.

Before Ellis could say anything, Angeline spoke first. "Laic will be joining us as he has business in the next stop for us. I want you to come and I want him to come. You will have to live with it or go your own way. I never asked you along anyway, but for the most part I was glad you came."

Angeline had enough of Ellis's attitude and was letting him have an earful that he needed. "I know you aren't here to actually help me and that you could care less what happens to our mom, whether she is alive or dead. If you want to see Paelencien, then there are many other ways to accomplish that besides coming with me." She then stopped to watch the expression on her brother's face. She had never been so bold and blunt with him before.

He was speechless because this the most his sister had ever said to him and she certainly never spoke to anyone like that before. She was laughing inside at the expression on his face, but she wasn't laughing on the outside.

Ellis was stunned for a few minutes at what he heard his sister say to him, but then gained his composure as if nothing happened. "I just came along to protect you and don't you ever say I never did anything for you or that I never even cared about you." Ellis then simply walked away. He wasn't thinking that of course, but his sister's actions that morning had intrigued him enough to lie and want to stay. He could still make her miserable. He thought that it might be easier anyway. He sat back at the table and proceeded to finish his breakfast. He said nothing to Laic upon his return to the table. She returned a few moments after her brother and sat in between them again.

Like nothing had happened she asked, "Enjoying your meal, Laic?"

"Yes." Laic smiled, but wondered what was said during the conversation. "Is everything okay, my lady?"

"Yes, we are ready to set out with you traveling with us."

Laic was rather surprised by this, and was happy to hear it.

After the meal, they left to go further east again. There was still a lot more forested land left to go.

They made their way through the bad side of town and out of the eastern gates, which were not really large gates as one would suspect, but more like fences. The forest in this area was getting thicker and thicker so there wasn't much light to be had, even during daytime. Their luck wasn't the greatest either because it started to become cloudy with a storm in the distance. If they did not find shelter soon, the trip through the forest would take a turn for the worse.

Laic said, "I heard there are plenty of caves around here on fairly high ground and we could at least have some shelter there."

Angeline responded, "We should get as far as we can before stopping. I am worried that each minute we waste needlessly, our mother is closer and closer to danger, if not already in danger."

They traveled for a few more hours until it was starting to get really dark. So they finally went in search for some shelter. They managed to find a small cave nearby that would at least keep them dry. It wasn't comfortable because they had to scrunch together, but they were dry. None of them spoke during the downpour of cold rain. An uncomfortable silence remained among them. Angeline was usually quiet, Ellis had nothing to say to either of them, and Laic didn't know what to say to break the ice.

So they all just sat there quietly and awkwardly as the rainstorm continued to get worse. The thunder and lightning worsened and a bolt of lightning even struck a nearby tree. Ellis found a bit of dry wood and an opening into a larger cave as they sat there. He decided to check it. He could at least start a fire and keep warm. The opening to the larger cave was just big enough for one person to go through at a time. After Ellis went through, the other two followed. This cave was definitely drier and big enough to start a small fire to keep warm. Ellis put the wood he found down and sparked it up mentally. All Laic could do was watch in awe as the brother lit the campfire without any more effort than a single thought.

The fire was lit, so they could keep warm. Laic eventually thanked Ellis for lighting the fire. He was trying to break the long silence between the three. Ellis was surprised to hear Laic thank him and responded, "you're welcome" before he even thought about what he was saying. After he realized what he said, Ellis clammed up again and stared through the opening they came through.

Angeline was shocked to hear her brother say that and smiled when she could hear him cussing in his head for speaking without thinking first. She wanted to have a conversation with Laic, but didn't know what to say to him. She was so use to not saying anything that this was rather odd for her. She decided to start drawing cave art to occupy herself and Laic watched as she drew. He was impressed by her skill with art and told her that he hadn't seen anyone who could draw that well.

"I am better with a paintbrush, but I could draw with anything if I needed to."

Just as their conversation started, it was ended abruptly by a loud crash of lightning that struck the tree closest to the cave entrance. They all jumped at the loud, sudden crash.

"Storms have never been this bad before, not around here that I know of since I was born." Laic was slightly concerned as to why the weather was worsening now.

Angeline said quietly, "I've seen some bad storms and they bother me less than some other things. Lightning, I can handle. There are other things that scare me." She glanced over to Ellis, but he seemed to be ignoring the conversation altogether. As Angeline looked down at her drawing she saw that it was ruined since she jumped when the lightning struck. There was a horrible scar down the drawing, but she wasn't concerned about it. It was just a way to pass the time. She just wanted to find her mother and she wished the storm would end soon.

She needed to move around so she got up to look around the cave. She spotted another tunnel leading off of the cave room they occupied. Laic saw it as well as he was watching her get up from the floor. They both decided to take a look at it to see if there was another room nearby while they had to wait for the storm to pass. They peered into the hole and found only darkness. The tunnel sloped downward, that much they could tell. They couldn't tell how far though because all they had to go by was the firelight. Laic felt along the ground and could feel that near the hole, the ground was damp. If they didn't watch it, they'd end up in the hole! He started to tell Angeline the discovery, but it was too late. She had already slipped and he was unable to catch her in time. He called out to her as he could hear her falling down the tunnel.

At this point Ellis was at the mouth of the tunnel trying to look in after her, but she couldn't be seen by either of them.

"We need to go after her Ellis!"

"Yes, I believe we should as well, but we should wait until we have more light."

"What if she's injured and needs our attention immediately? She could die if we wait too long."

Ellis spoke the words neither wanted to admit. "She could already be dead for all we know. I hear her no longer."

They could hear no sound from the dark tunnel before them now and they didn't receive any answers except their own voices when they tried to call down to her. Laic wasn't going to wait. He had to go in after her. Ellis thought he was insane for going in after her, but he wasn't going to stop him. Laic slid down the tunnel after her and hit the floor with a loud thud. His rump really hurt, but he didn't think anything was broken. He took out a torch from his pack and lit it so he could see. He searched the area and found no trace of her anywhere. That concerned him. Laic called back up to Ellis and he heard Ellis call back in reply.

"She's not here, not where she should have landed!" Laic tried to make sure he could still be heard.

"She has to be. She would've answered us or called to us were she at all able to." Ellis was now concerned, but too preoccupied with the situation at the moment to realize he was concerned. "Unconscious or dead people do not just get up and walk away...unless they're undead, and that's highly unlikely."

"I'm going to look for her, see if I can tell where she went." He searched the floor for evidence of her and found nothing. He kept looking and finally something shiny caught his eye. He went over to the shiny object and found a gold necklace with a ruby pendant in the shape of a "s". He didn't remember seeing Angeline wearing such a thing, but then again he wasn't looking at what jewelry she had on. "I found something, a necklace! I do not know if it's hers or not. You should help me look! Come down! This will happen faster with two of us."

If I'm going to continue to make her miserable I should probably go after her. She's not getting off this easy. But how to approach this... I could do that, but I haven't done it in such a long time. As children of 4 years old, they once held hands, one of the few times they did, and as they concentrated they managed to make each other float a few inches off the ground. He could try it without her and see if it worked. He concentrated on the moment years ago when they did it together and began to slowly rise in the air. He kept concentrating and began to travel into the darkness down the tunnel, using his hands along the walls as propulsion. He stopped when he caught sight of Laic's torchlight. He floated down as landed softly as Laic just stared at him. Laic was awestruck and a bit jealous.

Laic couldn't help but ask, "How many more things can you do with just your mind?" He didn't get a response back.

"We should find her quickly." Ellis ignored the previous question and looked at the necklace. "I have never seen this before; it is not my sister's necklace. I don't know who it belongs to." The two men searched the room and found nothing. They didn't even find an exit out of there except the way they entered.

Laic was sure that there was another way out of the room and was determined to find it. Ellis helped him search and after a while, the men began to hear chanting and screaming. The screams seemed to belong to not only one, but several females. Their cries echoed through the room and they filled Laic's heart with terror. The horrific noises made him feel urgency of finding an exit to that chamber. He thought he would be searching forever, but after only a few minutes he found a moveable rock with a passage behind it. The sounds of terror came through the hole very audibly and Laic did not hesitate to go into the chamber. He found himself once again sliding down another tunnel. This tunnel was different though, because it was lit the entire way down. Laic landed easily at the bottom of the tunnel sloping steeply downward. What he saw in the instant he had a chance to take in the situation made him freeze.

At the bottom of the tunnel there was a grand cavern with a lake of water surrounding a walkway and round piece of cavern limestone made into an altar. The altar had one large symbol and several smaller symbols surrounding it. There were candles lit in certain places on the larger symbol. The bodies of several dead women lay strewn about the floor on the symbol and Angeline was laid out on the altar with a goblin chanting over her with a black dagger in his hand. Assessing the situation, he quickly realized Angeline did not have long. The goblin was about to strike.

There were several other voices chanting around but he could not see anyone else except the one with the dagger. His heart felt like it stopped yet still pounded at the same time. Ellis soon broke his state of shock as his feet kicked Laic in the back. The shock of the event sent Laic face first into the cavern floor. Ellis was just as shocked as Laic by the gruesome scene. Blood seemed to drip from everywhere, even the places they could not think it logically could. The bodies that littered the center symbol lay bleeding on it. Both Ellis and Laic rushed forward at the same time to stop the goblin from plunging the wicked, black dagger into her chest. Ellis stopped shortly after his oddly instinctive rush forward. His thoughts turned to the goblin drowned in a sea of flame. No sooner had he thought it, than the event instantly happened. The helpless goblin burst into flames and charred bits. It's wicked dagger nearly plunging into her on its way down.

Laic had the misfortune that he could not stop his dive forward in time. He dove into the flames and past them straight into the cavern lake! Ellis had no time to go to his sister's aid due to the rush of goblins from all sides of the cavern. They were headed straight for him. They seemed to be infuriated and rushed in unison to attack, traveling along the outskirts of the lake to get to him. A few managed to stab him in the legs just before he was able to burst them into flames as well.

After the flames died down the pain in his legs worsened. Ellis could barely move. His head hurt horribly as well! With the bombardment of sudden intense pain, he failed to rush to his sister's aid and check on her. For some strange reason, he wanted to make sure she was not hurt too badly. Why should I care? I hate her! But his head and his body disagreed with one another resulting in more confusion. All of it left him reeling. The pain was too great for him to move and he had no idea if Laic drowned or not. Ellis lay there in pain with his eyes closed for some time. He had no idea how long he had been there, unable to move. He began to see his sister in the darkness of his mind and thought he was hallucinating.

She called to him repeatedly and came closer with each passing moment, though it felt like time stopped. Angeline wore a white flowing gown and floated towards him, calling his name repeatedly. She kept getting closer and closer or so it appeared; yet she wasn't any closer than she was when the vision started. Ellis was sure he had lost his sanity. She called his name several times more and reached out her hand to him. He instinctively reached out for her hand in return and touched it. It was soft and soothing, a loving touch unlike he had ever felt. A bright flash of light followed and he slowly returned to his senses. His legs still hurt, but they were seemingly healed. His head didn't hurt nearly as much as it had before. Once he felt able to, he surveyed the surroundings.

There was still light in the chamber, but this time coming from a crack in the ceiling. It was daylight outside. Hours had passed in the dark cave while he was in the dark place in his head where he saw his sister. He looked and saw the daylight shining over his sister's body still unmoving on the altar. He could see no sign of Laic from his current position. He decided to brave moving in closer to get a look around. Of course, there were charred pieces of little body parts all over as well and he could smell the other women. The smell from the bodies stung his nose. Ellis walked to a spot where he could see the whole chamber. From there, he could see a motionless Laic on the other side of the cavern.

He decided to go to his sister first. He had to see the damage that had been done. He was sure the goblin was destroyed before it could cut her. Bodies had to be moved out of the way to be able to reach her. In doing so he could see that most of the women had been mutilated before the final stab. He was surprised at how ill he was beginning to feel when he would normally not feel that way. What is happening to me? He could see no visible wound on his sister except from some scrapes and bruises that were most likely from her fall down the tunnel. Angeline still had breath, but she would not wake up no matter how hard he tried. He tried to wake her to no avail. A nasty head wound was found as he inspected the damage. The wound, he realized, made him feel something he never really felt before. It was new and he didn't know what it was exactly. To try to rid himself of the strange new feeling he went to check on Laic. At least his sister was still alive for the time being. He was uncertain for how long.

Upon the inspection of Laic's body, he too was alive and breathing, but seemed to be unable to wake. Ellis couldn't very well transport both of them out and himself as well so he went in search for another way out. He struggled to walk through numerous caverns with odd symbols etched into the walls. He remembered seeing those symbols around the larger center symbol in the other room. There were numerous other bodies in some side caverns and probable religious items in others. Ellis was not the religious sort. He never thought studying it was worth anything.

Finally a cavern opening that let out into the forest was found. Stepping out into the forest from the cave was a breath of fresh air, literally. He had no idea how long some of those bodies were in there and he had to get a few more breaths before going back into the caves again. Unfortunately, he found no sign of a road close by and he knew predators would be attracted to this place soon if not on their way already.

Ellis traveled back into the cave and to the room with the lake. He noticed something odd when he came back in that he was too focused with other things to notice earlier. No blood spilled over the side of the altar into the lake water. All of the blood was now contained by that odd large symbol and the blood was still disappearing. The symbol seemed to be absorbing the blood from the unfortunate women that were slain. In checking out his own body he found no trace of blood on him either. He decided that he should try to get both of them out of this room and closer to the exit. The symbol was too creepy, even for him. Still, there was a curiosity that it created. One by one he gathered them both closer to the entrance, and then decided to go looking for help. He found the wicked dagger that nearly stabbed his sister, and took that as well. It was of an odd make and black as black could be. He could already see scavengers on their way to the caves. Unable to destroy the impending scavengers, he knew he had to get help soon while avoiding confrontation.

Ellis traveled through the forest looking for signs of anyone or anything. He managed to travel a few hours out and then decided to turn back so he could make the cave before nightfall. He wondered how long he was out of sorts. The vision was what disturbed him most. Was that really her or just my imagination? He could not control his mind wondering about it.

By the time Ellis returned, a number of scavengers had already arrived and were anxiously partaking in the feast to be had. There were 2-foot tall carnivorous rodents that were dangerous in numbers and large carnivorous blackbirds. The birds were waiting their turn while contemplating attacking the rodents to be able to feast sooner. Careful not to disturb the scavengers, he snuck by them even though some of them watched him closely. He found that none had managed to feast on his sister and her friend. He was disappointed that he couldn't find help. Ellis knew he had to get those two out of there and soon. He finally decided to try to get them out in the morning and travel back towards Raist. It can't be too far. Ellis went to sleep and again he dreamt about his sister, but it was different than before. She just lingered there, smiling at him. He saw the surroundings of the dream change and he saw a troop of hunters traveling through the forest and he recognized the area. His trek had led him through that area of the forest. Then the scenery changed and returned to the white abyss that was usually there. The flowing Angeline came up to him and touched his face this time causing Ellis to awake to see sunlight. It was morning already and he knew what he had to do. If he managed to get the two to safety as directed, they had a chance to be found.

He moved his sister with his mind and carried Laic. After using a variant on the ability, he seemed to have awoken a more powerful version he had no idea he could do. It was hard on him, giving him another headache to carry them, but he had to. His mind was still grasping hold of his new development. Ellis reached the spot in the forest and there was no sign yet of anyone. He sat there near his sister in the grass and in a moment when his mind wandered to other things, his hand found his way to hers. He held her hand for a few minutes when he all at once remembered his pride and stubbornness. I'm holding her hand and saving the jerk?! At the realization he suddenly dropped her hand and backed away from both of them. Why would I save them? What is happening to me? He was stunned at his actions and was determined to separate himself from them. Leave them here and refuse to take them anywhere else. Why would I do such a thing as save them?! It was her, she made me! Damn you. You cannot control me. You will not! I refuse to let this atrocity continue. I don't care if you die!

But he did care; he just could not admit it to himself. He would learn this in time, but it would take time. This was especially true when it came to himself. She knew he cared and that it was his pride and stubbornness that refused to allow it to take root. Yes, he did and could do some pretty awful things to people and not think twice about it, but when it came to his sister, he wasn't completely evil. Ellis just could not be honest with himself in that part of his life. His heart was full of resentment, pain, and vengeance, but love and caring was there...just buried deep at the bottom of his soul where it could not see the light. Only when faced with his sister's light and instinct would it surface. What he longed to do most was to strike out at those around him that most affected him emotionally.

Ellis decided to try to head back to town without them and rid them from his company. He didn't want to be around them and decided he could care less whether or not someone came to rescue them. He was more concerned with himself at the moment. He eventually reached the town and went to the hospice to have his wounds looked at. In the cave and forest, the wound had healed pretty well, but now that he was back in town they grew worse. Even the nurse who looked at it said she had never seen such wounds.

"I have never seen a wound turn that color before. You have to stay here for the evening at the very least." She sounded concerned and inquisitive all at once.

Later on, the same hunters that were shown to him in his dream arrived in the hospice with Angeline and Laic. The nurses rushed to their aid and ended up putting Angeline in a bed right next to Ellis. Laic was put on the other side of Angeline. The nurses treated her head wound and cleaned the others wounds from the fall. They had a hard time trying to figure out what was keeping them from coming to their senses.

The hunters had more unfortunate news. "We found some of the missing women, but we regretfully confess they were found dead. They also had no more blood left." The hunters suspected Angeline and Laic to be the only survivors of the horror. "It appears as if they were all victims to Vernik."

The nurses did not recognize the name and looked at the hunters as such.

"Vernik is the god of murder and death. It would seem there is a cult following nearby. We have alerted the town guard. They should be on their way to the caves as we speak." The hunters described the scene at the cave as they found it with the charred body parts strewn about and the symbol.

Ellis decided to stop listening to the hunters and get some sleep. His legs were killing him again, but he had to try to get some sleep.

He dreamt of his sister again, but this time it was different. She was further and further away from him. He reached out to her only to have her fingers slip away from his hands. He felt an overwhelming sadness wash over him and it actually made him cry. He had never cried before so the experience was extremely confusing and disturbing. He began to panic the more she slipped away from him and was awoken by a concerned nurse. He noticed his leg wounds were hurting even more now than they did before. It was almost excruciating. He felt the overwhelming sadness hit him like a sack of bricks again and he fell to his knees at the side of his sister's bed. He cried out in pain, pain mixed with a great sadness. Nurses came running to help him and walked into the most bizarre scene they had ever witnessed.

Ellis was shouting at Angeline saying "If I have to live in this miserable existence then so do you! You've never made me happy before, why start now?" His voice sounded angry, but it was more than that...desperation, sadness, pain...things until now that he hadn't truly felt. "Open your eyes! If you give up now, you will know more pain than ever!" He then began repeating, "you can't give up you bitch! If I suffer, you have to suffer. That's how we work now, it seems. Open your eyes now!"

The stunned nurses had no idea what to do or say, so they watched in shock until he ran out of steam and fell asleep with his head next to his sister's side. It was also considered that he passed out from the sheer amount of pain in his legs, but they suspected a combination of variables. A few went over to him to inquire how he was feeling, thinking him to be asleep and were surprised when he spoke.

He was exhausted and experiencing emotions never felt before. "Just go away. There is nothing you can do for me. It is all her fault, and she's the only one who can mend it." His tone was monotone and almost a whisper.

One nurse tried to get him back in bed, but he refused. Even though his legs were now excruciatingly painful beyond what a normal human could withstand, something else inside him hurt worse.

\*\*\*

He fell asleep at her side and awoke to find her eyes still closed and her breathing very shallow. The nurses at that point made him get into bed and tried to examine his wounds. The wounds were starting to look better and were beginning to feel better. They moved his sister's bed closer to him, which made him content to stay in his bed. Ellis didn't say anything more for his stay at the hospice. He just held his sister's hand and looked as if he was meditating. The pain in his legs grew less painful day by day and after about a week of treatment the wounds were fine. They told Ellis he would always have scars on his legs, but at least they wouldn't have to remove them. The bed that he was in was given to another who had been injured in a brawl at the Naughty Man's Inn. Ellis went to investigate into what was happening about the missing murdered women and the cavern that they were found in.

He found out that the guard had retrieved the bodies and they were to be identified by the family members the following day. They would be displayed, after identification, in the center of town and the ones who were too mutilated would simply be covered and have their names on the outside of their box. Ellis decided to get something to eat. On his way to the Twilight,

Jacar ran into him.

Jacar was heading for the hospice to see the twins. He ended up having lunch with Ellis and Jacar was informed of what Ellis found in the caves. "How is your sister faring?" Jacar inquired.

Ellis merely responded, "she hasn't improved, but she isn't dead yet."

"What about Laic?"

"Same. He hasn't improved, but he's not dead yet."

Laic's condition still hadn't improved yet and the nurses couldn't figure out why. He just lay there in a coma. He was still breathing, but there was no logical explanation for him to be like that for so long. At the most he should've only been there for a few days but his condition was just not ending, for better or worse.

"I'm returning to the hospice after eating my lunch."

"And I intend to go with you to check on my co-worker." Jacar wasn't making it optional.

Ellis actually felt pity for Jacar that he had to work with the jackass, Laic. He didn't feel the need to advertise it though.

They finished eating and went over to the hospice again. Ellis went to his sister and took her hand once again. One of the nurses pulled up a couple of chairs for both of them to sit in. Ellis said nothing to her, but rested his head at Angeline's side again. He was content to just stay in that position for a while. Jacar was confused by what he was witnessing, but he was too concerned about Laic to give much thought to it at that moment.

Jacar tried talking to Laic. "Come on, man, join the living. Just wake up." He tried joking with him and other things, but nothing seemed wake his friend and co-worker. He then turned his attention to Angeline and held her other hand. He tried to give some encouraging words to help with her recovery and then sat silently with both of the twins for a while.

   ***

Laic was the first to wake that afternoon. He finally opened his eyes to everyone's surprise. Jacar noticed that he had an odd look upon his face upon waking. It hardly looked like his friend even though it was the same body. The look he had on his face was more of a cruel expression. Before anyone could stop him, Laic sat straight up and got out of bed. Without a single word, Laic walked out of the hospice, seemingly in some kind of daze. He had no regard for anyone and as Jacar followed him out, he lost him in the crowds in the street.

Jacar returned to the hospice. "I'm going to try and find out what happened to Laic. I just wanted to say that I hope she wakes soon."

Ellis just said "thanks", and went back into his daze.

Jacar left to try to find out what the hell was going on with his friend.

Evening came and Ellis slept at her side again. He began to dream about her again. This time she was there. For a few days she never came to him in his dreams. They were a cold, lonely, and empty space. Now she was back in his dreams, but she was still out of reach. No matter how much he tried to go to her, she remained the same distance away from him. She was just floating there silently. He longed for her to speak, but she didn't say a word. He awoke in the morning and her breathing was beginning to speed up slowly. She still didn't open her eyes, but her breathing was starting to return to normal. He remained by her side still, leaving only to eat meals and run necessary errands.

Jacar talked to some co-workers and friends about Laic and found out he had gone to visit his parents and sister. Jacar traveled to the home only to find that Laic had murdered his family and now was nowhere to be seen. Guards were pulling the bodies from the home. Not all were entirely intact. It was a gruesome scene to witness. The condition of Laic's family seemed to be worse than those who were retrieved from the cave. Jacar was disturbed and perplexed. It was so uncharacteristic of Laic to be so violent. It saddened Laic's friends and co-workers to find out about it. The word was that he slaughtered them and just vanished. The guard had searched all over town and some even went to the caves to search for him. Two of the men who went to the caves drowned in the cavern lake during that search.

Events in town just seemed to be getting worse and now the guards were frequent in the streets. The activity on the bad side of town had nearly ceased. The relatives of the dead picked out their family members and went about the mourning process.

That evening, the priestess of Aria that Angeline spoke to entered the hospice to visit Angeline and to thank her for what she had done. Ellis paid the woman no attention and still seemed to be meditating near his sister. She asked Ellis if she could give Angeline a token of her appreciation and held out her hand to Ellis. Inside her hand was a silver cloak clasp with small rubies in the shape of their holy symbol, a heart with a rose in the center. Ellis took it from her and placed it in his sister's opposite hand for when she awoke. The priestess said a blessing over both of them and left to attend to her duties in the temple. Ellis didn't really pay attention to much going on around him and stayed with his sister until he fell asleep again at her side. He dreamt again of his sister and this time she was smiling and looking at the clasp that was put in her hand earlier. She looked at her brother, yet still said nothing to him. This night she was closer than the night before. She was getting closer to him again. Her breathing was steadily gaining its normal speed and a few more nights passed before she awoke from her long rest.

*** 

Ellis was at her side and meditating when he heard her voice call to him. I'm so tired and I feel strange. He looked up in excitement at his sister's voice, but was confused because her lips weren't moving and her eyes were still shut. Ellis was trying to figure out if he'd gone crazy.

Suddenly she spoke to him in his mind again. "You aren't crazy Ellis, this is the only way I can communicate with you and connect with you for now. I know you were there for me all this time and I am still confused as to why I was slipping. I should be unable to die. You know that. I am life and life never dies."

He tried to reply back to her mentally. "I left you for the hunters, but that was the only time I truly left you."

"I have no intentions, brother, of making you happy and it is my duty to continue to make you miserable with my company so long as we exist." He could hear a light laughter in his head.

He smiled slightly on the outside and thought to her "welcome back and don't ever scare me like that again." Suddenly he felt like his normal self again. "I'll be waiting for you at the inn. Better get your ass moving. You know how impatient I can be. We need to move on from this wretched town." His tone was icy with a hint of happiness. As he was getting up to leave, he felt her hand squeeze his. He turned to look at her and she opened her eyes.

Oddly enough he could still hear her in his mind; I will be leaving this place in a few hours, brother.

He began to walk back to the inn and tavern and Angeline asked him about Laic. "I was with him for a few days, but then darkness came and engulfed him. He did not return to me. I called and called for him but he never answered me." Angeline's concern for Laic was obvious.

In Ellis' normal speaking tone…"Laic woke up and left very abruptly. He left without a word to anyone. That's all I know and all I care to know. He's your friend, not mine."

"Thank you for saving him as well."

"Think nothing more of it." He paused. "Can you constantly pester me like this now? Or is there a way I can block this out when I want to?"

She simply asked, "How much is it worth to you?" She chuckled to herself.

He chuckled as well for a moment and then stopped abruptly. He was having too much fun with his sister now. He had a reputation and an ego to protect.

He went to the Twilight and started to pack up his items. Soon there was a knock at his door and when he answered the door he found his sister there. She was still a little weak, but was up and walking around at least.

"You'd better pack quickly if you want to keep up with me. I left your stuff scattered in your own room a few doors down. Don't want it contaminating my things after all. Needs some distance."

She went over to him and gave him a hug and a kiss on the cheek.

He just said "yeah, yeah, enough already. I get it. You're happy, now get to packing and don't hug me again. I might catch something. Get." He shoed her out of the doorway and into her own room. She packed and they started out again.

She asked him on their way out, "was mom in the cave?"

"She was…and she's already been buried here. That's all I know and all I care to know." He tried to push their journey along as fast as he could.

"I want to see her grave before we leave." She didn't know whether to believe him or not. His thoughts were silent on the matter.

"It's already done. It won't help you any. It'll just be an annoyance on the trip."

She reluctantly went along with her brother, but she wondered if he was telling her the truth about their mother.


## Chapter 8: The Outpost


As they left, Angeline could feel that her heart was unsure of what had become of their mother. Hope remained for her mother in Angeline's heart. She felt there was some connection between the cave and her mother but she didn't believe that her mother was dead yet. He's just trying to put my mind to rest on the subject rather than annoying him by dwelling. If she really is buried, then where are we going? What is Ellis up to now?

Ever since Ellis realized that they could now communicate through their mental bond, he now pondered how to utilize it only when he wanted to. His sister never gave him an answer to his question of how to block it. She was smart and knew him well. He saw some aspects about his sister blossom since the cave incident. She was more alert somehow and stronger in her personality where he had viewed her as frail before. That change in her intrigued him enough to stay with her on the journey. How else will she change and grow?

Angeline wanted to find Laic to see how he was doing. She remembered that he had something to pick up in the next town so she thought that maybe she could find him there. She hoped she would anyway. It was a decent distance away. She never found out how far it actually was. The forest was still thick and light was dim due to all of the foliage from the trees. They wandered down the pathway through the woods. The road and the woods seemed endless. They came to a ruined outpost by nightfall and decided to check it out as a possible shelter for the night. Angeline was weary from walking all day. Although she was slowly getting use to it, she still had a ways to go.

The towers leaned overhead from the outpost. The walls were crumbled in spots and the doors hung off of their hinges. She wondered how the place could have ended up that way. Whatever happened to it, it happened a long time before their arrival. There were a number of doorways they could enter, but they weren't sure if they should split up. Both agreed to split up after a few minutes of debating. They figured they could handle themselves, but if need be, they would stay fairly close. That way, if one of them cried out due to an unfriendly encounter, then the other could respond quickly.

Ellis went through a doorway on the right-hand side and Angeline went to the left. Ellis came into what seemed to be a room where guards would've been stationed for a quick exit or for a quick defense. The room was in disarray upon entering. There was a table in the center of the room that had been crushed and overturned. He found an axe stuck in the side of it. There were also some arrows stuck in various places in the room. Chairs were overturned and crushed by something large that came through there. A few decaying limbs from the previous occupants were strewn about the room. The smell from them was awful, almost as bad as the caves. It seemed to be older than the bodies in the cave. He wasn't sure what really happened there, but it must have been one hell of a battle. He wished he could have seen it for himself.

Angeline went to the left and forwards a bit. She decided to go into one of the middle buildings. She found some kind of training room with rotten wooden racks for weapons. There were still a few weapons in the racks, but most were in pieces on the floor. She decided she should probably grab the two spears on the rack on the left side of the room. She searched lightly over the room for other evidence and found a few various limbs strewn about that room as well. She was surprised at how the smell in the room worsened ten fold as she broke the top layer of a slimy pool near one of the limbs on the floor. She reeled back from the stench and tripped as she was trying to back out of the door. She checked herself and found she didn't hurt herself in the process. She had to take a moment to compose herself before entering again. She tore a piece of her shirt to cover her face as she braved the room again.

As she went around the room, there was a glimmer of warmth that caught her eye. She picked the item up and examined it and found it to be a short sword of sorts. Sure it was filthy, but it could be cleaned and polished. It seemed different from others she'd seen, especially because it had an aura of warmth about it. No one else would notice it, but since Angeline was in tune with the cold element, she could tell. She figured her brother could use it. She searched a little more and found an iron-covered staff in the corner. She thought she could definitely use that. She preferred not to use weapons at all, but she figured there would be some point when she would have to defend herself and her mind would be too drained to use her abilities. She was satisfied with her search and left to meet up with her brother again.

Ellis was beginning to wonder about his sister and caught her as she came around the corner of the building. She gave the short sword to him and suggested that maybe he could use it. Ellis knew how to use it well and had it wrapped up in cloth until he could clean it. In his rush to catch up with his sister upon leaving their home in Ishta, he left his daggers and knives and poisons that he made. He did pick some up in the secret place in Raist. He hadn't put any poison on his weapons yet, but he would when he needed to. While he was in the first room he decided to gather the arrows he found and put them in the front of the outpost until he could find a quiver for them and a bow. He knew how to use those well too, but not to the extent of his expertise with blades.

He noticed the spears and the staff and looked at his sister curiously. "So what do you plan on doing with those?"

"You can have a spear if you want one. I just thought there might be some fights along our travels and I don't want anything getting to close enough to me to touch."

He took one and told her, "I could teach you to use those." He knew she only took martial art classes in school, so she didn't know how to use those weapons effectively.

She said "I shouldn't need to use them often enough to have to learn the weapons use in battle. I don't plan on fighting that much."

Ellis just shrugged. "If you ever want to learn how to use them skillfully, you can come to me. I won't charge you too much..." and chuckled about it.

She just looked at him and reminded him that they'd need to find a place for them to rest for the evening. She was really beginning to get sleepy.

Together they went to another building and found a room with beds and it seemed to be undisturbed. Whatever untold events happened to this place, this room was spared the destruction. They decided that was the best place to rest. There were three beds and even though they were old, it seemed like they wouldn't fall apart. There were no body parts in the room so the only thing to smell in there was old bed. The beds were nicely made and though there were no blankets in sight, they had their own. They slept okay that evening. Since the beds were old they weren't very comfortable, but they were beds nonetheless.

Ellis woke up first and cleaned the weapons found the prior night. He also gathered some water from a nearby crystal clear stream. The water was cool and refreshing to drink. He took some to Angeline when she awoke. She didn't think he realized what he was doing. She was curious about the rest of the place and in the light they would be able to see well. Ellis agreed and was curious about the place himself. They agreed to continue looking around the outpost.

The twins went to a door in the back of the outpost, passing up the stairways leading up to the tops of the outer walls. The twins headed down a set of stairs that were just inside the door. This part of the outpost was starting to smell very ripe. Both of them could tell that they were heading into the worst part of that place.

They continued down a spiraling staircase and it ended just before a room that was about twenty by thirty feet with three doors. This place was worse than those buildings above. The stench was great and they could see no bodies that would make the place smell so horribly. The doors were not broken, but were open wide. It was wet from the two inches of standing rain water with leaves and broken wood pieces floating in it. Clothing, obviously torn to shreds, was also in the water so they had to be careful not to walk near it or it would have stuck to them. The main chamber had a few doors leading to other areas. They decided upon the right-hand door to start with.   There were once some plants growing in pots here, but the leaves and plants rotted and the pots were broken. They went on through to find some kind of recreational room. The twins assumed it was meant for the soldiers stationed here once upon a time. There were soaked cards floating about and furniture rotted at the bottoms. Some even tipped over due to the water level in the room.

The bottom of the outpost was so silent that the only thing they could hear was the sound of the water sloshing around as they walked through it. That sound echoed through the halls as they went. They investigated a few more empty rooms, which seemed to be the sleeping quarters for the former residents. The beds were ruined. Nothing down there was salvage-able due to the water on the floor. They went back to the main room and went through the middle doorway. It led to a larger training room. Dark squishy mat stains were splotched around. The stains on the top of the mat were dry at one point, the twins could tell, and it seemed to be blood. There were weapon racks next to the walls, but nothing could be salvaged there either. The good ones must have been taken by whom or whatever destroyed the place.

There was another room off of that one and upon getting close to the door, the stench got much worse. Ellis opened the door and the stench sent both of them reeling back. They were forced to cover their noses. Although it didn't really help much, it still helped a little. Angeline had to pause a moment before continuing forward. Ellis looked into the room first and left quickly after glancing around the room. He seemed to be sick and about to vomit.

Angeline was unsure if she should really look at that point.   She thought about it and figured she should.  She peered carefully into the room and the sight stunned her for a few minutes. The room was full of bodies of slain soldiers and they were just piled up on top of each oth-er.   The stench was unfathomable and the sight was too gruesome for words. The twins were both in disbelief. Angeline closed her eyes after just a short glimpse into the room.  She wished she hadn't looked.  She left quickly to follow after her brother.

By the time she caught up to him in the main room, he had already composed himself again. They were both too shocked to say anything to each other.  They both agreed not to go back into that room.  They then went to the doorway to the left. It seemed to lead into a dining room. Of course, everything was trashed, but it was better than the previous room they encountered. There were dishes and silverware strewn about the bro-ken table and floor, but luckily no food. They continued into the next room which was a kitchen in quite a bit of disarray, but there still wasn't any food on the floor or left standing anywhere else. The cabinet was the same way. The food, they rationalized, must have been taken by the people or things that raided this outpost.

They found no other ways to go so they walked back towards the main room, but upon reaching the dining room they could hear moans coming from that direction. They looked at each other for a moment, confused, and then continued to see what was going on.

Upon the horrific sight of what was coming toward them, Ellis immediately took his sword and dagger out to attack. "Take a step back and stay behind me." His tone told her that he was serious.

She did as he ordered and took out her staff that she found the day before. Ellis tried to focus his mind on them, but was too spooked to use his powers. He was too distracted to set them on fire. Angeline wasn't however, though she wasn't sure what was going on. She tried to freeze one, but all that did was slow it down.

There were at least seven of the soldiers walking slowly toward them. One of them wasn't positioned well to be able to reach the twins. The twins would be able to attack opportunistically before they could reach. The soldiers reached Ellis and were trying to claw wildly at him. They missed Ellis, though a few came close. Two more undead soldiers tried to grab him, but were unsuccessful. The other three tried to get at Ellis from behind their fellow undead, but were unable to reach. Ellis took the head off of the second one with one mighty swing of his sword. The dagger barely wounded the third one as he tried to stab it. Angeline raised her staff and tried to hit one of them from behind her brother, but missed poorly. There wasn't room for her to get next to him and try to hit them with her hands though she really didn't want to anyway.

Ellis took another swing and the unnatural being was cleaved in half. It fell over the top the one who just had its head cut off. His dagger wildly missed another. In retaliation, it clawed Ellis, scraping skin across his chest. Fortunately it was one who had been stuck in the water and the nails were softer, so the nails caused him little damage. Two more came up to take the fallen undead's places. One missed, but the other didn't, and since that one had been above the water, the nails raked skin off his arm and dug into his flesh. This caused great pain to shoot through his arm. Ellis gritted his teeth in pain, but he didn't yell out. Angeline took another swing at one of them and hit one in the head, crushing its eye. Angeline's facial expression showed disgust by what just happened, but she had to protect her brother. The last soldier was still unable to attack Ellis, though it was not for a lack of trying.

Ellis swung his sword around again and caught two across their faces sending them flying back up against the wall and his dagger stabbed another one in the arm. Angeline struck the first one in the right shoulder and the limb fell off into the water, but that didn't seem to stop it from attacking. The last one could finally reach him. It clawed Ellis from his face, across his chest, and into his arm causing him to yell out curses at it. The other two tried to claw him, but missed terribly.

"Set them on fire Ellis, now!"

Ellis wasn't sure he could because the pain from the last hit was still shooting through his body, but he couldn't let another one get a hit in on him so he tried to concentrate enough and managed to send the one in the back into a fury of flames that caught onto two others. The undead soldiers were frantic and distracted from attacking. They began to wander around aimlessly while burning. It didn't take long before they crumbled into the water on the floor.

A couple were merely injured and began to rise again. They began to shamble back over to the twins and with the last of Ellis' strength; he sent them into the air and slammed them into the wall. The soldiers didn't get up again after their fall.

Angeline helped her brother back up to the room they stayed in the night prior and had him sit on the edge of the bed. She knelt in front of him. "Do not move," she instructed.

He tried to object to her putting her hands on him, but he was too late for the objection once she put them on his chest.

"Hold still and relax."

Ellis seemed reluctant, but knew that objecting wouldn't do him any good at that point. He did as she said and she began to concentrate. Her hands glowed green and his wounds began to heal. She managed to heal his chest and face before she drained herself mentally and had to go rest herself. She was so weakened that Ellis had to assist her to the bed. Ellis wanted to thank her, but decided not to say anything to her. He had forgotten for a moment that she could read his mind and that was alright with her. She figured it would be for the best if he didn't think she heard him. They rested again for the evening and got up bright and early to continue along their way.

## Chapter 9:  Separated in the Grasslands

The day began darkened so the twins expected rain.  They were in a hurry to travel as far as they could before it began.  The twins didn't speak to each other on their trip as usual.  They noticed the trees were becoming sparser the further they traveled.  Soon they arrived at the edge of the forest and into fields of tall grass.  They had never seen such a thing before so it was exciting.  The only problem they realized was that things could easily hide in the grass.  They felt comfortable with their ability to handle anything.

They took their first steps into this new land they just discovered.  It felt odd walking through the grass because neither of them were use to walking in grass up to their hips or higher.  They thought the grass they'd traveled through so far was tall.  The new terrain slowed them down a bit and they knew they couldn't afford to be slowed down.  They had to cross it anyway so they continued.  Soon enough, it started to rain and they had no shelter.  To make things worse, they couldn't start a fire because of the wetland.  They saw a small copse of trees a little ways up and off to the side of their path.  They decided to make for that.  At least they wouldn't be rained on; the foliage on the trees would afford them some cover.  Ellis just hoped that lightning wouldn't strike the tree they were about to lean on while they were near it.

They made a run for the few trees and upon making it there they had to warm up.  Angeline decided to get out of her wet clothes and get warm.  She went around the trees and to change out of her clothes and into her blanket in a place out of view from her brother.  Both of them tried to find the place under a tree with the least bit of water dripping down.  It wasn't too cold out that night, except for the chilled rain, so they both thought they could manage without a fire.  Ellis got out of his clothes and wrapped his blanket around him while his sister slept.  Upon waking they saw the rain had stopped, but the area was still wet, so they still couldn't build a fire.  They decided to let their clothes air dry before continuing and stayed there under the trees until the clothes dried and they hoped some of the grass would dry as well.  It took most of the day to dry their clothes so they figured they'd just stay the evening under the cover of the trees again.  They slept well and awoke well rested and ready to continue.

The days were becoming brighter and warmer, so their trip was easier to manage.  They continued on their way through the tall grass, and though some of it was damp, most of the grass was dry.  The ground was still quite wet, but they expected that due to not much sun reaching the ground.  They traveled on for a few hours, stopped briefly to snack, and then resumed their trek. They could now see a line of trees from a small forest up ahead. They figured they could make it to those trees during the night, but they had to travel while tired for a few hours to do it.

They were just trying to keep moving when a sudden hissing noise erupted around them. They couldn't see anything, but they heard it. The hissing became louder and louder as if several things were joining in. Ellis knew what these were. They were a poisonous snake whose poison could cause several possible side effects in people, but it was deadly to smaller animals. He had fun testing the poison out on some animals around town that didn't like him. He was concerned for himself and his sister at the moment. It sounded like a nest of them and they stepped right into it.

He commanded his sister to get on his back so they couldn't reach her. He actually thought it would be interesting to find out what it would do to her, but he couldn't afford for her to get ill or die right then. He actually had a chance of resisting the poison due to his mistakes in trying to use it on the weapons he made and trying to get it into containers. He knew his sister couldn't resist it though, which piqued his darker curiosity, but he didn't want to test it there. He helped her up and ran through the nest as quickly as he could. Out of probably twenty snakes in the nest, only a few actually struck him, which was a good thing for him. He went as fast as he could to get away from them. He knew that those particular snakes would chase their fleeing prey. They're fast too, but they give up the chase after they get so far away from the nest. All he had to do was keep running and eventually they'd give up.

He ran and ran until his legs were cramping and he was heaving to catch his breath. His sister tumbled down and off of him when he collapsed from the leg cramps. He had never had leg cramps before and they made him immobile due to the pain. Angeline got to her feet and went to check on her brother. When she reached him, he wasn't moving. She started to panic and tried to shake him awake. That didn't work and he still lay motionless in the grass. She tried to keep herself rational in her panicked state. She stayed by his side for many hours and he didn't wake up. She tried to use her healing powers, but they had no other effect than the wounds on his arms from the outpost healing up. She didn't know what to do. They were too far from home and as far as she knew, they were too far from anywhere civilized.

She couldn't hold back her tears and she stayed by his side until she fell asleep. When she awoke, his condition hadn't worsened, but it didn't get better either. He was still breathing, but he was completely unresponsive to anything she did.  She knew she had to do something so she sat down and concentrated to try to think of a plan.  She meditated there until she remembered something.  *He can make things float sometimes with his mind…if I could do it too, we might get somewhere, even if it was little by little.*  She knew that would exhaust her though.  *I'd be useless if anything tried to attack us.*  She opted to think about it some more.

She meditated there for quite a few moments when she felt a gust of wind all around her and she felt something like claws scrape her back.  When she opened her eyes she saw herself quickly lifted off the ground and being drawn into the air by some immense bird.  It was black and spotted with light brown marks.  The bird carried her far above the ground and she knew if she tried to make it let go of her, she'd fall to her death, or great injury at least.  She was scared, but tried to remain calm.  The bird carried her to a mountain range and to one of the peaks.  She got a good look at the landscape around the area so she at least knew a little bit of what to expect when she tried to get back to her brother.

The bird flew over a nest of chirping babies her size or slightly larger.  They were hungry and they acted as if she was their meal.  The bird, mother or father, dropped her into the nest and flew off again in the opposite direction they came from.  The babies were already starting to tear her clothes up with their beaks.  She was lucky that she was dealing with the babies, because their beaks were still soft.  She knew the mother would have been able to kill her without a problem at all.  She tried to struggle out of the nest and to safety, but every time she got close, she found herself being dragged back in by the babies.  They were starting to tear at her flesh now and pain was shooting through her body.  She was starting to feel faint and passed out moments later.

Ellis woke from his "sleep" and looked around him.  He wasn't sure how long he'd been out, but it was getting towards evening.  His whole body felt stiff, so he tried to move as much as possible.  He looked around for his sister and saw nothing.  He looked in his pack and found that he had little food left.  He'd have to go hunting.  Then it occurred to him that maybe that's what his sister was out doing.  He decided he'd wait for a few hours before trying to find her.  He tried to speak to her mentally and received no response.  Even if she had closed her mind to him, she would've given off some sort of signal.  He was beginning to get very worried about her.  He decided that he shouldn't wait to call for her, so he yelled out her name as loud as he could.  "ANGELINE!"  He listened for a few moments and found no reply from anywhere around him.  He repeated the call.  Still no response.

He began to travel towards the forest, though he knew he'd have to rest soon. Even though he had just come to his senses, he was still weakened from the poison. Apparently his resistance to it failed him that time. He wondered if she was struck and if she was confused and wandered off, but still, he figured he'd receive some sort of signal from her. He got nothing aloud or mentally from her. He wasn't sure what happened to her or where she was. Maybe, he thought, she was just good enough to block her mind from me and she tried to ditch me. If that were the case, he'd give her a lesson she'd never forget.

Still, he couldn't shake the feeling that she was in danger. Unless he found her though, he wouldn't know if his instinct was correct. You're getting soft on her Ellis, she's making you soft, he scolded himself. I'm spending way too much time with her. She's making me go soft. I'm wondering if it is intentional manipulation. He found a good spot to recover for the evening and rested as well as he could have. The morning sun arose bright and it stung his eyes before he even opened them. The birds were singing and the breeze was cool, though the temperature from the sun was hot. It was a good day to travel so long as the breeze kept on.

## Chapter 10: Disappearing Act

Ellis ate his breakfast and found that to be the last of his food. He'd have to go hunting for food so that he'd have enough to last him until he arrived in the next town. He figured that at least if he didn't find his sister in the forest, he might find clues as to where she was when he reached the next town. He went hunting for some deer and found one just big enough for him to be able to eat off of for a few days. He took out a dagger in both hands and prepared to attack the deer. He had never hunted before, but at that point he felt that he had to. He certainly couldn't use the sword Angeline gave him and go charging at it, though it was an amusing mental image. He thought he'd be better skilled with the daggers than the spear as well. After all, skill with the hunting weapons mattered just as much as what kind it was. You could have the best hunting weapon, but still fail in the task if the skill wasn't there to back it up. He wasn't even sure if the daggers would suffice in the situation, but he felt they were the best option. He never found a bow to go with his arrows that he collected from the outpost.

With lightning speed, he flung the daggers straight at the deer's head and throat. The head shot missed, but the throat dagger hit its target well.  The deer tried to bolt and couldn't get far before it fell to the ground.  He went over to it and hauled his kill over to his camp.  He made food that he could eat off of over the next few days and went on his way.  By the time he was finished with the deer, it was afternoon.  He'd have to get a move on as soon as possible.  He traveled until evening and found he still hadn't made it near a town yet.  He was hoping that he would find one soon.  He set up a camp to rest that evening and awoke refreshed.

He continued along his way through the forest.  Not much later past the afternoon he began to see some smoke on the horizon.  At last, there is something around other than grass and weeds.  He was in a hurry to find out the source.  I hope it is a home, town, or inn.  He hurriedly made his way along towards the smoke.  He reached the mystery location in a few hours and found it to be an old farmhouse.

"Hello!  Anyone home?"  He called out.  No one answered him, so he went to check around for himself.

When in need of a good place to begin, the back of the house is always preferable.  He went around the back and found that there use to be a garden, but it was overgrown with weeds.  The smoke he spotted from afar was a plant that was known as burning weed.  He had heard about it, but had never seen it before.  This plant seemed to unendingly burn.  If it was what he'd heard of, they burned for a few years before the fire would eventually consume the whole plant.  He only assumed that the plant was one in the same.  As he looked around further he found that a field, used to grow a decent number of crops, was so overgrown with weeds that he didn't recognize it until he was upon it.  The house seemed to be in decent shape, though it could've been better.  He was sure it wouldn't fall on him if he went in to look around.

Well, time to see if anyone is home.  He entered the old wooden house to have a look around.  Looks like someone could live here.  It isn't' too far gone yet.  There was a layer of dust on everything, but it wasn't thick.

"Hello!  Anyone here?"  He waited a few minutes for a response.  Again, there was no answer.

The entry foyer was small and sufficient.  I suppose they didn't get a lot of company out here.  He glanced around the foyer.  There were vases with dead dried flowers hanging stiffly over the rims.  Paintings covered in so much dust that he couldn't automatically tell what the paintings were of.  There were three ways off into other parts on the house.  The forward path was next to some stairs going up to a second floor.  Nearby the stairwell was an open doorway with stairs going down into some sort of basement.  The place smelled simply of dust.  Guess I start with upstairs.  He searched upstairs and saw only some unused beds, which were still made. The basement was full of useful farming items but little else. It was really nothing he would be able to use. He searched the main floor and found a kitchen, dining room, and living room. They were all dusty but he found that if he cleaned some of the pans out, that he could still use them to cook with. All of the metal knick-knacks were stained and tarnished with age and moisture.

He could hear the chirping of several small birds coming from the attic. Probably a nest. He thought. It would be a nice place to live if I cleaned it up some and repaired some boards. I'd have to find out where the town was from here and buy some supplies, as long as I find some more money. Where are the people who used to live here? Oh well, their loss is my gain.

He went out back again and found a small barn covered in vines on the outside. He started to go in when suddenly, as he opened the doors, a number of owls flew out and into the forest nearby. He could still see unknown black speckling the ceiling. He figured it was bats but wasn't going to get too close to find out. Searching the barn, he found a number of things that would help him repair the place, but little else of use. All of the food that was once good was now spoiled or stale. He figured he'd rest there that evening and try to head for town the following day.

And that he did. He woke up and traveled on. His path led into forest again and he hoped it wouldn't last long. He was sick and tired of the trees and the tall grass. It seems the landscape never changes around here. He only had to travel a few hours to find a small town the size of his own. There was no sign of people though. It seemed odd because normal people are out during the day running their errands, but not in this one it seems. I should be watchful.

"Is anyone here?!" He called out, but no answer. He noticed some kind of platform with two poles sticking straight up in the middle of it. There were ropes stained some dark color tied to the poles. The platform had bright yellow and red feathers glued to it for some odd reason. Then he noticed a large pile of bones behind the platform. It was an odd sight for him to see, but since leaving Ishta, he'd seen more and more corpses in one form or another. "Hello! Is anyone here?!" Once again, he received no reply.

What is going on here? I feel a strange sense of similarity. He closed his eyes, concentrated, and recognized the feeling there and knew it well. The sense of death and evil pervades this town. But what happened?

Ellis searched all of the buildings and found everything he needed except to talk to people. He found the supply of rations in the general store with other items he felt he would need for the farmhouse. Once satisfied there was no sign of people, he took what he needed from the town and brought it back to the farmhouse. He'd spend another evening fixing the place up a little and then going to sleep again. He awoke in the morning, unsure of where to go next to find his sister. He walked outside to think and came to a conclusion that hit him like a ton of bricks. As he stared out towards the landscape from the porch, he realized that he went the wrong direction to the town he intended to end up in. He'd gone north instead of more easterly so he missed the place he should've been at. In his excitement over that discovery, he hurried to gather his things. There is still a chance to find her after all.

He rushed out of the house, eating his breakfast along the way. He went through more grassland, keeping an eye out for any more nests of isils, the snakes that bit him earlier. He seemed to be heading towards a mountain range and would reach them in a few days. Surely she wouldn't have gone into the mountains alone, but if she was headed towards the town we intended to go to, she'd have to go that way. He came upon the forest again a day out from the farmhouse going northeast. He knew he wouldn't have to spend long in there and he hoped that nothing would run into him on the way.

Ellis traveled a day through the forest and made camp at a small clearing. The moon was nearly full that night and was very large in the sky. It wasn't normally so large, but Isis, the second moon, was usually large in the sky when it came around. Isis was a purple colored moon that shone beautifully. Isis corresponded to the purple sun. Isis and the purple sun were the most common bodies in the sky. The other moon, Cassius, was blue with a hint of green. Another sun with a greenish tint to it was rarely seen. Its green tint was faint and could hardly be seen unless one knew how to look for it. Once about every ten years a light pink moon and a peach sun could be seen, but they didn't last long. Ellis couldn't remember what the names of the light pink moon and peach sun. Not much was known about them other than they were there once every ten years. Ellis had only seen them during a small portion of a year in his life. He was about to turn ten years old when he saw them. The day the twins were born was the day right after those celestial bodies had moved on. And apparently, from what he'd been told, they glowed brighter than usual the period just before the twins were born, and then when those bodies passed on it seemed darker than usual. The weather became dreary after they passed.

The tired, raven-haired teen set out after his morning breakfast again and somehow he felt as if he was getting closer to her. He was sure he would find her past the mountains. His journey continued until he came to the mountains and he found that he'd have to circumvent the side of the mountains till he found a safe path through. The mountains were too steep in most areas. He could only go a few more hours easterly along the mountains before night was setting and he had to rest. He was sure he'd find a path the in the following day's journey.

That evening he heard odd sounds coming from the near forest. The noises kept him up for a while before he went to investigate what was out there. He moved closer to the forest and found beady red eyes staring at him. He heard tiny growls coming from that vicinity. As he was trying to figure out what they were, he started to feel dizzy all of the sudden and dropped to the ground. He awoke in his camp with everything of his gone. All he had was the blanket he was sleeping on and his clothes. Luckily for him, he kept his moneybags out of sight and he was glad because they were still there. He would have to hunt, but most of his weapons were stolen. He still had a few that were purchased from Jacar's place. They were hidden as well, for which he was glad.

He still had three daggers after he counted them. He vowed to himself that he would find his stuff and kill all who were involved with the theft. He was quite angry at the thought of his items being stolen, but there wasn't much he could do about it at the moment. He still had to find a mountain path to get through the mountains. These were particularly rocky and treacherous mountains so he had to keep his mind focused on the main objective. He'd go back and hunt the thieves at a later and more convenient time.

## Chapter 11: Uncertainty and a New City

Ellis traveled on the mountain path until he became tired. As he was getting ready to rest, he spotted a large nest and decided to investigate. It was a slight climb, but not too bad. In the nest there was an assortment of items in addition to several dead adult-person-sized chicks. Not wanting to be there when the creature that made the nest and had the chicks came back, he gathered up everything he could without really scrutinizing what he was taking. He traveled back to his camp and began to pick through the items.  Ellis found a number of jewelry items and some torn cloth.  He found a nice looking long sword with sapphires in the hilt in the shape of a star.  He claimed it immediately and vowed never let anything happen to it.  It was a stunning sword, unlike anything he'd seen yet.  He found a book, that when he opened it, realized he couldn't understand the writing contained in it.  It was full of symbols and letters unknown to him.  Setting the book aside in with his things, he moved on.  He found other broken and rusty weapons that he devised he would discard along the mountain path.  As he was going through the jewelry he saw something disturbing.  He recognized one necklace that he had come across on his trip with his sister.  He slipped it in her pockets one night while they slept.  What am I gonna do with it?  Better that she has it.  It was the ruby pendant in the shape of a "c" with the gold chain.

His heart sunk as he realized that his sister was once in the nest.  He wasn't sure what to think, because he was trying to deny to himself that she was dead.  He didn't see her in the nest or in the pile of bones.  Not that he could recognize her just as bones anyway.  He tried not to think about it, but the newfound evidence was all he could think about.  He held the necklace in his hand tighter and tighter as something wet started to run from his eyes.  Ellis was crying…again!  He wasn't accustomed to crying, so it was odd for him.  His heart was sadder than it had ever had been.  He tried to think that she was fine.  He hoped that she got away, but there was always the doubt that she was gone.  He fell asleep not long after finding the red pendant, as he cried himself to sleep.

Ellis awoke and he just couldn't motivate himself.  He felt weakened, and all he could do that morning was lay there and stare at the sky.  He got up later, but before he knew it, he realized that it wouldn't be long before the sun would set.  He just couldn't move even though part of him wanted to get moving.  Eventually his angrier side got a hold of him, and he made himself stop thinking about his sister as much.  I will continue on my way.  He had a strange feeling that his sister wasn't dead, but he wasn't sure what to believe.  If she were dead, he would be torturing himself to think that she was still alive.

He traveled for a few hours and rested again.  I will go to the next city as planned in the morning.  Perhaps I can get some rest there.  As he set his camp, he noticed wagon marks on the ground.  If the area was traveled by wagons, then perhaps she really was still alive.  Maybe someone rescued her from the creature with the nest, he thought.  It was a new hope that he was going to cling to instead of thinking the worst.  Considering the new possibility gave him more motivation to set out for the next leg of the trip.

He left in the morning and hurried through the mountains as fast as he could. Before he knew it, he was almost out of the mountains. He set up camp and rested for the evening. He awoke in the morning to find the giant bird flying in the air near a close peak. It didn't seem to notice him, but some unlucky traveler instead. It grabbed the person and flew away. He vowed to himself, I will get that bird back one day. Perhaps by controlling it mentally, or by burning it out of the sky. The thought of burning it out of the sky tickled his stomach. He looked forward to the day they met again, but for the moment he needed to find out what became of his sister.

He headed out of the mountains and into more grassland. He didn't think he had far to go through them, but he had to be careful crossing the grass because of the isils. He knew he was resistant to the poison, but the last time he was bitten, the poison worked on him. He ended up losing his sister by the time he awoke from the bite's effect. He went through the grass carefully and fully alert to anything and everything around him. He had to rest again before reaching the forest past the grasslands. There were birds singing on that fine morning when he awoke. The sun was bright and hot. He was a bit cooler by the time he got into the forest. The shade helped quite a bit. There was a road winding through the forest ahead of him. He stuck to the side of the road most of the time. He eventually came to a wagon along the road, but it appeared that no one was near it at that moment.

Ellis decided to wait for someone to return to the wagon, but no one did. So he rested, and in the morning he claimed the wagon as his own. He figured that it belonged to the person who was unfortunate enough to get eaten by the bird. He inspected the wagon and its horses. Everything seemed to be fine structurally. The horses were fine and quite healthy. The back of the wagon contained chests of clothes of numerous sorts. There was women's and children's clothing as well as men's. There were silks, satins, velvety, and plain clothing. It seemed that the wagon was owned by a tailor who had met an unfortunate fate. Now the clothes and the wagon were his. He decided he wouldn't sell any of the clothes. He wanted to keep them for himself. He knew he wouldn't be wearing the women's and children's clothing, but he could possibly make use of them later on.

He traveled down the road in the wagon, and had to camp once more before reaching the town ahead. He continued anew in the morning and was at the next town by midday. The new town was actually a port city with a vast expanse of blue beyond it. The water stretched as far as the eye could see. The city was a larger place than he had seen before. The city had a huge wall surrounding it. There were guard towers frequently spaced along the wall. Many men were patrolling on the top of the wall. He saw a great iron and stone gate before him that stood closed. There were guards standing to attention by the giant gate with pole arms. As he approached the gate, the guards lowered their weapons in a cross pattern to signal him to stop. He did.

"What is your business in Terrah?"

"I am searching for my injured sister."

They returned their pikes to an upright position and let him through the gate.

The gate was slow to open, but it eventually did. As the gate opened, he saw a grand city sprawled out before him. There were houses near, and they were made of some kind of stone he had never seen before. They were in many assortments of colors. There were old trees all over and wide roads for the busy people of the city to be able to get to places faster. The city was bustling with activity. There was a plethora of people, wagons, and horses. Apparently there was going to be some sort of celebration soon. Some of the residents were already beginning to decorate. He entered the city and found an inn and tavern where he could get a room. He unloaded his things, and then went to park the wagon in a rather large area devoted to them.

The Tumbling Boulder Inn and Tavern was near the gates he went through. It seemed to be bustling with activity as well, and there was only one room left when he arrived. *Guess I'm lucky I don't have to go further in. I think I'd get lost here easily.* He unpacked his things in his room, and decided to look around the city. First he intended on getting a meal, just in case he became as lost as he figured he would. The meal was good, but it was too spicy. He wasn't use to having much spice in his food, since his family couldn't afford it. He would have to adapt to the numerous changes that were upcoming.

Ellis went over to a bulletin board in the inn and tavern and checked it for any possible helpful information. He found that there was indeed a celebration about to happen. They were going to celebrate a citizen of the city named Rokk. Rokk seemed to be some sort of town hero that had just returned from a war. Ellis wasn't aware of the war. It had nothing to do with Ishta. The gossip about Rokk described him as a strong and great warrior. Rokk was said to have been taught by the best weapons master in the city. The town hero had gone to defend a neighboring town, one Ellis hadn't heard of, from goblin activity that nearly destroyed it. Ellis heard the hero's name several times in conversations around him. *He sounds tough, wonder why we've never heard of him before?*

He turned his attention back to the board's postings after listening in on nearby conversations for a few minutes. He noticed another announcement. There was another series of events with women ending up missing and that no women were to go out by themselves. All women were required to have an escort and were encouraged to only come out during the day. Well, well, doesn't this sound familiar? He also noticed that Kirlan, the entertainer would be coming to town to perform for Rokk and the rest of Terrah. Ellis had never heard of Kirlan either, but the postings made him sound important.

Ellis was about to head out, when he heard a familiar voice. When he turned around to look for someone familiar, all he could see was a room full of strangers. He left the inn and tavern after a few moments of looking for a familiar face without any luck. He started down the street, from where he was, and he could see several tall towers towards the center of town. He saw several temples to deities he knew nothing about. He had never studied about religions in his youth. He just found out information from travelers that happen to come into his town. He counted at least five temples in the city and he was sure he would find more.

As he went on through the street, he came to an open market area. There were different kinds of wares being sold at small tents along the sides of the road. The people in that town tended to wear more brown, grey, and white clothing. They seemed to love rocks for jewelry. Ellis didn't care much for the rocks or the clothing. He was wandering around the city looking for any clue he could find. He decided to look in a hospice for his sister, and then he planned to search the gravesites of the town, if they had any.

Going over to the hospice, he could see it was fairly busy. He walked in, and saw several people that looked similar to those he had found in the cave. The strange thing was that the people from Terrah were still alive, though not by much. He looked all over the area and didn't see his sister.

One of the nurses noticed he was looking for someone, and came over to him. "Can I help you, sir?"

"I'm looking for my sister." He described her to the nurse.

The nurse was in thought for a moment, and then said, "I don't remember seeing anyone of that description, sir, but I will keep an eye out for her."

"Thank you," and reluctantly he went to the graveyards around the city. He found nothing that indicated his sister was there either.

He decided to ask some guards. "Have you seen my sister, whether she was with someone or alone?" Ellis described his sister to them.

One guard said "I remember seeing a woman by that description coming into town a few days ago. She came in and I thought she was sleeping. She was in the back of a wagon driven by a man with sandy blond hair and green eyes. The man driving was about thirty years old. But I don't know where the man lives within the city. He is a resident of Terrah though."

"Thank you for the information," Ellis said. He started looking around the more residential areas of the city.

Ellis wandered around the city residential areas for hours. He finally saw a man fitting the description the guard gave him. He hurried to the man and tried to get his attention. The man knew Ellis was there, and turned around to face Ellis before he even reached him.

"I'm looking for my sister, and was given description of someone who looks just like you. You brought her into town in the back of a wagon didn't you?" Ellis paid close attention to the man's face as he began to speak to him.

"I found a woman that was nearly dead in the mountains, and brought her to my place. I've been taking care of her for the last few days, and that she still hasn't awakened yet. My name is Edward, yours is…?"

"Ellis."

Edward invited Ellis into his home to look at the woman he'd found. Ellis followed the man to his home nearby the area they were in. Edward led Ellis up some stairs and into a room on the second floor of the man's house. Edward checked her over and she still didn't wake up.

Ellis went up to the bed and confirmed that it was indeed Angeline. I found you. He smiled and he felt a sense of accomplishment and relief. "Do you have a chair I can sit in for a bit, Edward?"

Edward gladly retrieved a chair and thought to bring a second one in for him as well. Ellis looked her over, and she didn't seem too damaged from being in the nest. That confused him, but then he realized something that he didn't think about before. Ellis realized what happened between her and the chicks. During our pass through the snake nest, one must have bitten her. Then the mother bird must have picked Angeline up and taken her to feed the chicks. Since his sister had been poisoned, and that particular poison was more potent than others, the birds must have poisoned themselves trying to eat her. The realization of what happened made him laugh out loud.

Edward looked at him oddly.

"What do you think is wrong with her?" Ellis' curiosity was clear.

"She seemed to be poisoned, but was attacked while the poison was setting in."

Ellis laughed again. He now knew what the poison would do to her; it would put her into a coma. Ellis wondered if she could hear him and he tried to reach her mind, but was unsuccessful in his attempt. Her mind was silent to him.

Suddenly, there was a commotion outside of the house. A woman's scream in protest could be heard loud and clear, and then it was silenced. Both men went to the window in mere seconds, but by then they could see nothing. It was becoming dark and there would be little hope of finding the woman.

"Would you continue to care for my sister, Edward? I'm going to see what I can do about what we just heard. I will come to visit her often." This is for the best, Angeline. You have to stay here.

"Yes, she should remain here. I will see to her. You are more than welcome to visit her anytime, Ellis. I will be here."

Ellis nodded his head in acknowledgement and left. Ellis realized he was saying thanks more often than ever before. I am being too polite. What the hell am I doing? This "thank you" crap has to change! I will just nod from now on.

## Chapter 12:  A Familiar Voice Returns

Ellis headed down the stairs in haste, and out of the door of Edwards house. He looked around, but saw nothing other than darkness and shadows. He stood still and listened intently for any noise. He then heard the sound of a muffled female voice in distress. He went left, and the sound became fainter than before. He realized he went the wrong way. He misjudged the direction that the voice came from. He never was great on directions, but he considered himself lucky that most of the time he actually guessed directions correctly. That was one moment that his luck was less than generous. He doubled back the direction he came from and further past the house with his sister. He checked down the alleys that he passed, and if he saw nothing he passed them up.

He kept on going, and then he heard the muffled cry again. He followed it into an alley, but saw nothing. All of the sudden there was a flash of light and it turned to pure darkness quickly. During the flash, Ellis heard the sound of the woman's scream silenced as quickly as it happened. When the darkness lifted, he looked into the alley, and once again there was nothing. He went further down the alley and found a blood spot on the ground. There wasn't a body or a culprit anywhere to be seen, however. Ellis was quite confused about what just happened. He was sure that the woman was killed. He couldn't figure out how the body disappeared without a trace except the blood. The funny thing to him was that he had no intentions on saving her; rather, he just wanted to know what was going on in more detail. Denied the chance for either option, he left for his inn room disappointed but still determined to find out.

He managed to remember the way back to the inn without any problem, and when he got there, it was still bustling with activity. There were many drunken people by that time of night, making the scene quite humorous. There were a few musicians playing on a small stage. The song was an upbeat tune with horns. He didn't think he would be getting to sleep anytime soon, so he stayed up and had a few drinks before going to bed. He got a well-needed nights rest and was up bright and early to check out the town. He went down to get a meal, and during the meal, some guards came in and posted a few more notes on the bulletin board. After finishing his food and waiting for others to read the notes, he went over to do the same.

The first bulletin he read said "Notice: more attacks have been reported and several more women have disappeared into the night. If anyone has any information please contact the sheriff right away. Let us not lose more of our precious population. If any female residents of Terrah venture outside their homes, you MUST have an escort of 2 appropriately armed men. This is not optional.

Furthermore, the guard in the street will be doubled to ensure that the abductions will not continue. This warning is not meant as a daily deterrent to the normal activities in your lives, but mainly as notification to ensure everyone's awareness of the severity of the situation. The citizens are to continue their daily routines, but are to be extra cautious. No one is to travel during the night. The night watch will be increased especially." Ellis could see how things could be bad for anyone who got arrested on suspicion.

He would have to make sure he didn't do much in the middle of the night unless he wanted to get arrested, which he had no desire to accomplish. I don't really care much for the guards here, but so far I've only run into a few. One was helpful. Ishta never had near this much guard activity. But aside from the sheriff of Ishta, his lackeys still need to be taught a lesson. That is something I will do when I ever get back. It just hasn't been the right time, but it will come. He still had many goals of revenge yet to fulfill. He would eventually fulfill those goals when the time was right.

The second notice on the bulletin board was a wanted poster for an apparently famous villain that kept escaping the law in the area. "Wanted: a dark haired man that kills for mere pleasure, and is very good at escaping from jails, he is wanted on charges of murder and theft. No one is immune to this mad man's killing sprees, and this person is wanted and avidly sought out in several other cities as well. He especially likes preying upon the rich, and making off with their fortunes by robbing them before the guards are able to get to the victims' homes. The villain has brown hair, blue eyes, is 5'9" and well built. He is known in the area as The Shadow of Death. If captured, dead or alive, preferred dead, a reward of up to 5000 tils will be given. This reign of terror has gone on for a week, and has occurred in nearby cities and towns."

Most people did not even have 30 tils to their name. Tils was the currency of Terrah. Ellis was quite intrigued about this Shadow of Death and thought he would be an interesting person to travel with. It would be better than traveling with his "angelic" sister, although she seems to be growing on me. I will keep an eye out for that person while I'm in Terrah and the surrounding land. He was sure that many others were hunting for this stranger as well, so he had to be careful about approaching the situation.

The festivities were going to begin soon, which could be guessed by the bustling activity on the streets during the day. Shopkeepers were busy setting up more shops and tents, and their wares had increased. As Ellis went about looking through town, he thought he noticed Laic in the crowd. He ended up losing track of him. I must be seeing things. He found several tents that had many interesting wares to buy. He bought a few small things as replacement rations and replacement weapons. He stopped in a park in the middle of town and thought about past and future events. How will I continue these travels? There is no telling when or if she will ever wake from her current state. Do I stay and wait for her? Or do I go, explore, learn, and feel my way around this world? He was torn as to whether he should leave his sister behind and start a new life without her. He certainly wasn't going to continue the search for Judith.

He decided to return to his sister after some thought, and along the way he found an animal peddler. He thought that a pet for her would be a great companion in his place. He wanted to travel on his own, but until that moment he hadn't figured out a way to give her a companion since it was obvious that she needed one. The peddler noticed him looking at the animals and asked him to go inside the building most of the animals were housed in. Ellis went in willingly and browsed through the available animals.

The man was selling horses, farm animals, domesticated and trained animals, and exotic animals. The animals disliked Ellis, and the horses were very restless. The horses shied away from the stable doors as he passed. Ellis expected as much though.

"I'm shopping for a companion for my sister. She is unable to be here in person, but she really needs one," he told the peddler. Ellis looked over the animals and tried to stay away from the horses. He narrowed his choice down to a trained falcon, a blue panther, or a bear cub. Since he couldn't decide on just one, he figured he would get her two of the three. "I'll take the falcon and the panther." He paid for the animals and asked for the animals to be delivered to a stable closest to the Edward's house.

"Very well sir, but I must advise you there will be a handling fee for the transferal."

Of course, Ellis would also have to go to the stables to pay for the animals to stay there as well. Ellis got the man to sign a note and then a copy of it so that he could give his sister one copy and the stables another copy.

"Thank you for your business," the peddler said with a smile.

Ellis went on his way to the stables. He made it there in no time, and made the arrangements with the stable. It cost Ellis extra, but he was more than willing to pay the amount needed. He then went to Edward's house and set the note on the table next to his sister. She still hadn't awoken, so Ellis said his goodbyes to his twin. "Goodbye, sister, may you wake and find the path you seek. I hope you appreciate all I've sacrificed for you. You are on your own now…at least without me. I must live my life and you must live yours." Ellis nodded to Edward, and while Edward was looking at Ellis' face, Ellis was secretly giving his sister's hand one last squeeze.

Ellis told Edward, "I am leaving town soon, and I've left a note on the table for her should she wake. It is my parting gift to her. I trust you will see to it that she gets the note upon her waking."

"I will do exactly that, and I will care for her as long as she needs."

Ellis nodded in return and left to go to the festivities that were beginning.

As he went down the street, people were rushing in one direction in a hurry. He was pretty far away, but he could still see what was passing through the part in the crowd up ahead of him. A woman that had a long sword and a mace at her sides rode into town first. She had dark brown hair and was tall for a woman in these lands. She rode her horse like she knew just how to control it. She probably grew up with horses and was taught how to deal with them. She rode in gracefully and almost regally. She was dressed in fine clothes, though they were a little worn.

Following her, a very muscular man with a giant metal club and a morning star came riding in. He had black hair and tan skin. He was massive compared to most people, and it looked like the horse had a hard time carrying him because it went at a slower pace than the first horse. The massive man smiled and waved to the crowd as the people cheered loudly for him. Ellis assumed that he was the "hero" of the city, Rokk. Ellis could just envision him smashing goblins left and right into the ground. The man was almost frightening because of his size. But of course Ellis would never openly say that.

Two thinner men followed Rokk in the processional into town. They carried short and long swords at their sides and they seemed to be very injured even though their wounds were closed and cleaned. They rode in faster than Rokk, and had to slow down so they didn't run into him. They tried to keep distance between Rokk and themselves. They seemed to be discomforted by the loud cheering made by the crowd. He couldn't blame them for looking that way since the noise of the crowd was giving Ellis a headache as well.

The last people to come through were a group of musicians on horseback. One looked considerably more colorful and rich than the others around him. The group of musicians had a wagon behind them. Presumably, the contents of the wagon were most likely instruments and such. They rode through gracefully, and in a showy fashion. The musicians weren't bothered by the noise of the crowd. In fact, they seemed to love it. They waved at the people on the sidelines, and kept traveling towards the center of the city. The crowd followed the processional down the street and further into the city. Ellis joined the crowd, but stayed behind a little so that the people weren't yelling in his ears.

As he followed the group, he noticed a familiar voice nearby and turned to see Laic. Laic appeared distinctly more malicious than before. He didn't seem to recognize Ellis, and Ellis found that odd. He approached Laic and said "hello". Laic just gave him the coldest look that Ellis had ever seen before. Ellis knew the look was pure evil. Ellis stood there in surprise, and Laic ignored him as he brushed by him. Laic went further into the crowd. Ellis was stunned by the look he was given. Ellis had never known anyone other than himself to radiate that kind of aura, but in his travels with his sister, he had gone slightly soft. That was why he wanted to continue without her, but he was confused about Laic. Laic turned into something to be respected instead of the annoying loser that was interested in Angeline. Ellis decided to keep tabs on Laic, and find out what he was up to.

The crowd continued to cheer and shout for their hero and the entourage. The band played well, and late into the evening. The guards were tripled once the sun started to set. The band packed up their things, and Rokk stayed out to converse with the townsfolk. People slowly filed into their homes as the sunset, but a large group of men stayed and drank with Rokk. The woman with Rokk also stayed and talked to the men conversing with the city hero. She danced with a few people during the night, but not many. She eventually went to a house down an unexplored street surrounded by guards who were escorting her home.

Rokk stayed out quite late, and eventually went to a nearby house for the evening. Ellis had kept an eye on Laic ever since the look of death he gave him. Laic seemed to just be observing the situation. After most people were in there homes, Laic went to a different side of town with a seedier bar. Along the way, they saw a woman being escorted by a few men. Ellis noticed Laic take an interest in the woman, but he kept going. As Ellis watched the group go by him, he saw Laic turn around and look back at the woman wickedly. Laic had the scariest grin on his face that Ellis had ever seen. Luckily, Laic didn't notice Ellis following him around town.

Laic kept moving, and came upon the seedy bar and entered. Ellis waited for a few moments and went in after him. Both men noticed each other, as he entered the bar. Laic raised his eyebrow, but said nothing. He kept a close eye on Ellis after that. Ellis was keeping an eye on Laic as well, and even as the barmaid came to take his order, Ellis didn't take his eyes off of Laic. Before the barmaid came back with Ellis's food, both men got up simultaneously to go to the other's table. They both smiled at that, and Laic motioned for Ellis sit as he walked forward to Ellis's table. Laic sat down at the other end of the table when he reached it. For a few minutes, the two just looked at each other, not really knowing what to say to each other.

It was Laic that spoke first. Even the speech seemed different to Ellis. "I vaguely have memory of you, but I do not know from where."

"You traveled with my sister and me for a bit before you were sent to the hospice. You were interested in my sister and followed her like a horny dog."

A look of recognition crossed Laic's face at the mention of the hospice. "I remember seeing you as I left that place."

There was a moment of silence on both sides, and the barmaid came to the table to drop off Ellis's food. The barmaid seemed to be very nervous for some reason as she approached the table.

Laic finally spoke. "Why are you following me?"

"I found it odd that you didn't remember me."

Laic looked to be in thought for a moment, and said "I sense a kindred spirit in you," though Laic's was more pure.

Ellis looked at him questionably and said nothing to the comment.

Laic just smiled wickedly at Ellis, and said "we will meet again." As Laic got up from the table, Ellis agreed and watched Laic exit the bar to go upstairs to a room.

Ellis ate, watched the patrons of the bar for a few more hours, and thought about the conversation that just took place. Ellis observed several cheats and scoundrels doing what they were best at. The women that were there weren't very attractive. Most looked like "used goods", and there was no way Ellis would touch any of them. It made him wonder though if there was a brothel around. He thought that perhaps that was something he should go look for. It wouldn't have been wise at that time of night though. After a few hours he saw Laic return to the bar and gather one of the women. The two returned to the second floor. Ellis decided to wait to see if she came back down or not. Ellis knew he would be tired, but he could sleep during the day if he needed to. There wasn't anything pressing.

Ellis waited all night, and managed not to fall asleep. In the morning he noticed Laic come down without the girl. He even waited a little longer, and she never came back down. Ellis's instincts told him that Laic killed her in the night, but he wasn't going to look. Laic noticed him still sitting at the table and approached him.

"Morning."

"Morning."

Laic looked at Ellis oddly, but didn't say anything. Ellis could almost hear what Laic was thinking, and answered Laic's question as he was about to ask it. Have you been up all night waiting for me? Laic thought. Did you see me with the girl?

Ellis said only "yes" to Laic and answered both questions with one word. Ellis then asked, "Are my suspicions about the girl correct?"

Laic just nodded. Then both just nodded, and Laic said "I will find you before you leave the city."

Ellis nodded and left the bar. He went back to his room and slept into the afternoon. The celebration was still going on from the morning till the evening. He awoke to the sound of a musician in the inn and tavern. The music was loud and fast, and could wake anything from its slumber. He went to eat a meal before venturing out to look for the brothel. He had never been to one, but had known about their existence from knowing Judith.

He had lied to his sister about their mother and the cave. He had never seen their mother in the cave, and she was never buried, but it kept him from having to see her again. Now his sister could look for her, and he wouldn't have to deal with their mother at all.

He ate and went out into the city. He found the brothel in about a half hour, and decided to look around. He figured he could enjoy the festivities until sunset. He would visit the brothel then. He walked around, sight-seeing in the city, and explored other ways in the city that he had not been to. He almost ended up lost, but he managed to find his way around. Ellis was wandering the streets while sight-seeing; he wasn't watching where he was going. Distracted, Ellis ran straight into someone. Both of them fell down from the impact, and had to take a moment to regain their composure.

As Ellis got to his feet, he saw that he had run into the most beautiful woman he had ever seen in his life. He didn't get the feeling from her that she was some sort of good person, but she seemed to be more neutral in nature. All Ellis could do was stare at her for a few moments. He wasn't sure what to say to her, because he had never seen someone so beautiful in his life. She had long, straight blond hair and deep blue eyes. She was approximately 5'6" and nicely shaped. She wore a blue and green swirled silk dress. The dress was now a little dirty and it was his fault.

She looked angry and proceeded to tell him to watch where he was going. She was trying to get the dirt off of her dress, but wasn't having much luck. She just said, "Great, now it'll have to be washed again." She started past him, and as she was walking away he could hear her say, "jerk". Before he got his senses back, she had already disappeared into the crowd. She also stunned him because he sensed a similar spirit in her as he and Angeline had. He was determined to stay at that point, and try to apologize to his desirable mystery woman. He quickly followed in her direction.

## Chapter 13: New Groups Formed

Ellis followed after the blond with the silk dress, and quickly caught up to her. He saw her enter the inn and tavern where he was staying. My lucky day, he thought with a smile. He went in after her, and overheard her talking to the innkeeper.

"I need someone to draw a bath for me, and this dress will have to be cleaned. I trust you have someone who can clean it properly?" She sounded a bit spoiled, and probably well off.

He quickly went to the innkeeper after she went upstairs. "I will draw her bath and wash her dress."

The innkeeper looked unsure about it, but he also couldn't get any of his own help to do anything. All employees at the inn were either busy or out with the celebration. After some thought, the innkeeper finally agreed. "Very well, but you must understand I won't be able to pay you." The innkeeper was still skeptical about the decision. He gave Ellis the key to her room, and Ellis smiled. The innkeeper instructed Ellis how to draw up a bath properly, and said, "As for the dress, bring it to me and I will clean it."

Ellis agreed and went up to the room and knocked. She answered the door, and the look of shock swept over her face. His presence stunned her momentarily. He took the advantage. "I am here to draw your bath for you," he said with a grin that never left his face as hard as he tried. He had to try to turn it to a smile instead so she didn't feel creeped out. He opened the door and entered before she could object. A moment went by, and she gained her composure.

"Do you work here? Or are you just following me to get me dirty again?"

Ellis smiled and just looked at her for a moment.

"You can speak, I know you can. So are you avoiding my question?" She seemed slightly annoyed.

He finally answered her after a long pause and just staring at her beautiful face. "I admit, I am not an employee, but the staff is too busy to fulfill your request so I offered my services. After all, I was the one who got you dirty. I wanted a chance to apologize for knocking you down. I am not normally so clumsy. So sorry, my lady, for earlier events. Are you ready for your dress to be taken down to be cleaned? It is the least I can do."

She wasn't sure what to say, and was a bit wary of him, but accepted his apology. "Draw the bath then; the dress will be ready momentarily." She went into the walk in closet and closed the door. She came out in a couple minutes with her dress in her hands, and was wearing a robe.

Seeing her in a robe set Ellis' mind spinning with overlapping thoughts.

She handed him the dress. "You will instruct whoever washes this dress to be careful of the fabric. It is delicate and rare, and I will be very upset should this dress get ruined."

"I will pass the message along as you wish, of course." He watched her for a few moments, and asked "do you need help washing?"

She looked at him almost coldly, and said "you've done quite enough to me for one day."

He took it coolly and said, "I will take the dress down to be cleaned." He left and did just that. Ellis then went back upstairs and realized that her room was right next to his room. Ellis formed a wicked idea in his head. He went into his room and found a spot on the adjoining wall to her room. He put a ring of water on the wall so there was about an inch of dry wood in the middle of the circle. He carefully set the center of the circle on fire to make a small hole. He would find out if she noticed or not when he looked through it. I hope she doesn't notice; this should be quite entertaining.

He looked through the hole and he saw her in the bath in all her glory. He was feeling things that he had never felt so strongly while he watched her bathe.

He didn't know, but she was well aware of what he did. She decided she would play along. She planned to make him wish he had never done that. In a way she felt it was a compliment, and had never met anyone so annoyingly direct before. It turned her on like she never knew she could be. I will keep my cool and play along like I am oblivious. This should be entertaining.

He watched her bathe and just couldn't pull himself away from the hole in the wall. He was so entranced on the bath, that he almost missed her getting out of the bath and drying off. Of course she gave him the best shots from his view, but didn't look at the hole. She mentioned to herself that the bath would need to be drained. The mention of it made Ellis snap out of his trance. He jumped away from the hole and went to knock on her door with good timing. She was robed again, but he could still picture her naked. He yearned to touch her badly. He refrained from even attempting such a thing, and drained the bath for her. He could smell the perfume on her, and it was intoxicating.

"Are you finished yet? And when will my dress be finished?"

He snapped out of the trance at her speech. "I will check on it." He ran downstairs as well as he could in his... condition, and got her dress for her. It was hard for him to run or walk due to stiffness. Her dress had just been finished when he inquired about it. The innkeeper noticed his condition but didn't say anything.

While he was getting the dress, she was giggling to herself about what she was doing to him. I'm not done having my fun with him yet. There is still much more in store for him. By the end of the next few hours, he'll be burning down the entire wall! She could feel he was different from others and similar to herself, just as well as he could. She found it curious. She could read his mind and knew she was torturing him, but she was still having her fun with him. He ran back up to her room with the dress. She took it and thanked him.

Quickly he replied, "You're very welcome". He kept the exchange short and returned to the hole in his room quickly. He began peeping again.

As he watched her, she got out of her robe and stayed naked. She set the dress down carefully on the dresser top after inspecting it and finding the dirt stain gone. "I don't feel like wearing this at the moment, "she was speaking to herself. Lotion...that should do it. She spread the lotion all over her body, and she did it slowly as to get the maximum tease from it. Ellis was beside himself at that point, and was quickly losing control of his emotions. Then she went in for the kill. She lay on the bed and decided to play with herself a little bit. It was too much for him to handle.

He hurried out of his room, and without a knock or any advance warning he opened the door and closed it behind him. She tried to look shocked, but she had a smile from ear to ear at the sight of him in his emotional state. She was about to ask a redundant question, but decided to just end his suffering. She motioned for him to come to her, and he willingly obeyed. The blond woman and Ellis shared her room for the evening. The whole time all of it went on, he never learned her name, and she never asked for his.

Ellis awoke in the morning to find himself in her bed, but she wasn't there. She was nowhere to be found in the room. He got up and put his dirty clothes on just long enough to get back to his room. He rang for his own bath to be had, and after he was done there he put a clean pair of clothes on. He went downstairs to find that his sex interest wasn't there either. After a meal he had a few questions for the bartender. "Have you seen the blond woman check out yet?"

"No, but she left the inn about half an hour ago."

Ellis finished his meal, and set out about the town. No sooner did he get out of the door, than he ran into Laic who had been coming to talk to him. He went back into the inn and tavern and sat at a table in the corner with Laic and talked.

"I'm leaving this city tomorrow, you can accompany me if you would like," Laic offered.

"Sounds good, but I want another person to come as well, if I can find them again."

Laic looked unsure, but agreed anyway. "Meet me at the docks at noon tomorrow."

Ellis agreed.

"Dock 5 and it's called 'Crashing Waves'. Ask for Captain Dewey." Laic left Ellis to his business.

Ellis went in search of the blond. He realized he never caught her name. He started through the streets, and saw that the celebration was pretty much over. It was just life as usual for the people once again. He went through all the areas he knew to go, and found no trace of the blond. He was disappointed, but had a feeling he would run into her again soon. He continued on through the city, and went to find the docks since he hadn't been there before. After locating the docks, he headed back. I'm getting pretty good at navigating the city now.

As he went towards the inn and tavern, he thought he saw his sister and the animals traveling out of the northern gates of the city. Ellis didn't want to be noticed by her, so he hid and watched her head her own way. I will miss her, oddly enough, but she seems to be up and around, which was what I hoped to see. It warmed his heart to see her up and about, but she seemed sad that he wasn't there. He tried to block his thoughts from her so she wouldn't know he was there or anywhere near her. He watched her walk out of the gates, and went back to the inn and tavern.

He felt a strange sadness. It was a sadness that he had only felt a few times and all because of his sister. I will miss her, but I am better off without her and she's better off without me. As he walked and pondered about his sister, he felt a wet hand touch him and it made him jump in surprise. He turned around and it was his blond staring at him with her deep blue eyes.

She looked at him curiously and then understandingly. "I'm sorry." She paused. "I will leave you to your thoughts." She started to walk away when he grabbed her around the waist and pulled her toward him and up against him. He stared into her beautiful eyes and held her there. She almost looked embarrassed, but wasn't quite feeling that way. "I probably won't see you again anytime soon. I too have to go my own way."

"Travel with me." He was sincere. He wanted to travel Paelencien with her.

"My path lies in a different direction from yours. I cannot come with you."

He held her close. "Please." And trust me, I don't say that often.

"I'm sorry. I cannot." She genuinely seemed sorry to refuse him, especially after he just watched his sister leave.

"Where are you going? Where is your path taking you?"

She just smiled. "I cannot tell you that. But I will tell you my name." She smiled at him. "I am Circe." She kissed him and left his arms. "We will meet again", then she turned to walk away.

He followed after her and grabbed her hand.

She looked at him understandingly, and said "I really have to be going."

"My name is Ellis."

"I already know," she smiled. Circe gave him another kiss and broke away again. This time he lost her in the crowd of people in the street, and was once again alone.

He went back to the inn after stopping for supplies he might have needed to go seafaring. He rested that evening. All he could think about was his night with Circe. He was disappointed she couldn't stay and travel with him. And why is it the women seem to know more about me than I let them know? I realize now how my sister did it, but it seemed like Circe could too. This is a common thing? Hmmm, Circe..... Visions of her still entranced his mind. Where was she going?

He hurried to the docks in the afternoon, and made his way to the Crashing Waves ship with Captain Dewey. This was the first time he'd seen ships up close. The ship he was boarding was gigantic. The ship set out, and he found Laic already on the ship.

"So...where's the other passenger?" Laic inquired as Ellis boarded the ship.

"They will not be joining us after all."

Both men left it at that.

\*\*\*

Angeline awoke not knowing how long she had been out sorts. She came to her senses to find herself in a bed that was in some strange house she had never seen before. A man came in, and found her awake and smiled at her.

"I'm so happy you're finally awake. Your brother was in town to see you and check upon your health. Ellis just left town though. You have a note on that table that he left for you."

Angeline found two pieces of paper. One was a note from Ellis.

"It is best we both go our separate ways, sister, from here on. It pleased me to see you had not been killed in the nest. And I hope you recovered quickly. I will miss you, but we must take separate paths. I thought you might need some companions, so I bought a few things for you.

Your brother,

Ellis"

The second piece of paper was a note from a vendor telling what animals were purchased, and where they were being held while she was unable to retrieve them. The note saddened her, and the strange man standing in the room noticed.

"Those are your brother's gifts to you, my lady. I am so sorry you had to awaken to the news of your brother having already left. My name is Edward, and you are free to stay as long as you need to. I rescued you and brought you here to recover."

"I will only stay for the remainder of the evening. I intend to set out tomorrow morning. Thank you for taking care of me. There is little I can do to repay you for your kindness."

"You are most welcome, and if should need anything, you have but to ask."

"Thank you, I will."

Edward left the room to let her adjust to her new situation, but was close by in case she needed anything.

Angeline just lay in bed and cried for a little bit. She would miss her brother greatly, no matter how much they fought. No matter how annoying or angry he was, she loved him. They were always with one another. Now he was gone. She was saddened by the situation. No matter what, I must continue my search for mother, Ellis or not.

She got some rest and awoke in the morning. She was a little wobbly trying to stand up and walk, but she quickly got the hang of it again. She was still weak, but she healed nicely from the wounds. She ran into Edward as she started to wander around. "What happened while I was out of my senses? The last thing I remember was large chicks were pecking at me."

"You actually passed out from poison in your system. The chicks wounded you, but the poison in your blood caused the chicks to die," he informed her.

She was surprised to hear that and was sad for the chicks, but was happy that she was still alive.

She finished her morning meal and Edward helped her find her new companions. He knew where the stables were, and it didn't take much time at all to get there. Edward helped her as long as she needed it. When they got to the stables, she was almost bombarded with the animals' thoughts. She tried to read her brother's thoughts and there was nothing. It seemed her gift between her and her brother was now between her and the animals. The stable boy showed them where the purchased animals were. Her companions began to talk to her mentally right away, and were attracted to her instantly. All of the animals in the stables acted favorably towards her, but the two that were to be hers were especially bonded. The falcon came to her immediately, and the blue panther started to purr and rub against her leg. Angeline froze in awe of the blue panther. You are truly beautiful and amazing. She read that they were extremely rare animals to find. The fur was short and had a deep royal blue sheen to them. She counted herself lucky for Ellis to have found one for her. She also met the falcon, and thought that it was beautifully marked. You are beautiful and amazing as well. She ruffled the belly feathers a bit, gently, and kissed the bird on the head. The falcon sent happy thoughts coursing through her head.

What to name you two...hmm? You are Sapphire, my beautiful blue friend. And you, I will name you Scope, as you will be my eyes and ears. Do you approve of these names?

The cat purred and the falcon bowed.

Good, then let us be underway.

"Edward, could you show me around to the shops? I will need to make sure I have all my supplies." He helped her as she asked, and she bought supplies and rations. She also bought a staff to lean on if she needed to and it was just what she needed. She didn't know what happened to most of her things. Apparently Ellis had left a few things of hers, but not everything. She was now able to walk and get around on her own. "Thank you Edward, for being so kind to me. I will be fine from here on."

He seemed sad for her to go, but wished her the best of luck. "If you are ever in Terrah again, please stop by and say hello."

"I would love to." She blushed a little bit.

He smiled at her, and she returned it as best she could. She was still weak and in a little pain. "Please be careful, my lady, and know should you ever need help, you can count on me."

"Thank you, sincerely, for everything." She waved goodbye to him.

He waved and turned to travel back to his home.

She was sad to see him go, but she couldn't stay there. Scope, would you give this necklace to him for me. It was one I've had since I was a child and I want him to have it. Scope grabbed hold of it and flew after Edward. He dropped it into Edward's hands, and Edward took it gratefully. Scope returned and told her Edward was thankful for it, and put it around his neck almost immediately. Angeline was glad to hear it, and thanked Scope for delivering it for her.

While visiting a few more shops, she ran into the largest man she had ever seen. His muscles bulged out and he carried a large metal club and a morning star at his sides. He almost ran over her, but caught himself just before impact.

"I am sorry ma'am," he apologized to her and smiled at her. "I am Rokk, great warrior and protector of this city." His voice seemed soothing to her and she felt a kindred spirit to hers within him.

"Pleased to meet you, sir."

He took a look at her companions, and had to comment. "Those are beautiful animals, my lady."

"Thank you, yes they are very beautiful in my eyes too."

"Are you okay ma'am? You seem injured." He noticed she was using the staff to lean on. Before she got a chance to answer, he asked her, "Would you do me the honor of having lunch with me?"

"Yes, I could stand to eat something before leaving. I don't want to be hungry on the road."

He noticed that she has to use the staff for support as they went over to a little restaurant nearby. They sat down at a table. "What happened to your legs?"

"I was traveling with my brother and I was unknowingly bitten by an isil. Then the largest bird I've ever seen swooped out of the sky and carried me off to its nest. As if that wasn't bad enough there were hungry chicks in the nest and they attacked me. I blacked out from there. When I awoke, I was being taken care of by a kind man named Edward. I just left his company when I ran into you." She continued her story. "The poison still has me a bit weakened still, but it will get better. Normally I heal very fast. I don't quite understand why things aren't working as they should lately."

Rokk seemed deeply concerned for her, and had a lot of sympathy for her. "Where are you headed to, my lady?"

"I am trying to find my mother who went missing from my home town and family. It seems so far away now."

Rokk felt badly about her going off out in the woods alone, and especially with so many more goblins around. "I will help you in your travels. I offer my services to you and I will not take 'no' for an answer." Rokk saw how helpless she was, and couldn't let her go alone. "Please stay here until I return. I will be packing my things immediately. Promise me, you will not leave without me."

"I promise."

Rokk left to notify his best friend, Nova. Nova said she would watch things around Terrah, and for him to have fun. He gathered his things, and came back to the restaurant as fast as he could. When he arrived, he didn't see Angeline right away. Then he then spotted her trying to walk around without her staff. He managed to catch her before she hit the ground from her weakened legs.

"You really should not press your luck. You should be taking it easy, or you'll end up hurting yourself." He was concerned for her.

She just smiled at him, and they set out for the north gates. He continued for a way down the street, and got ahead. Angeline stopped to look at the city one last time, knowing her brother wouldn't be with her. She got sad for a moment, and hoped he would be okay. She then tried to catch up to Rokk, and did so in just a couple of minutes.

"Are you okay? Do you need to rest?"

She put on a half smile, and said "I am well enough to get the journey underway. Thank you for coming along." And thank you my friends! All three said they were more than willing to help her. She smiled at that and they set out of the northern gates.

# Chapter 14: Rokk

Rokk was born in Terrah. Terrah is a port city that deals greatly in ores mined by a smaller town near the mountains. Rokk was born with the power to move and command earth. He was always a very muscular person. He grew up in the kind of home that most people in Terrah dreamed about. His mother, Laine, and father, Kall, were higher up in the chain of command over Terrah. Rokk never had as hard of a life as most others, but he didn't let that go to his head. He was always a very helpful person to the community, even as a child. Laine and Kall taught him to respect others and to help the needy.

Rokk grew up with best friend, Nova. Nova was great at swordplay and loved to roughhouse with the boys. Nova's parents never really approved of it, but there was no stopping her. Once she put her mind to something, Nova was unstoppable. It really didn't concern her, what was and wasn't lady-like behavior. As they grew up together, Rokk and Nova yearned to see the world. They wanted to travel the countryside and battle. Rokk couldn't do that however, since he became a protector of the town even from an early age. He was made to train under the strictest weapons masters in the land to improve upon his skills. They often traveled from the west to get to Terrah, but some went west after coming into port in Terrah. One such master was Kaahn.

As Rokk grew up the burden of being protector became much more serious as goblins began to terrorize the area. Rokk was often sent off on missions to protect surrounding towns as well. They were in much more of a need for his protection. Rokk killed hundreds of goblins since his childhood, and they still kept coming. Rokk and Nova often fought side-by-side; they were a force to be reckoned with.

The matter came up between the families that perhaps the two should get married since they were clearly fond of each other. Both families had a lot to gain by such a union. Unfortunately, Rokk and Nova were purely friends and would have no part in the wedding, even though the two knew how much it would benefit their families. The two of them just couldn't get married to each other when they didn't share the love a husband a wife should feel.

Both families agreed that the two should be married and tried to force it on the two of them. Neither Rokk, nor Nova wanted the marriage, so the two left Terrah for a few years. They traveled all over the countryside and had a grand time ridding the land of evil and being free. Eventually, the two were found and told the news that since they left Terrah, it was attacked. The informant told them that their families were both targeted and were slain in the attack upon Terrah. The people begged for the two to return to Terrah, but it didn't take much convincing.

After hearing the news that their families had been slain, the duo went immediately back to Terrah to defend it from further attack. New leadership was put in place and was not working for the people. Raphael Vinell, the new mayor of Terrah, was only in it for greed and power. He misused his power and caused several unnecessary deaths in Terrah and the surrounding towns. Raphael even secretly made a pact with the evil roaming the land.

After that secret was discovered the hard way, Rokk took matters into his own hands and had Raphael taken into custody. With the help of goblins and other evil creatures of the night, Raphael escaped his holdings. With the escape came a large wave of goblinoid creatures attacking several towns and even Terrah. Rokk and Nova fought along side to defend Terrah and new leadership was quickly formed. While the people were rebuilding Terrah, Rokk and Nova, along with others, went out in the land to rid the land of the horde of evil sweeping it.

The war on evil lasted a few years and Rokk was a key factor in leading the area into a safer time. Most of those who fought in the war died. Only two guard captains from surrounding towns, Rokk, and Nova survived the conflict. Upon their return journey to Terrah, The group of four ran into a famous musical troupe was also heading to Terrah.

## Chapter 15: On the Great Sea

Ellis and Laic set out to sea, and Ellis wasn't even sure where he would go or what he would do. It wasn't like he knew that at the beginning of his journey either. As they pulled away, he stared off towards Terrah, thinking about his sister. I hope she will be alright. He figured she would, but there was always some doubt in his mind. I had to do this. She was tainting me, the more time we spent together. It was time we separated. I wasn't born the way I was, just to be corrupted by her. This is best for both of us to grow and become who we are meant to be. We were tainting each other. That thought made him chuckle. He just couldn't stay with her any longer. He had a sign of the right time, because their communication by thought was not functioning anymore. He was happy about that part of their relationship, but I will miss it in time. I just know I will.

Laic saw him staring off the boat and came up to Ellis. Ellis just turned and looked at him. "Not that I really care, but are you okay?"

"I am fine," Ellis plainly stated. "Where are we going?"

Laic looked at him for a moment, obviously trying to choose his words carefully. "We are heading out to meet one of my friends that would be interested in meeting you."

Ellis just raised an eyebrow and said nothing. He nodded.

The captain walked up to Ellis, "I am Captain Dewey. What would your name be?"

"I am simply Ellis," and just slightly nodded at him.

The captain was a man in his late thirties that had salt and pepper hair. He had a beard and mustache with a slim face. He seemed well built, most likely due to his work on the ship. "Your rooms are on the first floor beneath us, right about where you are standing. Joe will show you to them."

Ellis thought perhaps *going to my room will take my mind off of her*, and went with Joe right away. Laic stayed out on the deck.

Ellis sat in the room and meditated for a while. He heard a card game going on a few hours later, and went to join the crew in their game. He had never played before, but was willing to try it at least once. In Ishta, he knew several people who played, but he was busy with other aspirations. As the card game played out, the conversation ended up being about people who use magic. The conversation intrigued Ellis, and he asked several questions about the topic. He had only heard about those sorts of people very briefly. It was a hushed topic in Ishta. No one that lived in town ever talked about people who cast spells. The only way he heard about the term was by eavesdropping on a conversation that a traveler, which was passing through, talked about it. Even then, others overheard and hushed the topic quickly. Ellis asked all kinds of questions about them to the crew, and the crew seemed quite surprised that he knew nothing of sorcerers.

"I haven't heard of too many that could cast magic, but those who do are very powerful."

"Most are neutral or good in nature, but I heard there are some evil ones too."

"What types of things can they do?" Ellis wondered.

"I heard they can control the very elements around us at will, lightning, fire, poison, you name it."

"Naw, they have to say a few words at least. Only the gods can do it at will."

"Some sorcerers," one sailor said in a hushed tone, "can bring people back from the dead, or slay even the greatest hero with a word or ceremony, depending on the wizard of course."

As far as the crew knew, wizards had their own unique abilities; that most didn't share magic with one another. Ellis found out quite a bit about wizards, and stored the information in his head for future use.

*Am I some sort of wizard? Wouldn't I know it if I were? I can do some of the things they mentioned, so can she. Maybe the other people that felt like kindred spirits could do these things too. What is a wizard, really? I thought only the gods could do those things, traditionally. There are so many unanswered questions. I will definitely have to keep my powers in check while on the ship.*

After the game and the conversation ended, Ellis went back to his room and tried to get some sleep. In the morning, he went above to the deck and found they were still at sea. There was no longer any sign of land. He knew he couldn't stare at the sea or he would go crazy, so he went back to his room and decided to look at his new fancy sword. He had never seen a sword with sapphires in it, or any other kind of jewelry. He was sure that the sword was worth a fortune if he tried to sell it. He had no intention of selling it though. Upon examining the sword further, he noticed several symbols that ran down the blade. They were tiny and very intricate. Whoever made the sword had a lot of patience to be able to put the designs on the blade. Of course, he figured they meant something, but he had no idea of what the meaning was. After a little while he decided to practice his skills with that sword in his room. The room was small so he would have to be careful. He would have to get use to it since it was a heavier weapon than he was use to dealing with. The jewels and the type of metal made it heavier than normal. It was a silvery metal, but wasn't silver. It almost had a bluish tint to it. He practiced until he got too tired, and only stopped to get something quick to eat. He then just went to sleep.

When he awoke, the ship was rocking strangely compared to what he had experienced on the trip up until then. He went up to the deck and found that they were in a storm, and the waves were crashing against the ship. Some water from the waves went on deck, but the storm wasn't too bad. It was pitch dark though, and dangerous to be up on the deck so he remained down below. He was having trouble with the rocking of the ship, and there were a few times when he had to grab onto a post so he wouldn't lose his balance and go rolling around. It was definitely quite a first boat trip for him. He started to feel queasy, but braved the wind and waves anyway. He went back up on deck and he had to hold on to whatever he could to keep stable. He finally made it to a side, and held on while he let loose. He couldn't hold the sickness in any longer.

After he was done, he went back down below. He was soaked from going up there, and had to change into spare clothing to keep dry. He was cold now, so he huddled under his blanket. The storm lasted about four hours, and he was glad when it was over. There were all kinds of activities on deck when the storm was past. The crew was busy repairing things and he figured he would just be in the way.

He was bored at that point and decided to look at the book he had found. Even though he couldn't read it, it would pass time away. He looked at the book for hours and then he came upon something interesting. He found that one of the symbols in the text was a symbol on the sword. He searched more through the book and found all of the symbols that were on the sword, were also in the book. He then tried to figure out what the words possibly meant. He spent several days trying to decipher the runes. He only left his room to eat and do other necessary activities.

He wasn't sure how long he actually spent on the deciphering, but he found that he was beginning to understand what some of the symbols meant. He was in the middle of reading one day, and the ship jerked oddly. He set the book down and went to check up on what was happening above. He was only able to open the door to the deck an inch, because something heavy was on top of it. He saw another ship connected to the Crashing Waves. There were planks connecting the two together.

He saw some bodies lying on the deck and they weren't moving. They were dead and bleeding from blade wounds in the back and chest. They weren't the crewmembers from the ship he was on though. They were more richly dressed. The crewmembers of the Crashing Waves ship were stripping them of the silks and valuables that they carried. He could hear the captain ordering his men to hurry with the bodies, and Ellis heard someone moving something lying on top of the door. Whatever the object on the door was, it wasn't able to be moved very far.

The crew finished and set the bodies on the other ship. They just piled them on and set the ship a blaze after the plank was off and they were headed away from the other ship. When the barrier to the deck hatch was finally removed, Ellis decided to go out on deck after the other ship was a little ways away.

Dewey noticed him come out, and said "You missed the excitement Ellis!"

"Obviously," as Ellis surveyed the scene.

Joe was swabbing the deck of blood. Other crewmembers were just spreading away from each other to go do other duties.

Ellis went back to the room and stayed there. He did many things to occupy his time and keep boredom away. He could hear the crew of the ship hard at work for the next few days, and then it began to settle down. He went up every now and then and found no trace of the slaughter the few days prior. They continued on the ship for quite some time, and it was getting hard for Ellis to know how long they had been out to sea. He would estimate it was approximately another two weeks on the ship, according to brief snippets of crew conversation in passing. They encountered storms on occasion, but they weren't bad. Other than that, it was the same actions on the ship, day in and day out.

One day Ellis felt an odd vibe about the air. He knew something was amiss and went to check it out. As he searched around the ship, he found the crew was quite a bit crankier than usual. The captain had his eyes on the lookout, and Ellis noticed that the captain was eyeing a few certain men in his crew. They also looked at the captain funny on several occasions. Laic was nowhere to be seen, but Ellis knew he was staying in the room next to him.

The odd stares continued on.

"Check the sail Nevis," the captain barked.

"Ney, Captain."

The captain went to him quickly. "You will do as I say crewman!"

"Ney, Captain, I will not." Nevis was quite defiant.

The captain's face was turning red as his anger rose. Ellis watched as the crewmember drew out a dagger from his belt on his backside. Other crewmembers were beginning to gather around and looked as if they were backing Nevis up. A few men came up behind the captain to support him.

The man suddenly tried to plunge his dagger into the captain's chest and missed. The man missed so terribly he fell to the side of the captain. The men caught him before he hit the ground.

"Get ye all back to work, lest I slay you and throw you overboard!" The captain took his sword out and threatened the crew. "I will not suffer mutiny on my ship!"

The men still stood there, refusing to budge. One man spoke up and said "we're takin' the treasure, and tossing you overboard! Hehehe, you'll make good shark food."

Dewey responded back, "the punishment for mutiny is death, and if you men don't get back to your duties, you will be the ones joining the sharks, in pieces."

The men acted as if they didn't hear him or just didn't care.

Laic joined Ellis at his side to watch the spectacle with quite a bit of interest. The captain suddenly thrust his sword into the outspoken crewman's chest. He fell to the floor bleeding to death. Four other men drew their weapons, and tried to strike the captain down, but Dewey got to them first. The rest of the crew went back to their posts, and left the bodies on the deck. Ellis and Laic just kept watching to see what the captain would do.

Speaking loudly so all could hear, "Anyone else wanna try to take my ship for their own, you'll end up worse than them! Let this be your warning. I do not brook mutiny." The men seemed to be paying attention to him now, and the captain threw the bodies off the ship.

Dewey went back to his favorite place on the ship and kept his eye on the other crew members that didn't back him up in the confrontation. Ellis went up to the captain, and Laic followed.

"I would be willing to help you if these men become a problem," Ellis offered.

"I too will assist if you need it." Laic offered help as well.

"Thank you both, but I am capable of dealing with traitors myself. You needn't worry about the situation, but I am gonna ask you to go back below deck for now."

Laic actually wanted to kill a few of them, but would respect the captain's wishes for the moment. Once they set out on dry land, he would have his fun with the other cowardly traitors. Ellis just planned on going to his room, and hoped they would reach land soon.

It would only be approximately another week till they got to land. During that week, Dewey kept his full attention on his crew, but no one tried to take him out again. They all obeyed the captain for the rest of the trip. They finally saw land in the distance, and made it to a smaller city than Terrah, though a bit darker.

## Chapter 16: The Shadow

Upon arrival and docking, Dewey told his two guests, "I hope the trip went well for you."

"I had a fine time, Captain, just kept to myself," Ellis said.

Laic agreed with Ellis. "Thank you for bringing us to Estare."

"No problem. Now if you will excuse me, I have my own business to take care of in town." Dewey excused himself. The crew took crates off of the ship.

"Follow me into the city Ellis."

Ellis and Laic traveled into the city. Estare was a dirty city full of bandits and wanderers. Ellis knew he would like it. He spotted a tower towards the center of the city. It loomed tall, dark, and high over the other buildings in the city. It was covered in vines that were half dead. It had odd markings on it, but Ellis couldn't tell what they were from that distance. Laic had Ellis follow him to an inn and tavern and told him, "Wait in Scarney's Inn and Tavern until I come back." Laic quickly left, and Ellis was left alone again. He paid for a room, and looked about his surroundings.

Laic left and ended up running into one of the sailors he had his eye on. "Follow me; I have something to tell you. It won't take but a moment." The crewman followed him, and Laic led him into an alley. Laic then grabbed the man by his arms, and absorbed the traitorous sailor's life into himself. The crewman fell limp to the ground, dead. Laic made sure no one was watching, and took everything the man had.

He left the alley after he was finished, and went to a shop. The shop seemed to sell a variety of spices. He walked into the store, straight into one of the backrooms, opened a secret panel in the wall, and went down a set of winding stairs into a room with a bar and entertainment. There were several people in the bar drinking their ales. Laic went over to a man dressed in a black robe wearing dark rings with a black mace at his side. Laic knew he also carried swords, but he didn't seem have them with him at the moment. The man in black robes looked at Laic expectantly for some information. The robed man had three other people dressed in black normal clothes at the table with him.

Laic started the conversation. "We traveled from Terrah by ship, which nearly had a full mutiny. They robbed and slew the crew of another ship. The booty was supposed to be the prize of the failed mutiny. The price just went up though, for you, but it was purely unintentional."

"Well then, I will just have to kill a few more people then." The robed man's voice was plain and calm.

"Ellis is capable of many things it seems. He can light things on fire with a mere thought, can wound with a thought, not to mention his weapons prowess and knowledge of poisons. I am unsure of what other powers he might have. He is ruthless when pressed. And I warn you to never back him into a corner, you will die. Death seems to be a gift of his."

The robed man seemed intrigued. "Bring him to me...better yet, I will come to him. I will join him at the inn." He looked at Laic. "You are excused."

Laic obeyed and started to leave for Scarney's Inn and Tavern.

Just as Laic was leaving, the man said, "better yet Laic, one of my men will accompany you, and get to know more about this, Ellis."

The man who was volunteered then said, "Would it not be better to send Jenn? She would be able to get more information than I would."

"Agreed." The black-robed man turned to Laic. "You are free to go Laic." He turned to the lackey initially volunteered, "And you may gather Jenn."

Laic made it back to the inn, and found Ellis easily. He was watching the events going on in the inn and tavern.

Laic walked over to Ellis. "I'm going to my room. I will see you in the morning, Ellis."

"Alright. I will remain here for now."

About a half hour later, a nicely, but scantily dressed female with long black hair and green eyes came into the inn. Ellis found her quite attractive, but wasn't going to approach first. He kept his eye on her though.

She went to the innkeeper and talked with him a moment, then she headed up the stairs over towards Ellis. She smiled at him. "Mind if I sit with you?" Her tone was just the right tone of seductive.

"I don't own the table. You're welcomed to sit here if you like, but you have to sit right next to me." Ellis grinned at her.

That made her smirk even more, and she sat down near him. "I'm Jenn."

"Ellis."

"You don't look like the usual scab from around here."

"You would be correct, I'm not."

She stared at him with her light green eyes, and almost had him entranced. "Do you like to dance?"

"I've never been good at it. Other things amuse me more."

"The way I intend to dance with you, doesn't take long to learn."

That piqued his interest. "Alright, I will attempt it."

She took him to a fairly open area of the room and danced closely with him. The whole time she danced with him he wondered what she was up to. He wasn't use to having women behave as such towards him.

*She's after something. Or maybe this area just has a different kind of women. Between Jenn and Circe, I've never seen such outgoing women. I'm definitely enjoying this though. It is one of the most amusing things I've seen so far.*

She danced with him for some time, and she was doing well arousing him.

"You wanna go somewhere else and 'talk'?"

Jenn gladly agreed, and she held onto his hand as they went upstairs to his room. He had her go in first so he could watch her walk from behind. He smiled at her as she passed him. He went in and closed and locked the door behind him. She went to the window, and looked out the window at the scenery of the town. He started walking up behind her and she turned around as he went over to her.

She put her arms around his waist and smiled at him. She then drew him over to the bed, and asked him to lie next to her. She then began to ask him questions. "So..." she kissed him gently on the neck, "what brings you here? I want to know about you." She kissed him gently every now and then as she asked questions.

He humored her. "I'm not a scab, like the ones around here," he smirked. "What is there to tell about me? I'm a traveler of Paelencien." He was leaving out answers about his family and his powers. He never mentioned anything about his sister or the rest of the people he had felt were similar. Jenn seemed to listen intently at what he had to say, as she kissed him. "I'm evil, I'm abrupt, and I'm very turned on right now." He smiled. "Why the questions?"

"I don't just jump into bed with people like this. I simply wanted to know about you and your travels. They make exciting stories to listen to. And I do mean exciting." She smiled.

"Well then, how about me trekking through super tall grasslands and having to avoid isils. Or me getting caught in torrential downpour and having to remove my clothes so they could dry." He winked at her. "All other stories will have to wait for later."

After realizing she wasn't getting anymore information from him that evening, she then took the lead and made the first moves on him before he could ask her about herself. By the time she was done with him, he was too tired to ask her questions. She was gone before he awoke, and went to the black robed man.

"Well? What have you to report?"

"He's still very tight-lipped about personal information, but given time with him, he might relax enough. Right now he's on edge and reluctant to talk. He seems to have arrived here that way. Something must have happened on the way here that made him cautious about talking about himself. Give me more time with him." When speaking to the dark robed man, Jenn was very serious and business minded.

"I will pay him a visit tonight. You set up the time to meet with him, and I will be there."

"Without question or delay, sir." She left to go find Ellis.

When Ellis awoke, he found that she was gone already and saw a pattern forming. He actually liked for them to stay on through the morning, because he was usually in the mood first thing in the morning as well. It was actually his favorite time to have sex, but most girls seemed to prefer sex in the evening. He was getting dressed when there was a knock on his door. He decided to answer it half dressed and found it was Jenn. Before she could say anything, he grabbed her and pulled her into the room. He threw her on the bed and had his way with her. She didn't really object, but seemed quite surprised.

After he was done, she thought it a good time to talk. "Have dinner with me tonight, at my house."

"I will go if I stay overnight, all night, and get to have my way with you again. Whatever, whenever, however I want." He smirked.

"Very well," she said as she looked at him oddly. She gave him directions to her house, and told him what time to be there. She put her clothes back on and went to get the dinner ready. She didn't expect him to be so bold, but it was a refreshing change that she liked. Most of the men she dated were losers, and she had given up on finding someone from Estare. She was often hit on amongst her guild members, but she wasn't keen about to get involved with her guild mates. She thought such a thing was unprofessional. She was the prettiest in the guild so she was often sent to meet, and seduce certain people as designated by her superior. Had she dated someone from the guild, they would likely object to some assignments. She wasn't sure about Ellis originally, but once she saw and met him, she had no problems doing her job.

Ellis went to eat breakfast, and found that most people in this city weren't up first thing in the morning. Most were probably too drunk to wake up so early. He decided to check the city out, but was stopped by Laic.

"You need to stay in the inn and tavern Ellis, until I return." Laic told Ellis bluntly and without explanation.

As soon as Laic left, then Ellis left in a different direction. He was curious about the tower. Even though the sun was out, the city was blanketed in darkness. With the sun out, it was as if he was sitting in shade, but at night it would've been completely dark without the streetlights.

He traveled to the center of the city, and went to the tower. As he closed in on the tower, he noticed the stones used to build the tower were black and white with white objects that looked like skulls inside the stones. The door was made of a very dark wood, and had a skull for a doorknocker. He knocked on the door, and the door opened about three minutes later. A teenager dressed in a grey and black robe answered the door. Ellis asked if there was anyone there who could read a book that he found. The boy didn't speak, but motioned for Ellis to go in.

The boy then went to a small desk, and rang a small bell. The boy said in a low voice that "it will be just a minute". Not too long after, a man in black clothes trimmed in blood red came down a set of winding stairs. The man looked to be in his forties and had jet-black hair and black eyes. He came down and introduced himself.

"I am Nirak, the Fallen."

"Ellis." He noticed Nirak looking at him strangely, but he didn't say why. It actually made Ellis uneasy, but he remained cool. It was almost as if Nirak recognized him, but he wouldn't know how.

Nirak grinned at him. "Follow me."

Ellis did and was led to a room. "Can you read this book and the corresponding runes from the book to this sword? Do you know anything about this sapphire sword?"

Nirak looked at the book, and grinned quite a bit more. "Where did you find this book?"

"In a nest."

Nirak examined the sword, and was smiling, almost laughing. "Do you realize what you've found?"

"I know nothing of either of them, what they read as, nor who owned them prior." Ellis could tell Nirak knew quite a bit about the items, and began to get uncomfortable. Then Nirak asked Ellis something that totally caught him off guard.

"What do you want most in this world, Ellis?"

Ellis didn't know what to say, and shrugged.

"There must be something you want above all else."

"I would have to think about that in greater length," Ellis said, not really trusting Nirak.

That surprised Nirak, but he would go along with it. He gave Ellis the book back, and told him, "Think about the question I asked. I will trade for the book."

"What is the book about?"

"If you do not know, then that book is useless to you. It would, however, be of great use to me. I could dig up a few things in trade for it. That is, so long as you still do not know what it is you want. Come back later on this evening."

"I am busy this evening, but I can return tomorrow."

"Then I bid you goodbye," and the whole while Nirak had a grin from ear to ear.

Ellis figured he would ask again about the sword on the next visit, and he wasn't willing to trade for that. He went back to the inn and tavern, and had lunch. He waited there for Laic, and Laic showed up shortly before Ellis had to leave for the dinner. Ellis and Laic talked about where to go next.

"I will need another day in the city, but I will be ready to leave after that."

Laic wondered what it was that Ellis had to do, but he didn't ask.

Ellis left for Jenn's house, and arrived in no time. Her house was a two-story house, that seemed to be pretty old, but she seemed to decorate it well enough to make it look newer than it really was. He went to her door, and she opened the door a few minutes later. She was wearing a revealing black dress with silver sparkles in a floral design on the fabric. The sides of the dress were slit and it showed off her fit legs. She looked so good that he wanted to grab her, and take her then and there. As soon as she let him in, he wrapped his arms around her waist and held her close. He did the maneuver so suddenly that she was absolutely surprised, and wasn't sure what to say. He looked at her hungrily, and she quickly realized what he wanted to do. His actions, though surprising, made her aroused, and she quickly led him upstairs. Perhaps I should come to expect this reaction every time I go to his door, she thought.

After they were finished, they came down to eat.

"You look amazing, more than I can appropriately express, in that dress."

She laughed lightly and said, "I could tell you like it."

"I would not be opposed to spending all night and morning upstairs in your room."

"We should eat something first, and I have a surprise for you."

Not long after dinner, there was a knock on the door. Jenn let in a man wearing a black robe and carrying a black metal mace at his side. Three men dressed in black followed him in.

Ellis looked at them, clearly annoyed. Who the hell are these clowns? They've interrupted such a great night with Jenn. This better be good.

The man walked up to Ellis and introduced himself. "I am Jakule. I've heard about you, and I wanted to meet you."

"Really, I'm flattered, but this isn't the best time to talk." Ellis noticed how Jenn's behavior changed when Jakule walked in. It seemed as if he were some sort of superior to her, because she was very obedient to him. Ellis was curious to know more about Jakule. Is he some kind of ex-boyfriend or something? "I haven't ever heard of you, but I suppose I can talk briefly. But I do mean briefly, you've interrupted something good here that I am anxious to return to."

"I am certain you know of me, perhaps not by this name though."

Ellis looked at him curiously.

Jakule went into the room, and sat down on one of Jenn's chairs. Jenn offered the new guests something to drink, but none were thirsty. "I will be brief in my discussion with you then. I am aware you are traveling with Laic, and want you to continue along side him. I will also send Jenn with you. There have been several towns taken over by disease, and they all need to be wiped out. It is not contagious through the air, but all of the people must be slain to ensure elimination of the infection. You should not be in danger of catching the infection."

As Ellis talked to Jakule, he noticed that he sensed the same thing in Jakule as he sensed with Circe, though Jakule was much more evil. It was a strange sense of familiarity that he could not place. Ellis decided to bring it up to Jakule. "There is something about you, Jakule, which seems familiar to me. I sense it, though you are much more evil than I am."

Jakule smiled at Ellis after the questioning statement. "I sense it as well, and you will find out why, sooner or later. It is something that you, Ellis, have to discover on your own." There was a slight pause from Jakule. "All ten of us have to or have already had to."

That last part confused Ellis. What did he mean by that? "What about 10?"

Jakule would say no more about it. "I'm afraid my time has come to leave, but I will keep in touch with the group of you. The sooner you set out for the other towns, the better." Jakule turned to Jenn, "Goodbye Jenn." Jakule promptly left with his men in tow.

There was an odd silence now between Jenn and Ellis. Neither knew what to say.

"What did Jakule mean when he talked about 10?"

But Ellis didn't get much out before Jenn just started kissing him to keep him from asking questions. She led him back upstairs, and they stayed up there all night. She was still there in the morning, and it was afternoon before Ellis really did anything productive. He went to the tower and was met at the door by Nirak. Nirak led him up to the room they were in before, and asked Ellis about what his answer to the question was.

"I haven't had a lot of time to think about it, so what will you trade me for the book? But before all of that, I want to know what the sword does."

"The sword belonged to the person who owned the book. The sword was magically imbued, and would cut better than most blades. He said it was one of ten weapons made at a certain time in history. He said the sword's name was Calimel. He said the sword would release bolts of lightning at enemies when its name was called out in battle. It belonged to one of The Ten, as did the book."

Ellis started to ask about the topic, but was quickly interrupted by Nirak.

"I can say no more than that. You should search out the Lady of Fire."

Nirak quickly changed the subject back to the trade at hand. Ellis was getting frustrated at the constant evasion of important details and information. He just wanted to trade and leave. Nirak presented two rings, one pair of thick bracelets, a cloak clasp, two talismans that hung on silver chains, and an ornate black stick.

"This ring can magically protect you from an enemy attacking you. Of course it depends on your opponent's skill. You can still be injured, but it is less likely to happen.

"This ring can hide your ...nature. It is helpful so that other people don't judge you before they know you.

"These bracers will give you more agility and strength, and make it easier and quicker for you to fight.

"This cloak clasp will make you unseen, invisible.

"This talisman gives you power to regenerate, while this other talisman will allow you to read people's minds.

"And last we come to the ornate black wand. This will return people from death; however, they will not be the same as they were before. And this wand can only be used once every other week."

Ellis sat in thought while looking at the items before him. "Just one?"

"Yes." Nirak watched Ellis curiously and he thought about which item to choose.

I want to pick more than one, and this book seems to be of importance to him. "This book holds some importance for you; I want to pick 2 items."

Nirak thought about it for a moment, and then agreed.

Good, now which to choose. I will likely be in peril a lot, so the first pendant could be useful, especially since I don't have Angeline with me. Hiding my true nature could be useful, but do I really care that much? The bracers could really help with faster blade-play. But then again, there is so much I could do with invisibility. The first talisman could help since Angeline isn't here. And the other talisman, I seem to have a harder time with mind reading than most of my kind it seems, but others would be more useful. Plus, just how are these items made, who is this guy?! Ellis grabbed the cloak clasp and the first talisman, invisibility and regeneration. He handed the book over to Nirak, and thanked him for the trade. With business done, and Ellis frustrated at the amount of evasion, Ellis just wanted to leave. "I will leave you to your book then."

"Thank you, I look forward to viewing it. Goodbye Ellis. Though I do not doubt you will be returning with further questions. Till then..." Nirak gave him a command word for the clasp. The talisman just had to be worn. And quite abruptly, Nirak walked off with the book, leaving the servant to see Ellis out.

Ellis left the tower, and was determined to find out what the hell was going on with "the ten". He went to a few shops, and stocked back up on his supplies. He went back to his room and decided to look at the items he'd just chosen. He found the clasp was in the shape of wisps and was made of silver. He put it on his cloak and took up the talisman. He put the talisman around his neck and decided to test the talisman out. He took out of his daggers, and cut his hand slightly. He watched in amazement as the wound on his hand healed before his eyes. He was quite happily surprised with the talisman. He would test the cloak clasp later on. He got his things ready to go and rested the evening.

Ellis met up with Laic and Jenn first thing in the morning. They all had breakfast, and set out for the town they were supposed to get to. Jenn and Laic were both supposed to know where it was. Jenn didn't pay much attention to Ellis along the way. She seemed quite alert to her surroundings, and it was an odd side for him to see of her. He felt it was fortunate though. Too much play creates distraction, and now is not the time.

She was now in traveling clothes that were much plainer than what he had seen her wear. She mostly wore dark grey and black clothing that consisted of a black body suit that was skintight, and a black and grey cloak. She wore black boots and dark grey gloves. She had a dagger sash and grey belt with several pouches hanging from it. He found that her clothing made her nice to look at and he did just that.

They traveled for a few hours and it was getting darker as they went further inland. He thought the darkness came from the town somehow, but he was wrong. As they went on, he could see a vague shape of a castle in the distance to the south. They stopped further on down the road to set camp. No one really said much to each other. It seemed that Laic and Jenn were intentionally trying not to talk to each other.

Ellis noticed that, and asked, "How well do the two of you know one another?"

Jenn said nothing.

"I'd only met her once before, a long time ago."

Each one took a turn watching over each other during the night. During Ellis's watch, he could hear odd cries and other sounds coming from the south. There seemed to be some sort of dead forest in that direction. The trees had unknown things hanging from the branches. It was a quite uneasy feeling that he was receiving from that direction. Soon he saw a giant bat fly overhead; at least that's what he assumed it was. It never came near the camp though.

The land was dry and cracked, though there was an odd moisture about the air. Ellis tried to think about why that would be, but no good answers came to mind. Some spots on the ground were soft, and almost mushy, yet others were completely hard. It was an odd place to visit, but he was enjoying his trip. His thoughts turned to his sister for a moment, and how she would never set foot there. The whole area seemed evil and partially alive, yet dead at the same time. It would've scared her. I wonder how she is faring. To make himself stop thinking about her he told himself, she is fine.

The night went by without incident, and the group was off again in the morning. They traveled even further the next day, and camped in the evening. The landscape was the same the whole way they traveled, but he could tell that they were about to head into one of those forests he saw in the direction of the castle. He saw that they would reach it by midday the next day. That night on his watch, he heard more of those odd cries, and they were louder. He figured it was coming from something within the forest. They weren't animal, no animal he knew of anyway. They didn't sound alive, but they sounded almost people like. The cries echoed eerily.

## Chapter 17: The Forest of No Return

Morning came for Ellis, Laic, and Jenn yet it was still dark as night. Only a little light emanated from the dark clouds above. They had their breakfast before setting out. It didn't take long for them to reach the forest. There were only a few leaves on some trees. Most were leafless and lifeless, or so it appeared. The trees were deceiving in that they were actually alive. They seemed to have spirits inside, controlling them. The whole area radiated evil. It was quite the odd place for Ellis to visit, but he noticed the other two weren't affected at all. They seemed as if they were accustomed to it.

As they traveled through the forest, Ellis saw the trees move as the three of them moved by. It almost seemed as if they were staring at the group. Oddly enough for Ellis, it didn't make him nervous at all, just cautious. They had been walking for a few hours, when all of the sudden a large wolf came out of nowhere. It bit Ellis on the leg before he could react, and then it turned on the others. It growled ferociously at the party, and seemed determined to continue to attack.

Ellis got the first jump on it and as he tried to act, a shot of pain coursed through his leg. The sudden pain made him lose the energy he was going to use. It turned on Jenn next, but missed her. She acted next, and in a flash, she had a dagger in each hand. She swung at it three times, one of which injured the wolf. It was injured, but not downed, and it still wasn't backing down. Laic went over to it, and tried to touch it with his hands. It jumped away from his touch before he could.

The wolf decided to attack Jenn again, and barely missed her. The fangs hit some sort of magical force surrounding her. It almost looked like a small shock of lightning struck the wolf as it hit the field around her. Laic was the next to attack it, and he tried to touch it again. This time he succeeded, and it yelped in pain at his touch. Both of them could see that his touch drained some of its life. The wolf was quite injured, but still alive. It seemed to be furious at Laic, and seemed intent on attacking him in return. Ellis drew his sword out, and called his sword by its name, "Calimel". A bolt of lightning shot out of the blade striking the wolf, and sending it flying back. The wolf hit a tree and fell to the ground, unmoving.

The next event took the entire group by surprise. The ground seemed to absorb the body, and in a few seconds, the wolf had disappeared into the ground. The ground just seemed to swallow the body down. Each one looked at each other and looked surprised, but not scared by any means.

Jenn said, "You should get that leg fixed in the next few weeks, or you'll be in trouble. That was a werewolf, and there's a chance it could've infected you. If you are indeed infected, then it will change you during the full moons. Since there were so many moons, the transformation would happen quite a lot."

"How would I reverse it, if that were the case?"

"You would have to find a priest to do it." If we get into town in the next few days, you should be fine. The unfortunate thing about the next town is that not all denizens are very friendly. Sometimes they kill and eat travelers they meet."

Ellis had heard of cannibals, but he had never been near any. "Well then I will just have to convince the priest to fix me rather than kill me."

"The next town is also under special rules by Tarax, the lord of the area. He is the one who owns and resides in the castle to the south. Tarax had decreed that the people of Kakul are not to be killed or hurt by any people passing through for any reason. They are allowed to kill and eat whom they wish. Tarax will torture any who would injure the tribe members. Revenge isn't allowed against the tribe."

Jenn continued further saying, "Torture by Tarax would not be anything pleasant or easy to deal with. He is known through the lands for his torture methods, and most who live in the area or know anything about his law of the land, know better than to anger Tarax. As he grew and adventured, he perfected his torture methods, and he will not hesitate to use those methods on any who anger him." She seemed to be quite serious while telling Ellis the news about the Lord of the area.

Ellis heeded the warning and would try to stay off Tarax's bad side. "What other rules has he demanded for the people to obey?"

"No one is to ever attack his knights or other nobility of the land, no matter how bad they may have been. It is punishable by humiliation and then death. There are rumors that those who die by him are not really dead, but have changed into something else. That is just a rumor as far as I know.

"Also, there is to be no poaching of the local animals of the land. Those who do become what they were poaching, and will suffer the same fate as what they killed. Most crimes are punishable by the same things that the people accused have done. So as long as you don't kill anything unnecessarily, or do anything against the upper class, you will be fine. It will be harmful to his health, and to those who travel with you if you do anger Tarax."

"I will honor the laws of the land while I am here. I have no interest in any of those punishments." Ellis didn't want to have to stay here as a permanent resident.

"Good."

They continued on their way and had to camp in the forest. The sounds of the night were the same sounds that could be heard in the day. The difference at night was that the sounds were louder. As they camped that evening, he could hear what sounded like screams of agony coming from the northeast. He awoke Jenn and Laic so they could all go investigate. Jenn heard the noises, and sat back down.

That is just the Tree of Souls, Ellis. It is not an uncommon thing to hear those screams every couple of days. The Tree of Souls is where Tarax keeps the souls of the worst kind of criminals. The tree supposedly eats their souls slowly, so it makes them suffer for what would feel like eternity. It is actually supposed to take around a hundred years for a soul to be devoured by the tree. The tree also has a mind of its own. If anyone but Tarax goes near the tree, they die at the tree's whim. It steals the souls out of the bodies of those foolish enough to get close to it. I am unsure what happens to the bodies left over, but I suppose the ground takes them."

Jenn continued, "I don't travel through this area much, but I've learned quickly what not to do. I will live longer."

Ellis took in the information with curiosity. While I don't want to stay here as a resident, I think I want to meet Tarax on one of the days I journey back through here.

The whole while Jenn was explaining the rules, Laic's face was expressionless. When she came to the part about the tree, his face smirked slightly and his fingers moved slightly.

Ellis couldn't sleep well with the constant moaning of the souls in the tree. He eventually fell asleep, and awoke in the morning. They ate breakfast, and went on their way again.

They traveled on for most of the day, and in the evening, came to a small village that Ellis assumed was the "town" that Jenn mentioned. The village was full of people with dark skinned faces with red paint of some sort, at least Ellis supposed it was paint. They wore little to no clothing, and as soon as the group approached the village, they were met by several villagers with spears and axes. The natives pointed the spears at the three travelers, and led the group into the village at spear point. They were forced to go to an exceptionally large hut that contained a man wearing a large bone helmet with bone jewelry decorating his minimal attire.

The oddly dressed man spoke to the party. "What are you doing in my village?"

Ellis let Jenn answer the man's questions.

"We are passing through to aid towns that have been afflicted with disease to keep it from spreading, and we needed to pass through your village to get to there. Also, Elder, one of our members has need of a cure for the 'wolf disease'."

The elder looked the party over, "you are a liar. I have seen those afflicted with the wolf disease, and no member of your crew has that look."

"Ellis," she motions a hand in his direction, "has been newly bitten, and will need to be cured before the moon is again full."

The elder walked over to Ellis. "Where were you bitten?"

"On this leg."

The elder looked at his leg and became visibly angrier with Jenn. "You lie! That wound is old, and done by a wolf changer." He cried out in a language no one could understand and some of the tribe members came in and took the group. The man spoke again in the other language, and they led all but Ellis out near the fire.

The man looked Ellis over and began chanting. The man chanted for several minutes until he finally stopped. "Navush had deemed Ellis unclean to eat, so he would be spared. The others are a sacrifice to Navush, and they will be as one once their flesh and meat are consumed."

"So what happens to me?" Ellis asked.

The elder just started chanting in the strange language. Ellis could hear that others outside were beginning to chant and dance. He could hear Jenn struggling to get loose from her bonds and could hear nothing from La-ic. Ellis was then tied up inside the tent.

After Ellis was tied up, the elder left the tent, and began talking to his tribe. The elder would say something Ellis didn't understand, the others would hum in unison in response. That continued for several minutes, and Ellis tried to free himself from his bonds. He decided to burn the bonds, since he knew he would heal from it. He was out of the bonds in no time, and surveyed the situation in the village before rushing out. Jenn and Laic were tied to thick branches and bone, and were about to be placed over a large fire. The man from the tent had a dagger made of bone and some oth-er component Ellis didn't recognize. He was about to slice their throats over what seemed to be bucket-like containers. Ellis thought they might have been made from clay.

Ellis had to do something fast to keep them alive. He rushed out of the tent, and shouted, "If you continue with this sacrifice, then Navush will get angry and punish you!"

The elder appeared angry that Ellis freed himself from the bonds that kept him in the hut. He moved over to Ellis and began chanting. Before Ellis could act, he was touched by the leader and felt his body go rigid. El-lis couldn't do anything but watch the sacrifice. He still had a way of mak-ing the god's vengeance happen, because he still had use of his mind and senses.

The man was about to plunge the dagger through Jenn's throat, when the totem and other various religious items near it burst into flames sud-denly. The villagers shrieked, and ran away from the totem. They got about ten feet away from the totem, dropped to their knees, and began to bow and chant to Navush. Probably for forgiveness, Ellis thought. The leader in bone was so startled by the fire that he missed as the dagger went towards her neck, but the aim was still not totally far off. He still cut the side of her throat, and she started bleeding all over the place. Her body went limp, and Ellis could do nothing but watch and keep the fire burn-ing. I could just slaughter them all, but to do so would land me in a situa-tion I have no desire to be in.

The elder ran off of the platform he was on, and started doing the same as the others. Ellis knew he had to get to Jenn as soon as possible, but he still couldn't move. He then directed a little bit of fire to burn the ropes off of Laic. Laic cursed in pain at being burnt, but was free. Instead of Laic going to help Jenn, he went to the leader and tried to suck the life from him. Ellis wanted to shout out to him, but was still unable to do so. With just a few touches from Laic, the leader was nothing but a shriveled lump on the ground. Laic looked stronger for having done that. All of the sudden, Ellis could fell his body unstiffen, and he rushed to Jenn's aid. He picked her body up, and carried it to the side and away from the fire. He immediately took his talisman off and placed it around her neck. He could see her wound start to heal, but he wasn't sure if he made it in time to save her. He wasn't sure how far gone someone had to be before it no longer worked.

Ellis set her down gently and turned to talk to Laic, when he saw that Laic was beginning to turn on the others. "Laic, stop! You do that, you doom us all! Help me get Jenn out of here!"

Laic stopped what he was doing and went to Ellis' aid. The three of them started to leave the village, when Laic went back in to get their possessions. That caught Ellis by surprise. They left quickly and got far away from the village before they even thought about making a camp.

Laic realized that he had broken the law given directly by Tarax, and knew he would be in trouble when he found out. Laic knew that Tarax could see all, and knew all that went on in his land. Tarax would be angry for what Laic had done that night. Ellis didn't know if he would suffer punishment for Laic sucking the soul out of the elder. He was hoping not, since Ellis had done what he could to not directly harm them. The situation was my fault though, since the regeneration healed the proof he was looking for. And now, I have no cure. He pondered the ramifications of that.

They didn't sleep as long as they normally would have so they could get out as soon as they could. They traveled hard that day to get far away from the village. By evening, they reached a more lit area. The dark cover was fading as they continued, but the sun was also going down. They got as far as they could before they were too tired to stay awake. Ellis kept Jenn next to him in the evenings, and that evening he noticed she was breathing. The wound was healed, but she still hadn't awakened yet. He took the necklace from around her neck and placed it back on his. He held her close in his sleeping bag as he slept the night.

When he awoke, he saw Jenn had moved into a different position. She was closer and had her arms wrapped around him. When he noticed, he began to examine how she was doing. His examination woke her up.

She opened her eyes and smiled at him. "Where are we?"

"On the run, far enough to the east that we now have some light in the sky," Ellis responded.

She started to inquire about what happened, but it was cut short by him kissing her. She took the hint and asked no more questions about what happened in the village.

"You okay?"

"I think so." Jenn smiled at Ellis. She examined herself, and nodded. She still wondered what happened. Why are we on the run?

# Chapter 18: The Slaughters

Laic didn't seem to have any emotion at all upon waking to find that Jenn was alive. He could've cared less about her finally coming around. He acted as if nothing had changed since they left the city. Laic just ate his breakfast, and suggested that they get moving before the guards came looking for them. Jenn gave a nervous look at that comment, and Ellis just gave her a look as if to not even ask. Jenn really didn't like being kept in the dark about something that could possibly have them arrested. Most people who were arrested there were never seen again. Some were heard screaming in pain from the torture rooms or screaming in agony from the Soul Tree. Either way, she didn't like being unaware of the situation at hand.

They traveled on and came to a bustling small town just after noon. The people showed no sign of sickness, but according to Jenn and Laic, the small town was one supposedly afflicted. Laic was in the middle of talking to Jenn and Ellis, when a young child ran up to him.

"Please sir, help my mother, she won't respond to me. She won't wake up." The boy sounded desperate, panicked, and sad.

Laic looked at the child as if he were a gnat annoying him. He then wore an evil smirk on his face, and said, "I will gladly help you." Then Laic turned to the group and said, "The duty has to be carried out." He wished the others luck, and Laic let the concerned child lead him to the child's home.

"Laic should probably work on his own. I will meet up with you later, Ellis, after this deed is finished." She walked off in a different direction and left Ellis standing by himself.

Ellis picked a random direction and walked that way. He came upon a woman and her child walking through the street, and tried to use his invisibility cloak clasp. He tried and tried to activate the item to no avail. The item wouldn't respond to his commands, and it made Ellis furious. He knew he would have to do things the old fashioned way.

Ellis walked up to her and began talking to her. He seemed nice enough to her, so she agreed to talk to him. "Did you know, ma'am, my cat is hiding in the alley. It only responds to my wife. When I call for it, it ignores me. Would you be kind enough to call out to the cat so I can tell my wife her cat is safe? My wife would be very disappointed if she lost the most precious thing to her."

The woman, touched by the story, happily agreed to help him. As she went into the alley to call the animal out, Ellis broke the child's neck when she wasn't looking. He then drew his sword and stabbed the woman from behind. The blade went all the way through her chest and quite a ways out of the front side of her. He then lured others into the same alley claiming he found a dead woman and her child.

He killed many others before he was done with that method of luring. He would have to think of another way to kill others. He went into an inn and tavern and found someone in their room. He slew that person and then had people call the guard. The guard came rushing to the inn and went to investigate. Many other people gathered in the inn to see what was going on. Ellis left the building and set it a blaze with many villagers and guards inside. Those who tried to escape burned to death from Ellis directly. Some tried to get out of the rooms through windows, and fell to their deaths.

Ellis could hear cries of alarm from the other side of the town. He figured it was Laic. As more people gathered around the inn to try to help the trapped people inside, he made the flames jump out and engulf those people as well. Soon he found that no one else was around to help those in the inn, and he moved along his way into the town. He started setting houses on fire, and when he was exhausted mentally he went with openly slaying the town's folk with his magic sword. Some were slain by the lightning and others by the blade itself.

The town was thoroughly dead by the time Jenn, Laic, and Ellis were through with it. Jenn just slew people outright with her blades, and Laic sucked the life out of them, leaving them shriveled clumps on the ground. He did put most of them in one house, and set it on fire. Jenn did the same with the ones she had slain. The town was cleared and they were to move on to the next. They did stay at one of the empty, untouched homes, and were on their way first thing in the morning.

After Dark View was dead, they had to travel to Midwai to contain the "disease". Ellis wasn't sure the whole while they were in Dark View that the people were even contaminated by anything. Most seemed quite healthy to him, but killing those people gave him a feeling that he had been missing since he started traveling with his sister. He didn't care if they were innocent or not. That felt like a good therapy.

The group traveled on, and Jenn said that Midwai was still a few days away. They could see the dark blanket and the dead forest in the distance. Soon they lost sight of either of them.

"From Dark View onward, the land is ruled by an opposing lord to Tarax. He is under King Harand from further north. This lord frequently tries to 'cleanse' Nighthold of its evil. Tarax and Lord Bastion are constantly fighting, because of their beliefs. Normally Lord Tarax would win the battles. Bastion is more of a pain in his side than anything," Jenn informed Ellis.

That was the explanation Ellis needed to understand why they were killing innocent people. He didn't have a problem with it, but he was glad to know the real reason why he was slaughtering the towns. He actually looked forward to the next town. It gave him a rush and a tingly feeling in his stomach thinking about it. It was almost becoming a hunger for him. Jenn noticed the smile on his face, and she examined the look and his reaction intently.

She was happy she finally found someone that didn't wimp out on such missions. She looked forward to working with Ellis often. She had several reasons, but sex was the lesser reason. She often found that sex could get in the way of things, but she knew it wouldn't get in the way with Ellis. That thought made her smile. She was happy about going to Midwai as well, because there was a knight from Midwai that killed her brother while he tried to defend Nighthold. She had never forgiven the knight, and was getting a happy, anxious feeling about killing him out of vengeance. I will make him suffer as much as possible before he dies. He will regret the day he ever touched my brother.

Laic was just happy to suck the life from frightened victims. He preferred them frightened so he would often display his power in front of several people that were helpless and they couldn't escape. He loved it when victims begged and pleaded for their lives. He loved having that power over the ones he wanted to kill. The more they begged, the more he wanted to do to them. Sometimes he had to kill quickly, but he preferred to do it as slowly as possible if he could get the time to do so. He preferred to kill women and children especially, because they begged much better than the men did. The men would just clam up and take whatever he did to them. Laic knew that if he killed the wives and children in front of the husbands, then it would make the men more emotional. Sometimes he found that it made them more furious and gave them more energy to fight, but most ended up weaker for having watched. It was all quite a bit of fun to him.

By evening, Jenn said they would have to travel two more days to get to Midwai. "I want to make a certain section of the city for my own personal reasons, when we get there. The rest of the city is fair game for you."

Neither of the guys had a problem with that, and said it was fine. Ellis was curious about why, and decided to ask her while they were camped that evening. As they camped, Ellis went to her and sat next to her. He reached out his hand and took her hand in his. She made no effort to resist his motion. The two looked at each other for a moment before anything was said.

Jenn was the first to speak, when words were finally spoken between them. "How do you feel about clearing the towns of their inhabitants?"

"Doesn't bother me in the slightest, even if they were innocent when killed. Sometimes lands needed to be cleared. Why do you want a specific area of Midwai?"

"Eldarin, a knight there, killed my brother in one of the conflicts, and he has to answer to my blades for it."

"Want help in torturing Eldarin?"

"Thank you for offering, but I must do this on my own. And I must ask that you not be around me when I am doing so. Don't get me wrong, I like you being around me, but that is something I must do alone. Any other time is great for me."

"I understand." Ellis kissed her. She kissed him back and smiled at him. They didn't say much more to each other, but their hands remained together for the evening.

Nothing else happened during the night, and they all awoke ready to be underway. They traveled for most of the day and as it came time to camp, they saw another campfire ahead of them. They were all intrigued about who it was, so Jenn decided she would scout ahead, and let Ellis and Laic know if it was okay to get near the camp. The guys wanted to go as well, but eventually agreed to let her go first. She went into shadows, and the guys could no longer see her. They waited there patiently for her to return with news.

She snuck up to the camp, and found that it was a group of seven green-skinned creatures about man sized. They were sitting down around a fire, and eating what looked to be lamb. They had pug nosed faces, and seemingly they had no concept of clean hygiene. They didn't notice her, and she stayed in the shadows for a while longer to observe them. She had never seen creatures like them before, so she wanted to observe them carefully.

"Let's kill more humans, it's fun!"

"I want to find an elven female to bring back home."

"Oh yes!" the first one agreed.

"That is a great idea, since what Grok did to the last one." The third one was a bit less talkative, but was very much in agreement over the idea.

"Grok spoiled the fun," the second creature said with a frown. "They taste so sweet."

They talk about what they want like it's a dessert! Jenn shuddered and she realized their intent. She would have to be sure they did not get their hands on her. I will have to make sure I am quiet and unseen. I don't know what those things are, but I'd hate to see what they are like.

She listened a little longer, and then returned to the guys to report her findings. "Well, I have never seen those types of creatures before, but they like killing humans and want to find a female elf to have their sick way with her. And I don't want to know anymore beyond that disgusting thought."

"Sounds like they've got a similar path as us, aside from whatever they intend to do to female elves. And don't worry, Laic and I will protect you if they come after you. We'll simply kill them."

Laic looked happy about the killing option, and was ready to go right away. That I would protect her, Ellis must be joking. I'd rather watch them do to Jenn what they would do. "I've heard of these creatures in the past. They are well known for pillaging, amongst other things. More the first part though. They do favor female elves from everything I've heard. This means they'd just kill you, Jenn. They have quick tempers, and are supposedly quite cautious of other races. We should leave as soon as we can."

The group headed for the camp, and the creatures had no idea that the three were approaching. The creatures were quite surprised when the three of them came into the camp. The green skinned creatures hurried to gather their weapons and to get into defensive positions.

Laic lead the group into the camp. He started to speak to them, and only one of them was willing to talk to him, though he was still guarding. "We would like to share the camp with you orcs, if you don't mind."

The one who seemed willing to speak to them seemed surprised to find out that Laic knew what they were.

In a gruff, gritty voice, the orc said, "If you stay in our camp, we take your female to do with whatever we please."

Laic laughed. "Fine by me!"

"But not by me, Laic." Ellis was glaring at Laic. "That female is mine, but there will be plenty of women in Midwai for you to do whatever you want to."

The orc started talking to the others in the camp. He spoke in another language and they decided that it would be agreeable to them.

Laic thanked them, and came into the camp fully to make himself at home. Ellis and Jenn stuck close together, but weren't afraid of the creatures by any means. With Jenn assured that she would not be accosted by any means, she was a little less leery. Ellis and Jenn were quite intrigued by how things turned out, and thought that the events about to happen in Midwai would be quite memorable. They looked forward to it.

In the morning, the group and seven orcs began the travel to Midwai. They reached the town by evening and the madness ensued. Jenn went off on her own, and the orcs began to capture women openly. They did what they wanted to right in the streets, unafraid of anyone seeing them. Laic just watched the events and smiled. He took an occasional life force from the peasants, but was quite intrigued to watch the orc behavior. Ellis set the guards on fire that tried to help the women. Soon the orcs had enough fun for the evening and they took the women with them as they left the town. They thanked Laic for letting them come along. Laic told them it was no problem. Many unfortunate women were taken away that evening for the orcs' pleasure.

Ellis went through town and killed people as he wanted. Some were spared by him, but they ended up dead at Laic's hands. Soon the town erupted into complete madness. Guards tried to keep order, and tried to keep people in their homes. The attempts to keep order in the city failed after some homes were set on fire as well. The people were completely unsure of what to do. All they could do was panic, and try to flee. All who tried to flee were slain and soon Laic and Ellis both had separate groups of guards upon them. Both men were able to take care of them easily, and move onto others. Once the full fury of the men started, it was next to impossible to stop.

Jenn went to the house where Sir Eldarin was supposed to live. She knocked on the door politely, but there was no answer. She wondered if he was out on patrol or if he wasn't in town. She snuck into his home to find out one way or the other. She searched his home and found that he had left quite some time ago on some kind of personal mission. She grew angry that he wasn't there for her revenge, and she stormed out of his house. She killed anyone she saw, because her rage was so furious. Many people died at her hands, and when she came upon the party, she was still quite angry. Ellis could tell she was pissed off and guessed she was unable to exact her revenge. Ellis would say nothing to her while she was that angry. Laic seemed curious at why Jenn was so furious, but was content to watch her be angry.

Laic found her angry face cute to some degree. It was intriguing to him at the least. He had quite a wonderful time in the town, and wanted to do it again. Ellis just traveled to an empty building and rested up. Laic and Jenn both followed him to the building, and when they got there, Jenn couldn't take it anymore.

She snapped at Laic. "Stop staring at me! If not, I'll have to slay you outright!"

Laic erupted in laughter. "You're cute when you're angry, but only then. You're average any other time."

That statement only made her angrier, and she left to go elsewhere to rest.

In the morning, they burned the town and the bodies, and went on their way. Jenn wanted to go back Estare. She was done with the assignment. Ellis wanted to go back as well, and Laic said he would go back with them.

"I suggest we take a different route back. We don't want to be detected by Tarax or his men." Laic didn't want to take chances. The others agreed, and they decided that they would take the northern road from Estare to get back there. They were all in agreement on the plan.

They had to head west to get to the northern road, and it would take them through another forest that was governed by elves. They all doubted that the elves would be friendly towards them, but they would stand better chances going through elven forests rather than the road back.

When Jenn was calmed down more, Ellis said, "I assume you did not find him?"

"He must have left a few weeks ago. I swear I will scour the land for him and slay him, but only after extreme torture first."

"I can try to help you find him, Jenn, if you want my help." Ellis felt the need to help.

"I want you to come along on the hunt, Ells, and Laic as well," Jenn offered.

Laic only heard the part of the conversation that said she wanted him to go along with them. Laic said he would be glad to.

None of them spoke much on the trip, and when they came to the elven forest, they were especially quiet and alert. It took the group about a day to get to the forest, and they rested before entering the woods. As soon as they entered the forest they could feel eyes watching them from all around. They didn't let it bother them much, at least not visibly. They got about halfway through the day, when they were assaulted by several arrow shots from the trees.

A round of arrows fired from all around, and then one elf came out and made himself seen. "You're not welcome in our forest. You turn around and go back from the darkness where you came from, or you can be taken prisoner and judged. The latter has us determining your fate."

Laic looked at the people longingly; ready to suck their lives from them at the drop of a pin. Ellis just stood there looking defiantly at the elf that made the demands. Jenn was surveying the trees to try to find out the number of elves in the trees. It was difficult for her, because they blended in nearly perfectly with the forest. The group was injured due to the first round of arrows fired. Ellis was struck twice, and both hits were quite solid and deep. He had an arrow sticking out of his left arm and one out of his right leg. They were both very painful, but he tried not to let it show. The wounds were healing, though it was only due to his talisman. He pulled the arrows out so they wouldn't seal up inside his body. He would let the wounds heal as time went by.

Arrows whizzed by Jenn and one hit the elf that was threatening them. That got a chuckle out of the group and a scornful look into the trees from the elf leader. Laic was grazed on the arm by one arrow and another elf injured himself. A cry of shock from the trees could be heard clearly from that elf. Laic, Ellis, and Jenn looked at each other and agreed about what to do unanimously. They didn't need to say a word to each other on their intended actions.

"Continue this and I will burn your home to the ground. You will live or die in the ashes of what you once loved," Ellis threatened. "We just want passage through to the north road."

"I have no problem killing every last one of you if I have to." Jenn was serious.

"Your souls will be mine if you stand in my way. We will get to the road one way or another!" Laic's fingers were twitching again. The three of them had no intentions of backing down, and were going to get to the road one way or another.

The elf leader said, "So be it. Fire at will upon the trespassers!" They did as he said and arrows flew everywhere. The elven leader took out two long swords that were well made, and got into an attack position. He remained guarded for the moment. Ellis immediately began to make good on his promise. He began to set the forest on fire. A few screams could be heard from the unfortunate elves that happened to be in the blazing trees. The flames were spreading quickly through the trees. Many cries from the elves could be heard as the fire blazed.

Laic was quite intent on the leader and tried to use the blaze as a distraction. He touched the leader and took some of his life force away from him. The leader still stood even as Laic touched him. That was surprising to Laic since most died with a touch. Of course the leader was waiting for him and guarding. Laic was swung at and barely missed. Jenn acted before the elves could fire upon her. She went to a tree that wasn't ablaze and quickly climbed up it to get to one of the elves. She cut the bowstring from the bow in front of her, and missed the elf as he quickly dodged her dagger thrusts. The elf was surprised at the bow being inoperable, and looked as if he were about to pull other weapons. The elf did just that, and swung short swords at her. He cut her right arm pretty well. Pain shot up her arm with the strike, but she held her ground. The other elves fired arrows at those on the ground. A few elves that had targeted Jenn earlier were still trying to get at her.

Two arrows sliced into her skin on her side and ear. She cursed in pain at the attack. An arrow grazed Ellis, but the damage from the hit was too minimal to worry about. Laic was struck by three arrows, and cursed in pain himself. Laic vowed that those people would die next. As he was cursing at the elves in the trees, the leader attacked Laic. Laic's arm was sliced open well, and the leader hit him with another strike. He cried out in pain, and had the most evil look on his face that the elves had ever seen. They also noticed that Laic wasn't bleeding red blood. Laic's blood was black and thick. It almost oozed out instead of flowing out of the wound. That slightly frightened the elves, but they were still determined to take down the demon and his companions.

In his pained state, Laic let out a frightening roar that was louder than any one person could make. He uttered a few words and a black wave of energy shot out from Laic's body. Five elves dropped from the trees motionless. The leader screamed, and turned to dust at Laic's feet. The remaining elves let out audible cries of shock, but were only infuriated and more resolved to attack. They sent a rain of arrows at Laic for slaughtering their friends. Of fifteen arrows, only three hit Laic, but one landed deeply into Laic's shoulder. Laic seemed only more intent upon the elves' deaths.

Ellis and Jenn were both quite shocked by what Laic had done, but kept their cool and continued to fight. Jenn was so distracted that with her first strike, one of her daggers flung to the ground and sunk in right next to Ellis's feet. The other attacks she made on the elf in front of her injured him greatly. He was bleeding severely from a few wounds... Ellis turned his fire upon a group of trees that most of the arrows were coming from and he could hear their cries loudly at first but then they faded quickly as they burned to death. The only one left was the severely injured elf that Jenn was attacking.

The elf acted before they could, and he decided to flee and get help. He managed to get away from the three evils that just came into their forest. The lone survivor became impossible to see once in the foliage, and moved faster than they had ever seen someone move. He went to the other elves to tell them of what transpired. He was told to stay there, and a group of elves were sent out to check things out. By the time the elves got there, the three were gone. The forest was in danger of burning to the ground, and it took all of their effort to put it out. The three of them had succeeded in making their mark with the elves that would seal their relations with them for eternity. Once the fire was put out, the elves noticed that the dead had been stripped of their possessions and were strewn about in lewd positions. The bodies were placed that way on purpose and the intended reactions had transpired.

## Chapter 19: Changes for Angeline

Angeline left Terrah with Rokk and her new animal companions for the first time. She was unsure of what was in store for her in the coming times. She hadn't ever been apart from her brother like that and especially for as long as she suspected their time apart might be. She had even lost her ability to talk to him or hear him in her head. That aspect frightened her most of all. Her life was changing radically, and she wasn't really ready for it to change. She was glad she had someone traveling with her at least. Rokk seemed to be quite noble and kind. She knew she would get along better with him than she did with her brother. She just couldn't stand the thought that her brother was out there by himself reeking havoc wherever he went. She felt bad for those he would encounter along his journey. At the same time, she hoped that he would stay well, and that he would return to her someday.

Rokk noticed Angeline was sad, and that she was still having a hard time getting around. He decided to alleviate some of her burden and carry her. She was light, and he had carried much heavier things for longer periods of time. She tried to object to him picking her up, but he wouldn't hear it.

"You seem to have enough trouble, and you're still weakened from the poison. Do not think that I don't care, I am trying to help you." He acted that way for her own good.

"Don't get me wrong, I am very thankful you're trying to help. I simply do not want to be a burden upon you. You're such a nice man."

"My Lady, you are no burden. I will help you for as long as you need me, gladly. That includes times when you are unwilling or unable to admit you need help."

"Thank you for your kindness." She blushed from being embarrassed about her health condition.

Rokk smiled at her. "It truly is no problem. Do not think twice about asking me for help."

"Again, thank you," she said humbly. She didn't know what more to say to such a kind offer.

They traveled the day and Rokk set up a small tent that he brought along. After he set it up, he insisted that she stay in it and that he would guard it.

"Rokk, it is your tent. I do not want to take away your place to sleep."

"I insist, my lady. You need it more than I do."

She felt bad for taking his tent and making him sleep outside. "Well then the only compromise that will make me feel better is if we share it. You should be able to sleep in your tent." She was insistent and it was the only way she could see the arrangement would work out. Plus she trusted him to be a gentleman.

That took him by surprise, but he realized that she felt bad about him sleeping outside while she slept in his tent. He had no problem with her staying in there, but he could see that she wouldn't like the arrangement fully.

Rokk wanted to confirm what she meant by what she said. "Are you saying you don't mind if both of us share it at the same time? I just want to confirm, my lady. I do not desire to make you feel uncomfortable at all."

"Yes, I am saying that. Please, you need your rest too. I would not have you giving up your tent for me, though the gesture is appreciated."

"I promise you, my lady, I will be a complete gentleman. Be assured."

She had no doubt he would be, and didn't mind him sleeping in there with her because of it. He obliged her wishes and stayed in the tent with her. He tucked her in, and kept his hands to himself. He awoke to her crying in her sleep, and tried to wipe her tears without disturbing her. She awoke to his touch, but wasn't startled by it. He was about to apologize for waking her and say that he was just trying to wipe her tears away, when she asked, "will you hold me please?"

He wasn't sure of what to say to that. Her question took him by surprise, but as he looked at her, he could tell that she needed the comfort. He just put his large, muscular arms around her to comfort her as she asked, and they both fell asleep again. They stayed asleep for the remainder of the evening.

In the morning, they awoke about the same time. Angeline said, "Thank you for being here with me, and for everything you've done so far."

"It is not a problem, my lady; I am here as you need me. You can rely upon me. Please do not hesitate to ask me for any help that you require."

"I will ask you for help if I need it, I promise. Thank you again for everything. I know last night was not what you expected, but I was glad you were there."

They got underway and were not accosted during their travel. During the day, Rokk asked, "Why are you so sad? Do your weakened legs sadden you?"

"No, it's not that. In all my life, I have never been separated from my brother like this. I always had a mental connection with him. Now, that he has gone his way, away from me, the connection is lost, and I feel like there's an empty space that cannot be filled. The separation still saddens me." She didn't mention how bad he could act towards her. "We were always near one another, as much of a discomfort as that was at times. How do I deal with an unfillable void? He's not near, and I don't know when he ever will be again."

Rokk looked understanding. "I am no replacement for sure, but it will be okay in time. It will all be okay. Do not worry. I am sure, when you see him again, that connection will return in an instant. Brother or no, I am here for you. I will help you search for your mother, and I will stay by your side as long as you want me to."

She blushed. "I'm afraid that I might need you around for a while."

"I do not mind in the slightest, my lady. Traveling with you is my pleasure. My shoulder is yours, whenever you want it or need it to lean on." He felt sorry for her situation, and couldn't believe that her brother would just leave her like that. He almost got annoyed with Ellis, even though Rokk didn't know everything about the situation. I will help Angeline in whatever journey she takes, and whatever pain she must handle, this I vow. I will not desert her like her brother did. She was weakened, trying to use a strength she does not have back yet. How could a brother abandon his sister in her time of need?

Sapphire slept in the tent with Angeline as well, and Scope kept a lookout for danger in the evenings. Sapphire liked Rokk, as did Scope, but it was clear that the two were very protective of Angeline with anyone else. They were faithful companions to Angeline, and would talk to her often. They tried to console her as well, and it did help Angeline a little. She was glad to have friends such as them traveling with her. She felt very lucky to have each one of them. While walking, Sapphire would stay at her side, and Scope would fly ahead to scout things out.

Rokk would often carry her when she started to look too weak to walk, but tried to give her space to do what she felt she needed to. Angeline gave up on protesting, since all of her companions were working together to watch her closely. If Rokk didn't notice her struggling, her animals would signal to him, and he would relieve her of the stress. She felt fortunate to have that happen, but part of her also wanted to suffer so she would have to face the poison head on. She was out voted though, between the animals and Rokk.

They reached a small clearing in the forest they were beginning to travel through, and Rokk set the tent up. He picked Angeline up and set her in the tent.

"Please get some sleep, my lady. It will strengthen you. The more rest you get, the faster you will recover."

She tried to sleep, but she couldn't. Every now and then a depression would hit her, and she would be quite sad. One such sadness struck her that evening, and Rokk heard her as he stayed up on his watch. By the time he got into the tent, she was already asleep and seemed to have calmed down mostly. It killed him inside when she cried. *She is such a sweet girl. Seeing and hearing her in pain is simply heartbreaking.*

As soon as he got into the tent to lie down, he felt her reaching for him unknowingly. He felt touched at the gesture, and wrapped his arms around her. He was always gentle with her, and would always be. He would be her support as long as she needed him there.

Morning came and she was surprised to find herself in his arms, but she was comforted by him so she didn't mind at all. *I must have reached out for him in the night.* He was the strength that she was missing while the poison made her weak. *She was grateful to see him every morning when she woke.*

Rokk awoke to find her staring at him with an odd expression. "Is anything wrong, my lady?"

"No." She was smiling at him and kept staring.

As Angeline stared at him, Rokk felt an odd feeling in his stomach. He almost felt like he was floating on air, while under her beautiful gaze. He had an urge to touch her face lightly, but he wasn't sure if he should. He was trying to be a gentleman to her and the situation was becoming a little awkward. He began to blush, and she noticed right away. She smiled wider, and blushed herself. They both tried to get up, but neither could bring themselves to pull away. To make it worse, neither one knew what to say either. For a few minutes, they both lay there together unmoving and unspeaking.

Finally she blushed more, but gained a little bit of bravery. She lightly brushed her hand on his cheek. Her touching him at that moment sent a feeling through him unlike any feeling he had ever felt. His skin felt tingly and warm. His body felt like it was definitely floating. It almost felt intoxicating, though he had no ale that morning. He was unable to move. He wanted to move any part of his body, but it was frozen. He closed his eyes, and let her touch his face as long as she wanted to. He tried to gather enough strength to do something, anything, and when he did, he kissed her on the forehead gently.

He finally regained the ability to speak. "We should…get up and moving," he said with hesitance. He still couldn't move his arms to let her go, and she still had her hand gently caressing the side of his face. They continued to stay where they were for a while. She was feeling butterflies in her stomach, and had a strong urge to kiss him. She wasn't brave enough to do it though. All she could manage was to keep her hand on his cheek, and stare at him. Without her realizing, she was gently twirling some of his hair around one of her fingers. He responded to it by closing his eyes and enjoying the caresses and the playing with the hair. She didn't know what she should do, but she knew she didn't want him to let go. She didn't want to move to go anywhere. They were almost in a limbo for several minutes.

She would open her mouth to say something, but no words would come out. She noticed that he was having the same problem. Her breathing was becoming irregular as she tried to figure out what to do. Rokk was also dealing with the dilemma of what he should do. He knew he should have been cooking breakfast and the two of them preparing to leave, but what he wanted most to do was to kiss her gently. Before he realized it he spoke his thoughts aloud.

"Would you allow me to kiss you lightly, my lady?" He blushed when he realized he had said his thought out loud.

All she could do was shake her head in a motion that let him know she didn't mind. She could not form the necessary words. As he tried to move, she could feel him tighten his arms around her in what she thought was anticipation. When she finally spoke, she said, "No, I do not mind at all. Please do." Her voice was soft spoken.

He wouldn't have done anything until she confirmed her answer verbally. He still wasn't able to move much so he had to work his way to the kiss. He held her tightly with one arm, but not too much so that it hurt her. It was just enough to comfort her with his strength. He touched her face and hair with his other hand, gently. He moved slowly, because it was the most he could move. He finally kissed her lightly on the lips, and it sent waves of tingles through both of them.

Though his kiss was light, she returned it slightly more than he did. They kissed for what seemed like an eternity to the both of them. For them, time had basically stopped. After they parted their lips, they still couldn't really move much. Angeline laid her head on his shoulder, and he held her in his arms. They had no idea what time it was getting to be, but neither one cared at that moment as they lay in the tent. They were disturbed by Scope's cry at some point during their eternity to let them both know that someone was approaching. They both jumped, and tried to get up quickly. Sapphire was guarding the entrance to the tent, until they came out. Angeline tried to get up, but with the poison in her body and the tingles from the kiss, she couldn't. Rokk noticed, and asked her to stay in the tent. She gladly listened to his advice. Rokk was able to get up but he was still tingly as well and had to steady himself from his intoxication.

Rokk waited for whoever was coming toward their camp. He was ready to pull weapons if he needed to, but he would wait till he could see who was approaching. His body still felt strange after a few minutes, but he stood his ground. A wagon came near the camp, and Rokk recognized who drove the wagon. It was a merchant he did business with often. Rokk greeted the merchant, and the two talked about how each other had been. Rokk bought supplies from him and the merchant went on his way. Rokk was getting hungry so he began to cook.

Angeline exited the tent after the merchant left, and neither of them said much as he cooked the food. They didn't really know what to say to each other. They were both still thinking about the kiss. They ate and debated on whether or not they should continue onward that day.

"Do you want to travel until it is time to camp again? Or would you prefer to stay here for the evening, rest, and then head out in the morning?" Rokk asked.

She thought about it. "I think it would be just as well to stay here for the evening. We have already spent the best travel times here. Why not stay the night again?" She was smiling and blushing.

The silence came again and both were blushing slightly. Sapphire was telling Angeline to enjoy the rest of the evening in the tent, and that she would guard them both. Scope agreed with Sapphire, and Angeline thought about it.

Angeline made the first bit of conversation. "The animals say we should enjoy the rest of our time in the tent."

Rokk smiled and blushed, but thought the idea was a good one.

He wanted to hold her in his arms again, but he didn't want to seem ungentlemanly or pushy. He didn't want to prod her into anything she didn't want to. "As the lady here, I will leave that choice to your discretion. I do not want to impose upon you, my lady. If you desire it, I will remain guarding the tent, protecting you within. I will gladly do that if it is your wish. I must admit, I enjoyed our moment earlier, but I do not wish to rush you or make you feel uncomfortable. I would never pressure you. I am at the whim of whatever pace you desire."

"I know, and I trust you completely. I too enjoyed our earlier moment. I hope you do not get the wrong impression of me. That was the first time I've ever felt that way, to that extent, and I will never hurt you." She blushed, and then admitted, "That was my first kiss, and it was lovely."

He knew she wouldn't hurt him. He picked her up and carried her back into the tent. He set her down gently.

"Rokk, will you hold me?"

"Gladly, my lady."

She rested her head on his chest, and tried to relax. She wasn't tired. She just wanted to be near him again like they were earlier. As they lay together, he gently caressed and played with her flame colored hair. He was careful not to hurt her by hitting any tangles that would've been in there. As time went by, she fell asleep and he made himself more comfortable so that he could sleep as well. He gave her a gentle kiss goodnight, and kept his arms around her for the evening. He had to make sure he wasn't holding her too tight, because it was hard for him to judge his strength at times.

## Chapter 20: Shadow's Trail

When they awoke, they had a good but brief breakfast, and then decided to get on their way so they could get further that day. She wanted to do as much walking as she could for one day without help. She thought that it would help her, but it only made her weaker. She tried to keep her discomfort from the animals so she would be able to go further. Eventually, after traveling most of the day, she collapsed from being so weak. The other three only noticed at the last minute, and Rokk barely caught her before she nearly hit the ground. He picked her up and kept on going after making sure she was still alive and alright. She was alive but she wasn't responding to him. He carried her the rest of the evening, and as he was about to set up camp, he noticed a small town ahead. He made for it quickly, but was shocked to find out the condition the town was in.

He went straight for the closest inn and tavern, and found that there was no one to be seen anywhere.

"Hello! Innkeeper?" There was no answer. The whole town was silent, and had no sign of people anywhere around. He went to a room, and found it to be empty. He set her down on a bed, and asked the animals to guard her. They stayed near her as he went around the town looking for signs of inhabitants. He searched everywhere and found nothing. There was absolutely no sign of another living person around. He raced back to the inn to find all were still safe in the room. He searched every other room and found no one in those areas as well.

He then directed his attention towards Angeline. She seemed to be out of sorts and unresponsive to anything he had to say still. Rokk and the animals remained by her side through the night, and protected her from anything that would enter the room. She awoke in the morning, but was still very weak.

"I found a town and an inn and tavern, but I have not seen or heard a living soul here yet.

She seemed concerned. She wanted to go investigate, but Rokk insisted she stay in bed and rest. He told her that it would be the only way she would get better. She agreed to stay in bed, but she didn't want him investigating the town without her. He agreed to do as she asked. He said he would stay by her side until she was better.

Rokk then tried to think about ways to cure the poison in her system so she would be able to travel again, and be free of the weakness. He had heard of a plant in the area that could cure any type of poison, but it only grew in the richest of soil and was very small. It was one of the hardest plants to find in the wild. He had to look for it a few times while he fought the war against the goblins. He knew that there were some people that tried to grow them in their gardens, but the plants usually died before the flowers used in the cures could bloom. Very few people in the land were successful in growing the plant in gardens.

He would have to hunt for food anyway, so he told Angeline he would search for the plant when he went out to hunt.

"Fine by me. I want this poison out of my system. It makes it hard for me to think, as well as doing any other normal activity. It takes double the energy to do normal things."

"I promise I will find it before we leave this town, my lady."

"Thank you for everything you do. I'm sorry I overexerted myself like this. I'm not good at being useless. I'm sorry I made you worry about me."

"Apology accepted. Do not stress about such things. I will go look for your cure." He smiled at her as he left.

He found some deer tracks near the area and tried to follow them. He lost the tracks soon after following the trail. He figured he might as well search for the plant while he was there. Rokk thought he found the plant once, but the one he found had been killed by the local wildlife. He continued to look for food and more plants. He found more deer tracks and tried to follow them. He found a deer near a stream and mentally commanded the earth below the deer to rise up to grab the deer and hold it there. He was then able to kill the deer, and take it back to town. He looked for the plant on his way back, but saw no sign of it.

He fixed the deer meat, and stored some for later. He stayed by Angeline's side and took care of her as she needed. She was weaker then he had ever seen her until now. The poison was working double time on her even as she rested in bed. He knew he had to find the cure soon, or the poison would claim her life. He couldn't handle the mere start of that thought, so he went in search for the flower the next day. He had worse luck that day than he did the day before. He was becoming quite frustrated, but tried not to let it show. He didn't want her to see him like that. She smiled less and less as time went by. The poison was beginning to cause her great pain in her limbs. It would shoot up her body as if it were an arrow inside her. He tried desperately to find the plant, because he knew it would get worse. He hated to see her in pain of any kind, and it was breaking his heart to see her condition worsening.

He went and searched several areas of the woods to find the plant. He was determined to stay out there as long as he would stand it so that he could find the cure quickly. It was well into the night when he spotted the plant reflecting in the moonlight. He was very tired from being out there all day and night. He was very anxious to get the cure underway and get some rest himself.

He returned with the flowers needed and started brewing the cure. He finished the brew, and woke her to drink the remedy. She could barely talk or move by the time he got the cure to her. She tried to drink, but she was too weak to move. Rokk had to sit her up, and help make her drink it. She almost spit it back up, but Rokk helped her in trying to get it down. He stayed by her side through the night and got well-needed sleep. He had to sleep in, because he was up so late.

When he awoke, she seemed a little better, but it would obviously take a few days to a week for the cure to work fully. The poison had been working overtime on her. She was able to talk lightly, and move her hand slightly. Besides food, all she asked of him was for him to stay with her and hold her. He gladly did what she asked of him. It was almost a week before she was feeling well enough to travel around, and by then she was insistent upon investigating the town since she was feeling better. Rokk told her the only way he would let her out of bed was if he went with her and they didn't split up.

She agreed, and they went in search of any trail of residents. They found none in town, but as they neared the west side of town, they could smell something foul. They hurried that way and found that the bodies of many people lay shriveled in a huge pile. They were drying out in the sun and collecting scavengers and insects. Oddly enough, there should have been more food for the scavengers but the bodies were shriveled and dry. That meant that there wasn't as much for scavengers to normally eat.

Angeline gasped upon sight of the pile, and turned around. She had to lean on Rokk for support. Rokk was equally disturbed about the pile, but he was at least able to look at it.

"What will we do to put them to rest, Rokk?"

"We should burn the bodies to lay them to rest, and say a few words on their behalf."

Angeline didn't know what to say about them. She started crying for them, and her tears soaked into the ground.

"We will need the proper supplies to burn them. Come." They went into the town and into the general store for supplies.

When the two of them returned, Angeline noticed one of the bodies, near the ground where her tears fell, was now no longer shriveled. She even noticed the hand twitch slightly.

"Rokk! I saw one move, they moved their hand!"

She and Rokk helped the body away from the others, and found that the man was alive. The resident seemed to be in a coma, but he was alive. They rushed him to the inn, and placed him in a room. They went back out to the pile, and they found three more bodies in the same condition. Some would wake up sooner than others, but they were reviving somehow.

They continued to find more bodies as they left and came back. Soon all of the bodies on the pile were moved into homes and inn rooms to recover. They spent several more days tending to the people, and some began to wake from their comas. They continued to help the townsfolk, and in another week all of the residents were up and around. They didn't look the greatest, but they were alive.

The leader of the town, Darin, called a meeting with everyone, and they all thanked Angeline and Rokk for what they had done for the people. The people had no recollection that they were dead before, and neither Rokk nor Angeline would share that detail. The townsfolk presented Rokk and Angeline each with a gift that was a token of the people's thanks for saving them. Rokk was given a golden goblet with yellow gems imbedded in it. Angeline was given a matching platinum necklace and bracelet set with small rubies, sapphires, and opals in a swirling design. The townsfolk began to get back to their normal lives as Angeline and Rokk were about to leave.

"I feel I should tell you what I remember about the incident before you arrived. I don't remember much of the event itself, but I can tell you what I remember just before it. A shadowy figure came into town, and spread his dark energy around. The people didn't have a chance to defend themselves. That's all I can remember, and I don't think anyone else remembers anything. I think it a mental blocking of the memories. Don't know if that helps you or not, but as our town saviors, I thought you should know." It was all the help Darin could be. "If you should run into him on your travels, it would be best to avoid him. However, I cannot help but desire some sort of vengeance upon him. If you could destroy him, it would be justice done."

"I will destroy him on sight should we find the thing that wronged all of you," Rokk said.

"I am sure it was a man using dark magics. Thank you both very much for saving us!"

The duo went on their way again. Angeline realized as they were leaving, that the whole while they were in the town, there was no sign of Mother. We will have to continue the search for her. And since Angeline was feeling much better, and the poison was gone from her system, she had plenty of energy to devote to the search.

They began north again, and soon the road veered in other directions. Rokk knew what direction they were going the whole time. The travel was much easier on Angeline with the poison released from her body. Rokk barely needed to help her at all, but still offered as they traveled on.

Along their way, they came across a wagon that had been overturned and broken. It had also been stripped of whatever goods it carried.

Angeline was concerned. "We should check around for survivors. They could be injured."

Scope responded immediately, and flew off into the woods around them. Sapphire went the other direction, and Rokk and Angeline went together in a separate direction from the animals.

Scope found small grey skinned creatures camped near a cave entrance having a meal. He related it to Angeline as he flew over the goblins camp. Sapphire found a camp of humans and grey skinned creatures together sharing a meal. Rokk and Angeline were traveling through the woods, and were suddenly surrounded in an ambush by four humans, ten goblins, five taller green skinned creatures neither had ever seen before, and three deformed creatures that were tall and lanky. All seemed to be aggressive, and ready to attack the pair. Most of them were eyeing Angeline, and some of the humans commanded the tall and lanky creatures to attack the brute, and their gaze turned to Rokk.

Scope and Sapphire knew what was going on from Angeline's thoughts, and came running and flying as fast as they could go. The three tall and lanky creatures immediately rushed toward Rokk. The others went after Angeline, and seemed to have evil intentions for her if they succeeded. Angeline was the first to react, and she tried to ice some of the creatures coming towards her. She stopped the goblins in their tracks, but the others were just slowed. The humans held back and seemed to wait and observe the happenings.

The lanky creatures attacked Rokk with their sharp teeth and diseased claws before he could make a move. He was struck by three out of four claw attacks from two of them. Rokk could feel something seeping into his skin from the wounds. The third one missed with his first swing at Rokk, but then clawed him badly in the back and bit him in his shoulder. Rokk grunted in pain as he was bitten. He could definitely feel something seeping into his skin after the last attacks upon him.

The humans stood and watched for the moment, doing nothing to help anyone. Rokk took hold of his mace with one hand and swung it around at the one behind him. It barely missed the creature, but it was enough to make the foul thing let go of his shoulder and it backed up in defense. Rokk swung again trying to get all three with passing strikes on each. His swing was mighty, and knocked them all on each other. The creatures went crashing to the ground, fumbling around to get up. They were all beaten badly by a well-placed ridge on the mace.

The taller green skinned creatures were slowed by the cold, and were too distracted to attack Angeline. The goblins were still frozen, but would thaw a little bit over the next few minutes. They would no doubt be quite angry with Angeline. The humans talked amongst themselves, seemingly about the way the fight was going. The taller green skins made it to Angeline even though they were cold, and tried to attack her with swords. She was hit with three swords swings, and was badly injured by the last swing that hit her.

She cried out in pain as the blade sliced into her skin upon impact. The wound was bleeding rapidly from the gash. She was having a hard time concentrating, but was trying to do her best. Rokk took more swings upon the creatures on the ground trying to get up. They all managed to dodge out of the way, but Rokk concentrated and made rocky spikes protrude out of the ground beneath them. The spikes separated each of the creatures, but some became, impaled upon the spikes. The creatures screamed with a shriek that made everyone, including the human counterparts, cringe. Rokk heard Angeline in distress and knew he had to make his way to her.

The taller green skins attacked Angeline again. Two of them struck her, and one hit himself. It cursed in a different language than she knew. Angeline concentrated as hard as she could to create an ice wall as a barrier between her and the assailants. It worked, but it wasn't as thick as she would have liked it to be. It would at least protect her for a few minutes. She couldn't take many more attacks by the green skinned creatures. The lanky creatures tried to attack Rokk back for what he had done to them. The first one missed him completely, but the second one delivered a harsh claw rake and a huge bite to his arm. Rokk was in a lot of pain, but it was just making him more furious. The third creature clawed himself, but it didn't affect him much.

Scope and Sapphire arrived just then, and attacked some of the creatures. Sapphire pounced on one of the tall green skins, but it struggled enough that the cat couldn't get a really good bite in on him. Scope went for one of the human's eyes, but the human dodged the bird quickly. The lanky creatures, in a fervor, continued to try to kill Rokk. The first one hit with one of its claws, and the second hit him with a claw and bite, though they were lesser than the others dealt to him. The third one bit him, but couldn't scratch Rokk with its claws.

The goblins were beginning to move just a little. They were still unable to reach Angeline. The goblins were considering running away once they could move. Angeline went just before the humans could act, and she used the rest of her concentration to try to protect herself and Rokk. She wasn't sure if what she wanted to happen would work, but it was worth a try. She was getting very cold and she was severely wounded, but she wasn't being struck by the creatures that surrounded her at the moment. She felt herself becoming weaker as she remained there. She barely had enough strength to try her protective idea.

Suddenly a bright flash of white could be seen by all. The creatures tried to shield their eyes, but they couldn't all manage it in time. When the light died down a little, Rokk and Angeline were both surrounded by a large illuminated bubble. The bubble was partially through the ice wall leaving half of the wall exposed. Angeline was motionless inside the half surrounded by bubble. She seemed to stare off into nowhere, but she was still alive. Their wounds began to heal. Rokk was still quite aware of what was going on around him and he remained in a defensive position, though was surprised at what had just happened. He was concerned about Angeline, and that she wasn't moving or responding to anything. It was as if she was in a trance.

When the humans saw the display that Angeline had shown, they separated from one another. The human who looked like the leader, just disappeared. He was just gone. The others barked orders at the creatures quickly and left. Rokk was still able to walk around while the bubble remained around him. He tried to swing the axe around at the lanky creatures, and found the weapon passed through the bubble as if it weren't there. He hit all three of them with a mighty swing and dropped the latter two. The first one was still hanging onto life by a thread.

The taller green skins tried to attack the cat mostly, but one of them tried to get through the ice still. The creature would still have to get through the bubble and the melting ice wall. He struck the ice wall and part of it went crumbling to the ground. There was now a hole in the wall, which would make it easier to get through the wall to get to her. The others attacked the cat to try to get it off of their fellow. One hit Sapphire with a graze, and the one it pounced on dropped his weapon as he tried to get the cat off of him.

Rokk swung his mace at the creature in front of him again, and struck it. The strike killed the last lanky creature instantly. Angeline was still motionless, but as the ice melted more around her, all could see that she appeared to be floating somehow. The tall green skins continued to attack Sapphire, except for the one that was trying to get to Angeline. Sapphire was struck twice, but was still doing fine. The other broke down the ice wall, and tried to enter the bubble. As it tried to reach its arm through the light field, the green skin seemed to become confused. It just stood there shaking its head.

The goblins were able to move finally, and ran as fast as they could away from the combat. They couldn't get far since they were still quite cold, but they had no intentions to staying to fight. The goblins believed that was what the bigger and dumber ones were for. Sapphire mauled the creature beneath it, and turned to growl menacingly at the others. Scope swooped down to blind one of the others, and missed again. Scope was coming around for another dive at the creatures.

The taller green skins were the only ones left to fight, and they noticed. They were still intent on fighting, to Rokk's surprise. The one trying to get to Angeline finally came to his senses, and grew enraged. It was forced out of the barrier by electric shock. The green skin was sent airborne backwards, and landed on its back. The other three tried to attack the cat.     Each one hit Sapphire, and she was very damaged from the strikes. Sapphire mewed pathetically, and tried to go into Angeline's bubble. Angeline had no change in her condition, and the cat went into the light. Sapphire remained there and healed while in the bubble.

Rokk went to attack the creatures left. He swung his mace around, and got all three with the top spike on the mace. They cried out in pain from the attack. Angeline's bubble was beginning to grow dimmer, and was about to fade away as she slowly floated to the ground. She was still in some kind of trance. Rokk swung his mace around again and caused more spikes to grow out of the ground and through the feet of the enemies. They howled in pain and dropped to the ground. Scope flew to a nearby branch to get a look at Angeline.

All enemies were dead at that point, so Rokk rushed over to Angeline as she was about to collapse once she landed on the ground.

"Scope, scout ahead and report if there is anything to impede further travel."     Rokk investigated the bodies of the slain, and stowed what they could use along the way. When Scope came back with nothing seemingly in their way, Rokk picked up Angeline, and carried her till it was time to camp.

# Chapter 21:  More Devastation

Rokk held her in his arms all night and kissed her on the forehead occasionally.  He told her how proud of her he was and how brave she had been in battle.  He could tell she wasn't use to using weapons in battle, or really even use to battling at all.  He took care of her as needed, and got some rest.  The animals never left her side in the night.

When she awoke in the morning, she was in Rokk's embrace, and she stayed that way till he awoke.  He was happy to find her awake when he opened his eyes.  They both smiled at each other.

"I could hear you the whole time you were talking to me last night.  During the battle yesterday, I was losing the ability to concentrate quickly.  I was becoming too injured, and tried something I'd never tried before.  When I tried my plan, I was filled with power suddenly.  It was as if someone else was inside me, controlling the power.  I was merely a witness to the events following; unable to move, speak, or act."

Rokk didn't know what to say.  He was just glad she was alright.

Angeline was bright and cheery that morning, and anxious to get on their way.  Rokk found some game birds that became breakfast.  Neither spoke much about the fight earlier except to say that it was odd that one of the humans just disappeared in mid air.  Both of them had never seen that before, and were just shocked that someone could do that.  Angeline got an odd feeling about him, but she couldn't place the feeling.  It was similar to being around her brother and Rokk, but slightly different.  She wasn't sure of what to make of it.

As they pressed on through down the road, they came to another town by late evening.  They went through the town looking for an inn and tavern and found that much of the town had been destroyed.  There were broken signs near their businesses and other buildings were crushed.  There wasn't a person in the town that they could see.  Even the sign that told the town's name was broken in many pieces on the ground.  They were worried about the situation, but were also tired from traveling

They agreed that they needed to rest before they looked around town.  The inn and tavern was deserted and it was starting to resemble the town before it.  Angeline and Rokk found some beds that were in fair condition and slept the evening.  They arose early to investigate what happened to the town.  They skirted the outside of town to see if there was another pile of bodies.  They found no bodies anywhere in town, even as they searched inside the town limits.  It was beginning to disturb Angeline and Rokk.  They searched through all of the houses, and found nothing.  There were also no valuables, but there were plenty of clothes and other things that the townsfolk would have taken with them if they left voluntarily.

As they searched around, Angeline stepped on a cracked floorboard, and fell through. She injured her ankle, but it healed quickly. She did notice a small box down in the hole. It was apparently a secret hiding place. Whoever ransacked the town had missed it. She opened the box, and found a black opal talisman on a golden chain. The craftsmanship on the talisman was extraordinary. She had never seen such work on jewelry before. She figured it was worth a fortune just by looking at it. Of course she was no jeweler, but she could tell the talisman was very expensive.

As she handled the talisman, she felt compelled to put it on. She resisted the urge. She held it for a few more minutes, and by then, she could no longer resist the temptation. She placed it around her neck, and tucked it behind her shirt. She left the house and caught back up with everyone. The animals communicated to Angeline that they found no luck finding much of anything except rubble and useless items. Angeline said she didn't find anything that could help them find out what happened to the people either.

Of course Scope and Sapphire knew about what she found, but they put no importance upon the item. Neither animal ever indicated to Rokk that she had it.

Angeline felt like she had to say something to the missing people. "I hope you are all safe." She seemed out of her senses for a few moments throughout their trek onward, but there didn't seem to be anything physically wrong with her. Other than those few moments, she was perfectly fine. She was still disturbed about the town though.

They traveled westward from the town with the broken sign. The forest became sparser as they went. It was becoming plains. It seemed to just be flat land without trees. The grass was very short and green. They could see that the terrain ahead them in the distance was hilly. They could see another town in the distance on top of one of the hills. It was faint though. Unfortunately, they couldn't tell the condition of those areas. At least nothing was on fire, they thought. A tall tower could also be spotted. It was in a valley, but was tall enough to spot from where they were.

It would still be a few days before they would reach that town. The hills were still quite far away as well. To make matters difficult, it looked like it was going to storm in a few hours. They had to set up shelter or they would be miserable for the rest of the night. They planned to set up the tent after they traveled a few more hours. They set it up and managed to get inside with the animals just before the downpour began to fall. Scope flew out a few times to take a bath in the rain, but came back in when he got too wet. Angeline was going to say something about it, but decided not to.

Rokk decided to work on his mace to pass some time. Angeline just took the time to relax since the hills would be hard on her. After Rokk was done, he decided to ask her questions about her family and her childhood.

"So can I ask you about your family and such? If it isn't too personal."

"Well," Angeline responded, "my mother was barely home because she was working to support us. It was my father who raised Ellis and me. My brother was always trying to take his attention away from me and keep daddy solely to himself. Daddy did a good job with us, considering how hard my brother was. He liked to pick fights with me and compete with me. All I've ever done was care about him and try to help him.

"I liked art in school and could paint future events. I liked landscapes the best though. I tended to focus on non-violent subjects. Ellis focused on weaponry and combat." She paused and chuckled for a bit, "and of course trying to annoy me. Daddy was really sad when mother went missing. I have to find her." Now her tone was a bit sad and serious. "Ellis just couldn't stand mother. He often thought how he didn't care if she lived or died. Well, I do care, and someone has to find her. Plus, it is nice to get out of Ishta and wander Paelencien."

"Of course you do, and I will assist you." He hesitated a moment, and looked like he was debating on asking question. "Did you have any boyfriends growing up?"

"I was never really interested in that growing up, though no one wanted to date me anyway for fear of my brother. The townsfolk were very apprehensive of him for the most part. He was enough to deal with." She smiled and laughed lightly. Rokk seemed a bit relieved that Angeline didn't have someone waiting for her upon her return home, at least no one in a romantic way.

"So what about you, Rokk?"

"Well, I grew up in a noble's household. That came with almost immediate responsibilities to the city. But I had Nova to keep me company. Our parents always wanted us to marry, but we were strictly best friends. And I would love to introduce you to her upon our return to Terrah. She would love you." He paused. "I too lost my parents, but I cannot search for them like you search for your mother. When our families tried to force Nova and myself to marry, we left Terrah. Sometime later we learned that our parents had been killed. We returned home and had to defend and protect the residents of the city. I've had to battle so many goblin forces in my life. I never had time for a girlfriend. Duty saw to that."

"I would be happy to meet your friend." Both smiled and blushed a bit.

Rokk appeared as if he needed to say something, but he just couldn't say it.

"You want to say something, I can tell. What is it?"

He smiled. "I really like you and I hope you will continue with me once we find your mother. I would like to go home with you and meet your father anyway. He sounds like a great man."

Angeline paused for a moment. "I would love for you to meet my father, as he would want to meet you. And I would also love to continue around with you after my mother is found." He seemed happy about that, and they both blushed.

Without warning, he gently pulled her closer to him so he could kiss her. She was surprised, but didn't stop him. She returned it and after their lips separated, they both lay down to get some sleep. The rain poured all evening, but it lulled them to sleep. When they awoke, everything was soaked. They would have quite a travel ahead of them. They ate rations and packed things up so they could set for the hills. Rokk spontaneously put his hand in hers gently as they started out, and held her hand for quite a while during their travel that day. Angeline had no problem with holding his hand. She hoped that he would never let go, though she knew he would have to eventually.

They traveled until around midday, and it was about to storm again. They set the tent back up, and had to stay in it again for the rest of the day and night. Not much was said, but they lay next to each other and shared jokes they'd heard. They laughed for a while at the jokes, and finally began to calm down. Rokk held her in his arms as they slept through the evening. They awoke early, and repeated the process they had started the previous day. They managed to make it into the evening, before it rained again. They were wondering if it was ever going to stop raining. The night went by as the others did and they awoke for an early start again.

The hills were difficult to manage due to all of the rain that had fallen recently. They finally made it to the town and were happy to see people again. It appeared as if that town was never touched by the devastation, luckily. It was about to rain again as they got into town so they rushed to the inn and tavern. Angeline insisted on bringing the cat and the bird inside, saying that she would pay extra for them to share her room. They got a well-needed sleep in a soft bed.

When they woke, they asked the innkeeper where the leader of the town was.

"He's actually gone currently to help out a town somewhat nearby, 2 days away. The sheriff is in charge until the mayor returns." He gave them directions to get to the sheriff's house.

It was still raining so they had to run to get to the house they were directed to. Luckily, the sheriff had a porch, or they would have had to wait in the rain for someone to answer the door. The sheriff recognized Rokk immediately and asked them inside. He gave them things to dry off with. "Why is the hero of Terrah so far away from home?"

"I was traveling from Terrah to here, to accompany Angeline. The other towns on the way are completely desolate. And one town had its entire population slaughtered by a dark unknown magic. They were dead, sir. Angeline brought them back to life. The other towns were destroyed with no bodies to be found anywhere."

The sheriff got a deeply concerned look on his face. The sheriff asked about details, and then called a soldier into the room. The sheriff spoke to the soldier quietly and the soldier left in a hurry.

Angeline asked the sheriff, "Have you seen my mother?" She described Judith, yet again.

"Yes, she was in town with a gentleman none of us have ever seen before. This sighting was some time ago."

"Could you please describe him?" Angeline was anxious. The description was the same as the man that disappeared into thin air a few nights prior. Angeline now had a concerned look on her face, and asked him which direction they went.

"I don't know, Angeline. I did not see them leave. I'm sorry. She was definitely here though."

"Rokk, I have to look around and ask about this."Angeline wanted to rush out the door. "Sapphire, you stay with Rokk. Scope, you come with me." She ran back to the inn and tavern, and listened to conversations.

"I was told a man was in town with my mother some time ago. My mother's name is Judith. Please have you seen her? Is there anything you can tell me that would help me find her?"

"All I can tell you is that your mother arrived first and I saw her go up to a man's room, which neither of them left. No one saw them since, and the room was empty when it came for our maid to clean the room."

Angeline felt like panicking, but tried not to. Rokk came in and saw how upset she was. He put his arm around her, and led Angeline to her room. He stayed with her for a while until she fell asleep, and then went over to his own room. He knew they would be heading back the way they came from very soon. When Angeline awoke, she was eager to get going so they could find her mother. The only clue was the area where they last saw

the disappearing man. She knew she had to hurry if they were to find anything out.

She readied herself as quickly as she could, and went to wake Rokk. To
her surprise, he was already awake and ready to leave as well. They ate
breakfast quickly, and resupplied the things they would need on the
trip. They set out and hurried back to the area where they last spotted the
disappearing man. It would take them a little while to get there so they
were going as fast as they could. The clouds still looked threatening, but it
was just an appearance. It never did start raining in their location.

They went as far as they could and rested. That evening Angeline had
a nightmare about the future. She saw the disappearing man confronting
Rokk and herself, and he was asking about the talisman she found. He demanded that she give it up, and she refused. She then saw everything go
dark, and the only thing she could see was a foreboding man holding the
talisman and laughing hysterically. Her dream then shifted to envisioning
fields of dead or tortured people. She made herself wake, because she
couldn't look at it any more. When she awoke, she noticed that her reactions to her nightmare woke Rokk up, and he was trying to calm her
down. He wore a look of concern on his face.

She took comfort in his embrace, but she couldn't go to sleep after the
dream. Upon waking, she felt she had to remedy a situation. "Rokk, I have
something I need to say. I had the worst dream last night, that we found
the person we seek, and he seems to be seeking something that I found...
recently. I didn't say anything about it then because I didn't think it important. But now..." She paused. "He's going to attack us for it, take it,
and it's going to lead to so many deaths. I cannot get the vision of the field
out of my head." She started sobbing.

He held her in silence, just trying to comfort her for a while until she
calmed down. "What is this item?"

Angeline pulled the black opal from underneath her shirt. "Please,
Rokk, he cannot take this. He can't. You have to keep him from getting his
hands on it!" She was determined not to let the disappearing man get his
hands on the talisman. She called Scope and Sapphire to her. As Scope was
waiting for her orders, she got out a small pouch and reluctantly took the
black opal off. She placed it in the pouch, and tied it well. She tied it to
Scope's leg so it wouldn't fall off during flight, but loose enough so that
Scope could get it off when he found a place to put it.

"Listen to me, Scope. You have to hide this talisman, and I need you
and Sapphire to go get help. Rokk will be attacked, and from what I saw,
the outcome will no go well." She pulled the cat and the bird over to her,

touched her forehead to theirs, and transmitted her dream vision to them so they would know what kind of help to go get.

She was sending them to go gather people to rescue her and Rokk, when or if they were captured. The whole thing disturbed her, because deep inside she knew what was going to happen, even if she refused to realize it then.

Scope flew off towards the hills, and Sapphire nudged her and purred before taking off further down the road from them in the direction they were heading. Rokk was disturbed by her nightmare, knowing then that she could see the future. Angeline and Rokk made their way again in the morning, and it began to rain again around the time they got to the forest. They tried to rest, but neither one of them could sleep. They were both too disturbed about what was coming.

"We can go a different direction, and perhaps avoid the situation," Rokk suggested.

"I don't think it's possible to avoid this, Rokk. If you haven't noticed, the disappearing man travels oddly. That means he will find us wherever we go." She seemed to come to a realization about the disappearing man that Rokk had not yet discovered.

Rokk tried to continue to think of a plan to take care of the approaching situation.

They eventually fell asleep, and awoke to find that it was still raining. They would have to stay put, and wait for something to happen. The rain let up for a few hours, and they decided to go back into the flatland. Their reasoning for it being, that no one could sneak up on them out there. The stop in the rain didn't last for long. A few hours later a very heavy down pour began.

"Angeline," Rokk said in a serious manner, "there is something I want to tell you. You fear we will be captured. And if you are right, and you get captured, I promise you, here and now, I will not let anything happen to you." He put his hands gently on her face. Then he moved one hand to hold and gently squeeze one of her hands in reassurance. "If you are captured, I will find you, rescue you, and take you to safety."

"Thank you." She tried to smile, and said nothing more about the situation. She was trying to keep herself calm. No matter how hard she tried to do so, she couldn't keep herself calm. She was panicking. She could feel danger ahead. She would be separated from Rokk. She was in danger, and nothing Rokk would do, not of any fault of his own, would save her.

She had a wretched feeling in the pit of her stomach that she couldn't get rid of. Rokk noticed, and tried to take her mind off things by holding her close and kissing her. It seemed to help her for a short while, but the feeling couldn't be dismissed so easily. She was scared for reasons she didn't fully realize, but she had every reason to be frightened. She wasn't aware of just what she would have to deal with in times ahead. Those events would affect her for the rest of her life. She would never be able to get rid of the pain she was about to endure.

## Chapter 22: Quantis and Tarax

Rokk and Angeline waited in the flatland, but they didn't have to wait long for company to arrive. During their next night, the disappearing man arrived with several dark clad men and a few women. The disappearing man looked quite intent on Angeline. His stare burned into her. Her feeling of him was one of rage and desperation. Rokk noticed the look, and went to stand between the enemies and his girlfriend. He unfortunately wasn't able to get to her in time. The other people surrounded him before he could reach her. The gang of dark clad people made the first move. Before Rokk could do anything the whole group threw him to the ground, and had him pinned down. He was absolutely shocked, because he was a very muscular and heavy man, but somehow they managed it.

The disappearing man came closer to Angeline, and she could get a better look at him than she could get before. He had medium length black hair and grey eyes. His skin was tan, and he was a few inches taller than her. She sensed the strange similarity between the aura Ellis gave off and the disappearing man. He smirked an evil smirk towards her, but then it quickly turned sour and frightening. She got to act before he could though, and she tried to place an ice block over his head so it would fall on him, and buy her some time. He quickly dodged out of the way, but it still caught his arm. The odd thing was that it went right through his arm as if he wasn't there. Her eyes grew wide as she realized she would be able to do nothing against him.

Rokk acted after Angeline, and just as quickly as they pinned him down, he burst out of their grasp. They were sent flying outward off of him  One of them hit their head on a fairly large rock that was placed as a marker for the road and was knocked unconscious...or dead, he wasn't sure which. Rokk rushed over to Angeline, but could not get an attack in before the disappearing man acted. The apparitional image pointed at Rokk and concentrated, and all of the sudden Rokk was gone. Rokk disappeared into thin air.

The apparition came towards her. "Give me that talisman!" His tone was demanding, icy, and frightening. He was definitely scarier than Ellis.

She tried to keep her nerves intact, but she was petrified in fear. Her heart was racing, and her voice slightly quivered. "I don't have it." She tried to move, but she just couldn't manage to.

He came towards her, and he went to knock her across the face. Angeline thought his hand would go right through, but it materialized just before hitting her. The blow knocked her backwards, and she noticed that she was now surrounded by all of the others except the one that hit his head on the rock. They grabbed onto her arms, and held her in place for the dark-haired assailant.

Her face stung where he hit her. He was becoming visibly more enraged, and looked willing to do just about anything to her to find the talisman. She was still frozen stiff with fear.

He asked again, with an angrier tone. "I...said...where...is...it?!" She could just feel his rage, more than anything else. He was driven by it.

Again responded, "I don't have it." He's going to kill me, but at least all those others won't have to die.

He struck her harder after she gave him what he thought was the wrong answer. She was on the verge of tears, but was trying to hold them back.

"Hey Quantis, after you're done roughing her up, can I have her?" The lackey was eyeing Angeline in a very uncomfortable manner.

Quantis just shot him an angry look, which apparently was enough of a reply. "If you don't tell me where that talisman is, you will suffer a greater torture than you could ever imagine. Having that idiot have his way with you will be sunshine compared to what you're about to endure."

She knew his breaking point was near, and she was in real danger. She didn't even have to look at his face to know it. His aura screamed it deafeningly. She took a breath and said again, "I don't have it." She couldn't let him get a hold of the talisman at any cost. She could only hope that Rokk could get to her, before anything really bad happened to her, like he promised. She hoped he was safer than she was at that moment.

Quantis snatched her from the others forcefully, and threw her on the ground. He pinned her down, his eyes narrowed at her, and he stared at her coldly. Quantis then calmly told her, "even if I am not the one to take it from you, someone much worse will. This is your last chance. You say those words again, and you will be forced to know a hell worse than my wrath. You will be going into the fiery depths of the worst underworld you can imagine." He spoke the last part even slower. "Confess the location of that talisman, or a hell you've never dreamed of awaits you. And you will…never…come…out."

Her heart raced. Even though he was speaking calmly and slowly now, it was still menacing. Yet, somehow in his threats, she realized he was truly trying to spare her what came next. Even he didn't want her there. Her breathing sputtered for a brief second, trying to catch up from her holding her breath. She opened her mouth, and said, "I don't have it, and I do not know where it is." She knew those words were going to be very bad for her. She believed him on the matter of what was about to happen after that.

"Too bad for you then. You had a chance to save your life, and do things the best way. Now you face the most evil person Paelencien holds. There is no mercy with him. He is a master at torture, and now you answer to him."

Angeline's vision went black, and she was once again in darkness, but this time her brother wasn't there. She wished he was. One of the others hit her on the head from behind and made her go unconscious. Quantis then disappeared into thin air with Angeline and the others.

When she came to her senses, she was in chains and being dragged into a large, gothic, columned room with a tall ceiling arches and a throne on the other end. The throne seemed so far away. The place was made from black and red marble and there were depictions of death, murder, and torture in pictures lining the hallway. There were statues of grotesquely deformed and bloodied people. There were torches in sconces on the walls. Some light was coming from red glowing eyes in some of the statues. Angeline had the worst feeling in her stomach that far succeeded the pain in her head from the surprise blow earlier. As they got closer to the throne, she could see that the man on the throne was the one she saw in her nightmare that was holding the talisman and laughing. He had a blank expression on his face as the troop came to the foot of the small stairway that led to the throne. She could see Quantis come forward and kneel at the base of the stairs.

The man on the throne had reddish skin and black eyes. He wore black armor that seemed fitted to his body. He had a black sword at his side with many black opals in the hilt. The man had brown hair, and what looked like two little horns sticking out of his head at the top sides. When she stared into his eyes she could see pure evil emanating from them. It was like looking into a black abyss, and she was extremely frightened.

"My Lord, Tarax," Quantis was carefully thinking about and choosing his words, "I..." He was careful of what he said and the way he said it so he wouldn't anger Tarax. It seemed even Quantis and everyone else feared him as well.

Tarax spoke in a deep growl for a voice to Quantis. The voice was piercing to all who listened to him. "Where is my talisman, Quantis? And why do you bring me a slave?"

"She has the talisman, my lord, and upon trying to retrieve it, she continued to lie to me, that she didn't have it. None of my methods were persuasive enough to make her admit the location. It is only right, then, that you interrogate her."

She could tell Quantis was afraid of Lord Tarax's reaction. She could tell there was something more to their relations that she wasn't made aware of, something deep. He is not a willing servant. He serves out of fear. Of what? Why? Quantis is one of us, I can feel it. Why so much rage? She wished she could read his thoughts. And thinking about Quantis was distracting her slightly from the utter fear she should have been feeling.

Tarax was getting irritated. "I assume, what you are telling me is that you failed to get my talisman from a measly wench."

Quantis lowered his head, still measuring his words carefully. "I am sure, master, that you can have much more fun trying to get the information from her. Would you not take pleasure in you being the one to discover where your talisman has been hiding?"

That seemed to quell some of the irritation, and kept Tarax from getting angry with Quantis for his failure. He was still very clearly irritated.

Just as they were talking, a servant came in, and Angeline could only watch how Tarax mistreated her. Then it dawned on her all of the sudden, that he was mishandling her mother! Her eyes grew wide, and before she could stop herself, she cried out the word "mother". The men holding the chains and Quantis looked at Angeline as she yelled it out. They were stunned for a few moments. Tarax however, got the most evil look on his face that she had ever seen. He was smirking evilly. Angeline regretted forming the word and blurting it out. She just put her mother's life in danger.

Tarax threw Judith into the hands of one of the troops. "Take the slave girl and her mother into 'The Room'. Even you can't screw that up." Quantis was clearly supposed to remain there to further speak with Tarax.

The men took her down several old spiraling stairways, through numerous halls, and down more stairs. As they transported her, she could hear countless screams of pain echoing throughout the corridors. She was determined to get her and her mother free, and try to make a break for it. She didn't know her way around the place, but she thought that her mother might. Judith seemed so out of it that she didn't seem to notice that Angeline was even there.

Angeline tried to ice the smooth floor beneath her escorts' feet. They were leading the two women down a staircase. Both of the men on Angeline slipped on the ice, and fell hard. Neither of them were knocked out, however. The men holding Judith still had a hold of her, and didn't fall. She managed to get the jump on them before they could react, and iced them down, which rendered them immobile. Angeline tore the chains from her mother's captors' frozen hands. She helped her mother down halls and stairways. She tried to get away whichever direction she could. She really wanted to find the front doors so she could make a break for it.

She had to do something to help or they would be in serious danger. She was hurrying through the halls and stairways, and finally found what she thought was the way out. She tried to get the doors open, but they wouldn't budge. They were huge and extremely heavy. They were made of very thick metal, which meant it was a very secure door. She tried and tried to get the doors open, but the doors refused to budge even an inch. She became frustrated, "I wish these doors would open!" The moment she said the word "open", the doors began to part and move. She was surprised, but then was getting anxious. Adrenaline was kicking in.

The doors weren't opening fast enough so she took a chance, and said the words "open faster". The doors swung open with such speed that it blew her and her mother back, and they hit the ground. She tried to get up as quickly as she could. Her nerves were shot and her adrenaline was pumping. She could move, but she would have problems when she stopped. She helped her mother up, and ran through the doors. Angeline was very disappointed when she saw they weren't outside. She seemed to be in some sort of courtyard full of knarly trees that seemed alive.

All she could think to do was run as fast as they could go, so that she could put more distance behind her. She could hear voices of guards that were searching for them. It sounded like it was up ahead of them. The only other ways to go were through the trees on either side. She definitely didn't want to do that, so she kept going straight ahead. She figured that she would deal with the guards ahead with ice. She timed it well enough that she managed to ice the floor where they were walking. They fell and had a hard time getting up. The guards' inconvenience gave her and Judith time to get by them quickly. She lucked out, and wasn't seen by the guards, because they were concentrating on the ice and trying to get up.

She raced down a few more stairways, and almost tripped a few times because she was running so fast. All she could think about was getting out of there quickly. She ran through a hall with more creepy paintings and tapestries on the walls. That hall, she knew, was a bad one to go through leisurely if it bothered her just to run through it. She saw numerous blood-stains on the carpet in that hall. She saw many other eerie decorations as she ran through the castle. There were skulls and other things made of bones. Statues with a fleshy covering could be seen here and there.

In some instances, there were actually people alive, and others who were dead in torture devices along the sides of the hallway. Those who were alive were screaming in pain, and when they stopped screaming, something would click on the machine they were on and they would scream again from the pain. It looked to Angeline like there were circular mechanisms on the device that had a number of blades on them. The people who were strapped to the device were impaled on the blades and when they stopped screaming, the blade circle would rotate, causing them to cry out in pain again.

She finally came to some doors that she could smell outside air coming through. It smelled rotten, but she could tell it was air from outside. She tried to open the doors with her strength and by saying what she said to the other door. Nothing worked, and she had no idea how to get the doors open. She was frantically pacing as she tried to think up a plan to get them out. She drew blanks in her head, and deep down inside her she knew that meant she wasn't getting out. She refused to believe there was no way out. She was determined to get her and her mother out of the wretched place.

She then decided, maybe we could get out through a tower, but that was shot down when she realized that she had no way to get out of that plan alive. She thought about the basement, perhaps sewage pipes. She would have to try. She ran down a flight of steps near her, and nearly tumbled down the stairs, though she caught herself in time. She came up to a door, and said the word "open" again. The door obeyed and she went through. She came upon a room with a sewage hole. The stench that came from the hole was quite foul. It made her sick to her stomach, but she knew it was their only way out. She pushed her mother in first and then jumped in after her. Her mother was still out of her senses, so Angeline took her hand and ran as fast as she could through the slime and muck.

She didn't notice until she was quite far into the pipes that she was also running over rotting corpses and pieces of them. When she fully realized the situation, she couldn't help but vomit. Her muscles were beginning to cramp from just stopping those few minutes. It slowed her down, because she kept cramping as she ran. She eventually had a cramp shoot up her leg, and it sent her flying into the muck. She was going to vomit again, but pulled herself together enough to take hold of her mom and continue through the tunnels.

The cramp was still in her leg, but she was trying not to think about the pain. She finally saw a grate that led outside. She tested it and found it was stuck on there quite well. As she was trying the bars, she could hear lots of moaning coming from behind them. She quickened her tries on the grate, but it wasn't budging. There wasn't room underneath the muck for them to get out. They were trapped.

The moaning was getting louder and louder, and she could hear more moans adding in number as they got closer. An arm at her feet grasped hold of her ankle, and dug its nasty nails into her flesh. She screamed in pain and in shock all at once. She jumped and was panicking. She hurriedly tried everything she could think of to get out, but nothing worked. She thought about freezing them in place in the muck, but there was no way she could do it. If it worked, she and her mother would have been frozen in place as well, and eventually the water would thaw. She couldn't concentrate hard enough anyway. The pain from her wound and her cramps would never allow her to concentrate well enough. The moans now rounded the corner and she could see the rotting dead shambling towards them, and the tunnel was choked with them. She knew she would surely die if they didn't find a way out.

She screamed for help, and banged on the bars as the walking dead came closer. The wound on her ankle was tingling and growing more painful each minute. She screamed out for help again as she could hear them getting closer and closer. Angeline was in tears, yelling for her life. Her mother was seemingly mindless, and was completely oblivious to what was about to happen. She could feel the filthy water vibrating and sloshing around as the dead got closer. Then they started saying "brains" really slowly, but it was clearly audible. Another kept saying "fresh meat".

She was in full panic mode as they were only ten feet away from her and her mother. She screamed and screamed for help, but it seemed as if no one heard her pleas for help. She turned around and held her mom close. She tried to concentrate as she did before, but her nerves were to shot and the pain in her leg was unbearable. She closed her eyes and tried not to watch the creatures get close to her. She knew she wouldn't be able to fight them all and most likely, only a few would fall before they all just started eating her. Her body went in to a state of shock as she closed her eyes. She could feel the fingernails and jagged teeth sinking into her skin before she passed out.

\*\*\*

Angeline went into some sort of dream state where reality and fantasy collided. She felt like she was swimming in a vast ocean of darkness, but she knew she was still alive, at least for the moment. Out of the darkness, I came, to give her hope. She wasn't dead, but I told her that she needed to be strong for herself and her mother. I managed to give her at least some comfort before He took her away from me. Who am I? That will be told later. As for now, there are always other sides to every story. There are more who share her fate and whose stories must be told. This story is far from over.

# WIND, WATER, and LIGHTNING

# Chapter 1: Wind and Lightning

Irisel never really knew who her parents were. She was raised in a big city named Faulkton. It was a port city with the largest trading guild. Hanmel, the guild leader was like a father to her. He and his wife took her in when she was just a child. Due to events in her childhood, her mind repressed everything before she went to live with Hanmel. After Hanmel's wife died, he became the sole parent. When she wanted to know about her childhood, he told her that she was left all alone when she was young, and he took her in and raised her as the daughter that he was never able to have. As she grew, of course there were boys who were interested in her, but Hanmel would force them to give up on their chances with Iri.

She understood why he did it, but sometimes it annoyed her. She would sometimes help on ships due to her unique ability to alter and control the winds. She was also helpful to the guild during poison testing due to her natural immunity to poisons. She had a pretty normal childhood as far as she could remember. Hanmel was not disturbed by what his ward could do. He was amazed by her.

Irisel also learned some of the skills of her guild friends. She learned how to pick locks and sneak around pretty well. She was also usually sent to spy on situations that Hanmel asked her to watch over. She met several kinds of people in her dealings with traders and guild contacts. One of the better contacts was a large man named Olaf. She didn't see him often, but he was very memorable. He was kind and funny. When he came to port, it was a good time. She learned how to use short swords pretty well so that she could defend herself from rowdy sailors that would be lonely from being out to sea for some time. It was something she had to deal with often.

She had one friend above all others that she trusted completely. Although Arnesti was a little more impulsive than she was, Arnesti was the only person, other than Hanmel, that Irisel could trust with her life. They were inseparable most times, and Hanmel had to often cater to Arnesti as well, since she stayed at his house so often. Arnesti and Irisel kept no secrets from each other, and vowed for things to remain that way.

Irisel had fair skin, dark green eyes, and very light green hair that went down to the middle of her back. She was about 5'4" after she stopped growing. She preferred to wear grays, greens, and whites for clothing. Though most women wore dresses, she wore pants or shorts and a shirt with a vest. She often had her hair let down, but if she was going to do anything with wind, she would put her hair up so that her hair wouldn't block her line of sight.

Arnesti had a little more than shoulder-length silver hair and light grey eyes. She wore silvers, blacks, and blues for her clothing. Her clothes were usually the same kinds as Irisel wore. Both girls were miserable in dresses and would rather die than wear one. It was because they both grew up around men and preferred comfort over beauty. They considered themselves beautiful even if they didn't wear dresses. The snobbish girls usually wore the "proper attire for women".

The two girls couldn't stand hanging around the high class girls in town. They made fun of Irisel and Arnesti often because they dressed like the common men. The two girls never really cared what those girls thought of them. Arnesti would usually make fun of them right back if something like that started. Irisel just ignored their snide remarks and went about whatever she was intending to do.

One noble girl in particular was the leader of those snobs, and could be quite cruel at times. If the two girls actually cared about the comments, they would be quite hurt by what Melissant Quennis would say. She was the daughter of the local lord, Lord Fadel, by another noblewoman, whose name was often kept secret. Anyone who pried into the question would be taken straight to her father, and he would "settle" the matter himself. There were rumors, but none were said publicly.

Some said that Melissant was the daughter of a whore from the nearest town. The girls favored that rumor. Other nobles speculated that she could have been the queen's secret child with the lord. Living near the docks and working there as well, the two heard all kinds of rumors. Most of those rumors were entertaining, but rarely did anyone say them officially. Melissant would often go to the docks to collect special silks for her father. That's when she would start in on insulting Irisel and Arnesti. Most of the time Melissant said the insults openly and publicly. Melissant had no shame when it came to Irisel and Arnesti. Arnesti would often poke fun that Melissant was a bastard, and that at least Arnesti knew who her parents were. Arnesti's parents died in one of the more recent wars, and Arne had to take care of herself from then on. She met Irisel while she wandered the city and docks, and the two became the best of friends.

Usually that parentage insult would shut "Miss Prissy" up and make her leave hastily. Then the routine went that Arnesti would get scolded for saying those things to Melissant, but the funniest thing was that Arnesti was never made to apologize for saying those things to her. They were all surprised that she never sent her father down to take Arnesti, and put her in jail or whatever he would do to punish those who insulted his family. They were lucky that she never did, or they would've been in a lot of trouble.

One day the girls were working hard, unloading a ship that had arrived with spices. They were so busy that neither of them noticed the contingent of guards coming down the road to the docks. The street cleared like rats going into hiding as they marched through the street. The girls were talking about some of the attractive guys off the new ship and were taken completely by surprise when the guards grabbed them both by the arms and were practically dragged off the ship. The guards seemed to be in a hurry to get the girls to the destination. The girls were informed along the way that they were summoned to the palace. The guards would not say why and kept a quick pace to the palace.

Hanmel was unfortunately unable to see what was going on, so no one stopped the guards as they dragged the girls away. After the guards passed by and far enough out of sight, a few guild members ran into the spice shop and told Hanmel what happened. He looked concerned, but there would be nothing he could do for them until Lord Fadel sent word to him officially stating the reason for their capture.

The girls were dragged through the city and to the palace. Arnesti argued, and tried to talk her way out of whatever trouble she was in. It didn't work no matter how hard she tried. Irisel just went along and said nothing. The less we say, Iri thought, the better off we will be. Arnesti insisted upon being let go, but the guards never even told the girls why they were being taken to the palace. They had a good idea why though. They had done nothing else to get taken away. They were certain Mel had something to do with it.

The guards took them into the palace, and through several winding hallways into the main audience chamber where Lord Fadel and Melissant were seated on the thrones. There was a blank expression on Fadel's face, and when Melissant saw how nearly panicked Arnesti was, she grinned from ear to ear. She looked so smug that both girls eyed her with contempt.

The two were brought before the two nobles and were made to kneel, if they didn't kneel without prompting. It looked as if Arnesti was about to start her defense story without knowing why they were there, but Fadel silenced her with a wave of his hand. It took a few waves for her to actually be willing to be patient. Irisel just waited calmly to hear what Lord Fadel wanted.

He was finally able to actually speak after several minutes. "I've had my eyes on the two of you for some time now. And I've noticed your behavior."

Arnesti looked like she was about to explode with her defense, and Melissant was on the verge of laughing aloud at the situation. Finally, Arnesti couldn't keep her story in. "It is Melissant's fault! You might think she's a lady, but in our part of town she's as far from a lady as a sailor is a virgin!"

Lord Fadel was taken aback by what Arnesti was rambling about. He stopped her in mid defense. "What are you talking about?" He seemed to be quite confused by her outburst.

Melissant was turning as red as a tomato and looking at her father. Then Melissant started in on her own defense. Soon it was nothing, but arguing between Mel and Arnesti. The noise was unending, and it was getting on Irisel's nerves.

She wasn't the only one who was getting quite tired of the arguing back and forth. Lord Fadel stopped them both dead in their tracks with one loud booming command. Both girls immediately shut up and looked frightened.

"I don't want to hear either of you speaking. Period! You will both remain silent and listen to me. Irisel and Arnesti, I need you to go rescue one of our ships that is dead in the water. I do not know if it has been attacked or if it is simply a lack of wind, but you are both to go and help that ship return home. I know you, Irisel, can create wind and command it at will. And I know that both of you are rarely ever separated, which is why you are going along Arnesti."

It seemed to the girls that he didn't know anything about Arnesti's ability to create lightning from nothingness and control it. It was probably fortunate since she would most likely end up using it on Mel's rear end when she became extra cruel. Arnesti and Mel were both surprised why Lord Fadel called the girls there. Apparently Mel and Arnesti both thought it to be the same reason, their fighting.

It actually made Iri want to laugh about the situation, but she refrained from doing so. She did smile about it though.

Lord Fadel sent Arnesti and his daughter out of the room. With the two out of the room, Fadel turned to Irisel and said, "thank you for being so well mannered Irisel. I will reward the two of you upon your return."

Iri curtsied and thanked him, though she was just thanking him purely to be polite. She was about to turn and walk away when Fadel stopped her.

"Wait a moment, what is the real situation between my daughter and your friend? There must be a reason for the argument."

Iri wasn't sure if she should talk, but knew that if he asked either girl, they would make it sound worse for the other side. I should just tell him the truth, but downplay some of the things Arnesti says. I don't want my best friend in jail. "Whenever Melissant comes down to gather the silks, she is always rude to Arnesti and me. She says some of the meanest things I've ever heard and I'm around sailors all day, sir." She paused. "Sometimes Arnesti just can't hold her irritation over the rudeness and words slip out aimed at Mel. But you must understand, sir, Arnesti doesn't mean those things. She just can't take it and lashes out. It is her defense against Mel's cruelty. We don't really care what Mel thinks of us though. If we did, we would both be very offended and would probably have left town by now."

Fadel took everything Iri said into his head, and thought about things for a moment. "Then I will have another gather the silks from now on. Mel will be forbidden from going to the docks. I don't like her going there anyway."

Iri just bowed courteously, and asked "do you require anything else, my lord?"

"No, you are free to leave. I wish you luck on your trip." After Iri left, Fadel went to speak with his daughter.

He would be mad at the things Mel would tell him Arnesti said to her, but he would be more prone to understand since Iri explained how his daughter acted.

I don't know if I want to return from this trip, Irisel thought. Iri left the palace and went home. She was met by her Hanmel as soon as she arrived.

"I was worried about you, especially after hearing you'd been taken by the guards," he said in a concerned but relieved tone. He was happy she was back home.

"Well, unfortunately the news doesn't get better…for the most part anyway. It looks like Arne and I are being sent out to sea. It isn't a punishment, but knowing I can control winds, Lord Fadel wanted me on the crew to search for one of his missing ships. And knowing I don't go anywhere without Arne, she's supposed to come too."

"For how long?"

"For as long as it takes, I suppose. Oh, and Mel will not be coming to the docks any longer."

"Why not?" He was curious.

"Well, Lord Fadel had a talk with me about Mel and Arne. Fadel decided that it would be best to keep her at home and away from the docks. He didn't like her going there anyway."

"Yes, it probably is for the best." He was powerless to stop the will of Fadel, so he had to send her away on the mission. He made sure she had everything she needed before she went.

Iri gave her father a hug, which was returned. "You know I'm going to miss you a lot!"

"As I will too. You come home safely, okay?"

She lowered her head a bit and said, "Well, I was thinking I might take my time after the mission is completed, and see some of the other lands. I could even possibly help the trade here by doing so."

Hanmel didn't know what to say, but he knew she was a big girl now, and she had to be free to explore the world as he did when he was younger. He still had reservations, and good ones that he could never speak of. "Well, regardless of how long it takes you and where you go, just come back safe."

"I will have to return after the mission to inform Lord Fadel of the results. So I will be back at some point. I will miss you!" She hugged him again, kissed him on the cheek, gathered her things, and she went to find her best friend so they could get underway.

She found Arnesti on her way to the house. "Hey! We will be going soon I think."

"What did he say after I left?" Arnesti was dying to hear the news.

"He asked me about the thing between Mel and us, or rather, you. I told him Mel is always cruel to you when she comes down here and that sometimes you just can't stand the amount of rudeness from her, so you say things back occasionally." Arnesti looked worried. "And then he said he had to go speak to his daughter and told me she will be banned from coming down to the docks for the silks." Arnesti was relieved that she wouldn't be in as much trouble upon their return. She was happy that Mel would be put on the spot and forbidden to invade their area.

The two girls went down to the docks, and saw the ship was full of guards and a few of Lord Fadel's knights. They were dressed in armor as if they expected trouble.

They were met by Sir Alltin. "Welcome aboard The Defender, ladies," he said with a smile. "Let me show you to your rooms."

The ship set off as soon as they were on board. It was a sunny day at least, so the girls didn't think they would have problems out at sea.

Sir Alltin was known for his kindness towards the people of Faulkton. He was the most favored knight of Lord Fadel and seemingly Melissant's crush. He was a tall man standing 6'1". He had long, straight brown hair that was admired by all of the ladies in town. His brown eyes were also the object of admiration. The word that most described his eyes was "gentle". Alltin was quite the favorite of visiting nobles as well. Because of that, Lord Fadel kept him busy in politics. Alltin frequently had to turn down several ladies gently who tried to keep him for themselves. Sir Taen and Sir Caladin were his best friends growing up. They teased him to no end about how much women chased him. They definitely didn't want to be in his shoes for any amount of time. They saw how much he had to deal with, and knew better than to get involved.

Sir Taen was blond man who stood 5'11' and had a mustache. He was glad that he didn't have to live like his friend. He supported Alltin, but didn't want to be like him. Sir Caladin had short red hair and was often thought of as a bold man. He had a bold, direct attitude about life and lived as he thought was right. He placed a lot of importance on the security of Faulkton and its residents. While Alltin entertained the ladies of Faulkton, Caladin watched the other people to make sure that no one was going to cause any unwanted surprises. Sir Taen dealt with the guards, and trained the men in weapons combat.

Sir Alltin kept the girls company while others up on deck kept control over the ship. Sir Taen and Sir Caladin were still up on deck helping out as best they could. It only took a few minutes for Arnesti to begin flirting with Alltin. She mostly was flirting with her eyes and body language. Alltin tried to safely dodge her advances without hurting her feelings. The thing about Arnesti was that she was never offended. She just loved to flirt. She did almost every time there was a cute guy around. Iri found it humorous most times. Arne was quite bold, in fact much more so than Iri. Most men couldn't handle Arne though, so she didn't have many boyfriends. She just liked to flirt.

Alltin kept the girls company for the duration of the trip out. He played games with them and shared some of his more exciting stories from past experiences. Approximately a day and a half away from Faulkton, they could all hear cries coming from deck. There were alerts to the location of the ship they were sent to find. Everyone rushed up, and they were all shocked at the state of the ship. It appeared as if another ship assaulted it, and then sent it to be stuck on a rock outcropping in the water.

The ship was badly damaged. It was so bad that everyone agreed that it wouldn't be able to be salvaged. The closer they neared the wrecked ship, the more bodies the crew began to see floating in the water. Some were strewn about the rock and were being preyed upon by nature. The guards and the knights, except for Alltin, climbed into a smaller boat, and went to investigate the situation. Alltin stayed with the girls. The crew that set out to search thought that they might find survivors, though it appeared to be a very slim chance.

The ship was stable enough for the moment to have people walking around its wreckage. The crew on the ship watched as the guards disappeared into the injured ship, and then the knights. The girls and Alltin watched and waited for the group to come out, but after a few hours went by, there was still no sign of the first group. Not a few minutes after Alltin was about to go in after them, screams could be heard from the wreckage. Still, no one came out of the wreckage, but there were several more screams.

Alltin and the girls decided to rush and find out what was going on. "Ladies, I must object to your presence in this task. You should remain here for your own safety."

"We're coming along, and you cannot persuade us otherwise," Arnesti responded. She winked at him, "You'll just have to protect us."

They boarded another small boat, and headed for the wreckage. About halfway there, the screams stopped, and everything was dead silent. Alltin went as fast as he could toward the wrecked ship. They reached the opening in the side of the ship, and were hit by a wave of stench that knocked them all back for a moment. They pressed forward, and Alltin made sure the girls stayed behind him. As they went further into the ship they found his friends, Taen and Caladin. They were severely injured by weapon wounds. They seemed to be alive, but were not responsive.

"Ladies, get the men out, gently. They are badly injured" Alltin ordered. This would allow Alltin to not have to worry about them as much as he investigated the scene.

Iri focused her powers of wind, and made a wind tunnel underneath the knights. She floated them to the ship, and the girls went back into the wreckage.

Alltin found several more bodies of guards, and finally found the location of the majority of the guards. They were all slain and still bleeding on the floor. As Alltin stepped into the room, the bodies of the old dead and the guards began to rise. They grabbed weapons and started toward Alltin. He unsheathed his sword and fought with the foul creatures. Alltin's sword was unusually long compared to the customary weapons of the region. It was nearly as long as he was tall. The sword was thin, but very sturdy, and cut things well. Within short order, Alltin struck two of them down with mighty blows with his extra long sword. The girls came upon the fight not long after he started attacking the walking dead.

When girls arrived to help him, there were still approximately fifteen undead creatures scrambling to attack them. Arnesti was quick to act, and she shot bolts of electricity from her fingers through the creatures. She slayed twelve of the creatures with her lightning attack alone. The electricity arched through body after body. Alltin took two others out with a mighty swing of his sword. Iri concentrated and made a wall of wind that kept the last undead creature held back until Alltin could attack it. The undead creature tried to get through the wind barrier, but was unable to. Alltin took its head off with a mighty swing, and Iri ended the wall.

Alltin had no idea Irisel had powers so intense. He had heard of her abilities on a smaller scale. Alltin was even more surprised that Arnesti had electricity originating from her fingers. "Amazing work ladies! Arne, I had no idea you could do that."

Arnesti winked at him. "Few do." She smirked.

"If you desire my silence, ladies, you have it."

"Yes," Iri spoke up, "it would be best if you did keep it to yourself, as much as possible anyway." Some people knew of Irisel's powers, but virtually none knew that Arnesti could manipulate and create lightning. All people knew about Arne was that she was just a normal girl.

Alltin and the girls collected a few of the guards' things to take back to their wives, when they could hear a cry from their ship. It was difficult to hear, but sounded like there was another ship coming. The three hurried out, and back to The Defender. The three of them looked at the approaching ship, and could see that the newly arrived ship was intent upon attacking. They climbed aboard quickly, and the crew was working hurriedly to get the ship underway.

As the girls looked at the ship, they didn't recognize the banner flying on it. It was green with a large white and red circle in the middle.

"Let me see that spyglass," Iri commanded. After a crewman handed it to Iri, she noticed that the approaching ship's crew was using their spyglass to survey The Defender. They stopped when they eyed Irisel, and began to quicken their attempts to catch the Faulkton ship. Those on the foreign ship were talking and even pointing at Irisel as they barked orders to their crew. They were preparing for battle and boarding.

Irisel made sure that the captain and the crew of The Defender knew what was going on. Irisel wondered why those people seemed to recognize her. She had never seen their banner or them before. She pulled Arne close to her and whispered in her ear. "They seem to recognize me, but I do not recognize them."

Arne suggested, "Perhaps we should go downstairs and hide until this is over."

"We can't leave these people defenseless. And if that ship is coming for me for whatever reason, I cannot let more of these people die for me."

Irisel went to the crow's nest and addressed attending crewman. "You need to climb down; I will take your post."

Arne climbed after her. Irisel took control of the wind and forced it to push the ship in the opposite direction. Arnesti used her powers of lightning to call down a bolt upon them from the sky and injure the ship. The lightning strike set part of their ship on fire, which distracted some of them. Their intent was to reroute the opposing ship.

The strange ship did fire a couple of shots at The Defender, which managed to hit their target, but the damage done was easily repaired.

The two girls managed to send the other ship away, to their relief. The crew on that ship seemed very confused and were busy trying to correct the situation to no avail.

"Thank you, ladies, once again. You are surely proving to be the greatest thing to happen to this mission." Alltin was grateful for their presence.

"Aye!" The crew seemed to agree with Alltin's words.

"Thank you for the kind sentiment, but this activity has been a bit much for me," Iri said, "I'm going below to rest up a bit."

Arnesti agreed. "We'll be below deck."

"Would you like me to join you ladies, after I check upon my friends?" Alltin needed to know his friends were taken care of, but wanted to convey his gratitude to the two people who just saved the lives of the rest of the crew remaining. Alltin would also have to write down a report of the events so that he could give it to Fadel upon their return. Of course he would leave out the information he promised to keep to himself.

Arnesti looked at him flirtatiously and said, "You are more than welcome to join us." She had a smirk from ear to ear.

He looked rather nervous. "If you ladies need anything, you have but to ask."

"I could think of a few things," Arne replied.

Iri just grabbed her friend by the hand led her down below. Iri was almost laughing aloud at how nervous Arne made Alltin feel. "You are such a flirt, Arne. It is hilarious to watch you make men squirm!"

"That, my friend, is the best part," Arne said with a wink. They both laughed and relaxed for the rest of the return trip home to Faulkton.

Iri came to the deck a few times during the evening, and found Alltin up on deck looking out across the water. "What are you looking at?"

"The beautiful ocean," he replied. "I wanted to thank you again for all you did for this mission. Were you not here, I fear things might have gone poorly. We would have likely suffered the same fate as our missing ship."

Iri noticed Alltin was looking at her differently, though he didn't seem to be aware of it. She thought she detected a twinge of interest in her as he spoke with her. *Perhaps it is respect, but it seems more than that.* "I was glad to help, Sir Alltin. I was just doing what I could for my people." She was loathed to mention her observations with the spyglass regarding her. While she considered Alltin a nice guy, she had no interest in a relationship with anyone. She was happy for whatever was there to remain a friendship.

# Chapter 2: Captured

Surprise came to all aboard the ship as it pulled up to the dock. There were no people in the street and it was unusually quiet. Aside from no people in the streets, everything seemed normal. The crew began to take the knights off the ship and carried them off to the palace. Alltin looked around curiously and kept a watchful eye on the area. He even looked into one of the bars and there weren't any people in the bar.

He was becoming concerned and hurried to catch up with the injured. He escorted the knights to the palace and found few guards at their posts. He quickly got the knights to their beds, and started off again to find some nurses. He didn't even notice that the girls were no longer following him. He ran into the audience chamber and found Lord Fadel and Melissant sitting in their chairs guarded by men wearing the same symbol as the one on the foreign ship. Lord Fadel seemed to want to say something, but as he tried, the man guarding him put his sword tip closer to Fadel's neck.

Alltin walked over to the men. "I demand to know the meaning of this! Where are the people of this city? And why do you hold my lord hostage?" He thought if he pulled his sword, they would make good their silent threat upon Fadel, and he did not want to be the cause of his lord's death.

A man dressed in a green and red robe came out from nowhere to answer his questions. "Your country has taken our princess. She was kidnapped and brought here. She's been spotted several times by one we have sent to hunt for her."

Alltin was shocked. "I know nothing of this. I assure you that my lord would have no part in such an action. And if you don't call off your dogs, I will remove their arms for good. They will never again be able to wield anything."

When the robed man just laughed at Alltin's threat, Alltin had his sword out in the blink of an eye. Before the man threatening Fadel could react, Alltin had his sword firmly pressed against the man's arm. It was a risk Alltin felt he needed to take.

The man was so surprised that he dropped his sword while trying to pull his hand out of the way. Before the other man holding Melissant captive could react, Alltin repeated the action upon him as well. Both men on the sides of the lord and his daughter began to back away from all three. Alltin kept his guard while standing in front of Fadel and his daughter.

"I demand to know your name and what country you are from!" Alltin was addressing the green robed man.

The robed man simply and calmly stated, "I'm not leaving without the princess."

Melissant spoke up. "The green-haired girl you are looking for is in town somewhere, or should be. She was sent on the same mission as my knight, here. If he's returned, surely she has too."

Before Alltin realized what he was doing, he instinctively began to defend Irisel. "She can't be the one you are looking for, because she was born and raised here in Faulkton. I grew up with her, so I know she is native to this area."

Lord Fadel looked confused, but didn't say anything.

"I have my men searching the city for her, and if she is found, Faulkton will have open war upon it." The robed man also made his own personal threat by saying, "if anyone tries to impede the search or if any of my men are injured, then they will respond in kind."

Alltin could tell from the look in his eyes that he wasn't joking. The robed man and his lackeys left the palace to check on the progress. After the men left, Alltin realized that the girls had not followed him and they were nowhere to be seen in the palace. If they had followed him, they would likely have been found already. He hoped they were safe until he could find them. He thought about his friends, injured and in need of a nurse. He informed Fadel in a brief statement about his friends needs, handed him the report of the events at sea, and left quickly to find the girls. He knew Fadel would see to Taen and Caladin's needs.

As Alltin rushed out of the palace and into the streets, he failed to witness the girls being grabbed from behind and pulled into an alley. They couldn't see who grabbed them, but whoever it was had their mouths covered so they couldn't scream.  The captor turned Irisel and Arne around, and they discovered that it was Hanmel who had grabbed them so quickly.  Noises could be heard down the street like several people walking their direction.  Hanmel signaled to them to keep quiet and hidden until the people passed.  He then motioned for the girls to quickly climb up the ladder on the side of a nearby building as the footsteps approached.  He thought the roof would be the best hiding place.

The girls obeyed, but they were quite confused at what was going on.  After the girls climbed up, Hanmel soon followed.  He made it up to the top just in time.  Lights were shone down the alley, as if the people were searching for something or someone.  The men were dressed in green and white robes with red trim.  They bore the symbols of that flag on the foreign ship.  After the men left, Hanmel started to explain what was going on, since he could see that they were clearly confused.

He spoke very quietly so as not to let others know that they were on the roof.  He looked at Irisel.  "You have to stay hidden.  These men are here to take you away from me."

Irisel still wanted answers about the men and the flag.  "Where are they from and why would they want to take me away?  The ship we were searching for was attacked by these people, and they seemed to be after me.  We managed to reroute them.  But they killed everyone on our missing ship."

Hanmel looked concerned after she told the story of the trip.  "We need to get to a safe place to talk."  He pointed off in the distance at a movement of shadows on rooftops a few blocks down.  They checked to make sure the coast was clear and went for a dark spot.  "They think you are someone else, and intend to take you back to their homeland.  They are from a kingdom far across the ocean.  They are here to look for their princess that also has green hair.  You must believe me, you are not the person they are looking for."

"Do not worry father, I have no intentions of going with them, even if I was some sort of lost princess.  I am happy with you.  And I have had more than enough dealings with prissy women to last me a lifetime thanks to Mel."

They hugged, and Hanmel turned to Arne.  "Whatever happens, Arnesti, you must watch over Iri.  She will need you in the times to come.  It is time to put your friendship to the test."  He turned to both and said, "We have to get you to a safer place."  He then went to look around.  He had to be sure the foreigners were nowhere around so the girls could get away.  He managed to get them as far as a block from their house, when the group of them was ambushed.

Irisel, Arne, and Hanmel prepared for a fight, and guarded. One of the men spoke to Irisel. "You are safe now, Princess. We will take you to your father."

"I don't know what you're talking about; I was born here in Faulkton. My father is here."

They didn't believe her. "Come now, Princess, you will not be harmed. These people have brainwashed you. Please, come home." When that didn't work, they threatened her. "If you do not come willingly we will be forced to take you against your will, because if we do not, the king will be furious with us."

"I don't care if you get in trouble or not. You've got the wrong girl." She spoke plainly. While, the men had their attention on Irisel, Arnesti and Hanmel slipped into the darkness. Both were separately intending to sneak up behind the forces in front to Iri. They had to go around the buildings on both sides to do so, leaving Iri standing there by herself.

When the men noticed Hanmel and Arne missing, the leader of the group had some of his men spread out and try to "find the 'kidnappers'".

"My father is not a kidnapper, but you will be if you take me against my will."

The leader of the troop seemed unphased, and went to grab for her.

She dodged out of the way and said with determination, "You're not taking me without a fight."

"Yes, it will happen that way if you are not more cooperative. I ask you again, your highness, please come with us."

She remained guarded as he ordered some of the other men to return and try to restrain her. As they approached her, she swiped a few of them pretty well with her short swords. They cursed from the pain, but continued to come at her. They managed to overtake her and hold her firmly only because of their numbers. Another nearby foreigner took her weapons from her and secured them.

Hanmel and Arne were delayed getting around, because there were too many enemies coming onto the scene, blocking their way through. Hanmel and Arne had to eliminate more people than they thought they would, which forced the plan to help her to slow. To avoid undue attention, the foreigners had to be taken out quickly and quietly, one at a time.

"You will regret ever touching me!" she threatened as she struggled against her opponents. They began to take her away. She made her own wind tunnel, which knocked two of the four off of her. It sent those two flying into the brick walls of the nearby buildings, making them unconscious. She struggled against the two remaining on her, but they held her firmly, and no matter what she did, she couldn't get them off of her. She kicked and used her power over wind, but they remained held onto her.

Hanmel and Arnesti were now in a race to get to her before they took her away. With the combat, some of the foreign group were at heightened alert and discovered the Hanmel and Arne trying to help Irisel, and engaged them. It detained them long enough for the men to take Irisel away, while all her friend and father could do was watch. Arne was not about to let them take Iri. Those men near Arne suffered electrocution and slumped to the ground. Arne ran after her friend once she was clear.

A few of the foreigners left the conflict before the electricity storm to gather the rest of the their forces in town still searching and all exited the city out of the south gates having accomplished what they came for. Their secretly hidden ships awaited them away from the city docks, anchored along the coast just south of the city. The overall conflict was far from over though. Blood had been spilt, men were dead, and they found the girl they thought was their princess. Open war was now upon the great city of Faulkton.

Once out of the city, the foreigners all converged upon their hidden ships they rode in on. After all left alive were aboard the ships, they set sail. Everyone relaxed and Irisel was placed in plush quarters guarded by four men. They refused to let her out for anything. Luckily for her, the robed man that Alltin came across was on a different ship. The guards did anything for Irisel except let her out. She couldn't stand it.

Shortly after the ships set sail, Iri heard an odd noise coming from one of her windows. She went to investigate. She took a closer look out of her window and discovered Arne, just hanging around outside her window. Irisel tried to open the window but couldn't. She motioned to her friend as such.

Arne didn't look concerned. She would take her opportunity to sneak around the vessel unseen. Eventually she could slip inside the room. Once the guards thought Irisel was asleep, Arne picked the key from one of them, opened the door just enough, and quietly enough, then replaced the key and closed the door. She managed to pull it off so well, none of the guards noticed.

Once Arne was in the room with Irisel, they hugged each other. Irisel was very happy to see her friend. They were together once more. The two friends spoke in code with their hands so they didn't rouse the guards' suspicions. They came up with the code so they could talk without nosey sailors overhearing their private conversations. They spoke of the situation and options until both became too tired. Arne found a comfortable hiding spot where she could get some sleep and remain hidden.

\*\*\*

Alltin came running as fast as he could once he realized where the conflict took place. Sadly he was too late and found only Hanmel, dealing with the bodies.

"I'm so sorry Hanmel. I tried to keep them from suspecting your daughter, but they'd already found out about her. They believed nothing I said. Apparently Melissant told them quite enough about Irisel to keep up her revenge on the girls. Hanmel, I promise you, I will find them and bring them home. But while I do this for you, you must help keep an eye out here and on my lord while I am away. You should be in contact with Taen and Caladin. You can trust them." Alltin felt awful for not finding the girls in time. He failed them.

"I will do as you ask, and thank you for going after them. I fear for them. My daughter is in more danger than she realizes."

"Lord Fadel has been filled in on the situation at sea already. Taen and Caladin are being treated for their wounds from the ordeal. You daughter and Arne were instrumental in the mission. We would all have been lost had they not been there. And I cannot let them be taken after what they've done for all of us." Alltin started to say goodbye to Hanmel and turn to gather his things when Hanmel gave him another bit of information.

"I have a ship you can use Alltin. Take it across the sea to the east to Nista, then by foot to the Harand Kingdom. That is where they are taking her." Hanmel gave Alltin detailed directions to get to Irisel and Arne as fast as he could, then was left to prepare for the trip.

Alltin hurried to get his supplies readied and he met with his lord. "My Lord, I must inform you I am leaving to go after Irisel. She and Arnesti have been taken and are enroute to the foreigners' lands as we speak. Plus if all works out, I might be able to avert open war. I do not have much time if I am to catch up with them. I will be back as soon as I can."

Melissant was visibly annoyed that Alltin was going after Irisel, and stormed off when she heard him say it. Alltin knew why Melissant was so mad, but she would just have to deal with it. Melissant had a crush on Alltin, and tried to come on to him all the time. He tried to be as polite and correct as he could be with her, but he just wasn't attracted to her in that way. Melissant just never took the hint, and she was definitely angry with him for leaving her to go after Irisel.

Lord Fadel wished him luck, and made Alltin promise that he would return.

"If it is possible, I will return to you my lord."  Alltin went to exit the palace.

Melissant met Alltin by the outer gates, and seemed as if she had been crying. "Please, do not go. I beg of you. I love you!"

Alltin just looked at her blankly, and said, "It is my job to go after Irisel, especially after your vindictive and jealous actions in the throne room earlier.  You led the enemy to her out of revenge, Melissant.  I cannot forget that.  She would never have done that to you, even after everything you've done to her."

Melissant became furious, and began yelling at Alltin. "It is your job to do as I say as well.  I am ordering you to stay and protect me and my family!"

He smiled halfway, and said, "I plan on protecting your family, but by going after Irisel and those men who took her."  Mel was a little cute when she tried to be firm, but was otherwise nothing other than a pain in the ass.

"I told you to stay here! If you choose to leave, then you are permanently released from your duties as a knight of this city."

He just looked at her, and responded, "Do what you want Melissant, but I am still leaving.  I know my duties better than you.  You are but a child to me.  And your personality reflects it.  You know, you shouldn't throw threats around so frivolously and needlessly just because the object of your childish crush is leaving town temporarily."

She stood there, speechless.  He had never insulted her like that before, and she didn't see anything childish about her love for him.  She was on the verge of tears, and tried to hold them back.

He noticed.   "I am sorry, Melissant, if my words hurt your feelings.  What I said is still true, and I meant it.  You have given them head start enough by detaining me.  I must go."  He pressed on past her, saying, "I am out of time to engage you in pointless discussion.  Goodbye for the time at hand.  I will return."

She shouted out angrily, "You needn't bother coming back, because you are no longer welcome!"

He continued towards his destination, with the last words to her being, "that decision is not up to you.  It is my Lord's decision.  He has the final say on that matter, not you."  Alltin was too far away after that.

She burst into tears, and noticed that the guards were standing around.  She assumed they saw most of the conversation and ran as fast as she could to her room. On top of being hurt emotionally, she was also very embarrassed that the entire lot of guards witnessed the scene. She stayed in her room for the rest of the evening and cried. She let no one in, including her father.

Fadel heard from several of the guards about the conversation, while he was checking on his injured knights. Of course that was juicy gossip for the palace servants and it spread quickly. Fadel felt bad for his daughter, but knew that what she wanted to happen, never would. He was proud of the way Alltin acted in the conversation, and knew that the conversation need-ed to happen for quite some time. He knew he would have to console his daughter, but would not willingly relieve Alltin of his post because of her hurt feelings.

Alltin rushed to the ship, and it set out that evening with a crew that Hanmel trusted completely. They were fortunate that the winds were on their side. Alltin did all he could to help while they were sailing towards the port city of Nista. He kept himself busy with practice and reading nor-mal books from his room when he wasn't needed. Several times, the wind didn't blow and the ship was stuck in place, but it soon picked back up. He kept thinking that if Irisel were there, it wouldn't be an issue. He wondered if the foreigners were using her talents as such. It ended up taking them approximately a month to get over to the Harand Kingdom. The trip was long, but everything went smoothly. There were a few storms and some moments when the wind just wasn't cooperating, but the trip went as well as it could have. They anchored near an island so they weren't spotted. They headed to the port town of Nista on foot.

*** 

On the trip for Iri and Arne, they set up ideas to send a plan into mo-tion. Arne made a light green wig out of various decorative items from the room and dressed in Iri's clothing. Iri went into the shadows where Arne was. They had a great surprise in store for her kidnappers. They liked the idea of the plan so well that they couldn't wait to get to their destination, wherever it was. It took approximately a month for the ship to arrive in Nista. "Iri" was led off the boat, and immediately into a well guarded coach. There was no way either girl would be able to escape the coach. Irisel hid amongst clothing and other belongings. She stayed still, and made sure she was in with the stuff that wouldn't be bothered on the trip.

Going through Nista was almost unnoticed by the two girls. Their coach was traveling as fast as it could and it didn't have many windows. Arne, dressed as Irisel, was too preoccupied with hassling the guards keeping her in the coach to watch the scenery. Before Arne realized it, they were already out of the port city.

There were a few close calls for Iri where a guard wanted to get something obscure, but was talked out of needing it by another guard. Both girls learned more from the conversations they overheard to use in their plan.

"Irisel" asked the men, "why would you take the princess against her will? Is it just to get in the king's good graces, or is there a reward to be had?"

One of the guards answered, "Both. But of course we're just happy to have you back, your Highness."

"What if I'm really not the princess and all of this is a huge mistake?"

They didn't seem phased and the other guard in the coach told her that she could still pass for the princess. "We are sure, however, that you indeed are the princess. You are the only born with green hair that we know of."

"You will regret taking me away from my home. You just doomed all of your trade ships. After all, you just abducted the daughter of the highest authority in trade in this region."

"Then he shouldn't have kidnapped the princess, because the king will wage a long hard war upon those who stole his daughter away. Now you will shut it for the remainder of the night."

"But I want to continue talking."

"Get some rest, your Highness."

"I couldn't sleep if I tried, because I don't trust you." The tone was mocking and snobbish. Arne was totally hamming it up and having fun with it.

"If you don't shut your mouth, your Highness, I will have to gag you and your father will understand!"

Arne huffed and rolled her eyes.

It took four days to get to the Castle Harand, east of Nista. They arrived and were rushed through the castle, and into the main audience chamber. It was a normal castle, built from dark grey stones. It had several towers, and was very large. There was a moat around the castle with some sort of steaming black liquid in it. Neither girl had seen that before. Once inside the castle, Iri jumped out of the supplies and hid, ready to trail them to wherever they went.

The two guard captains commanded the lesser guys to take a hold of "Iri", and the captains walked in front of the group. As they entered the audience chamber, an older man who was quite grey haired and quite muscular, was sitting on the throne. He had several men and women standing around him, but no one sat in the other chair upon the dais. He stood up as they entered the chamber.

"Your Majesty, we have found your princess, at long last. She was found in Faulkton, under the rule of a Lord Fadel. When we went to gather her, we met with some resistance, even from the princess. Not all of our men made it back home. In our search for her on the sea, we had to destroy one of Faulkton's ships."

The King Harand did not look pleased, but tried to turn his attention to the "princess".

Arne played it very cool as she listened to their story.

"Leave me alone with my daughter," the king asked of his court.

The men left, and Iri stayed in the shadows to watch their plan in action. This was better than she expected.

The king inspected Arnesti, and asked, "Is there anything you want to tell me?"

She said, with a trashy accent, that their story was a lie. It was such horrid speech, that Arne could barely keep a straight face and say it. "I were captured most brutally, and my life they threatened, were I did not cooperate. I am supposed to pretend a princess am I. This wig is atrocious, but was forced upon me as part of my disguise so I would convince more! Care I not if they go through with their nasty threats. Not willing to pretend to be your daughter just so's they can get booty and fame am I!"

Arne took her wig off, and continued with the plan. Irisel had to try hard to keep from laughing aloud at her story. The king had quite an angered face as Arne continued to tell him about all of the things they threatened to do to her. Arne was so good at acting, that the performance was excellent. The king bought every word of it, and almost blew his top when he found out that she was the daughter of the trade guild leader. His face was turning a deep shade of red that neither girl had ever seen on anyone before.

"Your name, miss?"

"Arne, sir my lord!" She loved watching his face cringe at every awful word phrasing and butchering! Her face wanted to do the same thing!

"Well, Arne, call your captors in for their 'rewards'"

She gladly did as he asked her to, and sat back eager to watch the next events unfold. She even got to sit in what was supposedly Irisel's seat. The delivering guards entered with smiles on their faces, and were completely caught unaware when the king yelled at them furiously. The king had a thunderous voice when he was angry. It boomed throughout the corridors. The last thing he told them was, "you are profoundly stupid if you think that passes for my lost daughter! You are unworthy to serve me!" He turned to his palace guards. "You will take these men into your custody and throw them in the dungeons!"

The surprised delivery guards tried to protest. They did not understand. "But your Majesty ...why...?"

"That is not my daughter and you well knew it!" He was fuming mad. "How dare you mock a father's pain by such a farce, for, for ...booty and fame!"

The delivering guards never even noticed that Arne had taken her wig off, and that it wasn't Irisel standing there. They protested all the way down the corridor to no avail.

The king asked for Arne to come forward. "I am profoundly sorry for the actions of those imbeciles. I do hope that what ties to the trade guild existed prior, are not severed now. I am so, so sorry about all of this. I haven't words enough to accurately express what I am feeling."

"Know nothing 'bout how home goes, but home soon I hope to be if possible it is." Arne continued to play her part well. It was like trying to decipher a puzzle at times.

"I insist upon tending to any needs you might have. Have you been hurt by these people?" The king tried to look over for any wounds they might have inflicted upon her.

He lavished her, and Iri unknowingly, with many fine gifts, and food, and anything else she wanted. The girls were in heaven as he tried to make up for his soldiers' mistake. Arne was very happy, and even had some gentlemen come into her large and lush room. Arne chose the best two of them, and ended up sending one away because Irisel still couldn't come out and enjoy such things.

Irisel just went around the castle as Arne had her fun, but Iri didn't leave her alone for long. She wanted to make sure Arne was okay. As Irisel went through the corridors she saw a familiarly dressed individual go towards the audience chamber. She remembered seeing him in Faulkton, staring at them. Arne even commented on how fine looking he was. Irisel decided to follow him into the chamber.

The king was speaking to a man in green, red, and white robes about the situation. He scolded the man for failing so miserably, and jeopardizing the relations with the trading guild. The robed man stood silent as the king spoke. The familiar man went in and listened to the scolding. The king addressed the robed man as Maruk, and the familiar looking man as Judah.

In a refined and regretful tone, Judah apologized for the mistake. "It was my fault, your Majesty. I was the one who told the guards who to search for and capture."

The king looked at him sternly and started to say something, when he just decided to kick both of them out of his chamber. On their way out he did say, "Keep looking for my daughter, but the next time a mission is underway, be quite sure it is the right princess!"

"Of course, your Majesty," they both said in unison, and then left the room. They walked towards a different part of the castle than she had been, and talked about the current situation.

Irisel returned to their room, and found the man putting on his clothes. He still had his shirt off when Iri walked in. He seemed surprised to see someone enter the room without knocking, but nodded to her. He didn't seem to recognize her at all, for which she felt glad. She did find that odd though. He left, and Iri told Arne what happened.

Arne was surprised, and said, "We should get out as soon as we can."

They packed their things in a hurry, and were about to leave when there was a knock on the door.

Iri hid and Arne answered the door. It was the king, and he was surprised to see she was leaving.

"You're leaving? Has the hospitality been lacking? Please, do stay a bit longer."

"Must home now, sir lord. Jumbled ties fixed to be. Soon to go home as possible." Iri cringed and laughed inside every time Arne spoke like that.

"I am sorry to see you leaving, but I understand. I will send my best knight with you to escort you safely, and to help clear up any misunderstandings. I want to be sure the relationship will remain intact."

Arne agreed to it. What could she do? "Must on my way, underway."

He gathered Sir Eldarin, and the knight got ready as fast as he could. Eldarin met up with Arne, and the king wished them both luck.

"Eldarin, I trust you will settle matters with the trade guild, and make sure Arne returns home alright."

"As you command of me, your Majesty," and bowed etiquettefully. The two, (three), of them set out that evening, and the king provided the coach to Nista.

Sir Eldarin stood 5'10" and had long brown hair and brown eyes. He was usually a quiet person. The people loved him for the concern he would usually show towards them. He was the favorite knight of the king for the way the people adored him.  Even if the king did things that the people didn't like, they were less likely to complain if Eldarin was involved.  The king also liked Eldarin for his ability to complete the assignments given to him.  He was efficient in most cases.

One thing Eldarin never experienced was the affections of a girlfriend.  He was usually kept too busy for such things.  He hadn't even considered the aspect since he was the target of several crushes.  He saw how women could be and decided that the comforts a girlfriend would offer were just not the best thing for him at that point in his life.  He had plenty of things to keep him busy so he didn't think about relationships.

# Chapter 3:  Heading Home

Arne and Eldarin didn't speak much on the coach.  He asked her a few questions and she answered them as she wanted to.  She had to keep up the ruse, the whole way home!  Eldarin was a handsome man, but he was quiet.  She liked the quiet ones on some days, because they were more fun to try to spark a conversation with.  Other days, Arne would just prefer not to deal with it.  Sometimes it was too much hassle than she cared to deal with.  She noticed he looked similar to Alltin in several ways, and even had a similar role.  She wondered if there was something more to that.

As the coach was about to stop, it hit a large rock that the driver was too distracted to see.  The rocks made one of the wheels loosen, and the coach tumbled.  The horses were spooked, but the coachman tried to calm them down enough to stop.  Everyone got out of the coach and needed to rest after that.  Arne could see that she would most likely hate traveling in the coach.  Eldarin made sure his charge was okay, and made camp.  He pitched a large tent that had separate rooms.  As he made the fire, Irisel came up to the camp and asked if she could join them for the evening.

Eldarin was surprised to see a lady walking out and about all alone in the middle of the night.

Arne said, "Iri, sister she is.  Long time gone."

Eldarin noticed the green hair on Irisel immediately, but said nothing.  He was knighted after the princess went missing, and her disappearance was when she was a baby.  He never knew the princess, but heard plenty about it.  If he had to get her back to the palace, then he would need to make her believe that he had no idea who she was for the moment.  He politely smiled and kissed her hand. "A pleasure my lady. I am Sir El-darin. Welcome to our camp. Please make yourself at home, I insist. You look cold; the fire is nice for warming up."

Irisel smiled politely back and sat down to warm up. She also noticed a slight resemblance to Alltin, and it made her wonder. She had a few bruis-es from the coach tumbling and Eldarin noticed.

"My lady, you look worse for ware. What may I ask happened to you?"

"I was in the forest, running from something. I tripped and fell a few times as I ran."

"What was it the frightened you so?"

"Sir, I did not get close enough to look at it. I am not accustomed to letting things get close enough to attack me, just so I can get a good look at it."

He smiled at that. "Well, if it were otherwise, I suppose you would not be here right now, in this camp."

"Agreed." Iri looked at the tent and wondered if he would let her stay in it. "How many rooms does that tent have?"

"Four, my lady. And you are most welcome to share a tent with Arne and me."

At this point, Arnesti had enough. In her normal voice and speech she spoke. "Okay, I have to confess, yes, Irisel is my sister, but I am not as un-educated as I sounded. I was just trying to make my point. They had the wrong girl. That is Irisel, my name is Arnesti... Iri and Arne for short."

Eldarin smiled and nodded in acknowledgement at the admission. He said nothing to let either girl know that he intended to bring the real prin-cess back after he took Arne home as he promised he would do.

Irisel was happy, but surprised Arne couldn't handle the ruse any long-er. Irisel definitely understood.

They eventually went to sleep and were awoken in the middle of the night by the ground shaking slightly. They got out of the tent just in time, before a giant rock hit and crushed the tent. Two giant men were throwing the rocks from the forest. Eldarin took his weapons out. He used two blades that were the size of long swords, but were curved and fattened on the ends. The girls had only seen those kinds of weapons once before, but could not recall where or when. He ran up to the giants and attacked them. He took slashes at the giants' knees and made them bellow out in pain and anger. The giants tried to squish the knight, but he managed to get out of the way of their fists. The girls came up behind him and helped him with weapons.

Before long, the battle was over and the giants were slain. They were looted, and luckily no one got hurt. The three of them found a bag of items on both of the giants. Most items were unusable, but there were a few weapons and jewelry items, as well as some clothing items that were of exceptional quality. They went back to the camp and Eldarin set the tent back up. He was happy that the rocks just missed the poles so they didn't break.

They went back to bed and in the morning the coachman had to fix the wheel on the coach. The girls were hungry, and so was Eldarin. He went out and hunted for some food for them. He wasn't very good at hunting, but managed to catch something. He came back with a pheasant and cooked it for the girls since they didn't know how to cook. Irisel pretty much kept to herself, but Arne was beginning to see aspects about the knight that she was becoming fond of. She began to flirt and Eldarin seemed to be interested in Arne slightly as well. Eldarin gladly talked and flirted back, but not to the degree that Arne did. It was enough to make her smile a lot.

Irisel was curious about the situation, and wasn't as talkative with him as Arne was. Eldarin tried to bring up a few conversations with her, but Iri would keep her responses short. He knew that he had his work cut out for him if he was going to lower Irisel's guard enough for her to trust him. It was important that Irisel trust him for him to try to bring her back with him. Arne was easy for him to let her guard down. As long as he flirted with her, she would be more willing to talk to him and the better his chances with Irisel stood. He wasn't interested in Irisel romantically, though he did find Arne attractive. That part wasn't a lie, but he needed to befriend Iri. He had the coachman take his time with the coach repairs so he could spend some more time off the road with the girls.

Irisel was getting restless and just wanted to get home. A few times Eldarin asked Iri if she wanted to join his walks in the woods with Arne, but Iri refused his offer, though she thanked him for offering. He had to figure a way to get Irisel alone so he could talk to her. It was difficult since Arne was always near him flirting. They were there for another evening, and Arne was extra sleepy.

Irisel went to sleep, but was awoken by Eldarin.

"I need to speak with you, my lady, alone," he whispered. He motioned to let Arne sleep. He held out his hand to Irisel. "Please come with me."

She looked at him skeptically, but finally took his hand after a few minutes of debating whether or not she should have.

He led her into the forest away from the tent. "Would you indulge me by telling me a bit about yourself? I've gotten to know a bit about your sister, but you remain a mystery, my lady."

She knew what he wanted her to say, and wasn't sure if she should. She danced around the subject with the same things as she and Arne had said before until he called her out on it and asked her again.

"Please, tell me the truth. I can tell you are hiding something from me."

"Does my past matter to you so much that you would interrogate me this much? For as long as I can remember, I was born in Faulkton. I was raised by the trade guild, and ended up here after the men of this region kidnapped my sister. I just arrived, and luckily happened upon you and my sister broken down."

Eldarin didn't buy her story for one minute, but listened to what she said intently. She could tell he was studying her, and she ended the conversation abruptly. He tried to stop her by taking hold of her hand.

Suddenly he heard a male voice from behind him in a commanding tone. "Take your hands off of her!"

Iri recognized the voice right away, and smiled as she waited for him to come out of the darkness.

Eldarin was surprised by the demand from behind, and whipped around quickly to see who was behind them.

Sir Alltin stepped out of the shadows with weapon drawn. He was seemingly quite serious about his demand. Eldarin recognized his mark of station and country, and let go of her hand. He also noticed somewhat of a resemblance between them. Eldarin didn't quite know what to say, and Alltin took the advantage to move in between Eldarin and Irisel. She smiled about Alltin's arrival and placed a hand upon his shoulder. Alltin felt her hand touch his shoulder and smiled, but he wasn't letting Eldarin out of his sight. It was moments before either of them spoke.

Alltin broke the silence by speaking first to Iri. "Are you unharmed my lady?"

"I am fine, Sir Alltin," she answered. She was very happy to see him.

Then Alltin turned to Eldarin. "And what is your name?"

"I am Sir Eldarin, first knight of King Harand, whose lands you are in, and I demand you lower your weapons, Sir Alltin."

"Why should I lower my weapons when it is men from your lands who kidnapped her?"

A light shone in Eldarin's eyes and he knew that his suspicions were confirmed about Irisel. Eldarin still said nothing about it though. "My orders from the king are to escort Arnesti home and make good with the trade guild after the atrocity that occurred. King Harand is most apologetic for his men's' poor behavior. He seeks to make the wrongs, right again. So I escort these ladies home. The actions of our guards were uncalled for, and must be made right."

"Then why do you grab her and treat Irisel in such a manner as I witnessed just moments ago? That does not tell me you are simply returning her home." Alltin was getting angry just thinking about it.

"It was not meant as an affront upon her person. I do apologize, Irisel, if it seemed that way."

Alltin turned to Irisel, and looked her in the eyes. "Is that true?"

She thought about keeping up the charade, but she knew that Eldarin already knew who she was. "So far as I know, it is the truth, Alltin."

Alltin put his sword down, and turned around fully to check on her. She still had her hand on his shoulder and blushed when she realized how long she kept it there. Alltin just smiled, and the smile soon turned to concern as he saw the bruises from the accident.

Before she could say anything, Alltin turned to Eldarin in a demanding tone. "How did she come to be this bruised?"

Eldarin told him the story that Irisel told him, and Alltin looked confused.

"Sir Eldarin, give us a moment in private, if you would. We need some time to talk."

He reluctantly left for the tent. He stopped every few steps to see what they were doing.

"After being captured and locked away in a plush cabin, I was relieved when Arne showed up. We planned to get back at them for all of the wrongs they did to our people. We planned a switch. Arne dressed like me, even made a green wig." She laughed. "So when we docked, we switched. Arne took my place and upon being taken to the king, she showed him they had the wrong girl and they planned it from the start to trick him out of money and good graces...or as she put it, booty and fame." Irisel actually laughed about it out loud because she finally could.

Alltin studied her face as it went through the range of emotions the story invoked.

"Anyway, the king was so angry he sent the guards to the dungeons and scolded the two actually in charge. He released those two back into the world to look for me, "their princess", again." At that, her smile faded, but picked back up slowly with the remainder of the story. "He did everything he could to make sure Arne was comfortable, but we realized we needed to go, and fast. So he sent Sir Eldarin with Arne. I rode with the bags in the back. The coach hit something big and a wheel broke sending me tumbling around, hence the bruises. I entered the camp afterwards, she called me her sister, and we said I was looking for her. I told him I was running from something in the woods and fell when he asked about the bruises." She paused. "The worst part is that I think Eldarin knows who I am. When you came upon us, and I am so very glad to see you by the way, he was interrogating me about my past. I think you inadvertently confirmed his suspicions about me. Arne was supposed to be the one abducted." She looked into his eyes and said randomly to change the subject, "Hi, how are you?"

The randomness of the last part surprised Alltin into a smile. "I'm concerned about you of course, my lady." He took a moment, and then continued, "I apologize for ruining your cover story. We will have to be mindful, if he truly suspects you. And, we should check to make sure you are not wounded from your fall. Even small wounds can turn into big problems if not properly treated. Limbs have been lost over infected scrapes."

"Well, aside from all that, so far as I know, we are headed home. Eldarin has to beg my father for their traders to be back in his good graces again."

Alltin's expression went blank at that comment. After everything that happened, he didn't think good graces were where they belonged. He sighed a small sigh. "Well I'm glad you are alright, aside from the bruises," which he was still looking over. Alltin refused to let her be taken again. As far as he was concerned, she was raised and grew up in Faulkton. He felt that since that was where her family resided, then that was where she belonged. He looked her over for a few minutes more until he was satisfied she was okay, and then she led him back to the camp.

Fortunately, there was enough room in the tent for Alltin as well. Before they went to sleep, Alltin wanted to talk with her some more. They sat at the fire and chatted.

"I will stay in the room next to yours, if you don't mind. I want to make sure I am close by in case something happens. I will need to make sure I can protect you easier." Alltin sat closer to her next to the fire so he didn't have to speak as loud.

Irisel smiled at him. "Thank you for your help, Sir Alltin." She was playing at being formal. It made it seem things were like when they were on the boat before all the bad things happened.

"Not a problem, my lady. Shall we get some rest? You look like you could use some." Alltin motioned towards the tent, and Iri took the hint. They both slept until morning.

Eldarin wasn't very happy that Alltin was going to accompany them, and that he was planning on staying in the tent as well. Eldarin knew that complaining about it would just cause more problems than he needed, though.

Both knights went out for breakfast, but Alltin insisted that Irisel accompany him. She didn't mind, but she wasn't use to going out into woods first thing in the morning. She didn't even really do much to help the men hunt other than to spook animals towards the knights with wind. Alltin did most of the work.

She understood why he wanted her to go along. She understood that he seemed interested in her, which was also the reason he was being so protective of her. She was sure of that. She said nothing about it though. She wasn't sure if she wanted to be involved with anyone at that time. She thought he was cute, and his protectiveness over her was flattering, though she wasn't looking for a relationship. If it happened in time, she supposed she wouldn't mind, but she hardly knew him yet. She was genuinely happy to have him there though. He was a nice deterrent to keep Eldarin off her back. She could tell how badly Eldarin wanted to get her alone.

Arne was surprised that Alltin was there when she awoke, but she didn't mind. She was also surprised she slept through the whole thing. She started comparing the two now that they were near one another. "Alltin, how did you get here?"

"I followed the kidnappers all the way here after they left Faulkton."

Breakfast went well, although the two knights hardly said a word to each other. Eldarin kept an eye on Alltin and Iri, but he spent most of his attention on Arne. It was fine with Arne. She liked Eldarin more than Alltin, and she just loved attention anyway. The day was cloudy, but it didn't rain at all during the day. The coach was fixed finally, and they could get underway at last. The coachman ended up getting it repaired around midday, and all were glad to get on their way. They traveled until nightfall, and camped again.

The group said very little during the latter traveling, but when they stopped to camp, Arne wanted to talk to Iri alone. She pulled her friend aside and started talking about how nice Eldarin was. Iri listened to her friend as she spoke so well of Eldarin.

"What do you think? Is he boyfriend material?" Arne was definitely excited.

Iri smiled and said, "You should do what ever you want to do." Iri knew full well what was running through her best friends mind concerning Eldarin.

"I noticed a certain other knight who's getting a little clingy on you,"

Arne said in a teasing tone with a smirk.

"No boyfriend plans just yet Arne, but I will see how things go. I am waiting and getting to know him first before ever planning on doing what you have in mind for Eldarin."

Arne smiled and suggested, "Don't wait too long or he might not be around to consider. He's highly desired by many women, including Mel. And don't underestimate Mel. She usually gets what she wants."

Iri just smiled. "Mel doesn't concern me. Perhaps you should be focusing those words with you and Eldarin for the time being," she laughed. Arne was more than happy to do just that.

Arne ran back to the camp, and sat next to Eldarin. She slid her hand on his when he least expected it, but he didn't push her hand away. Those two talked for a bit and then decided to go for a walk.

"You know what, Eldarin?"

"What?"

"I like you. I don't know why exactly, but I do." She smiled playfully at him. "Once we get to Faulkton, I'll show you around, show you a good time."

He gave her a sweet smile and a look of agreement.

Arne stopped walking, placed herself closely in front of him. "What do you say we finish this conversation in your tent?" She smirked. "Plus it gives my sister some time alone with Alltin as well."

"Sounds like something I wouldn't mind." He smirked back.

Along the way back, Arne stopped long enough to give Eldarin a kiss, which he returned. Once in the tent, the two would not emerge for the rest of the night. They talked, kissed, laughed, cuddled, and then fell asleep.

While Arne and Eldarin were on their walk, Iri and Alltin tried to get to know each other better by asking about personal things, like favorite things and childhoods. They both seemed to be interested in what the other had to say. After Arne and Eldarin went into the tent, Iri knew what her friend was doing. Iri could tell that Arne really liked him. She didn't see what Arne saw in him, but as long as her friend was happy, that was all that mattered. She smiled and shook her head slightly at the thought of Arne flirting with Eldarin. She could never be as impulsive as Arne was. It was a quality that Iri actually admired in her friend, though it was just one of many qualities that she admired.

After Arne and Eldarin entered the tent, Alltin sat next to Irisel by the fire. Irisel wasn't sure of what she should do. She didn't move away from him, but for a moment it was a little uncomfortable until she came around to the idea of him being that close to her. She shivered slightly, and she hardly noticed it. Alltin did, and he put his cloak around her to help keep her warm. She didn't know what to say to him, so she thanked him, and unknowingly blushed.

He noticed her blush, but said nothing about it. He just smiled and said, "you're welcome, my lady."

His cloak smelled like a man's cologne, and it smelled good to her. The scent fit him well. It help set an entrancing mood combined with the fire. She noticed, now that he was sitting closer to her, that he smelled the same as the cloak. She had mixed signals going to her head about what should happen next. It was her side of reason that kept her from acting as impulsively as her friend. She thought about leaning on him or something else, but decided against it.

Alltin noticed her thinking about something. "What is on your mind, my lady?" He was looking at her in a caring but intent manner.

Before she thought about her answer, she let it slip. "You." She really did blush then.

"Good thoughts I hope?" He smiled.

She smiled, still embarrassed. She took a moment's pause as she was reluctant to admit it aloud. "Yes." She tried to avoid looking into his eyes, because she knew he was looking at her. She could feel his eyes fishing for an answer to questions running through his mind. Okay, I have to do something, anything, get up, just get up Iri! Iri had to do something to end the feeling of being stared at, so she stood up and tried to stretch. She lost her balance though, and Alltin had to catch her before she fell into the fire.

He caught her in such a way that she had no choice, but to look at him directly. She could see humor and concern in his eyes at her nearly falling into the fire, but she could also see deeper feelings that gave her a strange sensation in her body. She tried to keep herself composed, but she was having problems with it. She then tried to end the awkward, yet somewhat comfortable situation. "Clearly with that, I think I need some rest." This is what I get for being impulsive, ending up in a worse situation than before.

He looked at her peculiarly but understandingly, and agreed.

It was a good excuse, but as Alltin was helping her on her feet, they could both hear that Eldarin and Arne were still awake. It sounded to Irisel as if they were kissing, and neither one wanted to interrupt. She looked up at Alltin as she realized he heard it as well, and noticed that it was making him think about kissing her. Her eyes became wide, and she looked for a way to walk where she wouldn't fall over anything. She tried to walk that way and found she couldn't move, and Alltin was her support. He had his arms around her firmly so she wouldn't fall.

He seemed to be enjoying the grasp he had on her, and she was power-less to move. All she could do was look at him. She tried closing her eyes, but his scent drew her in closer to him. It truly was intoxicating to her, and she couldn't do anything but hold onto him for what seemed like forev-er. She was surprised that he didn't try to kiss her, but instead he rested his head on her shoulder as he held her. Little did she know, her sweet floral scent was having the same effect on him. He couldn't bring himself to let her go.

It was the loud call from an owl in the woods that brought both of them out of their trances. They both acted as if nothing happened, because they were both embarrassed that they had so little control over their actions. He helped her into the tent and they both ignored the kissing going on in the other room of the tent. After Alltin helped Iri to her room and checked to make sure she wasn't hurt. Alltin went to his room in the tent, and they both slept.

Alltin and Iri both dreamt about the other, but neither of them chose to remember the dream upon waking. They found that Arne and Eldarin were still asleep. Alltin and Iri just let them sleep as much as they need-ed. Iri was surprised to see Arne sleeping on her own side of the tent, but figured perhaps that Eldarin wasn't ready for her to stay on his side yet. Upon exiting the tent, Iri and Alltin could see the clouds were pretty dark, and it was very windy.

The coachman noticed it as well, and said "looks like it's going to storm."

Iri got a strange feeling throughout her body, and a strange look on her face to match. She closed her eyes and held her arms out to her sides. She didn't open her eyes while she spoke to the two men. "This is worse than just a storm. The winds are on the move today. There is a tornado coming our way." The coachman looked at her oddly. Alltin knew to trust her senses concerning weather.

From behind them came the voice of Arne who wore an odd expression on her face as well. "Yes, it is more than just a minor storm. I feel the elec-tricity becoming more active within me." Arne went to warn Eldarin while the others tried to find some shelter.

They weren't able to find any, and the girls kept saying, "We're run-ning out of time to search for shelter." Iri pulled Arne aside to discuss an idea she had. She put her hair up in anticipation.

"Ok, here's my idea. The camp remains where it is and I can try to di-rect the wind around the camp."

"I can ensure that we are not struck by any lightning. The tent will keep out any rain and remain intact if you do your part. The only problem is the horses. They're spooked enough by the impending storm. They will never stay in the camp."

Iri went to the coach driver. "You must take off with the coach and the horses."

He didn't seem to want to leave them, but agreed it would be best. The weather was worsening, minute by minute. He knew she was right.

Eldarin and Alltin noticed the coachman leaving and tried to stop him, but were unsuccessful.

Iri knew they wouldn't like it. "It is for the best, guys. It is for their safety and ours."

"Get in side the tent and stay there," both girls said to the men in near unison.

Arne took Eldarin aside. "Iri and I must take care of the situation now, get to safety."

Eldarin seemed confused. "But what can you do against such a storm?"

"Just trust me," Arne said as soothingly as she could.

"I don't like the sound of this; I'm staying out here if you are."

"Eldarin, please, for your own safety and ours, do as I ask. Iri and I are not like you. We can do things, special things, and to do so we need to concentrate. You, my dear," she smiled and touched his face sweetly, "are a distraction. I cannot protect us if you are not safe inside that tent. So please, we're running out of time."

"Very well, Arne, but I don't like this one bit."

"So noted. Now get in there!" He did and Arne turned her attentions to the growing threat.


"Alltin, Arne and I will take care of this, get in the tent please." Iri needed him safe.

"There is still time to find decent shelter. There must be something around here."

"The storm will hit us any minute now, please get to safety and hold on."

"The last time I left you, you were taken away, and this seems like it won't be any different. I am not leaving your side," Alltin said with determination. He refused to leave her side, and insisted upon being there for support in case she couldn't handle it.

"Go."

"No."

"Please," Iri could feel it getting closer. She needed him in the tent.

He refused to go.

She took both hands and firmly touched his face. "I need you in that tent now. If I kiss you like I know you want me too, will you go?"

"Alltin, please," Arne piped up.

Alltin just wasn't going to move from their sides. They finally prepared for their plan with him there. Eldarin came out as well once he realized that Alltin wasn't getting in the tent.

The girls had no time to concern themselves with it at that point. The tornado could be seen coming their way. Irisel planted herself firmly on the ground, and closed her eyes. Alltin wrapped his arms around her tightly in case they flew off. Eldarin had a hold of Arne as well. Eldarin could feel a surge of energy as he held onto Arne. It was coming from within her.

Iri began to concentrate as the winds picked up, and she continued to use her concentration to create a safe area around the four of them. She concentrated harder as she needed to, and before the tornado got to her, she realized that she didn't have the strength yet that she needed to match the power of the tornado.

She wasn't about to give up so she tried to concentrate on the funnel itself. She tried to move the path of the tornado in a different direction. She knew if she was able to change its direction slightly, they would only feel the winds from the tornado. She hoped it would be enough to keep them safe. She managed to move it off its direct path towards them, but it wasn't far enough off the path.

She was becoming mentally drained, and Alltin noticed. He could see the strain in her face to keep up her concentration. He held on tighter to her realizing that she had cleared them from the direct path, but she couldn't clear them from the indirect path. He could feel her body weakening as she struggled to maintain control over the sanctuary they were in after veering the tornado.

Arne noticed too, but she was busy concentrating on keeping lightning from hitting the group. She was concentrating as hard as she could to keep them from that danger at least. That was becoming increasingly difficult, because of the action going on in the clouds near them. The whole thing was exhilarating to her though. Arne's body was surging with energy. She felt more alive in that moment than she ever had in her life. There was a large churning energy in the nearby clouds that she would have to contend with. She herself was immune to lightning damage. She could absorb it safely, but the others couldn't do the same. She remained focused for her friends, and succeeded with her part of the plan.

Iri, however, couldn't control the winds any longer, as her energy was exhausted in her efforts. She grew especially concerned, because it wore her body and mind out completely. She was lucky Alltin had a hold of her, because she could not hold herself up by then. The outer winds from the windstorm raged as the sanctuary dropped. The wind knocked everyone back with almost concussive force. Alltin had a hold of Irisel as they flew high into the air, and were flung off into the forest together. Alltin tried to be Irisel's shield as best he could. They were flung into a large tree, and she could hear bones crack, as Alltin hit the tree instead of her. They fell onto the forest floor, and neither one was able to move. Iri couldn't tell if Alltin was dead or alive at that moment, but he wasn't moving. Arne's words popped into her head at that moment. "Don't wait too long or he might not be around to consider." While Arne meant it in a different manner, it still applied.

Eldarin's grasp on Arne was torn apart as he was jetted out into the forest in a different direction than Arne. He had a few close calls with tree branches flying in the wind. One scratched him but he considered himself lucky that it was just a scratch. He barely missed a tree on the way down, but was inadvertently in line for another. He hit the ground at the base of the tree, but he still slid towards the tree and hit his head. He was no longer conscious after his impact with the tree.

Arne, like the others, was flung off by the strong wind, but she didn't land in the forest. She landed further down the road, just off of it. She landed harshly, and broke her leg in the fall to the ground. She could do nothing else, but lay there in pain and try to keep conscious. The pain was unbearable in her leg, and it was shooting all over her body. She tried to move it a few times, just slightly, and she cried out in pain. She was rendered immobile and couldn't concentrate at all. It was all she could do to deal with the pain of her injury. She hoped everyone was better off than she was, but didn't know how they all fared.

## Chapter 4: After the Storm

"Alltin?" Irisel sat beside him trying to get him to respond, after she came to her senses. Alltin still hadn't awoken. She was near panic when she thought he might be dead. He looked horrible because of the bruises he suffered from hitting the tree and ground. She didn't look the greatest either, but she was able to function, which was more than he could do. She found he had a pulse, but he still didn't wake. She tried talking him out of his "sleep" but there was no response. "You're not allowed to die on me, you hear me? You said you had to protect me, but you can't do that if you're not awake and aware."

Nothing she said to him helped either of them. She was still able to concentrate, so she was determined to float him to help if she needed to. She did have a slight headache, but she could manage. She called out for help and her cry echoed through the forest. Unfortunately, there was no response. Iri was concerned for her friend and Eldarin as well. She didn't know what happened to either of them, and she hoped they were okay. She knew she had to get moving so that she could get help for Alltin. She concentrated and made wind form underneath Alltin, lifting him up off the ground gently.

They began to move, but Irisel had no idea which way to go. She had to make her best guess, and hoped it was the right direction. She would at least be happy if she made it to the road. They traveled slowly, but it was as fast as she could go while keeping control over the wind support under Alltin. She made a constant effort of watching her surroundings so she didn't run Alltin into a tree. She also wanted to avoid creatures that might want to attack them.

She could only travel three quarters of the day due to her concentration efforts on Alltin. Once she stopped, she called out to anyone who would listen. Once again, she got no response. She wouldn't be able to do much in the evenings since she was so worn by the travel, and the use of her power. Nothing attacked that evening as she slept and Alltin remained unconscious. She checked on him before resting and again after she woke up. He was still alive at least for the moment. All she could do was tell him to hold on, and that she was trying to get him to someone who could help.

She set out again, and she was still in the forest. There was no sign of a road anywhere. She traveled as far as she could stand to, and there was no change of scenery. It crossed her mind that maybe she was going the wrong direction, but then she thought that she could be going in the right direction. If that was the case, then changing her course could be devastating to Alltin. She decided to stick with the way she had been traveling. She checked on Alltin again, and was relieved that he was still alive. She knew she didn't have much more time though. She had to get him some help and quickly.

She set out again, and traveled as far as she could go. They were still in the forest, but she could now begin to smell the sea. She had been traveling in the right direction, but she would have to veer to find the road. She could hear animals that evening getting closer to camp. She made an odd noise, in the hopes that it would scare whatever animals were approaching. It worked and the two of them were undisturbed for the evening. She veered off in a direction, in the morning and went that way. She didn't know what direction they were going, but hoped to find something other than forest. She carried him as far as she could, and she found she could see the road in the distance.

She was so excited that she had chosen the right direction to travel. She could hardly sleep that night. "Look Alltin, a road! Fortune smiles upon us. Hang on just a little longer, please." She only got a few hours of sleep, but she was anxious to get into town. She traveled as fast as she could towards the road, and made it there in no time. She looked down the road and saw no one around. She took the direction towards the sea, and followed the road until she couldn't go any farther.

She looked around and she could see some lights not far off in the distance. She thought to herself that it must be a town. She tried screaming as loud as she could, and she even tried using what little energy she had left for the evening to carry her voice further in that direction. She figured that surly a guard or someone else would hear her. She did that several times until she could no longer concentrate. She fell asleep after her last attempt, and was shocked when she awoke.

She opened her eyes to see herself in a bed with a blanket on her. She looked around and found Alltin in the bed to her right. He was covered in blankets as well, but he had several things on him to try to get rid of his bruising. A nurse came in, and noticed she was awake.

"How is he doing?" Irisel asked the nurse.

"He will be here for a while. He has many broken bones and bruising all over his body. What happened to the two of you?"

"We were caught in the winds of the tornado. Sir Alltin broke our fall. He took the brunt of the damage to protect me."

"He sounds like a keeper to me," the nurse said with a smile. "There are few men out there that would be so selfless."

"Can I see how bad the bruising is?"

"Yes, but I warn you it might be a shock to you." She walked over to him and waited until Irisel was ready. Once ready, the nurse pulled the covers off of him. Alltin's body was nearly completely covered in black and dark purple bruises. He looked terrible.

Irisel gasped at the sight of his condition. It didn't look that bad while he was clothed. Had he not been there, that would have been me. The nurse has a point. Anyone willing to take that to save another should be held onto. It would be a foolish thing for me to deny the possibility of a relationship. Arne's words went through her head again too. Irisel should-n't wait too long to take advantage of her opportunity to be with him.

Iri just kept talking to Alltin while she was made to stay in bed. All she could do for him was to be there for him when he awoke from his co-ma. She turned her attentions to the nurse again. "What about my friends? My friend Arne and Sir Eldarin were also taken by the winds and I have not seen or heard from them since."

"Your friends have not arrived here, at least not yet. Sir Eldarin was with you?" The nurse had a look of recognition on her face. "If he was tak-en in the winds too, I hope he has made it to a hospice somewhere. If they are alive yet, I'm sure they are in a hospice somewhere." She said it to make Irisel feel better, but the nurse was definitely concerned.

Irisel was unsure of her friends' fates, and was very concerned for them. She could only hope they were okay or at least able to get to a hos-pice. She had to be positive about the situation and keep her hopes up. Irisel spent a week in the hospice, and then was let go. Her injuries weren't as severe as Alltin's, and she was glad, but she hoped that he would get better quickly. Over the week, his bruises changed color slightly, but he still looked awful.

She decided to look around town to see if she could find her friends. She quickly noticed that the town she was in was not Nista, at least from what little she could see of it on their way to the castle. She hadn't made it to Nista. She had made it to some other town along the coast in-stead. She looked around anyway, and came up empty-handed. She went back to the hospice and stayed by Alltin's side, breaking only for food. She even slept at his side.

A few days went by, and she was awoken to the feeling of someone gently caressing her hair. She looked immediately, and saw that it was Alltin. He was awake and looking at her deeply. Irisel was so happy, that before she could stop herself, she kissed him. He returned the kiss gen-tly. Once she realized what she did, she turned bright red and didn't know what to say.

Alltin just smiled, and gave her an assuring look. "What a nice sur-prise. To see you when I wake, and you are safe. So my holding onto you saved you after all, my intentions of protection worked. I am truly glad." He noticed not only her happiness to see him, but the concern over him behind the happiness. He gently ran his fingers through her hair and said, "Do not worry about me, my lady, I'll be fine. You're looking a bit ragged though." He chuckled. "You should sleep in a real bed. You should get yourself to an inn and get some real rest."

The nurse came in at that moment and was pleased to see that Alltin was awake. "Yes I quite agree with him. You should get some real sleep. The beds here are not as comfortable as the inn's. Alltin, you will still have to remain here for another month at least. You still have broken bones in need of mending."

Alltin didn't seem to mind. "I will be fine, my lady. You should go to the inn."

She reluctantly left his side at his request, and went to the local inn. She visited him everyday that he was in the hospice and after forty days he was finally released from the hospice. During those forty days, Irisel searched here and there for Arne and Eldarin. She also listened to the rumors around town. There was no sight, nor news of either of them.

The first thing Alltin did after his release was take Irisel by the hand and lead her towards the shore. They watched the ocean and the sunset, and he told her that they would get back home soon. He held her close, and kissed her gently on the forehead as they watched the sun go down. They went back to the inn, and he tried to pay for his own room, but Irisel insisted that he stay in her room. He did and all they did was hold onto each other through the night.

"There is still no word from or information about Arne or Eldarin. I'm still keeping up hope that they are alive and well."

"My lady, keep up those positive thoughts and I'm sure they will be fine. We will find them together." Alltin had every confidence that they could. Irisel did too.

\*\*\*

Eldarin awoke to find that he couldn't remember much about recent events, or who he was, or even much about his life. He could remember his training, but couldn't remember what the training was for. He could re-member the basics of his life, but not exact details. He had no idea why he was in the forest or what he had been doing. He knew that he had to get to a road or something. Perhaps someone would recognize him. He thought about which way to go to run into a road, and for a moment he vaguely remembered which way the road was.

He seemed to know where he was in the forest, though he had no idea how he knew. He went in the direction of the road, and it took him most of the day to reach it. He was able to see a wagon heading off northwesterly, but he didn't know what was in that direction. He couldn't remember. He figured he should probably go that way and perhaps he might run into a town. He could vaguely see a female figure with long blond hair, and dressed in blue-green clothing driving the wagon.

He followed the wagon, and came upon the camp in the evening. He tried to enter camp without scaring her. It didn't work as well as he expected, and he got drenched from water out of nowhere. He saw a stunning woman with long blond hair and deep blue eyes. She was around 5'6" in height and wore a silky blue and green swirled dress. She was a stunning vision. She was even cuter because she was so defensive. Her eyes were cool and deep. He could see intense emotion behind those eyes.

She spoke in an odd accent that he was sure he hadn't heard before, that he could remember anyway. He was sure he had never met her before. He was sure that he would remember a woman with such striking features.

"You will reveal who you are, or you'll get another round of drenching...or worse," She threatened. Her eyes were blue, but they almost swelled with emotion. In water terms, it would be like an ocean storm with the waves wild and out of control.

He smiled, and told her, "Would if I could, my lady, but I do not know what my name is. When I awoke this morning, I couldn't remember much of anything." He was, of course sincere, but she was unsure if it was true or not. She remained ready to attack, but let him enter the camp. "What may I ask is your name, my lady?"

"Until you remember yours, I temporarily forget mine too." She remained cautious of him throughout the night, and was relieved when morning came.

He awoke and found her dealing with camp and preparing to move on. "What is your destination, my lady?"

She just looked him up and down and huffed. "If you don't know that answer, you'll just have to try to remember harder. Good luck with that." She refused to take him with her, and left him to fend for his own breakfast.

He rummaged through the stuff in his backpack, and found rations. He looked himself up and down and wondered, what made her so mad? He knew it obviously didn't take much, but he was curious what about him offended her.

He found that his cloak clasp was some sort of symbol, and found that he carried a medallion of the same symbol. He had no idea what they symbolized though. He found that he was fairly richly dressed, even though the clothes were ripped and stained from whatever happened to him. He checked his scrapes and bruises to make sure none of them were becoming a problem. He set out in the same direction he was heading before. He traveled for a few days and began to smell the sea, or something like it.

He traveled the last day and came to a city, which the sign said was called Nista. The name rang a bell, and he began to realize where he was. He couldn't connect it with anything in his life before the trauma, but the name was familiar.

He reached the gate and the guards looked at him as if they knew him. They also seemed to be concerned about him. "Sir Eldarin, are you okay?" They quickly parted to let him through, but were waiting for him to answer.

Somehow Eldarin managed not to hear the title, and just heard the name "Eldarin". "Yes, that does seem to be my name. Thank you." He paused. "I am doing better after knowing that."

The guards still seemed to be concerned and confused.

He traveled into the city a little bit and found some children staring at him oddly. "You know me? I seem to have lost my memory in the night."

The children giggled. "Really? Truly?"

"Yes. It is true."

One of the children came forward. He was a little red-haired boy with many freckles. He smiled and put on the most sincere face he could. He really hated Eldarin because he had given him problems in the past. This was a perfect chance to get even with the knight. He smiled and looked at all of his friends. Eldarin couldn't see, but the boy mouthed instructions to the rest of the kids and had the wickedest smirk on his face. He turned around with the most innocent face and started his great lie. He got on his knees, as did all the children. "You are the prince of this land of course, and you're looking for a...bride!" The little boy continued. "My sister is of age, and is the most beautiful girl in the land, your highness. Would you like me to introduce you?"

"Thank you child, that will not be necessary. You are free to go play now." Eldarin seemed to remember, that he did have an important station before his memory issue, perhaps the child spoke the truth.

The reactions of the people regarding him, gave him confirmation that he was indeed someone of importance. He thought that maybe he really could be royalty as he looked himself over. He managed to convince himself that he must be the prince. Only the prince would be dressed so richly. Unfortunately, he couldn't remember where his castle was. He knew the memories would come to him in time. He perked up, and began to act like a prince. He strolled through the city making an embarrassment of himself, but he had no idea it was one. The people loved and respected him too much to tell him otherwise, so they just dismissed his behavior. He strode through Nista acting like he felt a prince should act. He was not as nice or helpful to the homeless as he normally would be. His display through Nista caught the attention of many people. He had no clue that his behavior would get such a reaction from people.

As he went through the streets, a pretty woman came up to him and smiled at him. "Hello, my little prince. You have not been to see me in a bit. You should come over more often," she flirted.

"I'm sorry, what was your name?" He didn't recognize her, but thought he might recognize her name. She obviously knew him, and he wondered to what extent?

She looked at him with an odd expression. "Oh stop kidding around. You know I'm the only woman for you. That's what you tell me anyway." She winked at him and smiled a flirtatious smile.

He began to think that the children had been right about the bride thing as well. He thought that perhaps the woman before him was one of the women he was considering. He decided he would have to be fair though, so he decided to make it an event and choose from the best the city had to offer. He thought about how he could get that lovely blond he ran into on the road into the mix. He went through Nista and posted a bulletin that the prince was looking for a bride, and that the women of the city were to meet him at one of the inn and taverns he'd passed that looked nice. Then he would make a choice between the women.

\*\*\*

Arne awoke in the morning, and her leg was hurting even more. She could hardly take the pain without wanting to scream. She tried to move even a little, but she couldn't stand the pain that shot through her body. The best she could do was hope that someone would come along the road in a timely manner to help her. She thought about Irisel, Alltin, and Eldarin. She hoped they were okay. She would definitely look for them when she could. The first thing she needed was a nurse, and she wouldn't get that until someone came along to help her.

As she lay there, she began to hear the sound of horses and a wagon. She was so excited that she was saved that she could hardly contain herself. She temporarily forgot about her pain, and waved and moved around to try to get the driver's attention. She managed a few movements before the pain shot through her leg again, and she yelled out in pain. The cry caught Circe's attention and she stopped for Arne.

Arne saw a beautiful woman with long blond hair, and pretty blue eyes wearing a silky dress. She seemed to be decently well off, or spoiled, or both.

"Oh my, that leg looks terrible." Circe climbed off the wagon and helped Arnesti onto it. "My name is Circe."

"I'm Arnesti, but you can just call me Arne, everyone does."

The two chatted about each other on their way to Nista. Both ladies noticed the kindred bond shared between a select few. The two seemed to get along great, and had a lot in common. Circe was even more unpredictable than Arne was, to Arne's surprise.

Arne noticed Circe was slightly annoyed about something, and thought she'd inquire. "You seem annoyed, why?"

"A stupid idiot that thought me gullible to fall for his act so he could push one over on me." Circe was still annoyed. How could he not think that was the worst line ever?

Arne nodded in understanding. "Yeah, I hate that." She thought of Iri and wondered if Circe had seen her. My friend and I got separated. You can't miss her. She's the only one I know with green hair. Have you seen her?"

"No, can't say that I have. I would remember that for sure."

"What about a brunette male with the longest sword you've ever seen?"

"Nope, sorry."

Arne began to ask about Eldarin, when they hit a bump in the road, and pain wracked Arne's leg again. It interrupted Arne before she got the chance to describe Eldarin.

# Chapter 5: Memory Trouble

Arne and Circe weren't far from the city, and she took Arne straight to the hospice. The nurses kept her in the hospice for a few days to make sure Arne didn't have to stay in the hospice. The nurses cleaned her wounds, and wrapped her leg up stiffly to try to make the leg heal. They suggested that Arne try to take it easy, and stay off her leg as much as possible. Circe let Arne use her strength to get around when she needed to. Arne was so tired and ready to get out of the hospice that she was almost rushing Circe in helping her.

The two girls tried to get into the inn, and saw a huge line of women stretching around several blocks. Arne and Circe just looked at each other oddly, and saw that they needed to break through the line to get into the inn. They were both hoping that they would find out why there was such a huge line of women streaming out of and into the inn. The women were gathered like a swarm in their best clothing to impress. The innkeeper came up with the idea of them coming in by lesser numbers like two or three. Of course that led to a line that streamed through the city. The choosing began, and the first group of three women was confused when they saw that it was Eldarin looking for the bride. They figured that the prince was entrusting the choice to his best knight.

Woman after woman flaunted themselves in front of the knight-prince. Eventually Arne and Circe came through the line, though they weren't actually in the line of possible brides. The two women went to the innkeeper, and paid for two rooms and extra room service for Arne. After that was settled, they turned to see what the spectacle was all about. Arne saw Eldarin inspecting several women at a time. He was looking at their legs and breasts and sometimes touching the women as he inspected them.

Circe could see the idiot she saw along the road, and tried to get Arne up the stairs. Circe didn't expect to see the look on Arnesti's face over the situation. When she looked at Arne, she could see a fury of small bolts flashing in her eyes. She noticed Arne was looking directly at the idiot with that angry expression on her face. Circe decided to help Arne over to him, and anxiously awaited what Arne would do next. Waves of blue seemed to crash in Circe's eyes as she watched. No one in the crowd noticed either pair of eyes though. They were all paying much more attention to Eldarin.

Arne marched as well as she could over to Eldarin, and removed his hands off of someone's breasts forcefully. Before he could react, Arne slapped Eldarin across the face so hard, it even stung her hand. Eldarin was hit so hard he cried out. He could feel electricity flowing through his head, and it made him feel very strange. Circe smiled and helped Arne to her room. She knew Arne would have to calm down before Circe would spend any more time with her. Circe went to her own room, and relaxed in a bath.

Eldarin was reeling from Arne's blow to the head. It did help him though, because he remembered who Arne was, at least he remembered her name and face. Other than that he knew nothing about her. He wondered if she was going to be his bride, and he just ruined his chance with her. He asked the girls to wait there, and asked the innkeeper what room Arne was staying in. The innkeeper told him, and Eldarin went to find out who she was before he inspected any more women.

He knocked on her door and there was no answer, but he could hear someone cursing inside the room. He could literally hear lightning crackling inside the room. He opened the door, and found Arne in quite an angry state of mind.

She was so busy ranting to herself, that she had no idea he was in there. "How stupid I was! Son of a bitch, it was all a lie. All those things we said and did. How could I have been so stupid? This is what I get I guess, for actually trusting a man. I won't make that mistake again. Nor will I forget that scene downstairs for the rest of my life. He wouldn't even touch me like that! If I wasn't stuck here because of my leg, I'd just leave. I guess I'll be reporting to the trade guild myself. He will pay for this hurt." She put her head in her hands, sighed, and said, "I just want to go home."

He could see the fury crackle all over her body as she spoke of how angry she was at him. She still didn't notice he was standing in the room. Watching her and hearing her voice brought back his memory of her and his relationship with her, but nothing about himself that he hadn't already figured out. He realized what she saw, and didn't blame her for being so angry with him. She began to cry as her anger turned to sadness, and he felt horrible for what he had just put her through.

He decided to be brave and make his presence known to her. "Arne, how did you injure your leg?"

She turned around and her eyes were furious and sad all at once. She was so emotional that she couldn't do anything, but look at him. If she said one word, the tears would flow out. If she moved toward him, she would hit him again. It would be a much harder and much more painful strike this time. Her silence and the look in her eyes spoke volumes.

Eldarin could feel the increase of energy in the room and it made the hair on his arm stand up. "I'm sorry for what you saw downstairs."

She turned her back to him and tried to ignore his presence. It didn't work. But the silent treatment was all she was willing to do at that moment.

He took the hint, and realized he made a huge blunder. The only right thing to do in his mind was to make all of those women go back to their homes. He felt a sadness, and wasn't fully sure why yet.

Eldarin exited her room, went downstairs, and asked all of the women to go home. The women were disappointed, and asked him if he wanted them to return the next day. He just said he would make that decision another day. He apologized that they wasted their valuable time, only to leave early. They reluctantly left and went back to their homes.

Circe, Arne and Eldarin didn't speak to each other the rest of the day or evening. Arne knew she had to calm down before confronting him again, but his actions were not easily forgivable. She really wanted to find Irisel and go home. Eldarin spent the evening trying to remember things from his past. He especially wanted to remember more about Arnesti.

They awoke in the morning, and Arnesti ate quickly. Circe helped her get around.

"Circe, would you like to travel to Faulkton with me?" Arne invited.

Circe had vaguely heard of Faulkton. She had never been there, but she knew a lot of sea trade occurred there. She had to go over the sea to get to her destination anyway. "Sure. That sounds like just what I need." Circe ate her breakfast and was about to leave to reprovision her supplies, when Eldarin came down.

Both girls were unaware he had come down. Circe left Arne at the table to gather supplies. They were to leave after Circe returned. Eldarin spotted Arne immediately and saw the moody, beautiful blond leave the inn. Eldarin took his chance to speak to Arnesti. She saw him as soon as he approached her. She shot him an angry look.

"Arne, might I speak with you, in private?"

She didn't know why, but she agreed reluctantly.

He tried to help her up to his room, but she made it clear that she didn't want him touching her for any reason. "Don't touch me," she hissed. She was having a difficult time getting around, and he helped her out anyway.

"You need help, my lady."

"Not from you," she protested. "And I'm not your lady anymore. Say it again and I hit you again." She looked for someone else to assist her, but no one seemed to respond.

He took her to his room and stood between her and the door. She glared at him. He could see white flashes in her eyes as she stared at him. "We need to talk, Arne."

She continued to glare.

"I woke up, not too long ago, not knowing who or where I was. I've been trying to piece everything together since, and mostly by myself. Some people like the guards and a child who seemed to pull a prank on me at the worst time have been my only clues as to who I am. I encounter that blond woman, and she was basically no help."

Arne realized why Circe was so annoyed the day they met. Arne was now starting to chuckle as Eldarin kept explaining.

"The guards tell me my name; let me know who I am at least. I go into town and this kid thinks it's funny to tell me I'm the prince, in town looking for a wife to share the throne. I saw nothing to tell me that he was wrong. From my clothing to the reactions of the people around me, it all seemed to be plausible."

Arne was laughing aloud at that point, listening to the ridiculous story he convinced himself of. Funny kid if it's true.

He looked at her oddly, but kept on telling her his story. "I only recognized you after you walked up to me and hit me, while I was looking for my wife. I could remember bits and pieces of you, and came after you to clarify things. I felt horrible after hearing how much my actions hurt you. And I released the women after our last encounter." He paused. "I'm asking you to forgive me for what angered you last night, because I did not know I was doing anything wrong when you came in. If you are the woman I was with, then I ask you if you will share my throne?"

Arne was laughing hysterically after he finished his last question.

"What is so funny?"

She couldn't answer him. She finally calmed down enough to talk to him. She just smiled at him, nearly laughing again, and said, "You have diplomatic issues to deal with before such a thing is even possible."

"I will do anything you ask of me to make up for the hurt I have caused you, my lady."

She chuckled and said, "Your Highness' has to get ready for sea travel in a few hours."

He came up to her and kneeled in front of her. He took her hand and kissed it. "As you wish", was all he said, before he left to gather supplies.

Arne burst with laughter after he left the room and intended to make him pay for his actions. She vowed to have fun with it though. She saw no harm in letting him believe he was the prince. She would have fun with his delusions. The energy in the room had calmed down from what it was. It was turned into a different kind of energy as her mood changed.

Eldarin went to the store and ran into Circe. She eyed him like a hawk as they were in the store together. He gathered what he needed and went over to her. "I apologize for any odd behavior on the road. I did not mean to scare you upon entering your camp. I have since realized my identity, and if you are going to be traveling with Arne, then we will all be traveling together. I did not get your name before. My name is Eldarin, my lady."

She smirked at him. "That's better. I am Circe." She was surprised that Arne was letting him go with them, but if she forgave him for whatever he did wrong, then Circe supposed it would be okay. She recognized the name Eldarin, from remembering Arne asking if she had seen him on the road. Circe chuckled a bit over the coincidence and paid for the things she gathered, as did Eldarin.

Circe talked to Eldarin as they went back to the inn to get Arne. Arne was ready and waiting for them to return, though she didn't expect them to travel around town together. She found it humorous. They were ready to leave, and left promptly. Circe was surprised to find a huge smile upon Arne's face as they traveled. Arne didn't stop smiling. The three of them boarded a ship that Circe had apparently arranged for. They were going to be riding on the Urchin with Captain Erinnt. Circe apparently knew him from before. Circe spent a lot of time talking to the captain.

Arne entertained herself with Eldarin's "discoveries" about himself. They kept her laughing and smiling for a while. He helped her around the ship and when her leg became too painful, she was taken below to lie down and rest. "Prince" Eldarin stayed by her side while they were ocean bound. He tried to kiss her a few times and she pulled away, saying, "I'm not ready for that yet. You will have to prove to me that you can be trusted around other women. Last thing I want to deal with is other women showing up with your children. It wouldn't look good to your people or mine."

He did as she asked him to.

They spent close to three weeks at sea and they barely got anywhere. The winds weren't cooperating with the ship. They didn't have Irisel to create winds either. Eventually, they came to a point in time when the winds were not blowing for days. When the winds did blow, it wasn't much at all. The ship ended up landing near a small tropical island out in the middle of nowhere. They exited the ship to have a look around while the winds weren't cooperating. They spent a few days on the island and the winds finally began to pick up.

When they tried to set sail again, the ship wouldn't budge. It didn't seem to be caught on anything, but it wouldn't move. The ship seemed to be held magically near the island. They went searching more thoroughly to find out why they couldn't leave. They went around the edge of the island first. It was mostly low-lying beaches, with some high cliffs. The inside of the island seemed to have higher land, hills and uplands. All they could see was ocean all around. It took them just a few hours to walk around it. They ventured inland to find answers after that.

# Chapter 6: Circe

Circe grew up in Oceansport. It was on an island out in the middle of the Paranj Ocean, sometimes called the Middle Ocean. Oceansport was a once thriving town until a wave of darkness took the island over. Most of the people died on that day. Circe was only 3 when the Day of Darkness came. A group of dark half-shadowy creatures dressed in black and red clothing came with the wave of darkness and slaughtered most of the townsfolk. Circe was able to survive by hiding in the water until the conflict was over.

Her mother and father were killed in the conflict. Her father was a notorious pirate in his younger days, and her mother a noblewoman from a distant land. Neither parent ever spoke of specifics. They didn't want anyone to know they were together. Her father, with the help of her mother, got their hands on a rare stone that was made into a talisman. It was created away from the island and her father kept it with him always. One day he gave it to his only daughter and told her to guard it with her life. She did the best she could. Her father ended up always getting attacked by others who wanted his talisman. They could never find it.

She later found out that the item the dark minions were searching for was the black opal talisman that had been given to Circe to protect. She was to keep it with her always and never let a terrible creature called Tarax take it from her. As she grew up, she was hunted by his dark minions who sought the talisman. She had always managed to keep it safe, but it meant that she was always on the run. If she stayed in one spot too long, she would be found and have to run away again.

As time went by, she kept running into a boy as young as she was who was always looking for something. He was evil, but had extraordinary powers. She was able to befriend him after meeting a few times. The two began to form a bond and soon turned into love. She and transporting were his only loves in the world. He would never tell anyone, but he must have had a terrible childhood because he hated the world so much. Only Circe and his powers were dependable according to him.

He searched tirelessly for an item that his lord desperately needed. The boy never found it, even though it was with him always. She realized eventually that the item her love was searching for was what she wore around her neck. He too searched for her talisman. She never told him for fear of how he would react towards her. The day came that the two of them thought of marriage. They were only interested in something quick and something that wouldn't cause too much attention to themselves. They decided to have the wedding on Oceansport Island. He even had a house built on the island especially for her.

The wedding went off without any trouble, until the night came. It was time for them to consummate the marriage. Circe tried to hide the talisman before her husband came into the room, but her worst fears came true. As she tried to take it off, he walked in and saw what he searched for his entire life. When she realized he saw her, she kept it close to her and they stared at each other.

He didn't know what to say. His love, his wife had lied to him their whole life together. She knew he searched for it and she purposefully hid it from him under the guise of love. He became furious at her for the life-long lie and struck her. He tried to take the talisman away from her, but she held on tight. He struck her again, this time drawing blood on her face. He acted like a beast and hit her several more times before she could get away from him. She finally dove out of the window of their home and ran to the cliff nearby.

He followed her threatening her and yelling at her as he chased her. She pleaded with him to stop, but he would not. She was on the edge of the cliff and he ran towards her. The two struggled as they fell to the water. He never got his talisman, and they were separated by the sting and force of the water. She sunk into the water and he barely made it to shore. He couldn't swim so he almost drowned. He waited for her to surface, but she never did.

He mourned her and his lost item. He loved her and felt guilty for killing her. He knew he could never go into the water to search for either of them. He went on with his life, all the while having nightmares of the look of fear and bloodied wounds from his hands on Circe's face as he tried to kill her. As far as he knew, he succeeded.

But he didn't succeed in killing her. Since she could manipulate water, she could breathe underwater. She made her way west, which was away from the island and her husband. A young man on a ship sailing by her found her. The boy, Erinnt, was a ship hand on the Urchin. They became friends and the ship took her to Terrah. She had some relatives that her family supposedly had in a nearby town. She went to stay with them for a little while until the creatures began to hunt her again. This time, little green creatures were sent from Tarax. She never saw her husband again. She kept on the move to keep the creatures away from her only known family left. She sailed to the east again to get away from the hordes of goblins after her. Through her travels, she never spoke of her husband to anyone, and tried to move on with her life as best she could.

## Chapter 7: The Island and Separations

Eldarin, Circe, and Arnesti went to investigate the inner island for clues as to why the Urchin couldn't move. The inner part of the island had many trees and vines. It appeared as if the island had been untouched for some time. Circe recognized some of the plants as those that grew on her island. She didn't share that information with the others though. They went farther in and found there to be caves in the area. There were also odd markers on the trees around them.

Circe froze when she saw the marks. Her eyes went wide and she could feel fear and sadness rushing over her. The place had changed so much since she was last on her island, that she hardly recognized it. She knew what those markings were. She was flooded with emotion and ran back to the beach. Erinnt, who was staying with the ship, didn't notice her come back to the beach, but Eldarin and Arne did.

"Eldarin, wait here by the cave. I'm going to check on her," Arne said.

Circe tried to regain her composure, but it was extremely difficult. Fear and sadness had washed over her, making her remember the night so long ago. It was a night that should've been the best in her life, but instead was the worst night ever. Arne came up behind Circe, and could see her rocking herself back and forth with her head in her hands. Arne could tell something was seriously wrong.

She came up next to Circe and sat down. She put her arm around her and tried to comfort her, even though she had no idea why Circe was so upset. Neither girl spoke for a while, and eventually Eldarin came up to them. He had enough of waiting for them. He saw that there was some kind of moment between the girls, so he went over to talk to Erinnt. Erinnt had no clue that Eldarin came up to him, and it startled him. Erinnt looked around and then saw how upset Circe was. He remembered the day they found her. She was just as sad, though at that time, her face was black, blue, and bloodied from wounds on it.

Erinnt apologized to Eldarin for not being able to talk to him at the moment, and ran over to Circe. With all of the attention she was getting, she broke into tears. Erinnt took over for Arne in comforting Circe. Circe wrapped her arms around him and wouldn't let go. Arne got up and shrugged to Eldarin. She and Eldarin went off together down the beach. The searching of the island had temporarily stopped for the rest of the day and evening.

Erinnt was deeply concerned about Circe. He completely and vividly remembered the day they found her in the water. She was so scared and hurt. Even though her face was black and blue and she was so scared, he fell in love with her that day. He knew she wasn't interested in a relationship. She already told him that years ago, but he still loved her. He always would. He vowed that whenever they were together, that no harm would ever come to her. He hated to see her cry. He learned to settle for being just a friend years ago, and he vowed to be her best friend. She knew that she could count on him if she needed him. She needed him on the beach that evening on the island. They didn't speak to each other. He just did all he could to calm her down and make her feel safe, like he did before.

The next morning they all awoke and prepared to face the cave. Circe put on a brave face and tried to act like nothing happened. Erinnt was concerned about Circe and was determined to go with them to the cave. He wouldn't let Circe talk him out of it. She was glad he was going with them. They went into the cave and found it to be just one large cavern chamber. The ceiling was approximately forty feet up, and as they looked around, they found there was a gemstone in the ceiling. The only way they could figure out how to get it down was to go above it and dig.

They did just that and in no time, the gem was free from the ceiling and they went inside to retrieve it. It was a deep blue sapphire with white sparkles inside the stone. When Circe went to the dig area, she could see the ruins of the house she and her husband made. It saddened her, but she tried to be strong. She turned her back on the ruins and suggested that they test the gem to see if it was what was keeping their ship near the island.

The closer they got to the ship, the more the ship was able to move. They were all excited about it and left as soon as they could. Circe was glad to get off of the island and away from her past. It still hurt her too much to deal with the trauma. She was relieved to be back out to sea. She loved the water. It was safe for her. It kept her alive when she needed it the most, twice. She went to her room on the ship. She decided to go to her mirror and look at what had given her so much grief. She pulled the talisman out and stared at it. Sometimes she felt like it was trying to talk to her. It can't because it is just an item, she thought, but sometimes it seemed like it could.

She placed it back under her dress as the ship began to slow down and she could hear calls from above about an approaching ship. She decided to stay in her room for the moment. The ship was a guild ship. Arne was so happy to see them. The two ships joined for the rest of the day and evening. Arne told the ship hands that Irisel and Alltin were presumed dead. There was no word or sign of them after the storm. To Arne's surprise, the crew didn't say anything about Eldarin. They should have reacted in someway, but they were just happy to see Arne.

There was a party that night that lasted until the morning and the guild ship had to take off again. Arne and Eldarin went to say goodbye to Circe. The goodbyes were said and Arne and Eldarin set off with the guild ship. Circe told them that she would join them, but she had to do something first. The ship was out of sight in no time and Circe was happy to still be on the Urchin. She felt safe there. She knew Erinnt liked her, but she wasn't ready for a serious relationship. She already tried it, and it didn't work out. She knew Erinnt wouldn't try to kill her, but she still couldn't bring herself to be with someone again like that. She knew Erinnt was okay with just being friends.

It took the Urchin just three more weeks to reach Terrah. Circe planned with Erinnt about meeting her on the coastline just east of Tumir in six days and then sailing to Faulkton to meet up with Arne and Eldarin. Erinnt was more than happy to help Circe as much as she needed it. Circe got off the ship once at Terrah and went through town to the inn and tavern. On her way she ran into a guy who wasn't watching where he was going. She wasn't in the mood for another jerk. She got up and went to the inn. Now she had to get cleaned up. Not long after she settled in, the jerk that ran into her knocked at her door. She decided to toy with him a little and ended up having a little more fun than she'd had in a while. Unfortunately, she couldn't spend much time with him. She had to get to her relatives. She was sick and tired of being driven and controlled by the damned talisman, that she was going to pass it on to her family.

She ran into the jerk again after their night of satisfying urges. He wanted her to go with him, but she couldn't. She had things to do. She was sure she would see him again, but she hoped he knew that it was just for one night. She would not trap herself like she did before. She gathered everything she needed and left Terrah. She was off to visit her Aunt Vivian and Uncle Edward in Tumir. It took four days to get to her destination.

When she got to her aunt and uncle's house they were happy to see her. She told them that she couldn't stay for long and that she needed to pass something very valuable on to the family. She finally gave the talisman over to someone else. It felt like a ton of weight had been lifted from her spirit. She felt free for once in her life, finally. Circe stayed the night and left in the morning to go meet up with the Urchin. She planned on having Erinnt take her to Faulkton. She knew Erinnt would be just as happy for her as she was. She was finally happy.

It took a day to get to the coastline and meet up with Erinnt. She felt like she didn't have to rush or run anymore. She ran into no one on her way to the coast. She had to cut through the forest to get to the coast. It rained a few times, but she loved water, so she didn't mind at all. She hurried to the Urchin as soon as the ship was in sight. She swam some of the way and rode in a boat the rest of the way.

She noticed that Erinnt was anxious to see her again. He always seemed to worry about her, especially after the island incident. The urchin set sail again as soon as she was aboard. It would take a while to get to Faulkton.

\*\*\*

The guild ship sailed home to Faulkton. The guild members on the ship were acting strangely. They should have given Eldarin more attention, be it good or bad. They didn't pay much attention to him at all. When Arne talked to them they acted just as strange. It was almost if the crew was under some sort of trance or something. Arne couldn't place why they were behaving so oddly. The ship sailed west for sixteen days and on the seventeenth day the ship stopped at a port that Arne didn't recognize. The crew was too busy to talk to her, as they were unloading supplies. With Eldarin's help, she asked some people in town and found out they had stopped in Nautica.

Nautica was a port city north of Faulkton, but it was part of the same kingdom as Faulkton. The city was considerably dirtier and rough looking. It looked as if it had seen some battle recently. No one in town would talk about the damage though. Arne and Eldarin just went back to the ship and stayed there until the ship set sail again. It only took a few hours to take care of business and the ship was again underway.

It took the ship three more weeks to get home with the wind being as temperamental as it was. Iri wasn't there to push it along again, so the ship was stopped several times due to a lack of wind.

The ship encountered a few storms along the way and the ship had some damage that needed to be repaired. That kept the ship stationary for a few days as well. The ship finally arrived in Faulkton and the crew and passengers were met at the docks by guards. The guards wore altered symbols of station and were acting just as strangely as the crew. The crew was free to leave without problem but Arne and Eldarin were taken into custody and told that Lady Mel wanted to see them right away.

Arne wasn't happy about it and Eldarin was rather nervous. He could sense Arne's vibe and he wasn't sure of what to make of things. He went willingly to see Lady Mel since it was customary for him to do for relations wherever he went. Arne didn't like the thought of seeing the spoiled brat so soon. Arne had a feeling she was up to something. The guards asked where Irisel was, and Arne told them Irisel was missing, and possibly dead. The guards showed little change of facial expression to the news. Arne expected more reaction. She was sure something was going on.

The guards took the two of them to the palace. Arne noticed the altered symbol on all of the guards. She looked at her surroundings intently as they went to the palace. The guards took them inside. Arne noticed that none of the guards said anything to her. There were no "welcome home's" from anyone as she passed. The guards escorted the two into the throne room and shut and barred the door behind them. Arne and Eldarin were both on edge by that point. Neither one knew what was about to happen.

Moments later, Mel walked into the room. She was dressed much more richly than she had been and wore the same altered symbol. She sat down slowly to prolong the two guest's discomfort. After she got comfortable, she spoke.

Arne interrupted her. "Is Lord Fadel going to join this discussion?"

Mel shot her a vicious glance and demanded that Arne be silent. "If you do not, I will have you gagged otherwise." Arne was taken aback by the venomous command. Arne could tell that Mel wasn't joking about the threat and remained silent.

Mel spoke again, this time uninterrupted. "Lord Fadel has passed on while you were gone. Now I am in charge. One of the men from the Harand Kingdom killed him while Alltin was away and the other knights were bed ridden." Mel shot an evil glance at Eldarin. "I demand you explain why you have brought the enemy here," asking Arne.

Eldarin spoke up. "I am the prince of Harand, and I am unaware that such an atrocity had occurred. I am deeply apologetic to you, Lady Mel, for such events upon your region."

"I am not interested in your apology or your ignorance. You will remain silent as well," she said with another venomous toned command.

He did as she asked and lowered his head.

"Arnesti, you consort with and harbor the enemy, the punishment for traitors is death."

Arnesti's eyes grew wide as she tried to protest her fate. She was again silenced by Mel and saw guards coming towards her with a gag in their hands.

"Before you die, I demand to know where Irisel and Alltin are."

"They are missing and most likely dead," Arne informed her.

Mel looked disappointed for some reason.

Arne figured that she was probably disappointed that she wouldn't get to punish Irisel for stealing Alltin away.

Mel stood up and addressed the guards. "Take hold of the prisoners."

The guards moved towards the two.

A male voice from an unseen location spoke up. "Stop."

The guards did as commanded.

Mel looked over towards the voice and looked confused at the command.

## Chapter 8: Confirmations

The throne chamber was silent as the man in silver and black strode in. The guards obeyed his command over Melissant's. Arne had never seen the man before but he wore the coronet that Lord Fadel used to wear. Eldarin was still surprised at the news that Mel had told them. He tried to be as respectful as he could.

Mel turned to the man in silver and black. "Why did you tell them to stand down? I would see justice for my father's murder."

The man responded coolly, "Calm yourself Melissant. There is plenty of time for you to see justice." He walked up to one of the thrones and sat next to Mel. "I am Lord Quantis, Lady Melissant's newly wedded husband."

Arne couldn't say anything due to the shock of the news. Quantis noticed and smirked at her. It wasn't the kind of reaction she wanted. His smirk sent chills up her spine.

Mel noticed the look and became jealous. She tried to get her husband's attention away from Arne by asking him, "Why do you insist I wait for justice?"

He turned to his wife and could tell what was happening. Quantis patted her hand and told her, "It will happen soon enough, my dear. You must be more patient."

Mel took it offensively and shot him an angry look. "I demand vengeance now, this moment. Guards, kill the traitor and her murderous companion."

"Stand down," Quantis repeated. The guards listened to Quantis and stood down again.

Melissant was furious by then and was about to unleash a mighty fury upon her husband.

He excused his wife and himself and pulled Mel off to a side chamber. Arne looked for a way to escape, but could find none by the time the two came back from the side chamber. Mel was still angry, but she was obviously trying to hold her tongue.

"Guards, take the prisoners into the dungeon and lock them in a cell together," Quantis ordered. The guards obeyed and took the two into custody. They were about to leave the room when he ordered them to halt momentarily.

Quantis could feel the energy running through Arne and knew that she had special powers as well. He walked over to her and placed a pair of bracelets on her wrists. He then gave them leave to take the prisoners away. Arne could feel all of her mental energy draining after he placed the bracelets on her wrists. She tried, but couldn't command her powers to do anything. She was truly scared for what would happen to her and Eldarin without the use of her powers.

The guards escorted the two into the dungeon and placed them in a cell. It was cold and damp and stunk from former prisoners. The guards shackled their feet to the wall and left them. They went back up to the door and stood guard there.

"I am so sorry for this welcome to Faulkton, Eldarin. It was not like this when we left here. And now I'm wishing we were somewhere else." She sounded sad for the situation.

"I am truly confused, and do not know what I should do. I do not think anything I say will get us out of this." Eldarin had added confusion to his existing confusion.

All they could do was wait for something to happen. Arne never thought that her end would happen at the hands of Mel. She tried not to get upset, but it wasn't working. Between, Irisel missing and nearing death by her worst enemy, she couldn't stop the breakdown. Tears began slowly coming from her eyes. Eldarin held her close as she wept. It was all he could do to be of any help.

The two of them were in the cell for a few days at least, when the guards finally came down and unlocked the door. There were several more guards than had escorted them down into the dungeon. They had firm grips on the prisoners and made sure the two could not escape. They unshackled the legs and took the prisoners back up to the throne room to face the noble couple.

Quantis and Mel sat in the thrones and watched as the prisoners were brought before them.   Both looked happy about the day's events to come. Mel smirked at Arne and Eldarin as she sat there.  She loved seeing Arne so worried and distraught.  She smiled at her husband and held his hand.  He smirked back at Mel and waited for everyone to get in their proper places around the room.  When all was silent again, Mel spoke to the prisoners.

"Your big day has arrived. It will be quick and painless."

Quantis let his wife have her moment of justice and stayed silent until she was finished gloating.  After she finished, he announced, "The execution of the prisoners will commence momentarily.  It will take place publicly so that the people can see justice done."

The noble couple motioned for the guards to ready themselves to escort the prisoners to their proper place.  They walked out of the room and the guards followed with the prisoners.  At one intersection in the palace, the couple separated from the troop of guards.  The guards led the prisoners outside to the execution site.  Mel and Quantis were on a balcony up above and were speaking to the people about the execution.  Arne and Eldarin were taken to stumps and tied down so their necks were lined up with the top of the stumps.  A large man with an axe came up and prepared.  The man was making sure the blade was sharp enough.  The two could hear him sharpening it further.  Arne couldn't help but wonder where Hanmel was during this whole time.  Surely he'd heard the news?  If he was able to, he would try to save her.

\*\*\*

The Urchin arrived in Faulkton to find there were very few people around. Circe was rather confused, but dismissed it as anything bad.

"Please be careful, Circe. I will await your return," said Erinnt.

She smiled at him and thanked him.  She tried not to let on that her gut feelings were going wild.  She had no idea why, but her stomach was in knots.

Circe ventured out into the city and searched for anyone to help her.  She finally managed to find someone to ask what was going on.  The citizen told her that there was a public execution taking place at the palace. The man told her that she should hurry if she wanted to witness it. Circe took his advice and went to the palace. It was easy enough to spot from the docks since it sat on the top of a hill.

She saw a large crowd of people gathered around the palace. There were so many people trying to get in that it was moving very slowly. As she tried to get in, she was becoming more and more impatient. Then she heard something that made her heart and body freeze.

"Ladies and gentlemen, your lord and lady, Quantis and Melissant!"

Circe froze in place and began to hyperventilate. The townsfolk paid no attention to her as she struggled to gain composure. Her body was fighting the initial urge to run while it was frozen.

The crowd was pushing her further in so they could get in and witness the execution. She made it in and tried to get against a wall to stabilize herself. She then heard the couple announce the execution of the traitor Arnesti and the murderer from Harand, Prince Eldarin. Circe became very concerned and it wasn't helping her recover from the state she was in. She couldn't move. She couldn't even look up to confirm her worst fears. Then she didn't need to look up to confirm her fears.

Quantis spoke about the execution and his voice pierced through the hard shell she built around her heart, and went straight on through to stab at it some more.

She could hear the prisoners being escorted out and saw them being tied up. People started to notice Circe and her fit. She began to catch a lot of attention from the spectators. All she could think to do was to run away as fast as she could before he noticed her there. It was too late for her to run though, and she couldn't move if she wanted to. Her body was reacting to the presence of Him nearby, and it was impossible for her to act at all.

Mel noticed the worst look on someone's face that she had ever seen. Her husband was wearing it very clearly. His eyes were wide and fury raged in his expression. He was surprised and very angry for some reason. He couldn't even speak even though he clearly wanted to say something. Mel tried to get her husband's attention, but he was in his own zone. She couldn't reach him no matter how hard she tried. She finally asked the guards to take him to his room where he could rest for a moment.

The guards reluctantly went to get a hold of him and had to drag him with them. Quantis was frozen in place as well. His gaze was stuck on Her, the deceiver. The guards got him inside and Mel followed them in to find out what was wrong with her husband. Circe could feel his gaze upon her and was relieved when he wasn't staring at her any longer. She forced herself to take her chance to free the other two. She made her body move and pushed her way through the crowd to the front. She used her powers to create a barrier of water around the prisoners and made it expand outward to force the people to move. She then untied the prisoners with her hands and helped them make a break for the ship. Circe used her powers to keep the stunned crowd at bay.

The group of them made it to the Urchin and Erinnt. When the group got there, Erinnt was very concerned for Circe. She was very pale and shaking violently. He didn't know how she was able to move at all. She told him in a quivering voice, "You need to set sail immediately!"

He ordered his men onto the ship quickly and they worked as fast as they could to get the ship underway immediately.

Once the ship was away from Faulkton, the concerned captain rushed to Circe's side. He had never seen her like that and wasn't sure what he could possibly do to make it better. He asked the others what happened because Circe was in a trance and not responding to his questioning. Arne told him what happened to them and how Circe saved them. Arne still didn't know why Circe was reacting the way she was.

Erinnt took Circe to his room and sat her on the bed. Her body was shaking intensely and the look on her face was frightening him. He tried to comfort her as best he could when a knock came on his door. Circe jumped at the knock and looked frantic. He tried to calm her as he told the person to enter. One of his men came in and told him that they were being pursued by Faulkton ships. He regretted leaving Circe alone, but he had to.

# Chapter 9: Searching

Alltin and Irisel thought about where they were going to go. Irisel didn't know where her best friend was or if she was okay. She still wanted to find Arne. Alltin was worried that Arne was possibly in the company of Eldarin. He wasn't fond of him ever since he saw the way Eldarin questioned Irisel. In Alltin's mind, Eldarin was disrespectful to her. He didn't like the tone he was using. It was no way to act towards their princess if Eldarin indeed suspected it. Alltin was concerned about Arne though. He was fond of her, but just as a possible friend. He knew that Irisel would go crazy if they didn't find her soon. They were inseparable, yet now separated friends. He didn't think either girl was faring well on that fact.

"We should find another coastal city traveling south," Alltin suggested. He was thinking that Nista would be close, probably within a few towns. They gathered food and necessities for the road and began their travel along the coast. It was beautiful oceanside. They were traveling along a long cliff that rose and fell in height as they traveled. There were no people on the road with them. They could hear the sea birds calling as they walked. The ocean waves crashed lightly on rocks out along the shore in the water. The waves were steady and lulling. By the time evening came, they were tired just from listening to the waves. They watched the sunset together as they set up camp. The sky was pink and purple and was quite a stunning sight from what they were use to seeing. The two fell asleep leaning on each other.

Morning came and they ate and quickly got underway. They traveled another day without incident other than a peddler traveling with his wagon. He stopped and they looked at his goods. They bought extra blankets since the nights were a bit chilly. The peddler also tried to sell them talismans and potions, but the two refused since they didn't see anything they liked. He went on his way, thanking them for their business before leaving.

"I must confess that I thought about purchasing something for you, my lady, but you didn't seem to see anything you liked," Alltin confessed.

She smiled at him, but said nothing.

Along the way, Irisel didn't speak much. She was concerned about something, which Alltin figured was about her best friend.

"We will find Arne if we have to search the entire world, my lady. Do not worry.

She smiled at him again and squeezed his hand in response. He held her hand as they walked and they watched the sunset again in the evening.

They awoke and set off again. They made it a few hours and Irisel spotted a cavern in the cliff ahead. "Do you want to check it out?" Irisel thought it sounded like fun.

"My lady, I am following you. Wherever you go, I go."

She took his hand and led him down to it. There was an easy path to it, so they didn't risk falling or injuring themselves. Alltin followed her as she jogged down to it. She seemed excited about checking the cave out. In her experience, there was usually treasure to be had in cave like that one.

The entrance was large enough for a small boat to get through. The water had formed quite the cavern at the base of the cliff. The first chamber was a grand room with a large lake of water in the center. There were several tunnels leading off of the right hand side of the main chamber. She was in awe of the first room when Alltin asked her, "Which way do you want to explore?"

She had a childish smile on her face that he had rarely seen before. "I've always wanted to go exploring caves like this one," she confessed. "My father would never let me go off with the other ships though. He was just protecting me from scoundrels, I know that. I saw several scoundrels come into town on the ships, and Hanmel would often ask me to stay in the house when they were rowdy in the streets."

"Your father cares a lot about you, my lady." Alltin thought of home and missed it. "We will get a ship to Faulkton when we arrive in Nista. I am certain we are sorely missed. We have been gone for some time now."

"I think we take the center one on the right," Irisel said distracted by the cave.

They had to cross a shallow stream leading to the small lake of water. Alltin picked her up so she wouldn't get her shoes wet yet. He set her down once they got to the dry side. Irisel walked towards the entrance in the center of the right-hand side wall and used some of her power in the main chamber just to hear the wind howl through the cavern. She chuckled and went into the natural corridor that led into a small cavern. Alltin lit a torch so they could see further down into the cavern offshoots.

The center of the room had a shallow pool of water and there were blue and green crabs living in the chamber. There were two smaller exits from the room. The tunnel on the left seemed to have a steep wet slope that looked dangerous to travel through. The other was the same level as the small cavern they were still in, so Irisel suggested going through the opening on the right. Going through the opening, she saw the tunnel immediately split off into four tunnels leading in different directions. She looked at Alltin as if it were his decision on which direction to go. The furthest tunnel on the right seemed the best way to go in his mind.

They went through, this time Alltin decided that it wasn't safe for Irisel to go into the chambers first, so he took point and decided he would just ask her which way she wanted to go. He didn't want her getting hurt in the caves. He held her hand going through the tunnels so that if she hit a slick spot, he would be able to keep a hold of her. Irisel didn't mind the holding of her hand at all. She was becoming rather fond of it actually. They went through the tunnel and in came into another small cavern. The tunnel continued at the end of the chamber with no other exits.

They followed on through and came to an intersection with another tunnel. Alltin could see the light from the main chamber coming from the right entrance to the tunnel. Irisel wanted to go left and further into the caverns. Alltin led her as she asked and the tunnel came into a slightly larger cavern than the small ones they had passed through. There were more shallow puddles of water in the cavern. There was some sort of symbol on the wall opposite of the tunnel entrance into the room. It looked like the symbol went onto the ground but it was covered by the sand and water. They couldn't read the bottom of the symbol. There were some sea birds in the cavern and they scattered as soon as the two entered the doorway. There were some nests along the tops of the wall where some outcroppings were. The two headed back to the four-way split in the tunnel and took the next to the left.

That tunnel went approximately eighty feet and ended in a deep-water pool. Neither wanted to swim down, so they went back and took the next passage over. It was approximately eighty feet as well and ended in another small cavern. There were rock pillars in here and a few shallow pools of water. The cavern had several more symbols that neither of them could decipher. Alltin thought about the symbols for a few minutes and remembered what they were. Irisel hadn't seen them before that she could remember.

Alltin told Iri, "Those symbols are associated with a certain group of pirates that I read about. They are the Black Skulls, and they have stolen quite a bit of wealth from the king." Alltin spoke of his own king, the one ruling over Fadel. There were rumors of the group disappearing with the king in the raid, but he had heard from Fadel that it was a lie and that the king was safe in his home. Alltin always wondered which the truth was, but there was no way he could find out. Alltin got excited that he might get his answer exploring the caverns.

"What happened to the pirates after they took the money?" Iri asked.

"The last time the Bloody Charger was seen, it was further north and a few years ago. The Bloody Charger was their ship and was said to be one of the fastest ships in the land. I hope we find it somewhere here in the cavern. If the ship is intact, it would be a great asset to us."

Iri hoped that he would at least get his answers about what happened to the king.

They took the last tunnel split and after fifty feet of curving tunnel there was a sharp drop, but the tunnel continued downward after the drop. The tunnel below was dark and neither of them could see down below to see how it ended up. Alltin had a feeling that there was something great down that tunnel but he didn't want to get either of them injured by going down there yet. "Perhaps, my lady, we explore other tunnels first."

Iri agreed, and they went out to the main cavern again.

They went over to the last opening on the right-hand side of the main cavern. It was the only one left to check on that side before having to cross the lake again. The last tunnel led in to a sizeable cavern with water in the middle of the room. There were more symbols on the walls, but they weren't in good condition. He could hardly tell what they were. Between the sea life and the water, the symbols were unreadable. He suggested heading back over the water to the other side of the cavern. Iri agreed and he carried her over the shallow part near the entrance again.

She chuckled at him. "I don't think you really want to put me down," she joked and smiled.

He smiled at her in return. "Do you want me to set you down, my lady?"

She smiled but didn't say anything.

He set her down after crossing and they went to a large cavern opening. There was a large cavern wall with pillars blocking the view of whatever was inside the next cavern. They went around the cavern wall and pillars and saw two ships. One of the ships had browned horns on the front of the ship. "That, my lady, is the Bloody Charger," he said with excitement. "I do not recognize the other one," pointing at a slightly smaller ship.

There was a large exit to the huge cavern. It was clearly the way the ships got in the caves. Irisel spotted another smaller exit from the cavern to her right. "We should check that out before boarding the ships," she suggested.

Alltin agreed and they went to check out the other way. It opened into a cavern and as they crossed a certain point, they heard a heavy thud. Neither of them expected to run into a trap and were surprised as a huge boulder that had been hanging above crashed between them and the entrance to the small cavern. The way was completely blocked and the cavern became pitch black instantly.

Irisel clung to Alltin's hand and mentioned, "I think I saw some chests at the end of the chamber."

"My lady, we have other things to worry about. I have a torch that can help us see, but if our air is cut off now, lighting it will eat up our air."

"I can try to force it aside with wind and you can try to help push." She said she could try to move the boulder by air. They tried and took them a few minutes to move it, but they managed. Light filled the room as the rock move out of the entranceway to the cavern. They both felt more at ease and spotted the chests.

"I bet those chests are trapped." Irisel and Alltin wanted to find out what was in the chests anyway. "I will try to open them." He took out a small knife and tried to pry the chest open. The attempt failed.

"I can try to break them in a few minutes if I can get some time to meditate," she offered.

He thought it was a good idea until he thought about coins. If the chests were full of coins, then they would spill everywhere. "On second thought, that might not be the best idea." He tried harder to open the lid and it finally sprung open. As the chest lid sprung open, a trap was set off. Alltin was unfortunately shot in the shoulder by a dart trap that had been set up in the chest.

He looked into the chest and it was empty. Iri came to check his wound and saw that the dart had something black on its tip. She got concerned that the trap might have poisoned him so she had him sit down. He mentioned after a few minutes that he had a funny feeling around his wound. It was as she feared and she didn't know what kind of poison it was. She decided to use her power to float the chest and break it open with a fall. The chest was heavy and broke into several pieces. Coins spilled out everywhere and some of the coins that spilled out touched her leg. She went to move the coins and realized a bit too late that they had a slimy feel to them. She realized that the coins were poisoned as well. She began to feel mildly faint, then fine again.

"I cannot move, my lady." Alltin went rigid.

Irisel recognized the poison and knew he would be fine. They just had to wait out its duration. It was clearly meant to make sure thieves were stuck there and found. She pulled him to the side of the cavern where it was dry so they could wait out the effect.

# Chapter 10: Dangerous Exploration

Alltin began to regain movement in his body sometime in the night. Neither one could see because of the darkness.

Irisel felt around for Alltin. "Alltin, are you alright?" She could feel small things moving around on the ground. She figured they were crabs.

"I am, just trying to unstiffin myself, my lady." Alltin felt around for her, and upon finding her pulled her close to him." She was cold and shivering. "You're shivering."

"I'm just a little cold."

"Body heat not warm enough, my lady?" They both smirked.

"Something in addition will be good."

Alltin took one of his blankets and wrapped it around both of them. He held her close to him for the evening. He felt that it would be better if they stayed where they were or they could have an accident from walking around blindly. He had a torch, but he thought it best to just stay where they were.

She stayed close to him for warmth and fell asleep in no time. He fell asleep as well and they both awoke to a sunlit chamber.

"Perhaps we should check the ships today, my lady. Maybe we can dry off a bit there."

She warmed up as morning turned to noontime. They went over to the ships and tried to find a way aboard. There was a rotten rope hanging that would have been very unsafe to try. There were no openings in the bodies of the ships to crawl in. He was glad to see they were intact. The sails were not usable anymore, but the oars were still in good condition.

"I can lift us by wind," Irisel suggested. She concentrated and floated the both of them up to the deck of the Bloody Charger. The ship was surprisingly in very good condition. Alltin and Irisel could tell that it was in much better shape than it should have been. They walked close to each other and searched the ship. They found nothing on deck. There weren't any signs of the crew at all.

They went into the captain's quarters. They found a logbook but the pages were brittle and yellow. Alltin tried to read one of the pages, but it crumbled as he touched it. He decided not to risk doing the same thing to the rest of the book. There were old colorful clothes. Most were red and black. There were some shirts in the captain's room that had gold trim as well. They ended up finding some wealth. They only found a few gold coins in the chest at the foot of the captain's bed.

They searched below deck and found many crates of dried rations and wine. There were barrels with rotten and dried fruit apart from the crates. They found some other rotten food with worms in it. There was nothing else of value on the Bloody Charger. They checked the other ship and found spices and clothing in crates. There were some porcelain dishes and utensils on the smaller ship as well. There were common goblets that contained odd stains on the insides of them. Neither one of the pair wanted to find out what those stains were from. They left the ships and decided to check the other ways they didn't go. They found a small opening that was just big enough for them to fit through but they would have to slide down the tunnel. They would be helpless if they ran into something in the tunnel. They had very little room for arm movement.

They were both sure that there was something down the tunnel. They were sure that there was something important down the other unexplored tunnel too. Alltin volunteered to go down the small tunnel first.

"I can assist with wind if I need to."

Alltin climbed in the tunnel and slid down first. Irisel climbed in after him and slid through the tunnel. They slid through the tunnel and landed in a cavern with a deep pool of water in the middle of the room. The tunnel continued past the cavern, but it was big enough to walk through.

There were more symbols on the wall in the chamber and they continued along the wall and further down the tunnel. They followed the tunnel into a chamber with loot. There were a few chests, piles of gold and gems. There were also some weapons and armor. The two wondered how best to get it out of the tunnel. Iri wasn't even sure how they were getting out. It was obvious that there was another way into those tunnels and chambers if they got the gold in there. Alltin and Irisel went to look for another way out.

They searched for approximately ten minutes before Alltin came up with an idea. "My lady, can you swim?" and he pointed to the deep pool of water. He thought it was quite possible that the pool connected with the water underneath the ships.

"Not enough to maneuver through a water tunnel. I could try to float them out of the other entrance with wind."

She tested the money for poison, but there was no sign of any. Alltin got in the water and was surprised how cold it was. It took his breath away for a moment, but he recovered quickly and was off to explore the deep water. He came back in a few moments and said his hunch was right. He said he would try to take half of the treasure through the water tunnel if she would float the loose coins out the other tunnel. She agreed and they managed to get the treasure on board the Bloody Charger after approximately two hours.

The only area left was the room with the steep drop off of the main cavern. They made for it as quickly as they could and reached it without trouble. Alltin tested the depth by dropping a lit torch down the tunnel. It fell and slid down the tunnel. They could see the light for a minute, but the light was soon gone from view. They could still hear the torch as it slid through the tunnel.

The two decided to go for it and slid down the tunnel. They got separated when the tunnel split but they both ended up in the same room. They landed in a large cavern with a very deep pool in the middle. There were

marks from some large creature in the sand. There were several bones lying scattered around the room. The evidence in the chamber visibly concerned Irisel. She was quite ready to leave quickly. They began to move
towards the entrance and were stopped by a large tentacle that flopped
down in front of them.

Alltin had his sword out in a flash and stood ready to defend
Irisel. Irisel was too stunned to think for the first minute. A large round
slimy body with several tentacles came out of the deep pool. Alltin
attacked the nearest tentacle and the creature roared in anger and pain. He
sliced part of the tentacle off and the creature was bleeding black ooze from
the tentacle stub.

The creature retaliated and hit him with two tentacles. The hits sent
Alltin flying back against the wall. It brought back memories of hitting the
tree. There were others that tried to strike him, but only two succeeded. Irisel was now the open target right in front of the large sea monster. She thought quick and tried to create a wall of wind to keep the tentacle attacks at bay for a few minutes. Alltin regained his composure and ran
to defend Irisel from its attacks. The wall of wind wasn't helping him
though. Just as the creature was having a hard time getting through, so was
Alltin. He decided to guard in place and attack anything that came near the
two of them.

The creature tried to attack with tentacles, but the wall of wind was
confusing it and the tentacles were bounced right back at it. The creature
called out in anger at the wall. It put more force in its further attempts to
break through. Irisel then changed her wall into a tunnel to go underneath
the creature. She lifted the creature out of the water, hoping that the air
would kill the creature. The creature thrashed the tentacles around furiously. One of the tentacles threw Alltin back up against the wall again, but the
tentacle was severed just as quickly with his guarded attack. The monster
roared louder as black ooze flowed more freely from the second severed
tentacle.

Alltin tried to get back up and get in position again to defend Iri. He
made it just before the creature attacked her. Alltin severed those tentacles
coming towards them. The creature was furious and grabbed hold of him
with a tentacle. The creature lifted him off of the ground by the waist. He
still had use of his arms and could still stab at the thing. The creature began
to squeeze him so tightly that he was having a hard time breathing. Irisel
continued keeping it out of the water and it seemed to work. The creature
was having a difficult time breathing.

Between the breathing and the fury from the severed tentacles, the monster was frantic.

The more frantic it became, the more it squeezed Alltin. Alltin could barely hold onto his sword because of the pressure from the squeezing. He almost dropped his sword, but he somehow kept his hold on it. He didn't want it to be lost in the pool. It was a rare sword and was a gift from his father. The monster gave one more frantic squeeze and slumped. It was still breathing, but barely. Alltin fell to the edge of the pool. He still kept a hold on his sword. He stabbed the monster with his sword and finished it off.

Irisel couldn't concentrate any longer and the body fell into the water. The body sunk into the depths and the water was completely black from blood. Alltin slumped himself after the final stab. He could barely breathe and his waist was in constant pain. Iri rushed over to him to help him. She tried to investigate how bad his wounds were and he wouldn't allow her to touch him. He shook his head when she tried. He was beginning to bruise badly from his injuries. She was concerned about him. She could tell he was in pain, but he wouldn't let her look. She didn't know what to do other than to meditate. "If I can gain some of my energies back, I can lift you out of here."

Alltin said in a whisper, "I want to stay here. I have a feeling the answers I am looking for are in the water. I will have to wait until I can manage to swim down and investigate though." He managed to start wheezing instead of whispering.

Irisel wanted to help him so badly, but he still didn't want her to touch him. She was starting to feel bad because he was pushing her away. All she wanted to do was help him.

He noticed that he hurt her feelings by keeping her at a distance. He tried to tell her that he was sorry his actions were making her feel bad, but she could hardly understand him since he was wheezing. She got up and went to another side of the room. She was trying to control her emotions.

He recovered after a few more hours. He was still bruised terribly, but he could finally breathe with some comfort. "Irisel, come here." He still didn't want to move much.

She was reluctant at first.

"Please, my lady? I am feeling a little better now."

She was visibly upset by his numerous rejections. She eventually came over.

He felt horrible, but it wasn't about the pain in his waist. He was thinking about her instead. He pulled her close to him. "I'm sorry if I upset you, my lady. I just didn't want to be moved or touched at the moment. I just needed to lay there and recover for a bit."

"Can I look at the damages?"

"If you're gentle. I am still very tender."

She pulled his shirt off gently.

"I think you just want to take my shirt off," he joked.

That comment made her smile. "Again."

"When did you..."

"When you were in the hospice, the nurse took it off for me, to show me how bad the bruising was." She looked at his upper body and saw his whole upper body was bruised terribly. She figured that it probably disturbed the wounds from the tree. "And it looked a lot like this, well okay, it was worse, but this isn't good. Are you able to get up?"

"I am not sure." He tried and pain shot through his back.

"You need to lie back down, and not try that again." She was concerned for him and he could tell. She stared at him as he lay there and he stared back at her. Her look was of concern and his was of a happiness that he felt as he looked at her. He was amazed that she was such a sweet woman. Her concern for him made him smile at her.

She noticed how he was staring at her and she smiled back at him. "What are you thinking about?"

"You."

She smiled and blushed slightly. "Good I hope." She chuckled as she realized they've had this conversation before, but reversed.

"Both good and bad actually."

She got an odd look on her face when he said that. "Explain?"

"It is good because you are so amazing and lovely. It's bad because all I can think of is kissing you, but I do not wish to make you uncomfortable."

She grasped his hand and held onto it while maintaining her smile. "I see."

## Chapter 11: Nista

Irisel and Alltin thought it would be best if they went to Nista and then returned to the caves. They could get provisions and someone to navigate the ship. Alltin wanted to wait until the morning so he could heal a little more. Irisel didn't have a problem with it, but she didn't want to stay in the room they were in. She figured that the water would probably be lower by the time they returned from Nista. Alltin agreed with her. He wanted to go down there and find out what was in the lower chambers. Irisel could tell he wanted to explore it, so she came up with a better idea than swimming. She rested for a while and then used her powers of wind to make a whirlpool.

She made a clear tunnel so they could see what was below after a few minutes. They could see bones and objects at the bottom. The body of the monster had been swept out of the way with the swirling water.

"Can you bring the items from the bottom up to the top with your powers at the same time?"

"I can certainly try." She concentrated harder on her task. She managed to get the items to float in a wind tunnel, but she almost lost the tunnel from exhaustion. She managed to gather the items before she was drained mentally.

Alltin began to look through the bones and articles found. He saw what he feared he would find. There was an amulet amongst the items that Alltin knew belonged to the king. His king had indeed been taken, and had lost his life here. The rumor of the king's presence at the castle was said to keep the people from becoming panicked. Alltin would have to get back home and prove that the king had died. Only then could the kingdom move on. To him, the proof should have more meaning with them sailing the Bloody Charger to the kingdom. Alltin said a few words over the amulet for the fallen king. Irisel just lowered her head and listened to Alltin say a few nice words for the king.

"My lady?"

"Yes, Alltin?"

"Thank you for this. You have just done something more for the kingdom than you ever thought possible. This is very important. Thank you."

"It is an amulet. What importance does it hold?"

"It proves that things must change, that we have all been living a lie. But no more."

The other items found were jewelry, money and gems. Three pieces of jewelry found were excellently made. They sparkled with the least amount of light upon them. The two rested for the remainder of the evening, and got ready to leave the caves. Irisel had to use wind to get them out to the cave entrance. To their surprise, it was pouring down rain. They needed to get to Nista, but they would risk getting ill from traveling through the rain. They decided to wait the rain out near the entrance.

Alltin kept looking at Iri to get reactions from her and they laughed about it for a little while. He kept doing it and she finally asked him about it.

"Why are you staring at me like that?"

He still felt guilty about how he had rejected her over and over down in the cave, when she was only being caring and concerned for him. He didn't tell her that that was the reason though. "It is because you are so beautiful of course."

His comment made her blush and smile. She didn't know what to say to him in response. "Thank you, that is most kind." She stood up to walk around. She was getting cold so she and got a few dry blankets to wrap around her.

The water rose slowly and the amount of dry land was becoming slim. The two had to move to another area with less water. Iri was still cold and beginning to shiver more. Alltin noticed and held her close to him to help keep her warm. They both shared the blankets as they waited for the rain to stop, or at least slow. The rain didn't stop all that day and kept on through the evening. They ended up falling asleep to the sounds of the rainfall. They awoke early and traveled on to Nista. Alltin still remembered the direction the city should have been in. The rain continued on and off.

They traveled a full day, but still they hadn't made it to Nista. They camped and arose early in the morning again. They only had to travel till midday to reach Nista. They were let in easily and they gathered supplies needed. They decided on buying a small wagon they could pull themselves to get the needed supplies to the caves faster. Alltin went to the docks to find a sailor who could navigate the ship well. Irisel went into town to ask about Arne and Eldarin. She ended up asking around at the inn where Eldarin had made a fool of himself.

"Pardon me, innkeeper, but I'm looking for a few of my friends. One of them is Sir Eldarin. He should have been the in company of my other friend, hopefully."

"I'm sorry to say, that you are too late. They were here nearly 2 months ago, and I have not seen them since. Sir Eldarin was helping out the Prince. When they left, a stunning blond woman was with them."

Iri was sad that she had missed them by so much time, but she was glad to hear her best friend survived. She missed Arne terribly. "Thank you sir, you have been a great help." Iri hurried to the docks to tell Alltin the news.

Alltin went to the bar near the docks and listened to the conversations. He wanted to be sure he was finding the right person for the job. He approached the bartender. "Is anyone here rumored to be extra skilled navigators or sailors? Also, who would you say is the most trustworthy?"

The bartender thought about it. "Olaf is your best bet. Olaf should be in his room at the inn, but I cannot divulge which inn he is staying at. I suggest you wait here for him to return later this evening."

"Thank you, I will wait then." He went to a table in the corner and sat down to wait.

Irisel went through the streets to the docks and looked around for Alltin. She didn't see him as she walked around the whole area and then thought about the tavern. As soon as she walked in, the room went silent. Most of the men turned to look at her in silence. It made her feel uncomfortable, and then Alltin stood up to get her attention. She didn't see Alltin, but noticed a few scruffy men at another table get up and walk towards her. They had wicked grins on their faces, but Iri wasn't scared yet. That was nothing new to her growing up at the docks in Faulkton.

They surrounded her before Alltin could get to her. "What does it take to land a wench like you? We could show you the time of your life. What do you say, you want to ride?"

Alltin turned their attention on him quickly by touching the end of his sword to one man's back. A small stain of red formed where the sword was touching. The man turned around quickly and the sword cut him more.

The blood flowed a little more freely and the guy freaked out. "Hey man, what the hell? You asshole!" The man tried to stop the bleeding while cursing at Alltin.

The other men looked at Alltin as if they were about to attack him.

Alltin spoke first. "You will step away from the lady quickly. And yes, I said lady, not wench." He said it commandingly, but calmly.

He said it with such authority that the men became slightly concerned, and did as he said. One of the other men tried to help the injured man.

Iri looked relieved to see Alltin and went over to him right away.

One of the sailors then spoke up. "Irisel?" He said it questioningly as if he knew who she was, but he was just making sure he was right.

She recognized the man. "Jack?" The tension eased up a bit as Irisel and Jack realized that they met briefly in Faulkton. She remembered that Jack was a crewman on one of the many ships that only came into port once a year. Jack didn't recognize Alltin though.

"Who's this?" Jack said pointing to Alltin.

"Please, Jack, join us at our table," she responded.

He agreed, and the three went over to the table in the corner. Alltin eyed the man suspiciously during the conversation. Jack noticed, and decided to comment on it.

"Who are you? I have never seen you before."

"I am her bodyguard," Alltin said. "While the lady is abroad, I protect her."

Irisel looked at Alltin oddly because his answer surprised her.

Alltin just smiled at her, but he didn't take his eyes off of Jack for a moment.

"Alltin is my friend, and he's a bit protective of me, if you can't tell."

"I don't recognize him Iri, where's he from?"

At that moment, a largely built man with a long scruffy beard walked into the tavern. All eyes turned to him as he walked in, and he waved at several people as he came in.

A sparkle shone in Irisel's eyes at his entrance. "Alltin, Jack, would you excuse me for a moment." She walked up to Olaf. She touched his arm to try to get his attention. As he turned around, she recognized him as another person she had met in Faulkton more than a few times.

He recognized her immediately, and gave her a hearty hug and a surprising laugh. He was surprised to see her in Nista. "Iris girl! Why are you in this city?"

"Olaf, won't you join me and my friends at our table?"

"Gladly, darling. But I must get something to drink first." He smiled a heartfelt smile at her.

Olaf was a very hearty man who was fond of reds and blacks for clothing. He stood about 5'10" and had brown thick hair. His hair was beginning to grow in white hairs that contrasted with his dark hair. He had a few long swords at his sides and pouches that were full. His boots seemed worn, but still usable. Olaf had a medium complexion that went well with his hair color. He seemed to be a jolly man. He seemed well-known and well liked amongst the locals.

He paid for a huge mug of ale and went over to the table. He sat down next to her and patted her on the back. Alltin twitched as he touched Irisel, but didn't pull out his sword. Olaf looked over at Alltin, and held out his hand for a firm handshake. It was apparent that Olaf remembered Alltin from his trips to Faulkton, but Alltin didn't remember Olaf. Alltin shook Olaf's hand and as he did, he remembered who Olaf was. It took him a few moments though.

Olaf laughed heartily. "Alltin! How have you been?"

"Can't complain too much right now, but crazy things happening back home."

"And what's little Iris doing here in Nista?"

"It is due to some unfortunate events back home that I will discuss later." Alltin didn't want to discuss it there in the bar.

Olaf shrugged. "I'm just tickled that the two of you are here! Oh and hello Jack, good to see you again."

Alltin and Irisel both asked Olaf if he would travel with them.

"Where is it you're planning on going?"

Alltin and Irisel answered simultaneously, "Faulkton."

Alltin continued the thought. "We have a ship, but we need someone who can navigate it and do some repairs. Neither of us are fully capable of steering and running a ship by ourselves."

Olaf thought about it for a moment. "Anything to help little Iris."

Irisel blushed from embarrassment as he called her that. All three men chuckled at her embarrassment.

Alltin told Olaf, "I've never heard her called that before, until now."

"You wouldn't. I'm the only one who calls her that. It is my pet name for her. She has always reminded me of the very rare, but beautiful green irises that grow in my homeland."

Iri blushed as the men spoke about her.

Jack spoke up. "Could I also help assist you on the ship?"

"I don't see why not," Olaf answered.

Alltin looked unsure about it, but if Olaf trusted him, then he supposed that it would be okay.

"Where is this ship, little Iris?"

"We have to travel a day and a half on foot to get there."

Olaf didn't seem to mind.

Jack did mind, but said nothing of his dislike for the idea.

"You should stay and party until tomorrow," Olaf invited.

Everyone at the table agreed and they did just that. Olaf called out for music to be played. Shortly afterwards, the musicians came into the room. The players performed a very lively tune that made everyone in the bar happy and made them feel as if they had to dance.

Olaf danced with Irisel a lot. It seemed to be his way of keeping the unsavory characters in the room away from her. None interrupted, while Olaf was with Irisel. Everyone seemed to respect Olaf enough to leave him be unless Olaf paid attention to them. Alltin got a few dances with her, but Olaf was the main person to keep her company. Alltin and Irisel didn't mind that Olaf was spending the time with her. Iri had a good time that evening. Olaf suggested, "You should stay at the Best Rest Inn. It is the best inn in town." Olaf even went to pay for their rooms, when Alltin surprised him.

"I must insist on sharing a room with Irisel, Olaf." Alltin thought nothing odd of the request.

Olaf gave Alltin a questionable look, but as long as Irisel agreed to it, Olaf agreed to it.

Irisel agreed that it was okay, though it surprised her a bit too.

Olaf said he would see both of them in the morning. Olaf was about to go to his room when he stopped for a moment. "Alltin, would you come speak with me in private?"

"Of course Olaf, but I am not comfortable leaving her alone for very long." Alltin went to Olaf's room and Olaf closed the door behind him. Olaf questioned Alltin. "What are your intentions with little Iris?"

"I am in love with her, and will defend her life with my own, just to see her safe." Alltin was sincere and frank with him. He had nothing to hide. "I will never do anything that my lady does not wish me to."

Olaf still seemed to question Alltin's motives, but was satisfied for the moment. "That's all I wanted to talk with you about. You are not the only one who cares about her well-being."

Alltin nodded. "I should get back to her."

Alltin was about to leave when Olaf gave him a warning. "If you ever hurt that girl, you will have to answer to me. She is like a daughter to me, and I too would see her protected from any harm that might want to befall her."

"That concern for her is something we have in common then." Alltin gave a respectful nod to Olaf, and then went to the room where Iri was already getting comfortable.

Iri watched him curiously as he entered. She looked at him as if she wanted to know what was said, but Alltin wouldn't say. She didn't know what to say to him. She was still a little hurt by the way he acted in the caves. She was less affectionate with him than she had been before. It caused an awkwardness that neither one of them knew how to remedy. The two just looked at each other for a few minutes without saying a word. Finally Alltin broke the silence.

"How many blankets do you need for the evening, my lady?"

"Two will suffice, but blankets are not the problem."

Alltin looked down for a moment and then walked over to her and put his arms around her before she had time to react. He held her gently. "I am so very sorry for the way I was with you down there. I never meant for your feelings to be hurt, and I still feel guilty for having been the cause."

She thought about her response for a moment. "I will forgive it only this once. If you never do that to me again, we will be fine. I was only trying to help you. For all I knew, you could've been dying."

He smiled and held her close. "Then we have a deal. I promise I will never do that to you again. Seeing your feelings hurt because of me was heartbreaking. I never want to feel that again either."

She let a small smile show, and held him in return. She rested her head on his shoulder and they remained that way for a while.

Finally he picked her up and took her over to the bed. He set her down gently and asked, "Would you rather me sleep on the floor, my lady?"

"You are the last person who should be sleeping on the floor, Alltin, after everything that has happened to you. I'm sure you're still a walking bruise. I don't mind if you sleep next to me."

He was happy to hear those words and he joined her. He held her throughout the night as they both slept.

Neither one of them realized that Olaf had been outside of the door listening to their conversation. Olaf would see how things turned out during the trip. He was still unsure about Alltin staying in the same room alone with her. Olaf went to bed once things were silent in the room and he was sure that Alltin wasn't trying to take advantage of Irisel.

## Chapter 12: Releasing the Past

Olaf, Jack, Irisel, and Alltin had a hearty breakfast before setting out to the ship cavern. The first day went by without a problem, but Olaf kept a watchful eye on Alltin. Iri and Alltin seemed to be back to their normal ways. The tension between them had lessened quite a bit after their agreement. While Olaf was watching Iri and Alltin, so was Jack. Jack didn't seem to like the way Alltin stayed near her either. Not much was said during their travel.

They camped for the evening and Olaf asked to speak to "little Iris" alone. "I feel like I must ask you about you and Alltin. What are your feelings towards him?"

"I like him. He's one of the kindest people I've ever met, and he has done so much to keep me safe." She chuckled. "I've never been fussed over so much, but it is nice."

"Is Alltin behaving himself around you?"

The question made Iri get a quizzical look on her face. She felt that question was a little too personal.

Olaf waited for an answer patiently.

"Alltin has done nothing but protect me and care for my needs." She didn't mention the way Alltin reacted to her in the caves because Alltin had done so much for her that the one incident could be forgiven so long as it didn't happen again. Olaf noticed there was more to the story than she was admitting.

Iri was becoming uncomfortable with the line of questioning and quickly changed the subject. "Olaf, tell me one of your stories."

They returned to camp and Olaf recounted the tale about the time he was sailing the seas and he came upon the Bloody Charger. "The ship was going so fast that they seemed like they were quite intent on getting somewhere quickly. My crew and I braced ourselves for a battle we were sure was going to happen. The crew was tense, and we were so surprised at what really ended up happening. The ship fired at us a few times with their cannons and then passed us by. The Bloody Charger scored a hit on my ship, but most of the crew survived and the Bloody Charger kept its speed and direction. Everyone aboard was thankful that their lives were spared due to whatever the pirates were more interested in. If the Bloody Charger had intended on attacking at full force and pillaging the ship, it would have succeeded. No one ship has ever been able to survive a full force attack from the Bloody Charger."

Alltin and Iri looked at each other and smiled as he told the story.

Olaf continued with his story about the Bloody Charger as they looked at each other. "It was the last time I ever saw that dreaded ship, but many sailors still insist it is out there. Some claim death took the crew, but that they live an undeath, just waiting for someone or something to find them. I am not sure if that is completely true, but I am sure it is still out there, taking prisoners and laying waste to everything it encounters."

Iri and Alltin were just smiling from ear to ear as he told the story. Iri decided to speak up. "We've encountered it ourselves recently."

Olaf looked surprised for several reasons. Iri watched his reaction to her comment. "Where? And how in Paelencien did you get away?"

"The ship has been locked away by time and the sea. When we searched it over, there was no crew, bodies, nor ghosts."

Olaf and Jack looked completely surprised at that.

Jack said, "Well it must not have been the Bloody Charger then. It must have been another ship that looked similar."

Iri and Alltin just smiled at each other and said, "We should probably get some rest."

Morning came and the four of them ate quickly. They set out and arrived at the caves midday. The skies were looking dark like it was going to storm again so Alltin and Iri got in the cave as quickly as they could with the supplies. They just left the wagon above. Olaf and Jack were surprised to find out that there was such a large cave system there. They looked around, and Iri asked Olaf and Jack to follow her. She led them into the ship cavern and watched as Olaf and Jack realized what floated before their eyes.

As Olaf came around the corner and he saw the ships. He nearly fell backwards from shock. He visibly jumped at the sight of the Bloody Charger. His skittish behavior quickly turned into curiosity behavior. He was anxious to investigate the ship.

Alltin spoke up. "We intend on breaking her free of her long time home."

Jack had no idea what they were talking about until he rounded the corner. He jumped and cursed aloud at the sight of the fearsome ship that had terrorized the seas. "You really weren't kidding or mistaken!" He then looked to Alltin to reaffirm what he said. "Is that the ship we're supposed to navigate?"

Alltin nodded his head and grinned.

Jack seemed spooked, and he wasn't sure if he should even touch the ship. "I will have to think about whether or not to step foot on that cursed ship."

"You're a cowardly dog, Jack!" Olaf moved closer to the ship to touch it. Olaf remembered that Iri and Alltin had said they had found no crew on the ship. "How did you get aboard it?"

"I got us up last time, but until I know who's going and who's staying, I prefer to wait," Irisel said.

Olaf came back to the shore and took hold of Jack's arm, pulling him over to the ship.

Jack tried to struggle, but Olaf had a firm grasp on Jack. Jack protested. "I don't want to be cursed, nor deal with an undead crew."

"Olaf?" Irisel asked, "Have you a good hold on Jack?"

"Indeed I do, little Iris."

She and Alltin went over to the other two and she used her powers to air lift them up to the ship.

Jack was really panicked by then. "The spirits are drawing us in! We are all doomed!"

Olaf had to grasp him firmly and shake him till he stopped ranting. Olaf laughed at him in his panicked state.

Irisel tried to calm him down. "Jack, it is not spirits, it is me."

He looked completely frightened about the whole thing and wasn't responding well.

Olaf took the time to search the ship and help place the things that Irisel and Alltin had bought from Nista. Olaf was very happy as he roamed the ship. He seemed like a child in a playland. Iri couldn't help but to smile at his childish manner. Jack was frozen in place on the deck, so they were certain he wouldn't go anywhere.

Olaf laughed a hearty laugh as he touched the wheel of the ship. He seemed anxious to get underway and take the ship for a ride.

Iri and Alltin informed Olaf, "We are ready and have a destination in mind."

Olaf was more than happy to oblige the two of them. They then went below as Olaf did what he needed to do to get the ship out of the cave. He knew he needed to get the ship out before the water rose, or they would have to wait to leave. He did what he could and tried to leave the cave. He had to dislodge the ship from a few places in the sand.

Irisel and Alltin began to clean up below and hid the treasure that they found earlier. They didn't really want to share it, since it was the two of them who took the risks of obtaining the treasure, not Olaf and Jack.

As the ship pulled out of the caves, Olaf could feel the wind blowing harder as the storm came closer. Jack started to ramble again frantically as the ship was pulling out of the cave. As Olaf was maneuvering the ship out, the wind was being counterproductive and trying to toss the ship on the sides of the cave opening. The ship narrowly escaped being injured on its way out. Olaf maneuvered the ship around once in more open waters, and they began to set sail in the direction the storm was going. Olaf tried to keep the storm behind them as they sailed off.

Jack remained frozen in place until a strong draft of wind took him by surprise and made him hit his head on the railing. He rubbed his head for a few minutes and got back up. Olaf barked some orders at him, but Jack just looked at him. Another strong gust of wind knocked Jack back down on the floor. He landed on his butt and cursed. As soon as Jack cursed, he immediately apologized to the ship.

Olaf knew Jack wouldn't be much help for a while. He didn't mind at all. He just loved the feel of the wind whipping around him and the thrill of being back on the sea. Olaf lived for sailing on the waters of Paelencien, and most of his fondest memories were of his sailing adventures.

Jack couldn't handle being up on deck any more, but there was no way he would go down below where he would be trapped. At least on deck, he could jump off if he needed to. He wouldn't be able to react quickly enough if he stayed below.

Eventually the storm caught up with the ship and Jack held onto the railing for dear life. Olaf was making joyful cries to the sea god as the waters became more dangerous. Olaf didn't look worried in the slightest. He was just having so much fun. He was giddy like a child as he tried to keep control of the ship.

Irisel and Alltin finished with the work below and began to get tossed around as the seas became rougher. Irisel even fell on top of Alltin during one of the tosses that the sea waves gave the ship. Alltin let out a slight noise of discomfort as she landed on him right where he was bruised the most.

"Sorry, I could not control that. Are you okay?" She tried to get up, but the sea was relentless and was not going to let the two stand up.

Alltin was rolled on top of her during the next rocking of the ship, and he smiled. "If the storm does not let up, then maybe we should stay here like this," he said with a playful smile.

Her cheeks turned a bright red as he said it. Her blush made him smile even more.

"You're adorable when you blush, you know that?" She blushed even more as he kept talking. "May I kiss you, my lady?"

She was surprised at the question. She didn't know what to say. Before she really thought about it, she said, "yes". It was too late to fully react to the situation and retract her "yes".

He kissed her deeply, yet sweetly. She could tell that he had been waiting to kiss her that way for a while.

It seemed like an eternity to Irisel, and then it seemed abruptly interrupted when the two were separated by another toss of the water. Alltin still had a hold of her, but after they rolled again she ended up on top of him for the second time. She could feel his arms around her snuggly. She knew that he wouldn't let her go.

She really enjoyed the kiss he gave her, and took her chance to kiss him while she was on top of him. That kiss was even more passionate than the first. Even though the waters were raging outside, the two paid the storm no attention. The kiss even distracted from any pain Alltin was feeling from getting tossed around. They were in their own happy world as the waters churned. They kissed and held each other the remainder of the time. They ended up falling asleep at some point in time, but there was no sense of time in their world that evening.

It was hard for Olaf, but he kept the ship under as much control as he could without Jack's help. It seemed as if there were several invisible ship hands helping him. Olaf enjoyed the whole evening. It was exhilarating for him. He felt that he was better off commanding the ship on his own that evening since Jack was useless anyway. He was exhausted by morning, but all survived the storm due to his years of experience navigating a ship and the invisible hands.

# Chapter 13: Homebound

Irisel was the first to wake the next morning. She found herself still in Alltin's embrace. She blushed slightly and got up as soon as she could. She tried not to wake him as she rose, but he awoke before she could fully make it up. She gave his hand a slight squeeze and continued to get to her feet. He let her hand slip through his and started to get up as well.

She helped him up. "I should look at your bruising after last night's events."

Alltin did feel a little more discomfort in the area where she landed on him, so he had no problem with her looking at it.

"It still looks bad, Alltin, but not too bad." She could tell that he was enjoying her company, especially her fussing over him.

Alltin placed his hands gently over hers, and pulled her closer to kiss her again. After the kiss, they went up top to see the damage caused by the storm.

Olaf was found sleeping on the wheel. He was snoring loudly and completely asleep. They tried to move him to a more comfortable position for his sleep. Jack awoke as Irisel came up from below with a few pillows for Olaf to rest his head on. Jack surveyed the ship as he tried to stand up. Unfortunately, he had been down for so long, that he had a very painful cramp shoot through his legs as he tried to get up. He quickly sat back down and tried to work the cramp out. He was cursing about it and saying, "We are all cursed. We will never make it back to Faulkton."

Alltin just plainly told Jack, "I am not interested in what you have to say Jack. I especially don't want to hear your predictions about the 4 of us. We will make it just fine. I'd say if there is one who doesn't, it would be you for your cowardess and your sniveling."

Jack was shocked by the comment and didn't know what to say in response.

Alltin took the wheel while Irisel surveyed the sea around the ship. She saw no sight of land. She hoped they were going in the right direction.

Jack stood up and walked over to Alltin. He was insulted by Alltin's comment. Alltin just watched him walk up and stood there with a blank expression on his face. Jack looked angry and then let his words fly. He said in a seething tone, "We are all going to die because no one paid any attention to the curse attached to this ship and those who ride it. It doesn't matter whether you believe me or not, we will all still die." Jack then stormed off, and was about to go down into the ship when Irisel stopped him.

Irisel looked at him with a scolding look. "Jack, you cannot go down there."

Jack wore a very confused look upon his face as he heard her say that. "Why can I not go below deck, you are not my boss."

She gave him a stern look and said, "Your cowardess and complaints about everything since we got to the ship is reason enough. I am certain you can be of use up here somehow like you were supposed to be. You make Olaf do everything," she scolded, "while you do nothing but cower and hide, clinging to the railing when you should have been helping to navigate the ship. You have no right to go and hide for the whole trip and leave the work to everyone else. Alltin is injured and is still helping out. He's the one who should be in bed resting. What are you good for?" She gave him a serious look. "You will help us from now on, or you will have to swim to a shore from here!"

Jack was appalled at what she commanded him to do and cursed at her. He disregarded her orders and tried to go below deck anyway.

She used her powers to force him away from the door and he went sliding across the deck until he hit the cabin wall. "You, Jack, will have to work before you do anything else."

Jack was furious by her actions and words to him. He walked quickly towards her. All could see his intent to hurt her worn upon his face clearly.

As Jack moved towards Iri, Alltin was about to leave the wheel to help Irisel when a large heavy hand was felt on his shoulders. He knew right away it was Olaf and he stayed at the wheel. The large man walked over to Irisel and put his hands on her shoulders to stop her from wasting her powers on Jack. She stopped and watched to see what Olaf intended to do.

Olaf stood in between her and Jack. Olaf wore an irritated expression upon his face and waited for Jack to make his move.

"Stand aside Olaf! I have business with the wench."

At the word wench, Olaf punched Jack in the face several times and the last punch sent Jack flying across the deck. Olaf moved in on Jack as he was lying still on the deck. Olaf picked him up and threw him against the mast. Olaf was very red in the face and clearly very perturbed at Jack. Jack could do little to nothing against Olaf, and then did the only thing he could think at the moment. Jack's head was still spinning around and all he could think to do was to spit on Olaf. The liquid landed directly on Olaf's face and Olaf twisted Jack's arm in response.

Jack cried out in pain as Olaf continued to twist. Jack started cursing at all three shipmates and Olaf punched Jack again. Jack told Olaf, "You will have to kill me and we're all dead men anyway."

"I can oblige," the irritated Olaf said, but Irisel stopped him.

She put her hand gently on his shoulder. "Olaf, just hold him still." Olaf did as she requested and she stayed far enough away to be out of spitting range.

Jack just eyed her coldly and spit some of the blood out of his mouth that ended up landing on the deck.

"Jack, your behavior is unwanted and unneeded. It is apparent you will not be of any use to us. Keep him up against the mast until we are closer to land. Tie him or something. When we get closer to land, we throw him overboard and he can swim to shore.

Olaf agreed to the idea and tied him to the mast. He then turned to Iri, "Are you okay?"

"I'm fine."

He was glad to hear it and went back to Alltin, who had been watching the whole thing. Olaf relieved Alltin from the wheel and said that he was no longer tired. Alltin went over to Irisel and put his arm around her. Jack eyed them all coldly and spit at them as they walked by him.

Alltin assured Jack that remaining tied to the pole was the best thing for him. "If you ever come near her again, Jack, you will regret it."

The two were about to go off to another part of the ship, when Jack said something very odd. "I know who you really are Irisel, and someone is looking for you. There are several actually." He then sneered and asked, "How's your mother faring?"

Irisel looked at him curiously, but then her expression worsened. Memories suddenly rushed into her head of her time before Hanmel. Memories her mind had repressed, and for good reason. She appeared to be thinking about something forgotten. Irisel's face went white and a little fear shone through her pale face. Alltin and Olaf both noticed and became concerned. She seemed troubled and withdrawn. She was mentally severed from what was going on around her.

"Exactly what do you mean by that? I suggest you respond quickly," Alltin demanded.

Jack just smiled evilly and turned his gaze away from all on deck.

"Olaf, I am going to take her down below so she can relax a bit," Alltin informed. "I will return in a few minutes."

Olaf nodded his approval and kept steering the ship.

Alltin took Irisel down to her room and had her sit. He kneeled in front of her and asked her, "What is wrong?"

Irisel still had a look of fear on her face that she could not get rid of as hard as she tried. "I don't want to talk about it. Can I just get some rest?" Reluctantly he left her side at her request and went above to help Olaf.

"Did you find out what was wrong, Alltin?"

"She said she didn't want to talk about. I'm not going to press it, but I am concerned that she might be hiding something big from everyone. My hope is that she will say something about it before it becomes required information, before the others find her." Alltin wanted to be prepared to defend her from everything. As long as she kept her secret, he would never be as prepared as he wanted. Olaf and Alltin were both very concerned but didn't want to pressure her to divulge the information that she didn't feel comfortable releasing. Jack refused to talk for the rest of his stay aboard the ship.

It took them three days to spot land off to their left. They were nearing some kind of natural rock bridge that spanned as far as they could see to their right. Jack was tossed off of the ship as it kept going. Everyone watched as they sailed away from him. Jack nearly drowned trying to get to the shore, but he did make it to the sandy beach.

Irisel didn't seem like her normal self ever since Jack spoke to them last. She seemed distant and scared. Olaf and Alltin tried their best to help her, but there was some secret deep inside her. It was obviously painful for her to think about. She told no one what it was. She did help navigate the ship and created wind when there was none.

It took them much of the third day out to pass completely under the rock bridge. After the rock bridge, it took them six more days to spot land again. They sailed in between the two large sand bars. The ship wasn't in any danger of getting stuck. They could see the sand bars in the distance, and saw them for three days until they emerged into the open sea again. From there they had to veer to the west. They sailed for nearly three weeks westward and still, Irisel said nothing about what her secret was. The men had given up on the secret and tried to enjoy the trip on the water regardless. They were enjoying the trip when one day, they spotted another ship. They wanted to sail to it, but Iri became a little frightened about the idea. Her fears were oddly lifted as they neared the foreign vessel. Irisel wasn't sure why, but her fears left her as a soothing feeling washed over her.

# Chapter 14: The Chase

The Urchin was sailing as fast as it could to try to get away from the Faulkton. Arne tried to slow their pursuers down with a lightning storm. It kept the ships from closing in on the Urchin, but the ships remained a constant distance away. Arne tried her best to keep them from closing any distance. While she was doing that, Eldarin was trying to do what he could to help Captain Erinnt. There was little that Eldarin could do, so he was sent below during the chase. He didn't stay there for long and came back to the deck to stay close to Arnesti.

As he watched the events going on, a wave surprised the ship and sent several men on the Urchin tumbling. Eldarin was also sent tumbling. He lost his balance and tumbled toward the mast. He hit his head on the mast and was dazed for a few minutes. Everyone recovered quickly from the startling wave and went back to working as much as they could. Eldarin stayed near the mast to let his head stop spinning, when all of his memories came back to him in a large wave. His eyes went wide and his face turned and bright red as he realized everything that happened after the storm. He just couldn't believe how foolish he acted and that he lost the princess and the jerk. He couldn't believe that Arne just laughed at him and let him think he was a prince. He wondered how she could just let him believe that, knowing otherwise.

As he thought more about that part of his trip, he turned more red and embarrassed. He knew that he would have much to explain and apologize to his liege for if they ever made it back there alive. He was shocked for several minutes as he thought about everything that happened. He was too stunned to do much of anything. The crew worked very hard to keep their distance from the other ships. Erinnt was very concerned about Circe and knew he had to keep her safe. He had to make sure the other ships never caught up to the Urchin or they would all be in trouble.

Circe remained in a trance-like state in the captain's cabin during the madness. She didn't move or talk. She just sat there staring at the floor like she was some sort of statue. Arne kept up the lightning as long as she could but then had to rest. The crew started working double time after her mental capabilities were spent. She started to head for the door that led below when she spotted Eldarin. She saw the facial expression on his face and became concerned about him. She approached him and he looked up at her as she did.

She saw the strangest look in Eldarin's eyes as she looked at him. It was as if he was so aware of the situation. As she thought about it, she realized that perhaps Eldarin remembered much more about himself. She sat next to him and held his hand. He held her hand, but his grip was looser compared to normal. "Eldarin, are you okay?"

He just looked at her. Neither of them spoke for a few minutes, and Eldarin finally broke the silence. "I am so sorry for everything I've put you through. I'm sorry you lost your friends. I'm sorry my hold on you wasn't good enough when we were swept up in the winds."

She watched his facial expressions change through many emotional faces. She knew he was back to himself again, and that he was truly sorry for the bad things that happened. As she watched him, she realized that she felt more emotions towards him than she had ever admitted even to herself. She realized that she loved him, and that was an emotion that she had never felt with anyone else. Most everyone else was just a fun time. She smiled a warm smile as he talked to her. He noticed her smile and it made him smile. All she could think about as he apologized to her was how adorable he was to her. He realized that she had forgiven him, and felt a little better, but not much. She couldn't resist wrapping her arms around him, so she did. They embraced for a few minutes and then decided to check on Circe.

They walked in to check on Circe, and she was as they left her. They stayed in the cabin with her while the crew worked hard outside of the room. Arne tried to get a response from Circe, but no response was given.

Arne and Eldarin talked for a while about the things that happened. Both were very surprised at how they were treated when they arrived in Faulkton and how oddly everyone in town had acted. Arne commented that it almost looked like they were zombies. Eldarin agreed, but could offer no further insight upon that subject. Arne's thoughts turned again to Hanmel, who was no where to be seen.

The opponents were gaining upon the Urchin until the winds died down. One of the good features of the Urchin was that it would still sail even if there were no winds to help it along. It was something that the first captain had put on the ship, but it was secret to everyone who commanded the ship after him. That captain never told how or why the ship could sail without wind, but all who commanded the ship were very happy that it could. The Urchin lost the other ships temporarily. After the chase died down, Erinnt went to his quarters to check on Circe.

Erinnt was surprised to see Arne and Eldarin in there with Circe. "Thank you Arne for the lightning storm, it really helped. And thank you Eldarin for trying to help as you can, even though he didn't really do anything."

Both Arne and Eldarin told Erinnt that they were glad to help. "So sorry you were involved with this chaos."

"Do not worry about it. I've been in worse situations. For the moment we've lost the Faulkton guild ships because of a loss of wind. It isn't over yet however. I suggest you two get below deck and relax. I would like to be alone with Circe."

Arne and Eldarin left and went below deck to their room and talked things out for the evening. "Arne, why did you let me believe I was the prince?"

"I wasn't likely to be able to talk you out of it, and it really was funny."

That didn't sit well with him at all. Then he thought about how upset she would be if she knew he was more focused on her friend than he was on her. He liked her, but he was beginning to see a whole other side of her that he really didn't like. He just decided to play it as he had been till then and keep her thinking that she was the most important thing to him. If he screwed up, it would be harder to get the princess, if she was even still alive. They kissed and held each other through the night.

Erinnt spent the remainder of his evening caressing Circe's hair and holding her close to him. He tried to get her to talk to him, but she seemed like she was in another world entirely. He tried to make her feel safe. He remembered the look on her face. It was the same look she had on her face the first day he met her when they rescued her out of the sea. He wanted to know what troubled her so, but it was something he knew he would probably never be told. He just wanted her to feel safe and secure with him. Her trance worried him tremendously.

\*\*\*

Quantis was on one of the ships chasing the Urchin. He was desperate to catch up to her rescue ship. He couldn't use his powers to get on the ship since it was in motion. He felt strange while he followed her. He felt desperation, guilt, love, hate, and anxiousness to get his hands on Circe again. More than that, he wanted to finally get his hands on the talisman so he could end his tiring search. He didn't want to settle down by any means, but he wanted to end the wretched search for the talisman.

Quantis thought about what he would do when his search for the talisman did end, and he realized that he would probably stay in Estare. He had no plans on staying with the brat from Faulkton. He couldn't stand her constant whining and her pining over him whenever he had to leave. She was spoiled and utterly irritating to him. He often longed to strangle her in the middle of the night while she slept. That was the only time he could get any peace. At least she was quiet while she slept. He had already taken Mel's virginity so she was useless to him anymore. He only married her because his master wanted him to for political reasons. He chuckled as he thought about the fact that he had killed and raped better women than Mel. If it were up to him he would put her out of everyone's misery. That was the only thing he enjoyed about her. Mel caused misery upon all who knew her. That often made Quantis smile.

Unfortunately Quantis's ships were unable to catch the Urchin and Quantis had other things he had to do. He made the ships follow the Urchin, but he had to return to other business. He decided to stay on the ship a little longer since he was so close to her. Then as he thought about her, he got the strange feeling that she no longer had the talisman. His feelings were confirmed when his master contacted him mentally. Tarax told him that his trail was cold and that, from what he could tell, the talisman was in the opposite direction. Tarax told him to go to the towns north of Terrah and that he felt it was somewhere in that region. Quantis had already been in that region prior to look for the stone, but he would have to search there again. He still wanted Circe though. Quantis left his commands with the ships to capture the escapees and any who helped them escape. He then disappeared from the ship to go back to the Terrah region.

\*\*\*

The following morning, the crew from the Urchin could see that the guild ships still followed the Urchin as it sailed, but couldn't catch up with it. Circe began to feel that Quantis wasn't near any longer and started to feel better. Erinnt stayed with her the whole night.

"Erinnt?" she said as she tried to gently wake him.

He awoke at the sound of her voice immediately. "Circe, oh good, there you are. You were so distant. I was and still am very concerned. Are you alright?"

"I am better now. He's no longer chasing us."

"Circe, when are you going to tell me what's going on?"

"I don't know, but thank you for being such a good friend to me."

She spent most of her time in the cabin. Erinnt stayed with her, though crewmen were always interrupting the quiet in the cabin to inform Erinnt that the ships still followed. Circe felt that they needed to head northeast and Erinnt listened to her instinct.

Soon Circe seemed normal and spunky again. The crew was happy to see that since her moods affected Erinnt's mood. Circe even started visiting with the crew again. To help keep the guild ships off of their tail, Circe created an obstacle with water. She made waves and whirlpools so that the ships would have no hope of catching the Urchin. It seemed to have worked, and everyone was glad to see the guild ships disappear.

The Urchin sailed northeast for nineteen days and spotted a ship in the distance. The ship seemed to get closer, and even veered to try to meet up with their ship. The closer the ships got to each other, the more Erinnt recognized it. Also the closer they were, the happier Arne became. She tried to urge Erinnt to go faster to meet with it, but Erinnt really didn't want to. He wanted to turn the other way as fast as he could. He made the decision up to Circe, and she said they might as well see who it was. Erinnt reluctantly veered towards the ship.

## Chapter 15: Reunion and Loss

The two ships sailed towards one other. The closer they were, the more uncomfortable Captain Erinnt became. He knew that they were heading straight for the Bloody Charger, and was planning on turning the ship around. He almost did, but then one of the crewmen announced that there were only three people aboard the Bloody Charger. Erinnt was surprised to hear that the infamous ship only had three aboard the ship, as far as the crewman could see anyway. It made Erinnt curious enough to keep the course to meet up with the ship.

Erinnt warned the crew to get ready just in case the Urchin needed a fast getaway. The crew stood ready for anything as the two ships approached each other. Irisel, Arne, and Circe all felt each other's presence. Arne rushed over to the side of the Urchin to look at the other ship. Arne and Iri immediately recognized each other and got excited. Irisel made a small wind tunnel, and Arne made it crackle with electricity. The two ships pulled aside each other, positioning the ships so that they could sail connected to each other.

The ships were attached, which allowed Arne and Irisel ran into each other's arms. They hugged each other for several minutes while all the others met up. Circe went over to the two girls and waited for them to part. Iri felt the presence of another power nearby, and turned to Circe when she was finished embracing her friend. The three girls went off together and Alltin and Eldarin let them. Erinnt struck up a conversation with Olaf and Alltin. Erinnt recognized both men, and welcomed the two men aboard the Urchin. Eldarin welcomed the two men as well, but said quite a bit less than Erinnt.

The four men went into Erinnt's cabin and had a discussion about everything that happened. Eldarin said nothing about his memory loss, but told of what happened in Faulkton. Alltin listened in shock as Eldarin spoke of the tragic news.

Why was Eldarin seen as a prince? Alltin decided not to ask just yet. "Did you see Sir Taen and Caladin at all?" Alltin described his knight friends.

"During what stay we had and what little hall wandering we did, no I did not see them."

Alltin looked more concerned than he had before the news. "Excuse me gentlemen," and he left the cabin to get some fresh air and think about the news. He was very saddened at the loss of his liege. He was very fond of him. The thought of Mel leading with her new husband made him uneasy. Alltin got on his knees. "May your eternal rest be everything your life could not have been. You will be missed, my lord. I am sorry I could not be there sooner." At the moment, it was all he could do.

Eldarin didn't follow the shocked knight and turned conversation to Olaf. He recognized Olaf immediately. He had several dealings with the captain before and knew him well. Olaf was happy to see Eldarin and Erinnt. He hadn't seen either man in several months since Olaf lost his ship and crew in a bad storm. At least that's what Eldarin was told when they found him on the shore near Nista.

Erinnt was anxious to ask how Olaf and the other two got their hands on the Bloody Charger.

"Alltin and little Iris found it," Olaf said. "I feel lucky they came to me to sail such a fine and mighty vessel. We had trouble with a man named Jack, not sure if you know of him Sir Eldarin. We kicked him off the ship a while ago. He should still be alive, at least last we saw."

Erinnt seemed to vaguely recognize who Olaf was speaking of.

Eldarin had no clue who Jack was.

"Eldarin," Olaf asked, "can I speak to Erinnt alone?"

"Of course." Eldarin left the cabin. He went to take a look at the infamous ship of the seas.

Olaf then spoke to Erinnt about what Jack said before he was thrown off of the ship.

"I know very little as to what that means, but I have heard there are many people looking for the Harand princess, a green haired beauty," Erinnt said.

Olaf was disappointed that Erinnt didn't know either, but he didn't really expect the young captain too know many details, if any. Olaf and Erinnt talked for several more hours about many things that had happened to them that weren't related to the current company.

The ladies went to Circe's room to talk. Arne just couldn't hold back her eagerness to tell her best friend what happened in Faulkton. Irisel was absolutely shocked by what her friend told her. She just couldn't believe what had transpired. Circe spoke up and told the girls about Quantis and their past. She didn't mention the talisman, but she mentioned all else.

Irisel went silent and lowered her head. Her facial expression was sad. "I have something to tell you, but it can never leave this room. I forbid you to repeat this to anyone, not even Alltin. You both must promise me you won't repeat this."

Both girls promised they wouldn't say anything.

She paused for a few minutes as she debated if it was a good idea to say anything, but then she spoke in a quiet voice so no one could even overhear what she had to say. "There are people looking for me and I am in terrible danger. I'm sorry, Arne, for not telling you this sooner. I did not remember any of this until someone triggered it. Apparently I've repressed it all these years. When I was very young, I was kidnapped by the court wizard. He promptly sold me in to slavery. I was sold to a very cruel man who had also gotten his hands on my mother. If I did anything that displeased him, he would torture her. I was never allowed to see her, but I could hear her screams of pain.

"The torture sessions only lasted for so long, because the sessions ended up killing my mother. I miraculously escaped, and ran as far and fast as I could. The only safe place to go was to my aunt's house who lived far away from that cruel man. She was Hanmel's wife. After my aunt died, uncle Hanmel took care of me as if I was his own daughter." Irisel's facial expression changed to fear. The man, Jack, who traveled with us on our ship, asked me how my mother fared and said he knew who I was. He was thrown off the ship some time ago but is still alive. I know that if that wizard manages to find us, I will be endangering you."

Arne didn't know what to say.

"I will not tell anyone, and I will help you however I can," Circe told Iri.

Arne went over to her best friend and gave her a large comforting hug as she told her friend that she would never let anyone take her away or harm her.

Iri was glad that they were so supportive, and then asked Circe, "Can I rest in your room?"

"I do not mind at all. You are both welcome to share it with me." The three girls agreed to share the room.

"Arne, what happened to you? I missed you so much!"

"Tons. The highlight was what happened when we made it back to Faulkton though. Mel ruling anything is the worst thing possible. On a funnier note, Eldarin lost his memory and some kids played a hilarious prank on him. He seriously thought he was the prince!" They both laughed. "Iri, what happened to you after the storm?" Arne was told the whole story. Arne raised an eyebrow when Iri came to the part when she kissed Alltin. The look on Arne's face made Irisel break a smile and blush.

Iri finished her recount of the events that happened to them and then felt she needed to rest a bit.

"Perhaps I should keep our knights company," Arne commented.

"I will stay here with her, Arne."

"Thank you, Circe." Iri tried to get some rest.

Arne went up to the deck and first saw Alltin leaning on the railing. He was obviously in thought. She walked over to him. "Greetings, Sir Alltin."

He smiled at her and saw that she was doing well. "Where's Iri?"

"Resting."

Alltin continued to talk to Arne as he stared out at the water.

"How are you holding up? It is nice to see you again."

"I am still sore from everything that has happened, but I am feeling much better than I had been. It is amazing to finally meet up with you. I cannot believe what has happened back home."

Arne sympathized with his shock. "I experienced that shock first hand."

"I am deeply sorry for what happened to you and Eldarin there."

She smiled and said, "I would guess that the events happening there are the results of having Mel for a ruler."

That comment made Alltin chuckle and smile.

Arne then felt a hand on her waist as Eldarin came up behind her. She smiled at Eldarin and then told Alltin, "See you later."

Alltin just nodded in response.

Arne and Eldarin went to Eldarin's room for the rest of the evening. Alltin stayed by the railing in thought. Eventually Iri woke up from her rest. She and Circe went to the deck. Iri wanted to introduce Circe to Alltin. The two walked up to him, and he noticed them right away. He thought that Circe was stunning. Of course he thought Iri was better looking, but he couldn't deny that Circe was exceedingly beautiful.

"Alltin," she smiled, "this is Circe. Apparently she's like myself and Arne."

"A pleasure, my lady. So what is it you can do? Iri can control the winds, Arne controls lightning, and you...?"

"I can control water. And what about you, Alltin? What can you do?"

Alltin laughed. "My job is protecting the ladies." He smiled at both of them.

Circe laughed in return. "Well you seem to be gaining enough to keep your hands full." She was still chuckling. "If you both will excuse me, I will see you later." Circe excused herself to go see Erinnt.

Iri had no problem with it, and after Circe left for the cabin, Iri wrapped her arms around Alltin's waist.

Alltin smiled warmly at her and wrapped his arms around her as well. "How are you holding up, my lady?"

"I am thrilled to see Arne again."

"I knew you would be. It pleases me greatly to see you happy again."

"What are we going to do since we can't go back to Faulkton?" Iri was concerned and unsure.

"I still intend to go back to Faulkton. I must know what happened there. But as you are my priority, I will go where you need me to first. I have no intentions on taking you with me to Faulkton. It is far too dangerous for you now, and besides that, they think you are dead. I am not proving them wrong."

Irisel put hers hands gently on his face. "I understand why you do not want me there, but it is your job to protect me. As such, that will require me going with you, wherever you go. Plus I need to find Hanmel. If they have done anything to him, Mel will pay dearly."

He chuckled and said, "You have a point. I can't let you out of my sight."

"I must confess, I don't ever want you to leave me."

He looked at her with a surprised expression on his face over her confession. She just smiled and placed her head on his chest and held him close. He held her in return, and they enjoyed the view.

Erinnt came up to them with Olaf not far behind. "Our course is continuing northeast."

"It is the direction my instincts are telling me to go in," Circe said as she came up from behind them.

No one disagreed to the direction, and the two ships stayed connected as they sailed northeast for two days. Not long before sundown, the ships came upon a huge whirlpool that they couldn't escape. The crew tried their best to maneuver the ships out of it, but nothing worked. It was as if the whirlpool suddenly started underneath them because no one saw it until the ships were caught.

Circe was called out to try to help. She responded, but did something that no one ever expected. She went over to Irisel and said, "I am sorry for what I am about to do." Circe walked over to Erinnt, who was barking orders at the crew. She gently kissed him on the cheek, walked to the front of the ship, climbed up on top of the railing, and dove off of the side into the whirlpool.

Erinnt was beside himself and ran to try to catch her. He called out to her, but his cries were in vain.

Iri was too late to use her powers to keep Circe from hitting the water. Arne rushed to the front after Circe, but didn't reach her in time. Circe disappeared deeper and deeper into the water. Soon she was completely out of sight. Circe made no effort to try to swim. She just sank into the deep blue water. The ship was nearing the center of the whirlpool when the waters suddenly went calm again. There were residual swirls, but the whirlpool just stopped. The entire crew and passengers were all shocked into silence and sorrow. No one knew what to say, especially to Erinnt who was panicking.

All were silent for several minutes as everyone just watched the water calm itself. There was a startling cry from the nest that there were approaching ships coming from behind them. The crewman called out that they were Faulkton guild ships. The skies were getting dark, and ahead of the ships a storm could be seen in the distance coming towards them.

Erinnt was beside himself, but he had to command his crew. He commanded the ship to sail forward into the storm. Everyone prepared for the worst as the connected ships sailed forward at the captain's command. The crew did all they could to prepare for what was coming. A third of Erinnt's crew was made to go on the Bloody Charger. Olaf, Alltin, Arne, Eldarin, and Irisel also tried to man the Bloody Charger.

The guild ships behind them were still advancing, and the best friends were worried. Irisel tried to push the ships farther back with wind gusts. Arne could only prepare to absorb any lightning that might try to strike the connected ships and divert the bolts if need be onto the oncoming ships. Eldarin held onto Arne as he did before the tornado that made him lose his memory. Alltin tied Irisel to him. Olaf tied a rope to her as well in hopes that his size and weight could keep them on the ship if they were swept overboard. The crew worked hard to do what they could. Although Erinnt was still saddened by Circe's leap into the whirlpool, he still had to command his crew.

Everyone knew that the storm would be a bad one to go through. Erinnt had seen only a few worse than the one ahead of them. As they neared the storm, the waves became very dangerous. Everyone did what they could to prepare so it was just a matter of surviving the storm. The guild ships would also have to brave the storm if they wanted to continue after them.

The waves were relentless. They crashed down hard on the deck and the people on it. Within the first few minutes, the turbulent water claimed a few crewmembers' lives from the Urchin. The waves rocked and tossed the two ships about like they were nothing. It didn't take long for the two ships to become forcefully separated and thrown away from each other, severing their link.

The ships lost sight of each other a few minutes later. More huge waves crashed onto the Bloody Charger. A giant ominous wave struck, and Arne lost her footing. Eldarin almost lost her, but he managed to keep her from going overboard. Another crewmember was not so lucky. A few minutes later another crewmember almost went over, but managed to somehow stay on the ship by a thread. The storm lasted many hours and the ships were severely damaged.

When the storm ended, the two ships had truly lost each other. The ships were severely damaged and would take days to fix for the ships to be ready to sail again. On the Bloody Charger, only Olaf and Alltin made it through unscathed. The other three had suffered injuries from the storm. Irisel suffered from a broken left leg from being slammed into the mast pole forcefully. Arne was unconscious from a head wound. Eldarin broke his right arm. If Arne was conscious, she would have made a joke about Irisel now having a broken leg to match. Of the crew on the Bloody Charger, only one more man was tossed overboard. They still had five men to help with the ship.

On the Urchin, all made it out of the storm relatively uninjured. Erinnt was fine, but the ship needed to be repaired. Of the three guild ships that were chasing the Urchin, two made it out of the storm scattered in different directions with heavy damages. As ill-fate would have it, the Urchin and the Bloody Charger were making repairs and noticed that each had a ship still following them. With as heavily damaged as the guild ships were, the guild ships seemed to have come out of the storm better off than the Urchin and the Bloody Charger. The ships were closing in on their targets. With all of the repairs that were needed to each ship, the guild ships were sure to catch up.

Irisel was beside herself at the news, and with her broken leg could do very little. Iri called Alltin to her. "I must somehow leave this ship; we cannot let them take me. If there is no way off, as it seems not, then I must be hidden somewhere that they cannot find me. If they take you and not me, it will likely stay whatever execution would happen otherwise. And give me a chance to free you. The problem is this damned leg! I can't walk. Alltin, what are we going to do?"

"I hate to suggest it, but perhaps we can put you in a crate below, and say you were washed overboard. I could stay with you, and we can save the rest once the coast is clear."

"I would attack them but I can't concentrate with this leg being broken. Arne is unconscious, or she could seriously mess them up. How many of us do you…?" She paused, in thought. A look of enlightenment crossed her face. "I know what we can do! Olaf, I need your assistance!"

\*\*\*

One more of the ten has not been introduced yet, but perhaps he will make an appearance in the stories to come. By now you must be anxious to return to Angeline, Ellis, Rokk, and to continue following Circe, Irisel, and Arne. The fates of those who control water, wind, and lightning have much further to travel and much more to experience. I will return to them in due time. Who am I? I still cannot say, but you will know me soon enough. It is now time to venture into the darker side again. Angeline's actions of sacrifice for all the people she saw dead, the consequences of keeping the amulet from Tarax's possession, will cost her more than she could imagine in her darkest nightmares. Not even I could save her from the worst she would face. What are her consequences? How will Ellis escape the justice of Tarax and his affliction? Where did Quantis send Rokk? And what can Irisel do to save those she loves most dearly, including the unconscious

Arnesti? Why did Circe jump ship and abandon her friends when she said she would remain and help Irisel?  Where has the sought out amulet been sent to? Why is it so important? Who are the other three beings of the elements? How do they fit and what can they do? What is their collective or individual purpose?  The beginnings have been told, for the most part. More will come. Many new and old questions remain. Now is the time to continue the adventure.


The End

Made in the USA
Columbia, SC
27 September 2023

23506221R00143